BOOK 1

THE FLOWERING OF THE ROSE

ROSEMARY HAWLEY JARMAN

TORC

Cover Illustration:

Reverie, by kind permission of the artist, Graham Turner

This edition first published 2006

Torc, an imprint of Tempus Publishing Limited
The Mill, Brimscombe Port,
Stroud, Gloucestershire, GL5 2QG
www.tempus-publishing.com

British Library Cataloguing in Publication Data.
A catalogue record for this book is available from the British Library.

ISBN 0 7524 3941 3

Typesetting and origination by Tempus Publishing Limited
Printed and bound in Great Britain

Foreword

Although this is a work of fiction, the principal characters therein actually existed as part of the vast and complex fifteenth-century society and had their recognized roles in history, sparsely documented though these may be.

I have therefore built around the lives of my narrators. They were all real people whose destiny was in various ways closely interwoven with that of the last Plantagenet king. I have endeavoured to adhere strictly to the date of actual occurrences, and none of the events described is beyond the realms of probability. Conversations are of necessity invented, but a proportion of King Richard's words are his own as recorded by contemporaries. The tomb at Greyfriars, Leicester, was sacked during the Dissolution of the Monasteries by Henry VIII. The remains were disinterred and thrown into the River Soar.

R.H.J.

THE HOUSE OF YORK

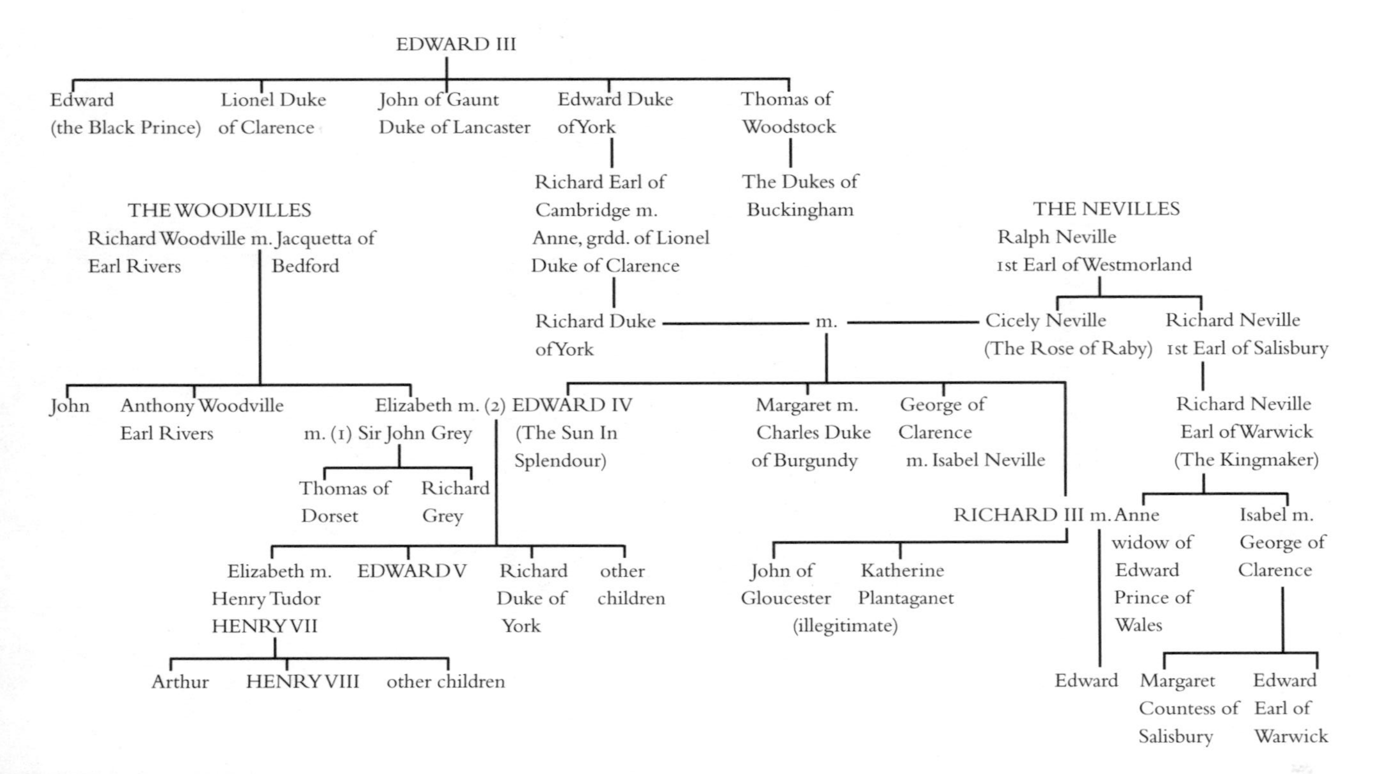

THE HOUSES OF LANCASTER AND TUDOR

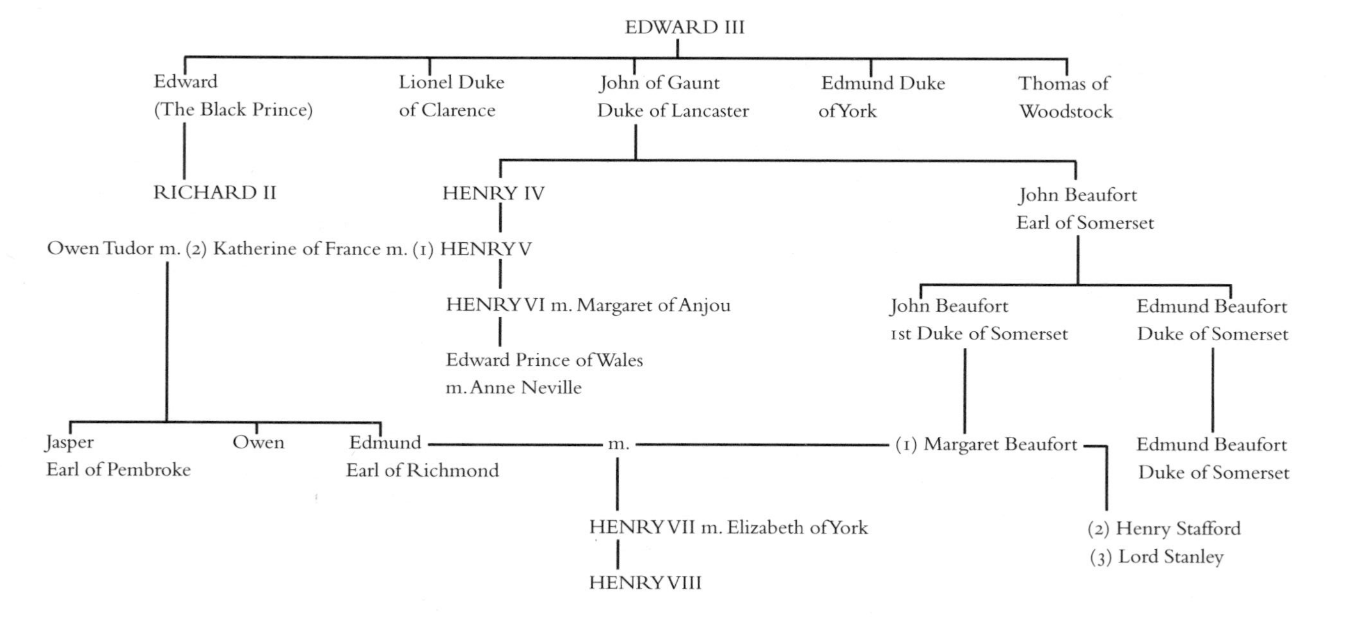

Gloucester: You may partake of anything we say;
We speak no treason, man; we say the King
Is wise and virtuous...

Shakespeare, Richard III, Act I, Sc. I

Part One

The Maiden

The maidens came
When I was in my mother's bower;
I had all that I would.
The bailey beareth the bell away;
The lily, the rose, the rose I lay.

The silver is white, red is the gold;
The robes, they lay in fold.
The bailey beareth the lull away;
The lily, the rose, the rose I lay.

And thro' the glass window shines the sun.
How should I love, and I so young?
The bailey beareth the lull away;
The lily, the rose, the rose I lay.

XVth Century: *Anon.*

Gardening is all of my pleasure. It was ever more a joy than a duty, to watch the tender shoots burst forth in spring, and to know that I had a part of them, in the cold season. When the scent of rose and gillyflower rises to mingle with the pungent breath of thyme and rosemary, chervil, basil and rue, I can close my eyes for a sinful instant, and be young again. Not old, and witless, and shattered by rheumatism like an oak after the lightning; but brimming with promise, as a fresh field awaiting the sower's careful hand. Like the good earth of England, made rich by the blood of strong men, slumbering in moist quietness yet, beneath, a moil of passionate life. Like my garden. I call it mine, but in secret; for nuns have no possessions, only their thoughts, and should the bishop and priest have power to read my mind, they might find me exceedingly worldly still. And I do not care. Sorrow is a sharper blade than penitence, and when a creature is bared to the bone she sees life as one might through a slanted glass, some of it faded, some of it out of true, some sharp and clear. I am very old. They say the old remember childhood best of all, and they do not lie, though this is a world of liars.

I have been thinking today about Elizabeth. Dame Elizabeth Grey, who was our Queen. I knew well that Elizabeth. I lived in her house, on the manor of Grafton Regis, when I was young, and reckoned myself so full of guile and cunning, and know now that I was not. Another Elizabeth is our Queen, and they say that she is ailing. May Our Lady of Sorrows have mercy upon her and guide her where I long to be. Though I have never seen her, I know that she is fair, like her mother; her mother of the herb garden. That brings me again to the flowers, and the neat rows of spices and the weeds which spread even unto the cloister with its tomb. Gardening too has its moments of truth, for a grave needs to be weeded, like everything else, and this is the grave of my beloved.

They buried him here, for there was nowhere else for them to lay him, in spite of the fact that he should have been entombed at

Westminster, not only for the good he wrought but because he came of the old royal line. No ordinary man was he; neither knight nor squire nor honest yeoman, but one possessed of such extraordinary strength and compassion that you would think he would ever be loved and revered. Mine is a strange, barren story: more joy, more sorrow, than is the lot of most. Yet the sorrow is sometimes almost forgotten and the joy, which supported me through the years while he lived, was such to make me smile and dream, refusing the knights who would have married me, and being content with the memory of a few hours. It is no heresy to love, and be mad. And there are times when, hearing the things now shouted about him whom I knew to be a good man, I wonder myself if I were once bewitched by the bright fiends of Fotheringhay.

I say the sorrow is almost forgotten, yet days come when an old woman has to look anxiously for the comforting Eye of God, in the mote of a sunbeam, in the passing glint of a chantry window, all the while cursing her frail tools and her weak hands. And I have betrayed my secret, an open secret these days, and one which I could mouth with pride. Yet had he been the lowest of the commonalty I would have run gladly towards the love we loved together. Daily the shouts of calumny and disfavour reach my ears; the shouts that once were whispers. I can but smile and shake my head for, being what they deem a witless old nun, my testimony is useless.

Always was he all my joy. And I first heard his name at the manor of Grafton Regis, when I was twelve years old.

A king once loved me.

1464

Two little boys played naked under an April sun. I leaned from the upper window, laughing at them. Tom, the elder, who was taller by a hair than Dick, had set up the quintain for lance-practice. It was a fearful Saracen's head, carved from wood and painted, and balanced so that the lightest thrust would send it spinning, arms opened wide to fell the jouster. Adding to the hazard was a bucket of water placed atop the Saracen. As I looked, little Dick, raising his weapon to shoulder height, made a charge untimely and unskilled. The infidel swung round. I heard a thud, saw the sparkling cascade then, howling, Dick sprawled on the sodden lawn, while his brother roared in triumph.

'They'll catch a chill.' Behind me came the grumbling voice of their nurse. 'Lord, Lord, what will their mother say?'

Say? Why, she will say naught, I thought to myself. She is too preoccupied these fair spring days. But I merely smiled at the nurse. I kept this secret as I kept my admiration for the absent Dame Elizabeth, for she was beautiful, my mistress. Tall and gilt-haired, with a small pouting mouth and heavy, mysterious eyes. I knew that, uncaring, she would let her boys run bare beneath the grudging sun, when they should be at their lessons. I imagined she had much on her mind.

So I said: 'They are hardy,' and went on watching them.

'Tchah!' said their nurse.

'Lady Grey approves of their sport,' I murmured. 'She says it will harden them for battle.'

And she had gone out riding, this day. Riding in Whittlebury Forest, where once she had met the man; the man with hair like the sun, and a body like a slim oak tree. I often wished that I were fair as Dame Elizabeth.

'Battle!' said the nurse.

''Twill be a long time yet,' I said comfortingly.

'Will it, in truth?' she answered crossly. 'I'm not so sure.' Her wrinkled eye was upon me and I searched my mind for a task undone, a duty neglected. I had been beaten once already that day; thus was I standing to watch Dick and Thomas Grey from the window. I could not sit down easily.

'From what I just heard,' she went on, 'babes and sucklings ride to battle.'

I was dying to know what the courier had said. From the moment of watching him ride through the crumbling courtyard an hour ago, I had been a-boil of curiosity. It was unusual enough, even in these days of fretful peace, to have such a messenger visit Grafton Regis. A real royal courier, with the *rose en soleil* shimmering on his surcote. There were so many things I was hot to know. He might even be able to tell the name of my lady's handsome stranger, the sun-haired knight. So I laid my cheek against the nurse's sleeve, fawningly.

'What said he, sweet dame?'

'He talked of the King's brothers,' she said grudgingly. 'One of them leads the levies to join the royal army. Like a real captain, and he only twelve years old. They are encamped at Leicester.'

Ah, Leicester. This gave me a pang. For it was at Leicester that I had been reared, in a nunnery, under the most virtuous Prioress that ever drew breath. Through war and peace and changing monarchs, in riches and penury, Leicester had been my home, both physical and spiritual. There I had lived with my mother until her death, and there had my father, dying, willed me to Grafton Regis and the service of Sir Richard Woodville's widowed daughter, Dame Elizabeth Grey.

'To my mind, it's shameful,' said the nurse, looking dolefully at the drenched boys. 'Nowadays, knaves are men before they're out of swaddling bands. Look at those two! And as for little Gloucester, I doubt he'll stand the journey.'

I knew hazily of King Edward's two brothers; there was George of Clarence, and this other, younger one, whom few had seen, who led an army, and who was of scant interest to me.

'Why did he not send my lord of Clarence instead?' I said. 'If this Gloucester is so young and weak besides...'

'George was appointed no commissions, the courier told me,' she replied. 'And the King thought it would be good for Richard. To give him confidence, courage.'

I dismissed this with a yawn. Then, eagerly, longingly, asked:

'Did the man... did he know aught of my lady's leman? The most handsome man, the hottest in love, for that he must be. Did he...'

Without warning, she boxed my ear. The wide sleeves of her worsted flew about.

'Leman! Lover!' she growled wrathfully. 'Cease this shameful talk! Remember always, there's none more chaste than Lady Grey!'

Had I been older, I might have mistrusted this fire-hot defence of virtue, and been wrong, for all that. Had I not witnessed a certain scene with my own eyes, I might have wondered on it. But, enthralled, scarcely comprehending, and a little afraid, I had seen the evidence of Dame Grey's incorruptible virtue. What I saw occurred not long after her first meeting with the great golden knight; a meeting which, in itself, had seemed a strange, oddly predestined thing. Elizabeth had gone out into Whittlebury one day, on foot, and unescorted save for the two little boys—and very sweet they looked, if a little ill-nourished and pale—hanging on her either hand. We had feared for her; the royal hunt was reputed to be about, and there was the hazard of her being trampled in the chase. Yet she returned at dusk, smiling, softly flushed, no harm having come to her save that the horse of a young nobleman had splashed her with some mire. It was soon after this that this man, terrifyingly handsome, like a saint or a sungod, had begun to visit Grafton Regis. I did not know his name, though I strongly suspected that others in the household did. He often called himself 'Ned'—sometimes 'poor Ned'—this with a rich laugh—or 'lovelorn Ned' in songs he composed himself and accompanied on the lute. My awe of him was great. For one thing he was so tall his golden head seemed to graze the clouds. That he came to Grafton at all was a kind of miracle; so might a saint step down from heaven, or the sun itself swing low for a brief space to bless our days. Young and sturdy, he had a happy voice and a purseful of gold angels ready to drop at any small favour done him. Once, he pinched my cheek. I blushed and shrank; he called me 'hinny'. Then, Lady Grey entered—he forgot me and grew pale with longing.

And my days were filled with pleasant duty, brushing out Elizabeth's long hair of spun silver, bathing and perfuming that white body. It grieved her that she had but a handful of dresses in which to receive her splendid guest, so that I was forever refurbishing them, taking the tassels from one, the gold passement from another, to make of a third a thing of beauty. We were poor at Grafton. Poor by any standards, for Sir John Grey, while he lived, had fought for Lancaster, and most of his estates had been forfeit to the Crown. I think this saddened Elizabeth; she had a passing tragic look at times, enhanced by the widow's barbe and wimple custom bade her wear. All her lovely hair was hidden, save for one little lovelock, a gilded promise that surmounted the broad brow, full lips and pointed chin. Lovesome was she, while she laughed gracefully and drank wine with the fair nobleman, she kept about her a cloak of chaste piety which might, I thought, have chilled his ardour. It did not; he was mad for her, as rams are mad in spring.

I rubbed my smarting ear and thought of the day I went to the herb garden on an errand for Elizabeth's mother. The old Duchess of Bedford, who lived with us at Grafton, kept her own small knot garden behind the long yew hedge next to the stables. A clipped, neat sward of lawn lay between beds which themselves were filled with strange plants and stranger fungi, most of whose names I did not know. Once, Jacquetta of Bedford had been as fair as her daughter, and now she spent hours brewing skin salves, or potions to revive her thinning hair. On this occasion she had sent me only for a few sprigs of rosemary and some cherry-blossom, should it be flowering yet. So I went down and the rich borders welcomed me with a joyous waft of perfume, so intense and inviting that my latest worry, the need of a new gown, fled from my mind, and I lay down, stretched out along the edge of the flowerbed, hidden by the bushes, watching a beetle staggering through the grasses, breathing thyme and sweet gale and pennyroyal, thoughtless and content. So their voices startled me, when Lady Grey and her tall young suitor came slowly down the lawn between the rectangles of raised shrubs. His velvet cap was tucked beneath one arm. With the bright light circling his head, he looked like the spirit of the sun. Yet he seemed ill-pleased about something, and a petulant smile lay on his mouth. Elizabeth's eyes were demurely downcast; as she walked she plucked a flower-head, a primrose growing in moss halfway up the garden wall. She held it for an instant to her lips. Instantly he snatched it from her, quite roughly, thrusting it deep into the breast of his doublet as one might plunge a sword into the heart. He took her hand. Their footsteps slowed. They stopped a few paces from where I lay; I dared not move or make a sound.

'Lady, be kind,' I heard him say. Then, desperately:

'Sweet Bess, why do you torment me so? I pray you, be kind. 'Tis little to you, and the whole world to me.'

She murmured something, low as her downcast eyes. She began to walk on, but he sprang, clasping her in his arms. She made no move to evade him; she merely stood, smiling that same, faint smile, and looking at the ground.

'Flesh and blood, Madame?' he asked gratingly. 'Or stone, Madame?' Then it was I became uneasy, frightened. He was so changed, so fierce. With a sharp movement of his great hands he tore the wimple from Elizabeth's head. Her silvery hair spilled over his arms. Bending, he crushed his face into her throat, while she stood, motionless. I gripped a bunch of rosemary and prayed they would not see me. Lying there, afraid, I thought I heard the pounding of their hearts.

'Yield to me Elizabeth!' he said in a terrible voice.

I could not hear her reply, it was so soft. Sunlight stabbed at the blade of a drawn dagger, and jewels burned at its hilt. He was holding the knife to her throat, the white throat bruised by kisses.

'Yield, Madame,' he said, like a madman. 'Or, by God's Blessed Lady, none other shall possess you. Bess, Bess,' he said, like a child, 'would you have me insane?'

Standing bravely, she said, calm and pleasant: 'Sir, I am too good to be your leman. Too good, Ned, to lie, even with you, in sin.'

Fierce colour mottled his face. He cursed and swore. He threw the knife, its hilt a jewelled rainbow, to the farthest end of the garden. Then he turned and strode, all swift anger, towards the house. For a moment Elizabeth stood musing, then coiled her hair deftly, rearranged her wimple and followed him, without haste, stopping only to pick up the dagger that quivered in the soft lawn. I rose and ran in the opposite direction, still clutching the bunch of rosemary for my lady of Bedford.

At one time I did wonder whether they were perchance enacting a scene from a play, or rehearsing some new disguising, some foolish romance, and that this was all in sport. Her calmness made me wonder thus. Yet I thought on it, and pondering, knew it had been no game. And so I learned of Elizabeth's stern chastity. He did not come again for some weeks; Elizabeth showed no sign of missing him, but her mother fell in a black fury, out of all proportion to the case. Her body-servant, Agnes, who was my dear friend, suffered the lash of Jacquetta's tongue, and nightly in whispers she and I surmised the reason for this wrath. We reached the conclusion that the old woman was in love herself with Elizabeth's suitor, and forgot our bruises in stifled mirth. But when he came again, all smiles and sweetness and contrition, we saw no signs of such a passion; in truth, Jacquetta withdrew into her private solar, and mixed more herbals. Agnes swore she was at work on an elixir to make her young again.

The pain in my ear was fading. I sought to placate the nurse.

'Is the courier still here, sweet dame?'

'Aye, he is,' she said gruffly. 'His horse cast a shoe, and that's why.'

I was disappointed. No news of battles, then. Not that I wanted a battle, God forbear. No summons to the Court of King Edward, either, for any of us. That had ever been a lackwit dream of mine. I had heard that the King, whose deeds of courage were legion, was wonderful to behold, and his court a splendour. But the nurse was babbling again of the King's brothers.

'Such a babe to lead an army,' she mused. 'So they say. And so frail. Unlike his brothers, I have learned. While both his Grace and George of Clarence are ruddy and fair, Richard is small, low statured. Blue eyes, nearly black. His hair is very dark. Almost that colour.' She touched the oak settle. 'Wistful of mien, not given to smiling.'

He sounded a passing dull fellow, 'Is he to fight already, this Richard?' I asked mockingly. 'And who's the foe?'

'He's only leading the levies,' she replied with restrained patience. 'Though, mark you, he could fight. They say he was trained in arms by the Earl of Warwick, at Middleham Castle in the north parts. And the King dotes on him.' She looked tenderly out of the window at

Dick and Thomas Grey. 'Babes in harness,' she said. 'Certes, these are terrible days.'

'One king is the same as any other': I had heard it many times, until the sack of Ludlow, when we at the nunnery had been so terribly afraid. It was Queen Margaret, the French vixen, who had bred in us this chilling fear. She had let her men pillage and burn and ravish; it was only King Edward Fourth who had put a stop to it. As for her spouse, the old Lancastrian king, Henry—folk said he had been mad for years. My own father had fought for Lancaster, and those days had been far more terrible than now. We were at peace, and King Edward, from all accounts, was a good king. It was what a man was by instinct, blood and loyalties, not what his policy made him, as the Prioress at Leicester–the Mother whom I still missed—used often to tell me.

'Have you naught to do, child?' the nurse said, suddenly sharp. 'What of my lady's mending? Her shifts are in ribbons. And there is work aplenty in the stillroom for those idle, lady-hands of yours.'

'Is the courier well-favoured? May I go down and see him?'

Gaze fixed again on the boys, she was not listening. They ran and leaped, the sun shifting on their pallid bodies. Thomas had captured the large black cat which belonged to the Duchess of Bedford. He was tying a rusty spur to its tail.

'Lord!' mourned the nurse. 'Dame Grey sets great store by those young knaves. But my lady Jacquetta loves her cat equally. Should I go down and chide them, I wonder?'

She looked at me stupidly; she was a stupid woman. Often she berated me, often she sought my counsel. The cat whimpered and squalled. Dick sat down heavily astride its twitching back.

'I'll go,' I said. 'They'll be killing it soon.' Her protests floated after me down the stairs.

It was a good excuse to escape her vigilant eyes. At any moment she would find me another piece of tiresome labour and I was weary from a morning laundering Dame Grey's delicate linen. My hands looked red and would have been redder still save for the application of rose-water cream filched from my lady's vial. (I think that was my only dishonesty. I always salved my conscience with the thought that, as she used it so lavishly, she must have a little to spare for those more needy.) In any event I misliked to see animals maltreated.

It was warm in the garden among the sheltering yews. Patches of violets edged the lawn. Like wicked frogs, Thomas and Dick grinned up at me. I rescued the struggling cat and smoothed its fur. Maddened to ingratitude, it sought to nip me.

'Poor Gyb is not a horse,' I said sternly.

'In faith, he did not mind being ridden,' little Dick argued, sucking a scratched wrist.

'Set up the quintain again,' I said.

Thomas heaved a great sigh. 'I am aweary of that game.' He gave me his sly smile. 'Play Hoodman Blind! You never play with us now!'

Summoning my new dignity, I said: 'Well, I'm a child no longer, sirs,' and was glad of it. Their play was rough, and sometimes they would treat me with a thin contempt, aping great lords. Once, Tom, in temper, had reminded me that my father had been but a landless knight. Now, at twelve, I was a woman, and the gulf between was almost absolute, but on that occasion I had been a crying child, reminding them that that same landless knight had died of wounds taken in the Lancastrian cause and the service of their own grandsire, Sir Richard Woodville.

'Put on your clothes,' I told them. 'You're wanton. Dick, get dressed.'

'I have no bonnet,' .he said, grinning. 'Lend me yours, lady.' Swift as a bat, he seized my dangling veil. My short black hennin with its tarnished gold braid was tweaked from my head, and my hair fell down, a life-time's heavy growth. It covered me like a cloak; the sun felt unfamiliar on my brow

'Wanton! Wanton!' mimicked Thomas, and they were off, flat-footedly racing, bearing my bonnet like a battle trophy. I was left with the echo of their floating laughter, and the slitted eyes of the cat, watching. It dabbed its coat with a quick tongue, then gazed at me again. Small boys were cruel, yet I felt a strange distaste for this particular beast, and marvelled that Jacquetta of Bedford should love it so. It slept in her bed all night. Its eyes were lines of amber, that looked on me with hate. Suddenly I clapped my hands.

'Shoo! Cursed Gyb!'

I know not why I called it cursed. It skipped, arching, behind the hedge. I walked on slowly. For a brief space I was free. At any time my mistress might return from her ride but, until then, I was at large to peek and glimpse, with fortune, a real royal courier. I tried to braid my hair. I loved my hair; it was long as Dame Grey's, and thicker, but a strange colour, seen by few, kept as it was in a great coil under my little blunt-pointed hat. Think of a fox, a chestnut, the setting sun on wine, a dying leaf. Those were the colours of my hair, and many more besides. I gave up trying to plait—it was too thick. I twisted it in a knot; it poured sleekly through my fingers like molten metal. I let it hang, and it waved and lifted about me as I walked, like the blown garment of an autumn tree.

I stepped into the kitchen and there was the courier. A courier off duty, by my faith, for he lay comfortably in a chair by the hearth, with its dusty andirons and smouldering peat, his boots extended to the warmth, while fat Agace, the cook, filled his tankard from the day's brewing. The blazing rose of York shone from his garment. He was laughing and, though he was past his youth, being at least eight-and-twenty, I thought him well-favoured; he lacked no teeth and his eye had an easy glint. He looked up when I entered, a little cautiously, as if unsure of whom he was about to see. Then he rose; he bowed. I found delight in that courtly bow. Agace, however, bustled over to me, proud and as insolent as she dared, full of outraged whispers. This was her kingdom, the scullions her subjects, my disarray her great displeasure.

'Bind your hair, mistress!' she growled. 'What will the gentleman think of us? My lady out riding, and you strutting like a wanton quean!'

The esquire caught her last words. He could scarcely help it. He said gently:

'Nay, nay, good cook. Like... a bride, I fancy. Yea, a bride.'

I felt the warm wash of pleasure. The dim kitchen seemed to glow.

'John Skelton, mistress,' he said, bowing again. 'At the service of Lady Grey's fair daughter, of whose existence I vow I did not know.'

Here was confusion. He had called me fair; yet Lady Grey had no daughter. I opened my mouth, foolishly, and heard Agace swiftly acquainting him of my life's history in one pompous breath. The kitchen was ordinary once more. I looked up at him, sadly spreading my hands. I was the child of charity, and fair no longer. Here the game must end.

'There you have my story, sir,' I said. 'Save that'—with an angry look at Agace—'my father was knighted ere he died.'

But he only smiled, gently. 'A tale of honourable misfortune,' he said. Then, half to himself: 'Mother of God, what a colour!'

He was gazing at my hair. I was little, I was unimportant, but he found me pleasant to look upon. I closed my ears to the scullions' giggling, and to Agace's disapproving sniff. I smiled into John Skelton's eyes, straightening my back. I liked the way he looked at me, though there was something oddly disturbing in it. Like finding a new, mysterious plant, lovely but unknown, in the herb garden.

'I have been in Calais, in Burgundy,' he said softly. 'Never did I see its like. By my soul, the Flemish artists would lose their wits over that hair. They would go mad while they mixed their paints. What is it? A bay horse's hide has it, and a beech leaf, but there's pure gold there, and red fire. Come to the light, child, that I may judge it better.' He drew me to the window.

Behind me, I heard Agace say, low-voiced: 'Court flattery. Certes, a right courtier!'

One of the stable-boys lurched in through the open door.

'Horse is ready, master,' he muttered. His tatters were shown up cruelly by John Skelton's bright robes. I went with him to the stable, while the boy slouched ahead, kicking pebbles. We walked through the herb garden, and I feigned in secret that the esquire was my leman, begging me to yield at dagger point. But he was old enough to have fathered me. I kept eyes downcast, as Elizabeth did.

'Are you betrothed?' he asked. I shook my head. My face must have expressed some hidden shame, for he tipped up my chin with a kindly finger.

'But you're still young,' he said. 'That hair! It would be shame to hide that hair in cloister.'

My spirit drooped. I thought, yes, a nunnery! The only alternative. Having no husband, to be exalted to Christ's Bride. What better fate? But he had called me fair.

'When Dame Grey comes to court,' he went on, 'I doubt not she will bring you also, and her other maidens to attend her.'

I stopped dead in the middle of the lawn. Even the trees held their breath, and the flowers.

'She is to go to court?' I whispered. And then, forgetting all warnings, said loudly: 'How her lover will miss her! Oh, Master Skelton, he's the handsomest man in the world.'

Now it was his turn to stop. He caught my hand and held it tight. 'Jesu,' he said quietly. 'She has a lover? What is his name?'

I described him, babbling of his beauty. I said his name was Ned, and that was all I knew. I never saw a man laugh so lustily as did John Skelton then. He clasped his own waist and leaned this way and that. I said stiffly:

'I think you mock me, sir. You asked, I answered. Now, is it true my lady is for London?'

He ceased laughing, and gave me the strangest look, saying quickly: 'Nay, put it from your mind absolutely. I did jest with you indeed. Forgive me.'

Being very cross, I grew even more polite than usual. Looking straight ahead, I asked him:

'You say that you have been abroad? Tell me of the fashions, if you please. I hear that in France and in Burgundy ladies no longer wear the tall hennin but a little cone-shaped hat, trimmed at the crown with braid. Is this but another rumour?'

He said again, very humbly: 'Forgive me. Yes, I have been to France, where the ladies can't hold a candle to our English maids, but I fear I've no eye for fashion. And as for Burgundy… by God! My last voyage there still gives me bad dreams. The most important commission of my life. And the most dangerous.'

His voice told me that this subject held neither flattery nor false rumour. His eyes were far-off, grey as the sea.

I said, 'Tell me.'

He looked down at me again, as if he had forgotten who I was. With sad face, he asked: 'Don't you recall the doings at Wakefield?' Then: 'Ah, certes, you would be but a young child.'

Seven years old, and in the nunnery. I remembered how the news came to us at Leicester. My mother had prayed for Lancaster, but the Mother of Leicester, the Prioress, had. prayed for both Lancaster and York. 'Tell me then, Master Skelton,' I said. 'Tell me the truth of Wakefield.'

'It was to be the final triumph for the House of York,' Skelton said slowly. 'The Duke of York, King Edward's father, his young son,

Edmund of Rutland and the Earl of Salisbury, marched for Yorkshire in hopes of defeating the French Queen at last. My lord of York had already claimed the throne by right of blood. He had been hailed Protector of the Realm in Westminster. But he had reckoned without the Scots and the men of the North—all of them heathens and hot for the Frenchwoman. When he halted at his castle at Sandal, it was Christmas, and both sides declared a truce for the holy season. Alas! the Lancastrians enjoyed their feast and their disguisings right speedily, for on the last day of December they fell upon the castle, where York lay unprepared. He and many of his followers were slain in a matter of moments. They lay with the remnants of their gaiety around them, the holly and mistletoe boughs all spattered with their blood. Salisbury was taken and beheaded at once. Young Edmund of Rutland fled to Wakefield, where the battle raged, and there Clifford, the Lancastrian lord near his own age, cut him down as he cried for mercy. "Your father slew mine, and so shall I slay you and all your kin."'

We stood quiet together, our feet damp with the lawn's dew. From the hedge a bird sang mournfully.

'He was seventeen,' said John Skelton. 'And they took his head, together with that of his father and Lord Salisbury, and exposed them to the people of York, speared on pikes at the Micklegate Bar, with paper crowns about their brows to mock their aspiration.'

'Yet we are at peace,' I said softly.

'Through Edward, gallant Edward. He was spared that disgrace and death. Eighteen years old, and chosen by God. Earl of March he was then... you heard of the vision he had at Mortimer's Cross? His Grace, rising on the battle morning, perceived not one sun in the sky, but three! Three suns! It was the sign, the Sun in Splendour!' He clapped a hand over the royal emblem on his heart, the fiery sun. 'I swear, I know, that God Himself gave him the victory. St Michael shielded him. Through Mortimer's Cross, through Towton Field—where the worst snowstorm ever known soaked up men's blood—Edward triumphed.'

'And you?'

'He had a task for me. The whole country was in uproar— churches were pillaged, children murdered—women were raped as though they were heathen women—men mad with looting-lust...'

'We prayed,' I told him. 'We prayed day-long, with the nuns. My knees were raw from the chapel stones.'

'Yes, the convent was safe for some. But not for those of the blood royal. It was January when the King sent for me at night, to escort his young brothers to Philip of Burgundy, where they would be best preserved. A risky adventure; I confess to being afraid. And, what was worse, the boys had been roused by the commotion and crept on to the gallery. They overheard our talk in the great Hall. I had hoped to bear them swiftly aboard ship without their knowing why, but Richard and George heard us speak of their father's and brother's deaths, and how their heads wept blood on Micklegate.'

I thought of my mother, slipping away in peaceful sleep; of my father, wounded and shriven, providing for me in death. To a Lancastrian household, Lancastrians, who had done these fearful things. But a Lancastrian household no more, since the King's pardon arrived last year. I thought: Death is a part of life, and a part of me. Held by John Skelton's story, it made me no less sad.

'Which is the right course, the right way?' I said. He did not hear me.

'The young princes had scarcely time to receive their mother's blessing. They call her the "Rose of Raby", that proud, brave woman. I saw her fighting her grief as she flung together a few necessaries for their journey... warm clothes, a missal, a jewelled dagger... She put little Richard in my arms. He was stiff with shock, like one dead. Jesu! How he favoured his father in face; he still does. When she kissed him I turned my head away—she knew not if she would see him again. The rebels were everywhere. London was in madness. Even the 'prentices were armed with clubs. Mayor Lee donned mail; the city flew to hide behind him. They said that the Frenchwoman's army was sweeping down like plague to murder us all, and that London was doomed. Many repented of their sins, that night.'

He was silent, thoughtful. 'Where did you take ship?' I asked.

'At Billingsgate, on a Flemish merchantman. Days and nights we tossed on the North Sea. George enjoyed it. He harassed me with questions while I nursed Richard, whom grief had thrown into a sharp fever. He moaned for hours, his flesh on fire. He was a frail child at the best of times; through his infancy men marvelled daily that he lived. So off the tortured sea came we to Duke Philip. Young Richard lives yet. Praise God.'

'Amen,' I said, out of customary politeness.

'Now,' he said, smiling, 'he is Knight of the Garter, Admiral of England, Ireland and Aquitaine. The King is proud of him. He is having him trained in arms under Warwick himself. At Middleham in the North. And Warwick is the most powerful knight in the world.' Even I knew of Warwick; the man who made kings great, by sword and by will.

Just then Dick and Thomas Grey came into view, sparring out on to the lawn with their wooden weapons. I was glad to see that they were dressed. Dick was wearing my hennin; he had torn its veil. A look of amiable scorn crossed John Skelton's face as he watched them. He said:

'I saw Richard of Gloucester training just lately. He fights like a man. He is so frail and weak it seems he would drive himself twice as hard as any of the other henchmen, to prove his worth to King Edward. All the young knights cry quarter...'

'Tell of Burgundy,' I begged. 'The court of Duke Philip...'

He smiled. 'We were royally welcomed, exiles though we were, and regaled with strong pleasures. Mistress, you would have loved a sight of Master Caxton's library. You know of Caxton?' I shook my head. 'A worthy mercer, friend of King Edward. In Bruges, he has hundreds of manuscripts, illuminated in the colours of the rainbow, their bindings crusted with gems. And at Duke Philip's manor at Hesdin, there is naught but engines of most cunning trickery—books which, when opened, blow dust into your face; a great hall where lightning shoots from the ceiling and thunder rolls overhead; marvellous birds and beasts, and bridges which collapse midway and tumble the unwary into a stream below.'

We had reached the stables by this time. I was about to ask more questions, when suddenly through the archway leading from the courtyard came the sound of hooves. Lady Grey was returning. Behind me, I heard a window in the east gable fly open. The Duchess of Bedford was on watch. I had wasted an hour.

'Farewell, sir,' I said at once. I gave him a curtsey, down to the ground. He laughed, tipped up my chin again.

'A kiss,' he said. I looked away, confused. ''Tis a courtly custom,' he said. 'Ned would tell you. Ned!' and laughed again, kissing me lightly on the laugh.

I might have been a whit enamoured of John Skelton. But he had told me naught of the court, naught of my lady's lover, had prattled only of King Edward's weakling brother.

He mounted and sat his horse, an ordinary enough man yet to me the emblem of glamour, with the *rose en soleil* shining from his breast. He smiled at me; the beast curvetted and sprang forward. I felt my hair whipping about my face, and his eyes upon it. Then he was gone, and a little space after, Lady Grey rode in, riding side-saddle, in the Bohemian fashion, her face fair and serene and haloed by the shabby wimple. Beside her rode an elegant figure. It was her brother, Anthony Lord Rivers. So he had come to visit us again. He frightened me.

Behind them came a scattering of ragtag henchmen and a man I had never seen before; a holy man, a black-robed clerk, with a wild, rolling eye and face the colour of whey.

I dreamed often of a knight, one whose countenance was never visible to me. Neither fair nor dark, pure nor swarthy, he would appear in dreams, mounted and armed, at the edge of a green meadow. The horse's legs were clothed in mist to the pastern, the rider's armour wore a sheen of fog. Always his visor was closed, but I would know that he watched me, with a deep, mailed look through his eye-slits, while I stared and stared, trying to penetrate that steely mist, in vain. Long after he had faded his essence remained, always a mystery. I told none of this dream; I knew it for what it was, a longing. Yet for what I longed, I had no knowledge. Once, the rider came close, and I touched the burning mail of his hand. The touch brought fear.

On the evening which changed my destiny I thought on him, my faceless knight. May Eve it was; I stood at the same window with which I began my tale, late and long past bedtime, a weird and weary hour, waiting to undress my lady when she rose from the parlour where she and her mother kept company with the pallid clerk. Agnes and I had discovered his name. This was his third visit to Grafton in as many weeks; from Stoke Newerne he came, a half-hour's ride off, and they called him Master Thomas Daunger. This night he had dined with them, and now it seemed that he would never leave. I left the window and crossed the landing to the stairhead, where I seated myself, yawning and shivering, upon the topmost stair. Below, the great curved balustrade disappeared where the motley-coloured tiles of the hall were lost in shadow. A thin line of candlelight licked under the parlour door; there was the constant low sound of voices, murmuring. I could distinguish Elizabeth's, now and again the harsh high rasp of her mother, and very occasionally the clerk's quavering tones. His voice, fit mate for his countenance, was milky and sour.

In contrast to the dim stillness of the house, the night outside blazed with life. A moon like a white, perfect fruit hung in a lattice of oak leaves, the humpbacked yews trembled as I watched from my vantage point near to a deep recessed window, and across the lawn long shadows flung their sleeping arms. A nightingale was singing, over and over the same careless tune, and was joined by another and another, until the fluid melody filled the night. From the border herb-scents rose, strong as incense in the Mass. Between the house's quietness and the perfumed song, I sat clasping knees on the top steps, my thoughts wandering; no doubt looking ridiculously small-statured, and wishing Agnes would come to me. I had not seen her since before supper, and on this, the last day of April, she had made me a promise.

Folk said it only worked on May Eve: the hawthorn-spray trick, that was. I had given mine to Agnes, and she had vowed it would be dropped at the nearest crossroads, where the wind should take it. And down whichever way the breeze snatched my spray, thence should my true love come. Agnes had no need to toss a thorn twig; she was already betrothed, to a silversmith's 'prentice in the south, and when he had made his masterpiece they would be wed and she would leave Grafton. I fell sad at this; I should be lonely. I wondered if my Lady Elizabeth had ever used a hawthorn spray. But then, she needed to even less than Agnes. Her own love had already come a-riding. Nay, she did not need it, any more than the face balms, the potions her mother made to beauty's cause. This set me thinking of the Duchess of Bedford's skilled alchemies, and the last time tall Ned had come to call. I had been very close to him that day; in truth, the Duchess asked my help in a small work, to please our guest. She had let me pour him a flagon of wine. But before pouring, she had taken a little vial from her pouch, filled with dark liquid fresh and sharp-smelling like the earth at night. I had to mix this with the wine, stirring in a special way: six times to the left, five to the right. A little strand of the herb clung on the tankard's lip, and she brushed it off. It looked like the five-leaf grass, ruled by Jupiter for strength, a flower whose purpose I did not know.

'Our guest is weary,' she said. 'Stir strong; that is good! He has a melancholy. Men mislike to be cosseted. So let this be a secret work, for his well-being.'

Then, of all things, she asked if I were virgin. Truly I thought she wandered in her mind, but gave her fair answer, and she nodded, with folds of skin over her small bright eyes, and seemed well pleased. She gave me a thrust towards the chamber where they sat. He did not seem melancholy to me, only with love. He sprawled, long and sturdy, and listened to Elizabeth playing her little harp, with his chin propped on one hand and his eyes making their slow hot journey over her body. I poured his wine, as the Duchess of Bedford had told me, and those love-lorn eyes, with the pupils large and lambent, like the middle of two blue flowers, never left my Lady Elizabeth, not even while he drained the cup as if he drank her lips. Later the Duchess prepared him a special supper, a rare mushroom with a sharp sauce. Sometimes, if they had some unusual delicacy, Agnes and I were allowed to share the remains. On this occasion, however, Agnes had tried to taste the mushroom on its way to the table and had been rewarded by the Duchess with a blow on the neck. After he had eaten, Ned fell quiet and muttered to himself, while Elizabeth knelt before him, stroking his lax hand. When I bent to fill his cup again, I stole another glance at his careless eyes, and saw that their blue flowers had folded inwards, and were tiny, like the eyes of a bird.

Now I am wise, and skilled in herbal knowledge, I know that dish was of the *Amanita muscaria*, the most wicked fruit ever to foul God's earth. But then, being innocent, ignorant beyond thought, I reckoned naught of it and recalled the incident with pleasure, for he seemed utterly content, and I had poured his wine.

I sat thinking forward to the morrow. Last year, and the year before that, neither Agnes nor I had been allowed to go to the Maying. In every part of England I knew they would be raising the great striped pole; there would be music, itinerant trinket-sellers, jugglers and the like. Gay clothes, strange faces, excitement. A country court in truth, just for one day, and, for both of us, forbidden. We could not be spared from duty. In a corner of my awakening judgement I knew this unfair—even the villeins and yeomen hirelings all around Grafton would be early on the road for Stoney Stratford tomorrow. 'They come home a disgrace, penniless and drunk,' fat Agace had told me tartly. Yet there was that in her face which told me she, withal her disdain, would gladly go, given the chance. Therefore I put it away from my mind, as a lost thing, and wondered for comfort about the destiny of my hawthorn twig, and where Agnes had got to.

I conjured her up, or so it seemed. In the next instant she was at my side, the flaring moonlight stroking the curve of her round face. Her hair escaped its kerchief in wisps. She sat down beside me on the step. I felt for her rough warm hand. Its touch comforted me.

'Oh, Agnes! You scared me,' I said.

'Lord Jesu! I lust for my bed!' she answered swiftly, squeezing my fingers. 'Why, you're nervous tonight! Are they still employed down below? Chatter, chatter. My lady will not be up to hear Mass in the morning. As for her mother, two hours I've waited to put her to bed. The warming-pan's cold. Such an evening I've had. Jesu! I mislike the looks of that fellow!'

'The clerk?'

'Yes, Master Daunger. When I was handing him his meat, he gave me such a look from those drooping lids I well-nigh dropped the salver. Like a black-beetle. Why does he come here, know you?'

'Maybe he's giving my lady spiritual instruction,' I murmured.

Agnes laughed shrilly. 'I would say rather she could instruct him. She's that pious... nay, sweeting, her drift tonight was something odd. As if a torch were lit inside her. And ill at ease. She knocked the chess-board off the table, and when I got down to pick the pieces up, that foul beast, Gyb, bit me.' She pulled up her skirt. On her moonlit flesh a neat set of fangs showed black. I rose and leaned on the window sill.

'Did you take my thorn twig?'

She came to stand by me. 'What a moon for May Eve!' she said softly. ''Tis like the sun. Nay, Jankin took it. He had to go to the maltster's.'

'Tell me,' I said eagerly.

'Well, mine blew southerly, as usual. But yours! It did but lie sorrowfully in the dust, and never moved.'

I whispered: 'Jankin speaks false.' Agnes often teased me but this time I was unsure. She should not jest about this anyway; it was a heathen practice, frowned on by the priests. Then she pinched me and laughed, and said:

''Tis I who's false, sweeting. All's well. Your true love will come from the north. The wind took it a little way north, then it caught in the hedge.' I knew no one in the north. None save the nuns at Leicester.

'Mayhap a Scotsman!' whispered Agnes gleefully. 'Yelling heathen foreign oaths, soaked in his foes' blood.'

I stared hard at the moonlit lawn, so as not to mind. Gyb's figure played in and out of the shadows, tossing up in his paws some luckless small beast. Only a little cat in the distance—I could hold him in my palm. He seemed unreal. At that moment I felt as I often did: something part of the moon and trees, intangible. One whose destiny was ordered, like my hawthorn spray, by the dictating breeze of others. Something that was shadow and not substance...

The parlour door opened abruptly. A voice said: ''Tis best he does not lie under our roof tonight.' And I heard the clerk answer: 'There is wisdom. Good night, my dames.'

'Till the morrow,' said the Duchess of Bedford. 'Speed our endeavour.'

'To our good fortunes.' Master Daunger was kissing hands in the doorway. Someone held up a light. His chalky face blazed in it; he looked like someone in Hell, like the pictures in my missal. Elizabeth said, very quietly: 'You are sure?'

'It cannot fail,' said Daunger. 'Do this night what I have said...' The tail of his words was swallowed up. They walked across the hall and went out.

'God be praised,' yawned Agnes. 'Now my lady will retire, and I can rest. If Gyb lets me. Last night he clawed me, even in sleep.' She ran upstairs, lighting her candle-end. She slept at the foot of the Duchess's bed, as I did with Elizabeth, in case they should wake in the night for food or drink or cosseting.

Lady Elizabeth came to the stairfoot, holding up the torch. The light fell about, casting quivering darknesses. Descending, I stole a look at her face; pale and marble-smooth, the blue eyes fire-bright, the lips like petals set firm. Demure and unyielding, and cool as spring water she was, but beautiful. I looked at her, marvelling; she was at least thirty years old and the mother of two great boys, but she had a maid's body, an angel's face. Yes, she was beautiful, that night.

'Who's there?' she asked sharply. 'Oh, 'tis you, wench. Where are the others? What's o'clock?'

'Nigh midnight, Madame, and everyone else is abed,' I said timorously. Then, 'It's May Eve, lady.'

In her hand the flame lurched suddenly. I wanted to explain: all I meant was—May Eve, the harbinger of May Day, when people pleasured themselves, and why not we? But I knew it to be useless. I stared at her like a moon-calf; she was tall and slender in the blue silk dress, a passing pretty gown, into which she had to be sewn. It had an intricate plastron under the kirtle, and she despised it as old-fashioned. She beckoned me with a long white finger. 'Why say you this?' she demanded. Saying naught, I looked at the floor, where fire and moonlight made patterns. She was ill-ease, in truth. I feared her swift temper. Then she said, quite kindly: 'How small you are, child,' and 'Get you to bed.'

'I'm ready to attend you, Madame.' I took the heavy torch in my hand. Its flame blew a hot breath.

'Go up,' she answered. 'I'll not need you.' She waved her long hands, a careless gesture. The wavering light etched hollows beneath her eyes. She went before me to the stairs, and the leaping darkness followed.

'I'll lie alone,' she said. 'I may spend the night in prayer. My mother likewise. Tell Agnes. She can sleep with you tonight.'

Something like joy ran through me, and I thought how pleased Agnes would be to be rid for a space of the Duchess's demands, of the fretting claws of Gyb. Neither did I think aught strange of my lady's whim; for I would rather share a truckle-bed with Agnes than snatch my rest at Elizabeth's feet. For the last two or three months she had kept me awake with her tossing and mutters, disturbing my own sweet mysterious dream; parting me from my fair faceless knight. He whose harness gleamed, who wore my favour in the tournament. She left me at the head of the stairs and went towards her little chapel. As she passed I noticed that her shoulder came level with my brow. How small you are, child! she had said. Shadow and not substance, that was I.

Agnes was sitting dolefully on a chest in the Duchess of Bedford's room. For moments I teased her, hinting at a treat, and got her to beg my pardon for jesting about the hawthorn twig.

'Ah! God be praised!' she cried when I told her. 'Maiden, let us to bed right lively before they change their minds.'

We ran tiptoeing to the attic. From next door, fat Agace's snores already shook the plaster. The moonlight mottled Agnes's lily flesh. 'There's a flea in this bed,' she complained, but was stripped and beneath the covers before I had unfastened my kirtle, throwing her clothes at the candle and leaving me to undress in gloom.

'Perchance they will even let us go a-Maying,' she said, while I struggled with my houpeland. 'You should have asked her, wench, while she was so full of charity.'

'And what should I wear, if they did?' I asked bitterly. 'I've no gowns fit to be seen. My best has a great rent where I tore it on a thorn. I should have all the knaves mocking me for a bawd, going naked in such fashion. And the one my lady gave me—why, I vow she wore it when she was great with young Dick—it swamps me, it's too long. I should be flat on my face in two paces.'

'I've made it to fit you,' Agnes said, in a little voice. 'While I was waiting for my lady. I'm sorry I vexed you over the hawthorn spell, sweeting.'

I flew to the bed and kissed her. 'Dear, kind Agnes!'

'Now, your Grace,' she said, mocking again, 'I'll help you disrobe. By the Rood, what fine jewels! I'll lay them in this coffer to be safe. There's a knot in your laces,' she said, fumbling. 'I'll have to cut you loose.'

I wrenched away. 'Oh Jesu!' I whispered. 'My Lady Elizabeth!'

A trivial thing, so completely forgotten. A trivial thing, enough to change my whole life.

'Now what's to do?' she said crossly. 'Is there no peace in this dwelling? Come to bed.'

Naught really, yet it loomed like the shadows. My lady was wearing her blue gown, the dress despised for its ancient cut, into whose intricacies she had to be sewn, and further, unsewn at bedtime. Elizabeth's possessions were jealously loved, none the less. In my mind I saw her careless disrobing, heard the split of cloth. She would burst from the plastron like the flesh of a ripened grape, with swift, high anger.

'I must find my lady,' I said wildly. 'I shall be sore beaten.' Groaning, Agnes pulled the covers over her head.

I ran downstairs, under the bright latticed moon. I knew my mistress. Useless to say she had dismissed me; useless to plead that she herself had vowed no need of me; I saw only her fury as I ran through the midnight house, now dark, now bright. She was not in the chapel, and her bedroom was deserted, save for the little dog snug-curled in the centre of the bed. I went next to the chamber of Jacquetta of Bedford, hoping Elizabeth might have tarried to bid good night. Only a candle burned there, slow and lonely. My hand slid like silk on the banister. Small and demented, I reached the hall. The parlour was unoccupied. More candles whispered there, softened tallow dropping like gentle tears.

I could have crept back to my bed. Years later, with all the mists gone from my eyes, I wished I had done that very thing, knowing that a thousand beatings would have been small sacrifice and, but for my witless pursuit of a duty, my whole existence changed.

I spun on my heel, shaking, as a sharp noise brought the blood to my face. I was unquiet, prowling the manor at this hour. Ghosts and demons rushed about me, catching at my breath, then the sound came again: a rough, grating buffet, and I knew it as the outer door swinging on its hinge. So, angry at my own dread, I went firm and resolute to make it fast. Even as I reached for the latch, it blew open again, and I saw my lady and her mother, limned clear upon the shining lawn. I opened my mouth to call to them and in that instant saw what they were about. My mouth stayed open. Unbelievingly, I watched the Duchess raising both hands to the moon's blank face. In one of them a small object gleamed. I put my foot over the doorsill to see better. It looked like a small manikin, a baby such as cottars' children play with, rough-cut from wood, or wrought in some fast-hardening substance. The Duchess leaned towards her daughter. Her voice came clearly through the soft white night.

'Have you his hair?'

Elizabeth scratched in the beaded pouch that never left her waist.

'Yes, Madame—I took three strands last time, but it grows less easy... I pray God...'

The Duchess hissed like a snake.

'Woman! Do not invoke *that Name* at this late hour in our work! Know you not that all power lies close... Our task is nearly done. Be still.'

'All power!' repeated Elizabeth. She looked about fretfully. I shrank back into the dark porch.

'Yea! All richness, all knowledge, all might! From the moment of your birth, all was written, and shall be. Give me the hair, then. I have his blood, mixed in the image. His blood; where his hand was torn upon your brooch.'

'Madame,' I heard Elizabeth say uneasily, 'is there still need for this? Is not the prize gained already, I ask you?'

Heedlessly, her mother stretched bony arms to the sky.

'Mithras attend me,' she said devoutly.

'Fortune defend me,' cried Elizabeth. Then: 'But, all is arranged—he will be here tomorrow, and were we caught at this craft... ah, Jesu! we should lose everything!'

I saw the Duchess's snarling teeth, like an animal's.

'Men are fickle, daughter, fickle, fickle!' she crooned. 'Let's leave naught to chance. Forget not the other! Had she slipped your mind?'

'Nay,' said Elizabeth, twisting her hands together. 'But he's mad for *me*!

Jacquetta of Bedford was busy with the manikin, binding something about its head. From her pouch Elizabeth took another small figure, one that had breasts and was crowned with a gilded wisp.

'Shall they embrace?' she asked, bringing the thing close to the larger one. As she spoke, a black shape trotted over the lawn with a little lilting noise. The Duchess stooped and lifted it in her arms.

'Ah, Gyb, my sweet!' she cried softly. 'See, daughter, I did not need to call him. Now he can bind the charm. Yea, place them together, so...' and I saw my lady mould the little dolls as one... 'And the pelt of a black beast can seal the matter.'

She rubbed the entwined manikins swiftly over Gyb's arched back. He let out a high hoarse cry and leapt from Jacquetta's grasp into the shadows. The Duchess laughed, a pleased noise, and muttering, elevated both figures towards the moon.

'Attend me, Mithras,' said Elizabeth, kneeling. 'And send me my heart's desire.'

A terrifying little wind arose. It swayed the dark massed yews and ruffled the pale flower-heads sleeping against the stone house wall. It passed curiously through my hiding-place, and with cold mocking fingers lifted my hair. A drum throbbed fiercely. I touched my breast with the Blessed Sign; I touched the drum; it was my heart. For a further instant I stood motionless, staring to where the Duchess held the figures high, like a priest raising the Eucharist to heaven. The wind dropped, leaving me more afraid than ever in my life. Even when Elizabeth and her mother began to cross the lawn towards me, I could not move. Then, at the last second I ran back; I slid into a little closet before they reached the door. In the passage without, a candle bloomed. I heard a man's voice, a deep, soft chuckle. So Anthony Woodville had also left his bed.

'Is it done?'

'Aye, my lord. I'm drained of strength.'

He laughed again, unquietly. 'May our lady mother's wiles bring fruit, sweet sister. Yet I doubt not that yours would have sufficed.'

'It will be a rich harvest, my son,' said the Duchess wearily. She said again: 'All is written.'

'It's heresy.' This, with a trace of fear. 'Remember Eleanor Cobham!'

'Bah!' said the Duchess scornfully. 'She grew careless. And this is worth any hazard. You will see, a year hence. Come, Gyb!'

Calling him softly, she went away. I stayed in the closet. A quivering ran up and down my sides, as if I were being stroked with feathers. Then I felt a soft nudging round my legs. A roaring purr filled the chamber, and I knew it to be, not the foul fiend, but Gyb. I dared not even shove him away with my foot. The Duchess was returning.

'To bed, Mother, I pray you.' Elizabeth's voice was alarmingly close. 'I'll need you in the morning, fresh and bright.'

'I can't find my sweeting,' said the Duchess petulantly. 'Puss? Where are you, poppet?'

'I will find the creature, Madame,' said Anthony Woodville easily. 'Go now. I'll bring him to your chamber.'

Lady Elizabeth soothed her mother away. As their slow steps faded, I stood, frantically plotting escape. There was no way out other than by the door into the passage. I heard Anthony Woodville calling the cat. Fiend that he was, Gyb yelled in answer. He pressed against my legs, uttering pleased chirps and a long, wise wail. The candlelight grew brighter. Filled with terror, I closed my eyes. A drop of hot wax fell on my neck. My eyes flew open: Anthony Woodville, tall, slender, elegant, looked musingly down at me. Gyb sprang to him, rubbing and roaring. Gently, he was pushed aside.

'Away, Gyb!' be said, just as if I were not trembling there in the flickering light. 'You are a plaguey monster. You have put hairs upon my new hose.'

His voice did not hold the anger I dreaded.

'Well, maiden?' he said. 'Why do you dawdle here? I was about to make fast the doors. We are late tonight.'

I swallowed. My throat was dry as old bread.

'Speak!' he said, more sternly. 'Are you moonstruck?'

I found my voice; I begged his pardon. I was but looking for my lady, I said—I was passing sorry. In my sight, his features looked long and thin. Sharp.

'Did you find her?' he said. His voice was gentle again.

'She was without.' I pointed to the door. I trembled. Then I heard him whisper a quiet oath, bitten off midway.

'Tell me, good maid,' he said, in the same even tone, 'how long were you here? You surely saw my sister and my mother in the garden—why did you not go out to them?'

Then, he needed no answer. My chattering teeth, my face, sufficed to inform him that I had seen something not for my eyes, bewildering and wholly bad, yet not altogether understood. I felt his long fingers on my arm. They gripped tight.

'What saw you, maiden?'

'They were playing with the cat.'

'What more?' His fingers bit my bones.

Suddenly something made me wise, more than I deserved. 'Naught else, my lord,' I said steadily.

He remained silent. I made a tiny flurried motion towards escape. His hand stayed firm.

'Do you dream o' nights?' he asked..

'Yes, sir, but why...'

'And your dreams are passing real, I doubt not,' he broke in. My arm was beginning to ache. 'So real, so true, that when you wake, you vow the dream was part of life. Is't so?'

'Yea.' My trembling stirred the candle flame. He smiled. His grasp relented. I rubbed my shoulder with an icy hand, my eyes fixed on his face.

'I've hurt you,' he said wonderingly. With great delicacy he drew aside the collar of my gown. 'How easy it is to bruise young flesh!' he murmured. 'Last week in London I saw a wench flogged at the cart's tail. The poor wretch had stolen a trifle of her mistress's beauty salve. And, though this good dame was fond of the child, she had no choice but to watch her punished. Unfair, think you? I vow there's no maid alive who does not snatch a morsel of this cream and that lotion, especially if the mistress be old and ugly, the maiden fair. Is it not fitting for hands that prepare the bath to take a little healing balm to cheer their soreness? Or perfume to lighten a weary heart?'

In his eyes I saw myself, a tiny, wavering figure. He knew about the rose-water cream. 'My lady is not old and ugly, sir,' I whispered. Through my lashes I saw on his face a look that reminded me of Gyb, after devouring a bird.

'Yes, whipped at the cart's tail,' he said, musing. 'Jesu! how that poor damsel's back was bloody! A pretty skin. But that was at the start of her journey.'

My stomach began to churn and plunge, like the courtier's horse. I began to cry. Anthony Woodville lifted my face with one finger.

'Do not weep,' he said. 'All shall be well, if you are wise. What saw you this night?'

'Naught, my lord,' I sobbed, and this time I myself believed it.

He smiled. 'You had a dream,' he said, and his eyes were large and sharp, eyes from a dream. 'Back to your bed. Tomorrow, you shall bring in the May.'

Agnes wondered why I wept. She held me in her arms and nursed me sleepily. But I would not tell her. I would tell no one of the dark and hateful things—then I had no wish to speak of them. And strangely, all was as my lord had said. The night faded, in the space of my drying tears, as if it had never been.

We were waked by a merry sun, and fat Agace banging on the door, dressed already in her scarlet kirtle, with glowing face to match—through joy, for we were to go a-Maying, all of us down to the smallest scullion; all of us, without exception.

'They will have to get their own dinner,' snickered Agnes. For a league she jested, making me laugh with images of my Lady Elizabeth's cherished hands cooking mutton, of her mother washing platters. I sat behind her astride the spavined palfrey, treading the road-ruts to Stoney Stratford. The day was merry. Great swathes of persil foamed in the ditches, the may-bloom hung low, and my heart lifted, through laced branches, to meet the blossom, its delicate cream and pale rose and its nested harvest of small birds, singing.

My head was bare, save for a chaplet of primroses, for Agnes said it was right seemly for a feast-day maid to go thus, and bother the priests! The sun turned my hair to gold, to fire; I saw it, falling so bright and sheen below the palfrey's dusty sides. My lady's cast-off gown fit snugly, slashed a thigh's length to reveal, under its gay russet, a glimpse of tender green silk. The neck was low; Agnes had pounched and padded my bosom to show it off. The sleeves were slit in twenty tiny fronds. Five years from fashion it might have been, but I was sore enamoured of it. And I had washed my face in May dew; nay, I had rolled in it naked, so that every limb had danced and tingled with the soft, gay tears of spring. Then I had made my lady Elizabeth ready for the day. Still pale, but with a hidden glow, like a may-bud, she had tossed aside the dark dress I offered her. 'Away with the old black gowns!' I dared not ask her reason, either for this or for her sudden disdain of the widow's headgear; her choice was a small gold hennin with a high veil to match a dress, shimmering and dawn-rosy, that I had not seen before. I merely knelt to straighten the long skirt and attach the broad gold cincture about my lady's weasel-waist. Before the sun was clear of the great oak's topmost bough, she drove me from the chamber.

'Lady Elizabeth gave me some money.' I stretched my arm past Agnes's cheek, to show the half-angel in my palm. 'And wished me good fortune at the fair.'

'The Duchess gave me a beating,' she answered tartly. 'Because I was not spry enough dressing her. Jesu, what masters! I must find me a great lord who will burn Grafton about their heads. There's a love-spell I wished I'd tried now. I'm sick of being whipped, and cursed, and virgin.'

'Don't, Agnes,' I whispered.

'Don't what?'

'Talk of spells, love-craft. I would not see you damned.'

She reined in to laugh like a woodpecker. 'Well, Mistress Pope-Holy!' she cried. 'And what's amiss? A little flower, a straw in the wind—all good customs, to hurt man nor beast. Hawthorn-wench, you're as guilty as I!'

Yea, my true love would come from the north. It was then that I began to hate the hawthorn, for, after what I had seen last night, which, though sunk deep in my mind's pit still brought unease, my little wistful ruse ranked itself with the worst spells of all.

'A great lord, then, Agnes?' I asked, for diversion. The pony grazed. 'Would you desert Master Silversmith?'

She half-turned. 'How should I do that?' she demanded. 'I'm his by troth-plight—no other marriage would be valid.' The sunlight caught her dimples. 'Besides, I lust for Master Jack right well. He's a strong leg, a lickerish eye...'

The groom escorting Dick and Thomas Grey ahead, came trotting back.

'Would to God you wenches would cease chattering,' he said discourteously. 'We'll not make Stoney Stratford before noon.'

'Bite your tongue,' said Agnes. 'Why all the haste? You're like my lady. She chivvied me out of the house an it were on fire.'

'Yea, they seemed passing anxious to see our backs,' muttered the groom, hauling the pony's head out of the succulent ditch.

'Why, here's another in a hurry!' cried Agnes, staring up the road. Towards us rode a horseman. A black cloak flew behind him like a dusty sail. His mount's hide boiled with sweat. He rode without skill; as he reached us, his horse swerved blindly and struck the groom's beast, sending horse and rider plunging towards the hedge. He stopped to ask no pardon, but spurred on hotly and galloped off the way we had come. The groom struggled out of the ditch, shaking off broken blossoms.

'Pox take you!' he yelled after the departing figure.

Agnes said wonderingly: 'Was that not Master Daunger?'

Yes, 'twas Daunger. He had swivelled his chalky whey-face and hanging lip towards us for an instant. Daunger, a dangerous name. Do-this-night-as-I-have-said Daunger. I kept silent.

'Is the clerk for Grafton again, then?' Agnes murmured. 'More pious instruction for my lady?'

'Not today,' I only whispered. She had been like a spray of may-bloom, ready to flower. Could the clerk be her lover? I did not know what it was that lovers did that was so pleasant and nice and full of sin. Yet whatever it was I knew that chaste Elizabeth did it not. Agnes stood in the stirrups and clapped her hands, and I forgot all about Master Daunger, and cried with her: 'Look! the May Pole!'

Stoney Stratford opened to us round a bend in the road. Every house door stood wide. More hawthorn, scattered with blossoms, stood in great branches at every porch. Garlands of meadow-sweet and cowslips hung from window and door frame. Folk thronged the narrow street, laughing, singing, crowned with flowers, with periwinkle, wild rose and young ivy; and in the square, with a breeze lifting its twelve gaudy streamers, the great ash-pole grew upwards to the sky. Dressed from tip to ground with wreaths of marsh-marigold, primroses and may, it stood winking in the sun. On its head lay a ring of royal lilies. 'Worship me,' it said.

Children ran to meet us. One pushed a nosegay into my hand, violets clustered with harebell and eglantine, still dew-damp.

'Oh, Agnes,' I said, lost in delight. 'Look, Agnes!'

Agnes's eyes darted about. She flirted her lashes at an elderly merchant, pursed her lips as a band of young clerks rolled by, arms linked. Flushed with ale, they bawled a chant far from holy. 'How wicked the world is!' she said, with dancing eyes.

We halted on the green, where there seemed to have congregated a host of young men. As we dismounted one fell in courtly pose upon his knee, clutched his heart and feigned a swoon. At the comical look on his face I burst out laughing. Agnes swept by with a hauteur worthy of the Duchess. I looked up at the ring of faces. A youth in a blue doublet held a buttercup under my chin and guffawed. I heard: 'Great Jesu, that maiden's hair!' and 'But maiden-hair's a herb, Will, and she's a flower, yea, by the Rood.' 'Deflower, say you?' A great burst of mirth, and Agnes's cross, seizing hand. 'Stay close.' I caught the tail of a voice, strange and yearning, like the look in John Skelton's eyes. 'Little and young, I grant you. But by my mother's soul, she lights my fire!'

So I was conscious of the hot stares of men. Their looks were like lances, to prick and delve, to consume me. I knew the object of their joy. It rippled about me, hued like autumn fire, cloth of gold, a beech-nut, taking the colour from the flowers, laughing back at the sun. I say this in no conceit, for from my hair's lustre came more fear than pride, that day.

Agnes whispered: 'Come! We'll lose the others, or we'll be put in charge of Tom and Dick!' and tugged me, squirming, through the crowd to the far side of the green, where men were shooting at the butts and slender wands, and the sweetmeat booths were set up cheek by jowl with the ale-wagons.

'We'll have wine,' she decided. I bought honey cakes to go with the thin sour brew. I watched Agnes drinking, her full creamy throat tipped back. Pink drops escaped the flagon's lip and trickled on her white bosom. I told her she was fair and she laughed.

'There's your great lord, Agnes.' I pointed towards a corpulent squire of sixty. 'Or him, look!' turning to a man who, skinny as a thong, contorted his body into horrible shapes before an admiring crowd.

'Nay, sweeting, he'd make too restless a bedfellow.' She pulled me on. A juggler threw up coloured platters. Two bold-faced women balanced themselves upside down on sword-points, their skirts falling about naked thighs. A group of 'prentices stood over-close, gibing shrilly. 'Flemish whores,' Agnes muttered.

Lovers there were, too. Walking close-twined, sitting lip-to-lip on benches. And from the depths of a scented bush came a rustling and a soft cry. At the entrance to a side street, I saw two soldiers gazing at the Fair. Their stare was a mixture of longing and feigned disinterest.

We sat down to watch the mummers. First the Green Giant, then Robin! I sat with hands clasped, loving him. In his suit of Kendal Green, he strutted and bragged, showing his prowess in archery. Maid Marian, a pretty boy with long golden hair, piped of her love. She followed him languidly, all over the green. Wherever he went, so did she. Robin sprang into easy attitudes; Marian tripped on her gown. They performed a courtly dance, and one of Marian's false breasts crept round the back of her waist. She fell prey to the Sheriff; Robin hammered with his broadsword, and the pair were united by Friar Tuck, much the worse for ale. Agnes and I shared a bench with four 'prentices, who leaped to their feet every minute to whistle and shoot peas at Maid Marian. Once, they upset the seat completely and began fighting among themselves. As Robin bore off his bride, the crowd bawled and chanted for more. A troupe of bagpipers who came next were hounded from the green in fury.

A strange creature capered into view. Clad in sparkling motley, one leg red, the other yellow, he frisked around the hem of the watching circle, tweaking the noses of the men, patting the women's cheeks. He had a face so comical that even had he not pulled it into hideous grimaces, men would have smiled at him. He rolled his eyes so high that only the whites showed, and pulled down his nose with his tongue.

'Certes! 'Tis the King's fool!' said a low voice behind me. 'Poor Patch. The richest man at court.'

'Edward must be hereabouts.'

'Leicester,' said the first voice cryptically. 'Ah, Jesu!' liquid with laughter. 'Will you look! He does my soul good!'

He was not a tall man, this jester; only about a head higher than I, and Agnes would have dwarfed him standing. Neither was he old, he was lithe and supple, but his face was patterned with lines, like a withered fruit. He came skipping, and stood before us, duck-fashion; he pinned the pike of one shoe to the ground with the other, scratching his head; he looked mournfully about, cried: 'Succour!' bent bow-legged and, agile as a monkey, seized the offending foot and tossed a backward somersault.

'Ah, bravely done!' cried Agnes.

The fool's head turned. Unerringly, he pranced over to Agnes, and grasped her hand. He pressed a lingering kiss into the palm, gazing into her face, with lifted, mocking brows. I stared at the fretted cheeks, the temples with the heavy painted lines from each eyelid, the curling mouth, still kiss-puckered. The eyes were a clear dove-grey, and shrewd. He took my hand next. I felt his teeth nip my thumb.

'You're gallant, Sir Fool,' I said shyly.

The fool gave a great cry of passion and clasped his breast. 'Beauty has spoken soft words,' he declared. Everyone watched, grinning. 'Madame, my heart is yours. Keep it.' He delved in his overlarge scrip and drew out the glistening, blood-clotted heart of some animal, sheep or calf, or man! I know not what it was, save that it made me scream. The men roared. I felt sick, as the horrid thing dripped before my face. And he knew it instantly—no fool, this fool—for he dropped the offal on the grass and bent close, asking: 'What ails the little maid?' his voice deeper than the high whine he gave his audience.

'It's a weakness,' Agnes sounded vexed. 'A certain delicacy.' They were giving me wine. 'And she hates cock-fights. And bear-baiting.'

We had already passed the bear, with his poor burned feet, stamping a chained, ceaseless circle. And that was only a dancer.

'Strange, but forgive me,' said the fool. ''Twas a crude jest. Am I pardoned, fair one?' This in a loud whine; the crowd was impatient for him to continue. I looked in his grey eyes, saw tenderness, touched his gay shoulder with a trembling hand. He sprang away, tipping himself on to his hands, and sped thus around the eager circle. The hobby-horse, gaudy-ribboned, chased the fool across the green as the Moorish dancers ran before us in a straggling file. They wore green and red fustian, dagged sleeves, bells. 'Clack!' went their staves as they feinted in the dance. The smell of trodden grass rose sweet and sour. But my joy in it was dulled by the fool's nasty jest. Though I had forgiven him, the bad taste of it lay heavy in my mouth, and when he bounded back to us I looked upon him without pleasure. He had a bauble on a stick, a monstrous moon-face, gilded with a smile on one side, a frown on the other.

'Ladies, follow me!' he pleaded, and Agnes rose from the bench. The fool's eyes travelled up her height.

'By the Rood, maiden, you are lofty,' he remarked.

''Tis you that is low,' she said haughtily, but I could see he charmed her in the same way as did the young birds, the flowers. He stretched out a hand to me, as I sat motionless.

'Marry! the little maid's still wroth,' he said. 'Come, my honey-comb. We'll find a friend of mine.'

He skipped ahead, Agnes admonishing him, but smiling, for as he went he sang about a lustful friar, and most of the words were nonsense. I lagged behind; Agnes nudged me on, like a dog herding sheep. Patch prodded a passing belly with his bauble; an important, a fine belly at that, clothed in murrey and fur with a broad gold pouch. And the belly's owner merely loosed a great guffaw and slapped Patch round the shoulders.

'Jesu, Agnes!' said I. 'He's bold.'

She gave a knowing little grin. 'Well 'tis the King's fool, forget it not,' she said; and I ran after him, eager at last, wanting to ask about the King, the unknown magnificences that were his daily fare. He threaded through the revellers, supple and broad in his motley, and once he turned with a grimace like some evil sprite leading me on to danger. I ran beneath the sun. Red and yellow, the day.

I thought he might be taking us to meet a courtier, but he halted at an old man's bench. Despite the fierce heat, this man was cowled to the ears in threadbare wool so that little of his face was visible. Across his knees he cradled a harp of most ancient design. Pale as lilies, his hands were translucent and veined. The fool stretched out a hand to pluck one string of the lyre. The sound was a drop of silver rain falling.

'Old friend, how goes it?' he said softly.

The minstrel opened eyes clear as water. ''Tis you, rascal,' he murmured. 'Methought I felt a cold wind blowing then.'

'Aged blood runs thin,' said Patch cheerily. 'How many summers, old one?'

With a twitching smile, he said: 'I know not. Yet I remember the second Richard, and the day Wat Tyler rode on London. Richard saved that day of blood. Sweet Richard, they called him.'

This is truth: I felt a strange little pang. It would be easy for me to seek sensation, to say that in an instant the future showed itself to me, but it was naught like that... Only something in me which heard those words, and moved to tenderness.

Patch pulled off his tight scarlet cap, and I saw that he was indeed young, no more than eighteen. Tight buttery curls covered his head. He said: 'I've brought you two fair maids. To mind you of other May Days!' and laughed, a whit churlishly, and nudged the minstrel with his elbow. The hood fell back. I felt the clear wise eyes upon my face. Thin he was, and passing frail. Any lusty wind could have taken him up like a puffball. One hand left the harp and beckoned to me.

'He has written a fair ballad,' Patch breathed in my ear. 'The ending troubles him. Is it finished, master?' he bawled.

'Sit by me, little maid,' said the minstrel. 'I have a song in mind, certes, it has lived in me for months. A tale of lovers. The knight, I know him well, child of my mind as he is. But the woman...' his head drooped, wearily.

'Is she a good maid?' I asked.

He said, with eyes closed: 'I am deathly sick.' Then: 'Yea, she is one who loved so true that she followed her love into the wilds and the desolate places. I knew such a one, once...'

Patch spat delicately. 'Nay, master!' he said challengingly. 'These creatures are things of song and romance. Angels, to haunt the imaginings of men—in truth I vow they're wayward harlots to draw a man's soul from his body. Then they depart, leaving him sick from lust and longing.'

'If only I could complete it,' said the old man, uncaring. 'The maiden's name escapes me... I cannot see her. The Forest Maid,' he murmured. 'The Faithful Maid. The Lily Maid... nay, nay!' he twanged his harp, vexed. 'Lilies are cold and holy—this maid is warm.'

Suddenly, Patch crouched close to me.

'Look, master!' he whispered. 'Look at her hair! Does this not inspire you?'

The veined hand stretched out. Taking a lock of my hair in his fingers, the old man gazed as it lay like a live thing, shining and reddening in his palm.

'Aye,' he said, after a long space. 'Nut-brown hair! A Nut-Brown Maid. Brown eyes, brown hair, sheen as a fairy woman's, and a heart faithful to death. Is that your nature?' he asked sharply. 'Before the dedication, I must know. Are you a true maid to your lover?'

'I have no lover,' I said. He smiled, a kind, veiled smile. 'Only a dream of one, to which I'm true.'

'A fair answer.' Sweet uneven chords issued from the harp. Patch cried: 'Sing! Make her immortal!'

'Cynical Sir Fool,' murmured the minstrel. 'My first verse then, shall echo your philosophy.'

'Be it right or wrong, these men among
On women do complain,
Affirming this, how that it is
A labour spent in vain
To love them well, for never a dele
They love a man again;
For let a man do what he can
Their favour to attain,

Yet if a new to them pursue,
Their first true lover then
Laboureth for naught; for from her thought
He is a banished man.'

I felt Patch stroking my hair, gently.

'We will have it in two voices,' said the rhymer. 'That first shall be sung by the man, in his ignorance. Now the damsel sets him right.'

'I say not nay, but that all day
It is both written and said
That woman's faith is, as who saith,
All utterly decayed.
But nevertheless, right good witness
In this case might be laid…'

His strange acute gaze fell on me, sweeping my hair, my face, my body. 'Can you write?' he asked. Someone thrust pen and paper before me. 'Set this down,' he said. 'I have but a little time.'

'That they love true and continue:
Record the Nut-Brown Maid,
Which, when her love came her to prove,
To her to make his moan,
Would not depart, for in her heart
She loved but him alone.'

A circle of listeners formed about us. They were quiet. The slow voice's tune was passing soft. The verses flowed by. I wrote feverishly, knowing my spelling poor. I blessed the nuns of Leicester, who had taught me my letters.

'It standeth so: a deed is do
Whereof great harm shall grow;
My destiny is for to die
A shameful death, I trow.
Or else to flee. The t'one must be:
None other way I know

But to withdraw as an outlaw
And take me to my bow.
Wherefore adieu, my own heart true!
None other rede I can;
For I must to the greenwood go,
Alone, a banished man.'

''Tis Robin Hood!' mocked Patch. His nose was out of joint by the attention the crowd was giving to the old ballad-maker, who only smiled.

'This is an allegory,' he said softly. 'Know you not that every tale can have two, three, an hundred meanings?'

'Are we not in the greenwood?' demanded Patch.

'Your mind is no sharper than it seems,' said the harpist. 'The greenwood can be the battlefield; the tomb, even. He of whom I sing, simple or noble. Construe it as you will.'

He struck a chord, I gripped the quill. Three or four filled sheets already lay on the grass. I found myself trembling at the words' beauty, glad that I should have aided their birth, if this was indeed truth and not the guile of a cunning showman. Then, glancing at the white fingers like crabbed stalks, I knew him too kindly, too much upon the next world's threshold to be counterfeit.

'Now sith that ye have showed to me
The secret of your mind,
I shall be plain to you again,
Like as ye shall me find.
Sith it is so that ye will go,
I will not leave behind.
Shall never be said the Nut-Brown Maid
Was to her love unkind.
Make you ready, for so am I,
Although it were anone,
For in my mind, of all mankind
I love but you alone.'

'Yea, that I do,' said Patch suddenly, close.

Rhyme snapped at the heels of rhyme. Frantic, I wrote.

'By Venus and St Valentine, I love thee, maiden,' he said, whispering.

'What next, what next?' chanted the crowd, as the ballad-maker paused.

'Good people, give me space to wet my throat,' he said wearily.

'I do not speak false,' muttered Patch. 'You've robbed me of wit. I think you even rob me of my soul. I love you.'

'Peace, Sir Fool,' I said, full of impatience. 'I cannot hear the minstrel's words. I'll laugh at your clowning later.'

But he leaped from the grass with an oath and swung away, broke through the crowd and was gone. A few turned to look after him, with little interest.

'I counsel you, remember how
It is no maiden's law
Nothing to doubt, but to run out
To wood with an outlaw.
For ye must there in your hand bear
A bow ready to draw;
And as a thief thus must you live
Ever in dread and awe;
Whereby to you great harm might grow:
Yet had I liefer than
That had I to the greenwood go,
Alone, a banished man.'

The tale of the Nut-Brown Maid leaped lightly from the ballad-maker's tongue, across the strings like sparkling rain, grew strong, sweet under my pen. She was constant and true, as I would be. She would cut her hair off by her ear, her kirtle at her knee, and so would I. The sheets of verse lay scattered like flowers. Now the lover tested his maid, tempered her steel with sorrow.

'If that ye went, ye should repent;
For in the forest now,
I have purveyed me of a maid
Whom I love more than you;
Another more fair than ever ye were
I dare it well avow,

And of you both each should be wroth
With other, as I trow;
It were mine ease to live in peace
So will I, if I can;
Wherefore I to the wood will go,
Alone, a banished man.'

Someone cried: 'Shame!' I set down my pen. 'Master, I am unworthy of the song,' I said. 'I think I could not brook such a betrayal.'

The ancient eyes scanned my face.

'Yea,' he said, softly, smiling. 'Yea. You could, you will. A loving woman does not cease to love. Child, so will it be, even though your tears flow; flow like wine on a feast day.'

I thought: how should he know? And then: I must strive to be the brave maid of his dreaming. I thought on my petty failings, and was ashamed.

'But a happy ending, I pray,' I breathed.

His mouth quirked on a smile. 'How fortunate that we can shape our romances to fit our will!'

'Though in the wood I understood
Ye had a paramour,
All this may nought remove my thought,
But that I will be your.
And she shall find me soft and kind
And courteous every hour;
Glad to fufil all that she will
Command me, to my power:
For had ye, lo, an hundred mo',
Yet would I be that one,
For in my mind, of all mankind
I love but you alone.

Mine own dear love, I see the prove
That ye be kind and true;
Of maid, of wife, in all my life,
The best that ever I knew.
Be merry and glad, be no more sad,
The case is changed new,

For it were ruth that for your truth
Ye should have cause to rue.
Be not dismayed, whatsoever I said
To you when I began:
I will not to the greenwood go,
I am no banished man.'

Fainter, the minstrel's words murmured on.

'...I will you bring, and with a ring
By way of marriage
I will you take, and lady make,
As shortly as I can:
Thus have you won an Earles son,
And not a banished man...'

His hand crept to his breast, as if it sought something long-lost. The wan face grew paler. I touched the hand gently.

'Are we finished?' I asked. Before my eyes, he was fading. Shrinking into the coarse cloth of his habit.

'The heavenly dedication,' he whispered. 'One verse more...' I could scarcely catch the words.

'Here may ye see that women be
In love meek, kind and stable,
Let never man reprove them than
Or call them variable;
But rather pray God that we may
To them be comfortable,
Which sometime proveth such as He loveth,
If they be charitable.
For sith men would that woman should
Be meek to them each one;
Much more ought they to God obey,
And serve but Him alone.'

His head bowed low. Two men with fiddles stepped up. 'Give us the air again, master,' they said. 'We have two here to do your ballad justice.'

A boy and a girl stood behind them, she with a chaplet of lilies on her head, he swarthy, eager. 'Bring wine for our poet, fellows!' they cried. 'The best there is, and we will pay!'

He was so still. I crept kneeling and touched his cheek with fingers soft as butterfly. The heavy head fell on my breast, the frail weight into my arms.

'The song is ended,' Agnes said sadly.

A priest came near, his sombre cloth ill-tuned with the flowers, the sunshine, and the cups of wine. He knelt by the silent form on the grass. Awkwardly, men doffed their caps, shuffled their feet, uneasy in the presence of this unseen, unbidden May Day guest. I turned away. I wept a little.

Agnes and I went together across the green. I looked up at the sky where the sun was tipping rosily towards the west. The minstrel seemed a good old man; I wondered if he were there already, young and strong again, playing a better lyre, smiling with those loved years ago. He, who had called me his Nut-Brown Maid, and dedicated a bright song, not to some great lord, but to me. Me, and none other.

Then Patch came running, catching at my hand, his words stumbling, and a different emotion for each of the comic lines on his face; humble and repentant and mocking and mischievous, and with an odd sad desperate gleam, like that in John Skelton's eyes, and the yearning voices of the men in the crowd who had touched my face and hair. Yea, he would be my lover, he said, and do me solemn duty, yet he begged my pardon for his churlishness and for speaking in an ill-advised, goatish way. Was he, once more, forgiven?

Again I had to say I was not offended, which was true, for at no time had I paid him much heed, being caught up with the joyous song and sorrow of the day, and I said, sadly:

'Your old friend died. Why do men die?'

He could not answer this, the silliest question in the world, but dropped his jaw and hung his head; then asked: 'May we still be dear friends?'

'I'll look for you next May Day.'

He shook his head. 'My life hangs on the King's whim,' he answered. 'This time next year I could be in France, or Byzantium. I ride for London tomorrow.'

'Back to court,' I said wistfully. 'Well, good fortune, Sir Fool. I doubt not with your skill his Grace is pleased to employ you. But we shall never meet, and that is truth. Never in a thousand years will I come to London. I am bound to serve at Grafton Regis with the Lady Grey.'

The fool's eyes narrowed. 'Elizabeth Woodville?' he said wonderingly. 'The widow with the virgin's face?' He began to laugh. 'Be not so sure, sweeting, you will never come to court!'

'Another jest?' I asked. A good one by the look of it; he rolled about and bounced off the palfrey which Jankin was holding for me to mount and go home on while the sky was still blue and gold.

'The King's Grey Mare!' he said, and seized me round the waist, laughing like a jaybird.

'I don't understand,' I said, dizzy.

'A jape, a folly!' he cried. 'Ah, maiden, I love you. Forget me not!' With a frisk, he was gone, bright red and yellow bird, plunging across the meadow.

'I mistrust that fellow,' said Agnes, glaring after him.

'He would have loved me,' I said, feeling foolish.

'Yea, to some tune.' Agnes slipped her foot in Jankin's hand and swung astride the palfrey. She pulled me up behind her, asking Jankin how he had fared. Quite well, said he. He had tried his skill in the archery and come second.

'I would not have been beat,' he said indignantly, 'had not one of the King's archers, a great lummox, sneaked in and hit the highest score before my eyes! I complained to the arbiters, saying that he should be on duty and had no business with May-games, but they would not have it, and he got the prize. A cask of Rhenish, it was.'

'You should have challenged him for it.'

'Well, the knave was courteous enough to give me a drink,' said Jankin, wiping dirt off his doublet. 'I asked him why he was not with his fellows at Leicester, and he said they would have been, had not the King halted at Stoney Stratford.'

'I did not see *him* at the Maying,' sighed Agnes covetously.

'Nay,' said Jankin. 'For he had taken a fancy to go hunting, the man-at-arms told me. They thought it strange, in the midst of an array, but off he rode, leaving his company blunting their weapons on apples among the village folk.'

'No royal whim is strange,' reproved Agnes.

'Jankin,' I said proudly, 'I have had a song written for me today. In praise of my nut-brown hair. What think you of that?'

We rode homeward in an untidy line, I loitering with my thoughts as dusk fell. In a senseless way I thought that the old ballad-maker's death was my fault. I managed to dismiss this, by thinking quite kindly of Patch. He would have loved me, despite what Agnes said. Several men would have loved me that day. I pulled off my garland and breathed its dying sweetness. Behind me I could hear the sounds of horseplay, snatches of song mingled with the blackbird's bedtime twittering, and I mused on love, wondering at its essence. Men had found me fair—that was enough. For I suspected there was something a whit frightening in this business of love. One could die of love; that I knew well.

When we came again to Grafton Regis, the sober house was lit as for a festival. Lady Elizabeth wore her dazzling gown and a smile like the crown jewels; and my lady of Bedford had been giving her cat wine, for he lay in the hearth, dead drunk.

Even then, they contrived to keep it from us for the best part of the summer, what had happened on May Day when we had all been chivvied out into the morning, and sent safely far from home. There had been a wedding at Grafton, most secretly celebrated, the bride my Lady Elizabeth, and the groom none other than tall Ned, twenty-one years of age, comely and omnipotent. King Edward the Fourth himself, besotted and bewitched and driven to the brink of madness by my lady and her scheming mother.

Certes, she wrought a fierce work that day, did Elizabeth. A seduction which, in twenty years, was to cause the ruin of one more precious than my own soul. For this I cannot forgive her, and I never shall.

Then between us let us discuss
What was all the manere
Between them two; we will also
Tell all the pain is fere
That she was in. Now I begin,
So that ye me answere;
Wherefore all ye that present be,

I pray you, give an ear.
I am the Knight. I come by night,
As secret as I can,
Saying, Alas! Thus standeth the case,
I am a banished man.
(The Nut-Brown Maid)

Agace the cook, as I have said, was an insolent old dame, stout and proud. She considered herself accomplished; she could recite the feast days and the Saints' Days without hesitation when she was in a good humour. As she had known me many years and had seen me beaten on more than one occasion, she afforded me scant respect. Our conversation was therefore akin to the parry-and-thrust of swordsmen.

I went often to her kitchen, that December of 1468. Four years I had languished at Grafton Regis after Elizabeth's departure. And I was still not resigned to the fact that she had left me behind. Even her sisters, gathered up from the length and breath of England, had gone with her to court. The Duchess of Bedford and her husband Richard Woodville, and Anthony Woodville, Lord Rivers (or Lord Scales, as he was sometimes called) were firmly ensconced there. So we heard, in fleeting spasms of news. In this bitterly cold manor I was sick with ennui. Dispirited, too. My dearest friend had left me: Agnes was in Kent, a respectable matron helping in Jack's silversmithy. Thomas and Dick were gone with their mother the Queen, to be trained at court. Their old nurse was dead. It seemed therefore that Agace and I were the last survivors of the Grafton we had known.

But this Christmastide Jacquetta of Bedford had come back. It was at least a familiar face, someone to whisper about. She had broken her journey at Grafton halfway through December, bringing an entourage of about twenty fashionable females, and complaining of the grippe. Straight to bed had she gone, and I remember it was I who had to fly around airing and sweetening chambers for the pack of them. As I stood by Agace's kitchen fire trying to keep warm, I thought I heard Jacquetta complaining from her bedroom aloft.

Stirring vigorously at a pan of food, Agace sweated and swore.

'By God's bones, let us hope this dish will pleasure my lady.' She ladled the egg mess on to soft toast. Herbelettes, she called it. The smell of the ginger and galyngale rose deliciously.

'I know not why she doesn't return to court,' I said.

The cook laughed derisively. 'Ha! I know why. This at least is her own domain. Despised, yet useful. Here she can be Queen in her own right. I trow my lady is still offended by the treatment she got two years ago!'

I thought on this for a moment. True, after the birth of the Princess Elizabeth, Jacquetta had come back to Grafton in a fine fury, swearing that she had not expected the Queen to use her thus. 'She babbled some wild talk that it was through her that Elizabeth was Queen at all, and now she must bid her aged mother do her obeisance like the humblest vassal,' said Agace, arraying a salver with the meal.

'And did she?' I wiped the foul table with a cloth.

'Oh, heard you not the tale? After the Queen's churching in Westminster, there was a banquet at the Palace like men have not seen in years, with four halls crammed with guests. The Queen sat in a separate chamber on a golden chair, while Margaret, the King's sister, and my lady of Bedford attended her. They dare not speak, and when Elizabeth addressed them, they must kneel. When the board had been cleared for revelry, my lady Jacquetta must kneel again, and she vowed that her gizzard has never been right since, for all the dust that the dancers kicked up. Princess Margaret, they say, was bidden to curtsey each time she passed the Queen's chair, even in the dance. This she did. She's a lovely wench. But her Grace's mother was far from pleased by her evening's entertainment.'

I choked on laughter. I pictured the old woman glowering on her knees, while Elizabeth, regal in her chair of estate, looked loftily over her head. There was probably a grain of truth in what Agace said. Although her husband was Constable of England, and, it was said, a bounty of treasure flowed constantly into her children's lap, Jacquetta still occasionally would rule a smaller realm. I took the tray in my hands.

'Yes, you bear it up to my lady,' said Agace, turning to warm her rump. 'Great idle wench,' she said, not unkindly. 'Sixteen, are you? And not betrothed? You should be professed as a nun.'

'What?' I said, lusting to kick her fat legs. 'This minute? While my lady of Bedford still needs me?'

'Yea,' she said grudgingly, 'she seems to like your touch with her hair and finery. Outrageous vanities, she has.' She pursed a pious mouth.

'She minds me of our one-time mistress,' I said, 'when she was awaiting a visit from Ned... from the King.'

Agace tittered coarsely. 'Mayhap she has thoughts of a leman, too. To while away time while the Earl is busy with affairs of state.'

Once I would have laughed. Now I was shocked.

'Jesu, mercy!' I cried. 'At her age? 'Twould be a shameful thing!'

'Seemingly not.' Agace winked. 'The Queen's brother John wed the Dowager Duchess of Norfolk, and she is nigh eighty years, and he nineteen. They call it the devil's marriage.'

'He cannot love her,' I said, sickened at the thought.

'I always vowed you were lack-wit,' said Agace with contempt. 'What has love to do with it, I ask you? Or with any of the marriages of the Queen's kin? The Duchess of Norfolk is passing rich, and of ancient line. Likewise the Duke of Exeter's daughter, lately wedded to young Thomas.'

Little Tom, who played with me, Hoodman Blind. A wedded husband.

'I trow my lord of Warwick was ill-pleased with that,' Agace went on cunningly. 'The maid was promised to his nephew.'

Here was a name to play soldiers with. The great Warwick. The man who had saved England by the sword. The King's strongest ally, who had set him on the throne.

'Yea, Warwick,' said Agace, watching me. 'He who roasts six oxen for a breakfast, then throws his doors wide to all. Did you know? He welcomes men, strangers and knaves from off the street, to take as much meat as their dagger can bear away.'

She laid a spoon beside the platter. 'Now, carry this up to my lady, and pray it's to her taste!'

What should I call her, I wondered, mounting the draughty stairs. Countess? Dowager Duchess? Among all the riches Edward had showered on his Queen's kin lay an earldom for her father, Sir Richard Woodville. I tapped and entered Jacquetta's chamber. The air was pungent from reeking herbal potions. Gyb, white-muzzled now, added his rank odour from the centre of the bed,

'Try to take a little, Madame,' I said, proffering the meal.

The Dowager Duchess sneezed, and glared at me.

'Her Grace was right,' she croaked. 'This is a plaguey chill place for such as I to spend the holy season of Christmas.'

I made her a curtsey, looking under my lashes at the ill-tempered old face. White bristles, like those of Gyb, sprouted on her chin.

'The court would be warmer, Madame,' I agreed. I picked up her satin robe from the floor and hung it on a hook. I waited patiently while she spooned a mouthful of Agace's egg dish between her lips. As I expected, she spat it out into the bowl, like a cross-grained infant.

'I cannot eat this pap,' she declared.

Fighting an urge to throw the tray, I sympathetically smiled. 'They have wondrous cooks at court, have they not, my lady?' I murmured. 'I hear that the subtleties are fashioned so cunningly that one can hardly bear to eat them. Yet when they are tasted one cannot leave their enjoyment.'

'Yes, yes, it's as you say.' She nodded grudgingly. 'Men gorge themselves on forty, fifty courses, and think naught of it.'

'I fear Agace cannot attain such heights,' I said. 'Will the Earl be here for Christmas? We must order more provisions.'

She shook her head. 'I know not what his plans are. Her Grace begs me to come to court for Yule.' (She gave the holy season its ancient name.) 'But I fear with this malaise I'll be unfit for the journey.'

A strategy so beautiful that it made me tremble began to form in my mind.

'I will have you well, Madame, I promise,' I murmured tenderly. Gyb stretched out a paw, talons spread, as I tucked the covers about his mistress. 'I will prepare you a posset myself. And I swear you will be recovered. Right speedily.'

The old eyes flickered in my direction. She looked surprised, and in my conceit, I thought, gratified. 'You are a good child,' she said, not for the last time.

Returning to the kitchen, I rudely pushed Agace away from the fire.

'Give me room, dame,' I said. 'I am to brew a simple to have my lady on her legs again before Christmas.'

The cook gave me a shove equally strong.

'What are you meddling with?' she demanded. 'I don't want her up! Certes, we have more peace while she's abed.'

'You will have peace aplenty, Agace,' I said, smiling a secret smile. I crushed herbs between my fingers. Already I knew what would cure a chest cough and the sniffles. I had some powdered dandelion, too, for her lost appetite. The cook peered slyly into my face.

'By the look of you, you're brewing more besides a posset,' she said. 'And it's no secret how you lust after the court. I've not forgotten how you bawled when the Queen left you behind! And she gave you all her old dresses!' she added enviously.

I stirred away, red-faced from the fire. 'I had liefer gone to court in my shift than remain in this place with a score of dresses.'

My thoughts turned round and round with the ladle. Tangy as the smell of boiled dandelion, they rose and hung above me in a secret cloud. Though I had never been an actual cozen of the Duchess, at no time had she shown signs of dislike. Now here she was, under our roof again, her will doubtless low-ebbed from sickness. Mine to approach in servitude, but in a servitude passing kind. I thought of my destiny as a ship, drifting anchorless. But if I, through stealth, could blow a strong breeze, hold back the tide, bend the gale—then might I come into the slack water of my heart's desire, and sail towards London, the city of gold.

'All the sisters went to court,' I said, half to myself. 'The cousins, and their cousins' cousins, a legion. And they went in a gilt coach. I would go in a cart.'

'Mistress,' said Agace slyly, 'you aren't the Queen's kin.'

'Is it my fault,' I demanded, 'that I have no royal blood?'

Agace had one black tooth-stump. It showed as she howled with laughter.

'Christ in Glory!' she said, wiping her eyes. 'Have they? Better than you or I, mistress, but common, none the less, common as English earth. Hence there's so many ducal tempers aflame!'

I knew naught of ducal tempers. I knew only that the Woodvilles were apart from me now, by reason of rank and greatness; aeons distant. Yet there was one close at hand, growling with the grippe, one who would like to be petted; that I knew well. I drained the posset into a jug.

'I will go up, Agace,' I said.

'Coddle her well,' the cook mocked me.

At the door I said: 'I did but think Bess Woodville would go to court as the King's leman. Not as Queen of England.'

'So did we all, mistress.' She started to laugh again. 'I can read you like a pack of cards. Do you have your way, speak, I pray you, for me also, and the stable churls. For it's as likely I should dance with the Duke of Clarence in Greenwich Great Hall, as you should accompany the Duchess to court.'

'Save my supper,' I said, closing the door.

But I got no supper that night. For from the moment I stepped into the bedchamber again, with my healing draught and words of honey, the breeze blew strong and my ship began to turn onto its course. I got no rest either, for from the instant I began to brush Jacquetta's hair, and held up the mirror with the murmured words: 'A queenly face, my lady, a right queenly face,' she would have the service of none other but me. I brushed and brushed her scanty hair, and at the right moment when she looked down to see the tress laid over her shoulder I whispered: 'Madame, it has the touch of gold.' Lie was it none; a strand of my own lay beneath it.

As we left the snowbound fields and came down Watling Street into Chepeside, I could not longer contain my excitement and started to ask questions, my voice raised through necessity over the bawling of the 'prentices—'Come buy! What d'ye lack!' and the constant clamour of church bells—the deep song of the Jesus Bells in their fat stone tower, the sweeter burden of St Paul's near by; the yells of the chestnut and apple sellers touting for custom and the cries of the cook-knaves at each shop door. Even while we approached through the milling street past the goldsmiths and silversmiths with the banners of their gilds and patrons in lavish display over the entrance, we caught the sharp strong odour of pigmeat and brawn, spiced venison and game, an advancing gale, pungent to the nose, weighty on the stomach. St Paul's steeple towered to half a thousand feet, monarch over the hundred other spires that pointed to Paradise. Houses huddled together, leaning dizzily, gilded and painted and bulging into the street, and the buzz of close life from within them dazzled the crisp urgent air. Shouts of song came from the taverns, the Mermaid, the Mitre, the King's Head, while the gay signs that hung outside, blazing blues and reds and gold, had been framed overnight by an angel with frosty fingers. Down along Chepe we came, and the dwellings leaned close and hugged each other lovingly, and my joy made me believe that they, too, wished one another fair Yuletide greetings, and that in all the world, every face smiled. One great mansion soared high above the rest; in the distance I could see its mighty roofs, silvered by snow and sun. I turned eagerly to the woman at my side. All the Dowager Duchess's ladies seemed to be larger than I, and in the swaying litter I was crushed in the corner, the end of a fur rug wrapped about my knees.

'What is that building—where is it?' I cried.

'Guess,' she said teasingly, addressing a bumpkin.

'Is it... her Grace's residence, Ormond's Inn?' I asked wildly. I had heard of the magnificence of the Queen's town house, with its hangings of French cloth of gold, exquisite ornaments, where her wards were trained, and the scores of retainers awaited her occasional visits.

She burst out laughing. 'That is at Smithfield!' she cried, and I felt foolish. Then, more kindly, she said: 'Nay, over there is Bishopsgate, and the high building, Crosby's Place.'

'Crosby's Place,' I repeated. A fleeting disappointment rose in me. The name said little.

''Tis Sir John Crosby's home,' she said reprovingly. 'He's a very important man.'

Still it meant naught, and how was I, no soothsayer, to know its very name would one day warm my cold blood?

A wintry wind blew off the Thames as we approached London Bridge and, to our left, saw the chalky pinnacles of the Tower. A few kites mingled with the seagulls, swooping and tearing at objects that were spiked upon the gates of the Bridge. I looked up in interest to see what it was they attacked so merrily, and looked hastily down again in the next instant. For they were the heads of what had once been men, empty-eyed skulls with tattered hair, whipped by the wind. A bird flew carelessly past our litter, a large piece of pallid flesh in its beak. 'Pirates,' said the woman next to me, and yawned. Still I gazed at my lap until the sight should be gone. Pirates, felons, thieves, they might have been, but once they were men, and mayhap well-favoured, and sometime loved.

The deep boom from Westminster Clock House calling the hour struck at my ears. The mighty river, choked with merchant galleys, rich barges, wherries and flotsam flowed strongly. A swift tide was running. Giant cranes lined the docks. Petermen offered penny-passage over the icy waters, their voices hoarse and salty. And on the crowded frosty river rode a thousand swans, like brave white blossoms fighting the swell. Our litter ventured cautiously towards the Bridge, for the road was foul with great wounds to catch at the horses' legs. I looked up at the score of arches formed by the joined house gables under which we were to pass, and was marvelling again, when we halted abruptly. The little brachet bitch on the lap of the lady opposite fell to the floor and set up a sharp yapping. Gently I picked it up, returning it with the sweet and docile smile which I had worn for days; I was thankful we had not brought Gyb. All the ladies seemed bored; they had made this journey before, and the Dowager Duchess was dozing in her corner. But I quivered like a lute when played by the master, and struggled to peer out of the side of the carriage.

'God's curse on this delay,' said one of the women languidly. 'What, is London drawbridge up at this hour? Why have we halted?'

Swaying gently, the litter waited. I could hear the shouts of men, the crisping of hooves on the snow, and as I looked out I saw a great body of horse advancing over the bridge. They will pass very close, I thought; there was small room for two such cavalcades and a crowd had suddenly gathered to swell the confusion. People lined the street: merchants, pedlars, monks, women with young children, ragged beggars, red-nosed with the cold—all pointing, gabbling in low excited voices. A milkmaid set down her pails in the dirty road, to arrange her gown in a becoming fashion. A father raised his infant high the better to see. What, is the King coming? I thought. The very air was alive. The King is coming to meet the Duchess, I thought, and was about to give my mind a voice, when a great roar went up from the people, a shouting tumult to make the heart beat fast.

'Warwick! Warwick!' they cried, like thunder. The echo rolled off the house gables and curled about our litter like a lash.

'Warwick! Warwick!' they roared, and the name was an anthem of praise.

All the gentlewomen lay back on their cushions, assuming disdain. I cared naught for their strange disinterest. I craned to see who rode towards us.

Had I not known the King by sight I would have hailed this one as his Grace, so royal was he, both of countenance and bearing. Astride a great black horse he came in magnificence. The beast was housed to the knee in cloth of silver, the bit and bridle and stirrups fashioned of gold and studded with pearls and diamonds. A score of archers on foot surrounded horse and man. They walked as one man who wears one badge, and that emblem, the snarling Bear and Ragged Staff, was painted clear and bold upon the banners waving above them. A score of noblemen, sumptuously clad, surrounded Richard Neville, Earl of Warwick, and none heeded them, for all eyes were on their master. He wore a long gown of dark blue velvet, the sleeves rich with ermine, over which, slung carelessly, lay a wide gold chain heavy with sapphires. A vast diamond flamed in his velvet bonnet. His eyes were a keen clear grey in his square dark face, and his hair fell in black curls to his jewelled collar.

For all his greatness, he halted to pinch the cheek of the waving child, doffed his cap in honour of the milkmaid, bowed to the priests and merchants and threw a fistful of gold among the beggars. His swift gaze swept our entourage, and in a flash the benign eyes changed. A cold look of contempt, a thin veil as of snow over black ice, entered them. He bowed to the Dowager Duchess's litter, spurred his horse through the narrow way and rode quickly past with his train, leaving the townsfolk in a turmoil of excitement. I sank back, trembling, and thought with admiration and wonder of the noble Earl right up unto Greenwich, where the King and Queen kept court for the holy season.

Dimly, I heard the women talking, fierce icy voices. 'Devil damn the popinjay!' said one. 'To make my lady wait!' The Duchess waked from her half-doze, chuckled and snarled, and I smiled at her. I knew and cared for naught, save that I was in London. I was too stupid to be afraid, and God guards fools, that I am sure; thus might I have thought had I thought at all, springing to the side of my lady as we ascended the Palace steps. Some of the gentlewomen's looks were like half- sheathed daggers, but I stayed milk-mild, taking from Jacquetta's limp hand the musk-ball she had carried against the stink of London, giving her the ivory cane with the jewelled handle. I whispered sweetly in her ear, ever solicitous for her comfort. False, was I? Nay, at that instant I was a true maid, for I could almost love the old woman for bringing me to this place, this glory. I wore the Queen's old gown, but I was in the Queen's household, for good or ill.

Agace had warned me, before I left:

'Guard well your tongue, mistress, and your ways. For I hear the court is not all you would have it be; trust few, for there's envy and hatred there. Let no fickle knight or false nobleman weasel into your bed. Without it be the King, of course.' I had scoffed: 'Peace, old dame!' in a flurry of preparation. She had said, to my amazement, for we had had many sharp words: 'St Catherine keep you.' I thanked her for her blessing, but tossed her counsel aside as an empty nutshell, for I believed in Providence and the armour of my own keen wit.

So, of this mind, I came to court, and never shall I forget that first evening, with its disappointment and its drama, its joy and disillusion. With a throng of gentlewomen, I was swept up a twisted staircase into the Duchess's apartments which, within minutes, became a bedlam of bright plumage and chatter, spilt vials of perfume and barking dogs. Women were delving into trunks and coffers, drawing out dresses, yelling for the laundry-pages. Harassed servants kindled the fire, smoothed damask sheets upon the Duchess's bed, hung wreaths of herbs around the curtained gardrobe, lest a stink should creep through heavy velvet to annoy my lady's nose. I stood alone, my back to a great tapestry, its threads grazing my hand. For something to do, I turned and studied this rich arras, and found it more beautiful than belief. Worked on red cloth of gold, each figure sprang to life in silver thread, real pearls, with here and there a diamond's gleam. Ruby blood spouted from the wounds of golden knights. All along one wall of the chamber the tapestry shook, a shimmering blaze of beauty. I had heard of the phrase 'a king's ransom'. This was it, in truth.

The Duchess was surrounded by chattering, ministering women. So I stayed, lonely and ill-ease, backed by beauty, and wondering how to occupy myself. Then a voice fragrant with a foreign accent spoke in my ear, a cool hand touched my wrist, and I turned to look into eyes so like Gyb's that I almost laughed. For how could a cat's eyes live in a woman's face? Yet they were shaped like Gyb's, uptilted, a sparkling hazel green; and so kindly that I could have wept at their kindness.

'Child,' said the soft voice, 'the Dowager Duchess needs you now. I'm right joyous to see her well again. We've missed her sorely at court. Come, sweet, she would have you dress her hair for the evening's revels.'

I went gladly. The rest of the women faded into an antechamber. I lifted the Duchess's hennin and lovingly began to pluck the stray hairs from her forehead to give it the noble height she needed, while the fair, cat-eyed lady knelt beside us.

'Fetch me a gown, Elysande,' the Duchess told her. 'There'll be dancing.' She shrugged under my touch. 'Make the brow right clean, child. By my faith! I can scarcely feel you. You're more skilled than those squawking abigails!' I could hear them, laughing in the antechamber as they dressed each other for the evening. My gladness grew, excitement began to ferment in me. When Elysande returned with a crimson gown I whispered 'Shall we be dancing, too?' and could not believe it when she, smiling, shook her head.

The lady Elysande sat with her arm lightly through mine. An hour earlier the Duchess had descended to the Great Hall with a stout train of attendant ladies, most of them ill-favoured, some of them downright ugly. In the antechamber full of truckle-beds, half a dozen of us were left; Elysande and I, and four stolid Flemish women who had shared the supper brought up to us by pages and who now slept resignedly on the floor, their backs against a linen-coffer. I was full of rich food and bad humour. Had it not been for Elysande's kind company, I might well have shed tears.

'Banquets are not for you and me,' she had said, giving me a quick kiss. 'We are *valetti* to her Grace. Is it not an honour to be left to guard her possessions while she adorns the court?'

Below, I could hear the sounds of music and laughter, drifting from the direction of the Great Hall. 'They have started the dancing,' I murmured.

'You don't want to dance!' said Elysande lightly. 'Think how wearisome it would be with all those clodpoll knights, and the women with claws out, each striving to outdo the other! You and I will dance together on the gallery, if you wish. That is a beauteous gown.'

She smiled. In many ways she minded me of Agnes: soft- voiced, but without Agnes's coarseness.

'Sweet Elysande, you lie,' I said. 'This gown is one the Queen gave me when she left Grafton, and it's four years out of style.'

My eyes wandered again to the great tapestry. I stretched out my fingers to touch it. In the candlelight the gold threads held mystery, you could almost step into the picture, and the rubies were real drops of blood.

'That's the Siege of Jerusalem,' said Elysande. 'It was a gift from Sir Richard Woodville to his wife.'

One of the Flemish women woke up. Suddenly I had the feeling she had not been asleep at all.

'So highly prized, so easy gained,' she remarked. I looked enquiringly. Elysande was silent.

'Yea,' pursued the woman. 'That arras was despoiled from the manor of Sir Thomas Cook, he that was lately Mayor of this city, on Woodville's orders. There was talk that he had Lancastrian sympathies—and the King was persuaded by the Earl of his guilt. The Duchess lusted for this arras, certes— and it was while the Earl and Sir John Fogge sought treason in Cook's house, they saw it there and seized it for my lady's pleasure! Then, on mere hearsay, the Earl had Sir Tom cast into jail and fined eight thousand pounds! Queen's gold, they call it, a fancy name for thievery!'

Elysande took a little tablet from her pouch, wrote something upon it, looking hard at the Flemish woman, then hid the writing away and smiled at me.

'Poor Gerta has been drinking deep. She lusts to lose her tongue,' she said, her voice so sweet that its message was blown away, like chaff in a breeze. She rose, retrieved a torn dress from the floor, swept some spilled face-paint up, snuffed a candle and, as another great roar of laughter reached us from below, looked at my downcast face.

'That will be the King's fool,' she murmured. 'They say he is the finest fool ever at court. Mine eyes have wept at his joculing.'

The thin savage note of the fiddles rose; if music has a taste, that was honey.

'They will be at it till dawn,' said Elysande. 'And I doubt not there will be some sore heads tomorrow at Mass. How my lord of Clarence does guzzle wine! I vow, down there, 'tis like the high days of ancient Rome!'

I could bear it no longer, and went and opened the door into the passage. Elysande came, and took my hand.

'Would you watch the gaiety, then?' she asked. ''Tis all artifice. But come with me. Soft, for God's love.'

It was cold on the gallery, and the stones were like ice as I touched them, to guide myself along the dark ways, for Elysande went ahead like a ghost. 'Stand well back,' her warm breath whispered, as we reached a little opening, a stone niche, with a torchlit embrasure through which I could peer. And down there was another world, which I surveyed, as a fallen angel might look on Paradise. There, in a blaze of colour and light, gambolled the royal court, its laughter high and loud. Along each wall a painted tapestry danced, aping the courtiers who moved and swirled on scented rushes, their feet crushing the petals of late white roses.

'Where's the fool?' I asked softly. 'I know him. His name is Patch.'

'He makes his exit,' said Elysande, pointing. 'Too late, but he'll be back, with a new jape. Now they dance again.' She shivered.

The music took hold of me by the bones. There was something older than Christian in the thump of the tabor, the rebec's jewelled wailing. Yet it had all the holy season in it too, with its passion and promise. I looked down at the joy, standing close to Elysande and thought: So might Salisbury, in his doomed Castle of Sandal, have heard such music with a weary smile. The cries of the dying would have sounded in its shrillness, and in the wind beating without the walls. So would Salisbury have listened, that Christmas, while his unknowing minstrels played through the hours to defeat and death.

I searched the room for the King, while the sweet high strains whirled about my head. Below, the dancers cavorted. In their leaping wind the painted knights upon the arras shuddered too, in a mocking fashion as of ghosts. Two pages with clarions blew a fanfare. From behind the great door I heard the rumbling wheels and grew rigid with sudden fear. For my thoughts were still with Lord Salisbury and that Christmas invasion. Elysande looked down at me and laughed.

'Watch the Storming of Troy!' she whispered.

There entered a walled city on wheels; a most wondrous sight, pushed by an hundred sweating yeomen. Banners fluttered from its heights. Women, clothed in flimsy stuffs of gold and peach and crimson, sat atop the battlements. In the wall nearest the royal dais was set a door fashioned from beaten brass, studded with bright beads and wide enough to admit a small army. Then slowly the candles around the outer edges of the hall were dimmed, bringing darkness broken only by the occasional flash of eyes, or the glitter of a jewel, so I could no longer see the vibrant, hot-breathing press of lords with their dragonfly ladies. Invisible were they, as were the butlers and guards, and waiting, quaffing unseen goblets, whispering in expectancy as through the great door, with only a faint rattle of pulley and chain, rolled the great Horse of Troy. Painted gold and white, garlanded with flowers and blowing real fire down its nostrils, it was, Elysande whispered, full of murdering Greeks.

'The King likes well this disguising,' she murmured. Pinching my arm gently: 'Jesu! It's cold in this place. I'm going back.'

She slid into the darkness and I was left alone, staring till my eyeballs ached at the mummery below. Though the whole court was mad with enthusiasm, smiting the tables with their hanaps and roaring bravos, I was not sorry to see the bloody battle finish. It was, after all, a man's sport, and I would liefer watch the dancing again, gazing at the rich gowns, the gracious gestures, jealous and a little sad.

Suddenly I saw Patch. He came riding a donkey, bringing light into the gloom with a blazing torch held high. His mount was caparisoned in red cloth of gold. Peacock feathers waved on his head and a blackamoor child ran at his stirrup like a hound. He circled the Hall smartly. As he passed below me I saw his face. Patch indeed, Patch, untrimmed by the years, still wrinkled and smiling wickedly, oddly dear to my sight. And the Hall was bright again, and I drank eagerly of the company, my eyes seeking first the royal chair of estate, beneath whose great broidered canopy King Edward lolled. His hair was ruffled, but he was more well-favoured than ever. His fine teeth showed in his laugh, he was tall as an oak, fair skinned and straight of limb, with diamonds flashing on his doublet. Behind his head, thirty yards in. measure, hung the royal dorsal with the leopards and lilies of England, watching with tapestry eyes the fickle splendour of their court.

Beside the King, Madonna-like, sat my late mistress, Elizabeth. Elizabeth the Queen, whose ivory face betrayed neither joy nor distaste for the scene under her eyes. The King drank, held his goblet to her lips, which pouted, smiled, declined. He dangled a bunch of grapes before her, made some jest, at which she smiled again, with downcast look. She took one grape, kissed it, and popped it into Edward's mouth.

Swiftly I scanned the others round the royal dais. I saw Earl Rivers, flushed and heavy faced, leaning close, talking earnestly in the King's ear. Anthony Woodville also bent his handsome head near the dais, smiling unceasingly. The torchlight flamed up and caught the coldness in his eyes for an instant. I remembered those eyes, how they had terrified me once as a foolish child. Never again would they affright me.

Patch was capering in the centre of the floor. Someone threw an orange, and he caught it deftly, speared it on his dagger, and strutted, mimicking the royal orb with his new-fashioned toy. The court howled with laughter, looking to the King for his approval, and seeing it, Patch turned a somersault, landed on a slippery square of rushes and fell on his rump. A great hound rushed snarling from under the King's table and flew at him. The fool yelled in fear and fled, round and round the Hall. Gales of laughter swept the company, and watching each face, anxious to share in their enjoyment in my unseen way, I realized that there were those who did not laugh.

The Earl of Warwick did not laugh. For the second time that day I marvelled at the icy splendour of his mien. In dark green satin crusted with rubies, the hilt of his dagger heavy with gems of price, he stood near the door, his arm about the neck of a tall, golden-haired youth, who held a brimming wine-cup. From his likeness to the King, I knew him instantly to be George, Duke of Clarence. Warwick was murmuring in his ear, gesturing the while with a glittering hand. I saw his glance fly to the little company about the King, and there again was the same disdain as when he passed the Countess's litter.

George of Clarence listened, nodded, laughed a little too loud, and drank more wine.

'All artifice,' Elysande had said. I pondered on this deeply, my eyes raking the crowd. Nay, not all were happy; that was sure. One small lady, in a rose-pink drift of gown, stood alone, wistfully smiling. Middle-aged, a woman alone; but those were not the reasons for her obvious sadness. Some strange intuition told me there was more. All artifice, was it? I searched the throng deeper and saw that some were the worse for wine, lolling white and heavy-eyed back in their chairs. From my eagles' eyrie, I saw sly fingerings of naked breast and arm, hot kisses pressed on cheeks in unlit corners, quiet speech between men and men, looks of love and hate and jealousy darting like lightnings from eye to eye.

Suddenly I thought: if the case stood thus, and I could choose, there is none here I would have for my lover! If this were the court, the true splendour, for the privilege of whose enjoyment men slew each other, I was sorely disappointed. Patch had finished his joculing, and was creeping back across the Hall, feigning a mortal hurt. His face a mask of pain, he crawled out of the door under my gallery and disappeared to roars of applause. Clarions sounded, and music swept into life again. The sweet wholesome sounds of viol and cithern, shawm and lute and psaltery soared to my ears. Earl Rivers bowed to the Queen and sought her in the dance. The King urged her from her chair, kissing her hand as she descended with cool grace.

It was the music. That was all my joy. The music froze me like ice, burned me like fire. It rose to unattainable heights, wailed and sobbed and laughed. The voices of spirits were in it, songs of the laughing dead, borne on the wind of rebec and string and cromorne, and the heartbeat of the lusty living too, struck from the skin of a joyous tabor. Poetry and battle, love and death, all grew strong in that music, and my skin had lumps like those on a plucked goose, as I clasped my hands and forgot my own existence, following the courtly pattern of bright dance with misted eyes.

Footsteps were approaching along the passage and I shrank into the concealing shadow. I heard a voice muttering to itself, rude oaths, but a voice that I knew, none the less. I stepped out into the flaring torchlight.

'Patch!' I cried.

All colour fled his face.

'Jesu!' he said with quiet gladness. ''Tis a ghost, a lovesome sprite. Come to taunt poor Patch.'

''Tis truly I, Patch,' I said merrily, and kissed him on both cheeks, while he swung me off my feet.

And all he could say was 'Well met, well met' and babble about love, his favourite jest and one which I thought he always saved for me, and he swore himself a prophet, for he had vowed that I should come to court, and here I was, and he also, with all the favourable planets swimming in Heaven for him, for he had thought often of his own true love.

'Give me space for a word,' I said, laughing and struggling from him. 'Are you well? Your skill is undimmed, I see.'

'I do well enough,' he answered. 'So my lady Jacquetta brought you? The Queen Mother. Mother of the King's Grey Mare!'

Now I could laugh at an old jest. We talked of Grafton for a while, then I turned back to the embrasure, which drew me like the moon the tide.

'I have been watching the merrymaking.' I looked again to where men and women disported themselves in the Hall. Patch leaned close to me against the stone.

'A fine spectacle,' he murmured. 'Often I come up here to watch—'tis better than any May-Games, and none know we are here.'

He pointed out several celebrated people, among them a group of Bohemian knights whom the King was entertaining; the Queen's sisters and the Duke of Buckingham. He even spotted Dick and Thomas Grey, playing merels together in a corner. Tom's wife, the Duke of Exeter's daughter, was the one in the green gown. She had a furious temper. I pointed to the small lady in rose-coloured silk, the sad lady, and asked her name.

'That is Katherine. Countess of Desmond,' said the fool, and all merriment left him. 'Poor lady.'

Then he was saying other things: possibly the Countess of Desmond's history, or he may have been reciting a psalm; or making his will, for whatever he said, I heard it not. I heard no more, though his voice went on and on, as a background to the beating of my heart, which started up enough to frighten me, as if I were in mortal fever. For my idle gaze had suddenly fallen on one who had not been in the Hall when I looked before. To this, I may swear.

And had I been an old old woman with three husbands buried and twice as many children, or had I been a coal-black queen from the East with the whole of Byzantium under my hand; or had I been an idiot with no tongue, no ears, and only eyes, eyes to see whom I saw then, and a heart to feel as my heart felt; had I been any of these, I would have done as I did. And being what I was, a virgin maid, with but an armoured dream to cherish, I looked that night upon a man, and loved.

Next to the Earl of Warwick he stood, but apart from him. He was solitary, young and slender, of less than medium stature. His face had the fragile pallor of one who has fought sickness for a long time, yet in its high fine bones there was strength, and in the thin lips, resolution. His hair was dark, which made him paler still. He was alone with his thoughts. Ceaselessly he toyed with the hilt of his dagger, or twisted the ring on one finger as if he wearied of indolence and longed for action. Then he turned; I saw his eyes. Dark depths of eyes, which in one moment of changing light carried the gleam of something dangerous, and in the next, utter melancholy. And kindness too... compassion. They were like no other eyes in the world. Like stone I stood, and loved.

The jester was babbling in my ear, and I could not answer him. With my whole heart I hoped that he might not be one too highborn to give me a glance. I longed to know that he was an esquire, mayhap the son of some lesser noble, or a member of his retinue. This, seeing the sumptuous fire of jewels on the restless fingers, the collar of suns and roses about his neck, I knew it all useless; my dreams but vapourings; and he on whom I looked with such love further removed than the topmost star. By rank more distant, and by riches far apart. Above all, by the way in which he stood, solitary, yet dignified by his solitude, among the noisy splendour.

In the face of this, I asked, trembling:

'Who is that young knight?'

Patch was acting craftily. 'Which one, madam? Madam, maiden, mistress, honeybee. Names, yea, names for one passing sweet, and she with many names would have a name to play with. Which name, my Venus, cozen and cuckoo-eye, which knight?'

A page was offering him wine. He waved it away.

'The one who does not drink tonight,' I said, and my voice was like a frog's croaking.

'Ho! a sober knight!' said Patch, and peered to follow my slowly pointing, wavering fingers. He dug his sharp chin into my neck.

'Certes, I had forgot you were fresh to the court,' he said with a little laugh. ''Tis young Dickon.'

'Dickon?'

'Yea, the sad one. The scant-worded one. The one who beds with his battle-axe. If my eye be not crossed, you point to Richard of Gloucester.'

'An Earl, a Duke?' I whispered.

'Both, and more besides. A prince. He is Richard Plantagenet, the King's brother.'

I loved. I loved, and to my surprise, the world went on its way as usual. As Elysande had foretold, there was much groaning and head-holding in the morning. Many lay abed, including the Duchess, but the King was up betimes, and after hearing Mass rode out hunting with a large train of knights and nobles, some looking as if they would liefer have stayed quiet in their chambers, nursing the quantities of wine that churned about their bellies. But King Edward was fresh as a flower, calling his friends in a voice like a clarion, mad to spear the otter. Elizabeth was serene, smiling gently with downcast eyes as she wished her lord a successful chase. Her own chase had been wondrous profitable, I thought, as we watched the King, at the head of his entourage, gallop out between the guard and disappear beneath the toothed portcullis. Yet as soon as his back was turned, her expression suffered a brisk change. The matron of Grafton Regis returned, and soon the whole Household was flying about like souls in torment in pursuit of their various duties. Little was seen of her, but her lightest wish was keenly felt. Even so, there was space for gossip—down the corridors it crept, the arras shivering with whispers: who had quarrelled with whom last evening; whose bed had remained bare till dawning; and once again, I came on Patch, whose face served as a beacon in a bewildering world of stares that were curious, and sometimes hostile.

He looked unwell, and was wearing a hermit's robe, all rags and tatters. 'To mock the Church,' he explained, and shook with laughter at my shocked face. 'Tarry a moment,' he said, catching my fingers in the passage.

I could scarcely bother to listen; my mind was floating high, my eyes burned with a memory.

'I've been speaking to my cousin,' he said. 'Men say there will be mischief shortly.'

'Oh, do they, Patch,' I murmured.

'You seem weary, maiden,' he said inconsequentially. 'Did you not sleep? I neither. My arse is sore. Did you see me fall last night? By St Denis, I thought my back was broken.' On and on, *ad infinitum*.

'Mischief,' I reminded him, after a long space, in which he had his thoughts, and I mine.

'There are signs in the heavens that England will have war again,' he said. 'At Bedford, two weeks ago, a dame laid out her bed linen to dry.

'So?' I said. A face crossed my mind, a young, noble, dangerous face; a face dark and pale; eyes of light and darkness, heat and cold, day and night. A face like the beginning and the ending of the world.

'And lo! it came on to rain, but the rain was not rain at all, but gouts of blood which stained the sheets and bolsters beyond repair, and all about shrieked and knelt in prayer, for this is a dread warning of things to come.'

I said naught. I wondered where the prince was, what he did. I had not seen him ride out hunting, but there had been so many in the train I could have missed seeing him, though this was unlikely. Patch, bursting with his fanciful tale, looked wounded at my inattention.

'By God's bones!' he cried. 'I might as well have speech with yonder arras, for the holy men broidered thereon would at least listen better than you!'

'Forgive me,' I said swiftly. 'Poor woman! Did she buy new sheets?'

'There is worse,' he said. His voice sank to a hollow groan. 'In Huntingdon County, there was a woman great with child. And at about the time that the washing was be-blooded, she heard the infant in her womb sobbing and crying with a great roaring noise, and she was sore affrighted, for this means sure sorrow in this realm and dolour for all men.'

This time I felt a prick of fear.

'Seek you to drive me witless with your tales, Sir Fool?'

'It is truth,' he begged.

'Once, you sickened me with a bloody heart,' I said, catching up my gown. 'Now you fright me with falseness. I'll hear no more.' And I ran, and the image of Richard Plantagenet ran with me in my mind, looking worried, and I wondered how he looked when he did laugh, and reckoned him passing fair, laughing; and ran into our chamber and slammed the door.

'Patch is like something possessed,' I told Elysande, who was sponging stains off the Duchess's red satin. I recounted the wild tales to her.

'War, hey?' she said, raising her plucked eyebrows, and went on sponging. Her calmness infected me and I put the whole matter aside. It was time to rouse the Duchess. I pinned on my sweetest smile as I sped to her chamber.

When night came, and all the upper apartments were deserted, and the merriment came loud from the Great Hall, I stole again to the gallery. Unseen, unheard, I gazed again at the bright scene below. Flattened against a pillar under the hissing torchlight, I stood for an hour. With my fingers I traced the carved faces in the embrasure, until the cold seemed to turn me to stone, as they were. I learned a great heaviness in that hour, for though the whole court assembled in glory beneath my eyes, all were effigies, without form or being. They swam like ghosts, devoid of colour or life. He was not there.

Patch came again midway through the evening, giving me sweet foolish words, snatching kisses on my cheek and neck. I smote at him as if he were a troublesome fly, and he called me cruel, so I gave him my hand to hold and together we watched the disguisings. Sir Gawayn and the Green Knight held sway on the floor below, the knight clothed in green branches, his horse also green, a little unsteady on its legs, but marvellously lifelike. I had begun to take pleasure in the play, when Patch brought back my dolour with a chance word.

'I see my lord of Warwick does not grace the company tonight,' he said. I do not care, I thought. They could all be missing, save one, and he alone would make for me a feast day.

'And George of Clarence, too, begs urgent business elsewhere,' went on the fool cunningly. 'Could it be, sweet mistress, that these two fair knights sup quietly somewhere together and talk of a lady?'

'What lady?' I said dully.

Cautiously yet pleased, Patch murmured: 'Men speak much before a fool. They think me truly *witless*, I trow, when they should but substitute an "n" for an "l", and be nearer the truth.'

'Go on,' I sighed, my eyes on the court.

'George of Clarence would wed Warwick's eldest maiden,' he whispered. 'It would be a right wealthy match for him, and the great Warwick knows his mind. Isabel is the lure to draw this falcon from his royal brother's side. And across the sea, waiting, sits an old spider, a French spider. King Louis...'

'I know naught of these intrigues,' I answered. 'And in any case, are they not cousins, George and Warwick's daughter?'

'Dispensations have been arranged,' muttered the fool. 'The Curia is greedy. And 'twould be a weapon in the hand of Warwick, to have

George as close ally. Warwick has never, will never, forgive Edward for his lowly marriage.'

I looked sharply at Patch. 'What's this?'

'Did I not love you, maiden, I would not tell you all these secrets, for you and I could be thrown in the Tower for such whisperings,' he replied, with a frightening grimace.

I pressed his hand. 'Pray, don't leave a tale in mid-air.'

'Warwick had planned a great marriage for his Grace,' Patch murmured in my ear. 'He had arranged for him to wed the Princess Bona of Savoy, sister-in-law of Louis of France. Imagine his fury when your fair widow of Grafton Regis filched the prize from under Europe's eyes! I trow the Earl writhed in his skin with rage. Think you, while we were at the May-Games that day, England was being set on its head!'

Yet I am glad, I thought, in my then arrant folly. Had all this not come about, I should not be here. I should not have seen what I have seen; should never have known this love, this love that tears my heart. I said: 'So now he seeks to wean Clarence from his Grace? Treason?'

'Of a kind,' replied the fool. 'Jesu! How the Earl must have fumed when he found his King was also a man, a frail man with a will of his own! No longer his mammet to raise to a height, to counsel and dangle...'

Suddenly, he stopped speaking, pointed down below. 'Here enters Lord Hastings. A great fighter, loves the King well.'

Lord Hastings was tall and fair, and I saw him not. For another came with him through the door, and again my heart was rent like the temple veil at Our Lord's Passing. There entered Richard, my soul's liking, Richard Plantagenet, my beloved.

This night he wore an air less lonely and distracted, and for the first time I saw him smile. He smiled when the King beckoned him over to the dais, and throwing an arm about him, placed in his brother's hands a little satin pouch or some such thing for holding jewellery. Richard opened it and drew out something small and shining, doubtless a Christmas gift from the King. A look of pleasure crossed his face. It was then I realized he was younger than I had thought; it was but his sombre expression that gave him years. He thanked the King, swiftly bent and kissed his hand, and Edward, cuffing him on the shoulder, roared with jovial laughter.

But the glad moment passed. I saw a pout forming on the Queen's lips, and with one of her white hands she touched Edward's sleeve. He turned from Richard in mid-sentence to gaze into Elizabeth's face. He looked at her as one bewitched, summoned an esquire with impatient fingers. A rosewood coffer was laid before the Queen. I craned to see what she drew from it; the white fire of diamonds leaped into life. It was a reliquary worked in beaten gold with three pearls of price dropping like tears from the lower edge. Elizabeth held it up for all to see, and whispers of admiration came from those who stepped forward to praise this kingly gift. In its lace of black enamel, diamonds big as hazel nuts vied with the pale blood of rubies dividing them.

Elizabeth also kissed the King's hand, but he kissed her mouth. Pages brought on the Christmas gifts, and Edward all but disappeared behind a veil of Woodvilles, bending the knee, kissing his fingers and the hem of his robe, smiling their thanks. Four of Elizabeth's five sisters came trailing yards of silk and sarcenet; the Lady Katherine in green, Anne in crimson, Elinor in palest blue and Mary in deep saffron. Miniver and marten banded their sleeves and veiling fell from the peak of their hennins in gem-scattered mists. Behind them, like meek lambs, came their new noble husbands: the young Duke of Buckingham; William Bourchier, son of the Earl of Essex; the young man who was the heir of the Earl of Kent; and Lord Dunster. John Woodville led his aged spouse, my lady of Norfolk, to the dais. She whispered her Yuletide greeting and looked weary, as if she lusted for her bed.

I had a sudden vision of a pack of hounds descending on a royal stag, their yelling mouths agape with greed and joy—which was strange, for all about the royal pair bore themselves demurely, with gentle looks, and courteous, loving gestures.

And Richard? Utterly isolated now from his brother the King, he turned slowly and walked across the Hall. Katherine, Countess of Desmond, came to meet him. She was smiling at him; my heart grew sore with envy. He was showing her the King's gift; she was admiring it, clipping it to the centre of the collar he wore about his neck. He looked down, fingered it, made some jest to her, and they laughed together.

Then the minstrels began a French tune, the old *basse-danse* with its slow and gliding steps. The Countess was giving Richard her hand. I turned away. No more could I have watched them dance together than plunge my fingers into the torch-flame overhead. The tears filled my eyes. I knew myself possessed by some demon. Only a demon could have conjured the thoughts and wild feelings in me at that moment. I was lonely too, for Patch had returned below some time ago. I had only my cold stones for company, with the blind carved faces.

I glanced back again, anguished. The Countess looked at Richard as if she found him pleasing indeed. But the dance was over soon, and she left him, to drink wine with a group of ladies, and he was alone again. He cast an eye over to the King, but Edward was occupied, laughing, his head a spot of gold between the greying skull of Earl Rivers and the sleek locks of Anthony Woodville, who once more leaned close, talking, talking, with smiles and frowns and wise, nodding looks, while Richard toyed with his rings again, pulling off the jewel on his last finger and replacing it, over and over, a maddening gesture of disquiet and heaviness. His eyes swept the Hall as one who looks for an ambush. Over the music the Woodvilles' laughter rose, as the dancing swirled about.

And he was solitary.

He was looking directly at me. I knew this could not be, as I was quite concealed in the lofty shadows, but it was as if our glances met through an arras of darkness, a tapestry woven of my dreams and desire. I made believe that he could really see me, and looked deep into his eyes, melting their coldness with the ardour of my gaze, playing a foolish game with him for my own comfort, before he suddenly turned and, to my sorrow, quit the Hall.

And it was then I knew why women stooped to mix potions and simples, to wreak strange works in moonlight, for there is naught one will not do to attain the object of such craving, and this gave me remembrance of the Duchess of Bedford and that night four years ago. In my childish way I thought I understood the actions of the Queen and her mother. For if Elizabeth felt for his Grace as did I for Richard of Gloucester, we were as one.

Fresh entertainment came forward, as a pair of singers, a youth and a maid, knelt before the King. Then a soft air, a simple melody, rose to the ears of the suddenly hushed court; and for me, it was May Day again, and I was no longer cold, for the sun burned bright and the grass smelled of its sour-sweet bruisings and an old man fashioned a ballad for the Nut-Brown Maid, who would ever be true to her lover. I leaned towards the brightness and, in an abandonment of joy and because there was none to see, tore off my hennin and let my nut-brown hair fall to my knees. For I would be a child again, for five minutes, and remember the time when men stopped to gaze at me, with my chaplet of flowers crowning that at which they all marvelled, and longed to touch and stroke and possess. The maiden sang:

'Mine own heart dear, with you what cheer?
I pray you, tell anone,
For in my mind, of all mankind
I love but you alone.'

I heard Patch's light step behind me in the passage, and without taking my joyful gaze from the scene below, stretched out my hand, crying:

'Ah, my friend, remember you this day! When all men called me fair, and the old ballad-maker said I would be a true maid, and fashioned this song for me ere he died! Take my hand, and say you have not forgotten!'

And I felt his hand in mine, and we stood together, listening to the music until it ended, and I turned with shining face to give him one kiss out of my true pleasure, for after all he was my friend and had shared this moment with me. And the hand which held mine did not belong to a fool, but to the King's youngest brother, who stood looking down at me with, God be praised, the same look I had seen in the eyes of men that May Day long ago.

He was there, he was real. His hand, slender and warm, held mine firmly. And I was bereft of speech, as completely as if my tongue were torn out. So, of necessity, I waited, and it seemed an hour before he spoke, which when he did was in a voice passing quiet; a deep, a gentle voice.

'Is it a custom, damoiselle, to stand alone in this cold place?' he asked. 'I know the court can be wearisome, but health can suffer from these chill vigils. You should be below, enjoying the festivities.'

There was irony in his last sentence.

The torch above his head blurred and came clear again. His face was in shadow, for he had moved closer, but I could see the gleam of his eyes in the flame. Belatedly I remembered who addressed me; a royal Duke, a Knight of the Garter. I sank to the ground in curtsey, and his hands raised me swiftly.

'You do not answer,' he said. 'And I know you have a voice, for it gave me fair words just now when you bade me listen to the song.'

'Most princely grace,' I whispered, 'I am not cold. And I've no place in the Great Hall, for—I am naught!' I bit my tongue at the witlessness of my words. He was silent for a moment, then he laughed. A right lovesome laugh he had. Was there aught of him that did not please me?

'Naught,' he said thoughtfully. 'Tell me, who shall say who is naught and who is otherwise? And, by St Paul, you do not look naught to me! Had I known you stood above I would have come before and spoken with you.'

His eyes travelled over me, as mine had over him many times, and that same awed gaze fell on my hair. I heard him breathing deeply, as if he were aroused by his thoughts; the last of my wits deserted me.

'My lord, I must go,' I said desperately. I longed to run away, to fall on my couch and weep for the tongue-tied fool I had shown myself, when the chance to be so near him might never come again. I tried to pull my hand away, but his clasp had become a grip of steel. I could not budge.

'Does my company prove so distasteful to you, then?' asked the quiet voice. 'I had hoped you would remain for a while. I tell you, I am dolorous tonight, and already you have cheered me more than a little.'

'I'm glad of it, my lord,' I murmured, and let my hand lie still. He asked my name and I told him, thinking even that sounded foolish. Yet he repeated it to himself, as if he took pleasure in it.

'Do you not dance, then, mistress?'

'Yea, my lord, I like it well,' I replied. And I thought: Richard, Richard, only would I love to dance with you, but how shall one, who has no quality, who is shadow and not substance, think in this wise? I glanced down at the minstrels, saw the smooth movement of the viol players bowing their instruments, the swift fingers plucking the wires, and the sharp cold strains turned my heart to ice, an ice that burned as it froze. The coloured court spun in a glittering skein. I trembled all over. My skirts quivered on my legs.

'But you are cold,' he said, and chafed my fingers between his hands. I shook my head, looking wildly over his shoulder, anywhere but at his face. He had the advantage of me, for the light fell on my countenance and he could see how my colour came and went.

'To dance would warm you,' he said; and from the subtle change in his voice it came to my mind that he was not so composed as he would seem, that mayhap *he* wished to dance with me, and a little of my courage returned. And as he bowed to me, just as he had done to the Countess of Desmond, there was naught in him save chivalry and kind graciousness. So I sank before him in accession as I had seen the Countess do, and we began to dance, slowly, with only the cold stones to watch us. Moving into the torchlight, I saw his face again, and the dark eyes were fixed on mine with an intensity that took my strength.

As the music reached its height and I the peak of my intoxication, he led me easily in a circle, passing me behind him so that our backs brushed lightly. As the last note sobbed to death, we came face to face, closer than was natural, our steps meshed in the confined space. My body touched his. Even in that instant I was conscious of the strength, full marvellous in one who looked so slight, dormant in him, like a coiled whip. I felt the catlike velvet of his doublet, the sharp pain of a cold object biting into my breast. I looked down: it was the King's gift that had touched me; a silver emblem shaped like a tusked boar rampant with ruby eyes. It seemed a ferocious, snarling creature for him to wear. Already I felt a bruise forming; wild thoughts of evil omens filled my mind. I gave a trembling laugh.

'I fear he mislikes our dancing, my lord,' I said, stupid and gay. 'For he drove his tusks into my skin as if to bid me begone from his master.'

Timidly I fingered the beast, bending my head over the pearl tusks, the fiery eyes. I felt the lightest touch, like a leaf falling, brush the crown of my hair, and stood motionless, staring at the boar's unwinking red orbs.

'Why did you choose this device, my lord?' I whispered.

His voice low and a trifle sad, he answered: 'The White Boar is my special cognizance. From the Roman name for our royal house.

Ebor*... Eboracum; his Grace and I thought it fitting. My late father's Duchy, too. So I took it for my blazon.'

Then I thought of York, Salisbury and Rutland. Their heads on Micklegate. I was lack-wit to ask, I thought. I have excelled myself in folly this night.

Restlessly, he walked away, turned like a sentinel in the passage and came back to me, while I leaned on the pillar and watched him. The torch flamed up in a sudden draught as a door at the stairfoot opened and loud voices, complaining, laughing, sounded disquietingly near. My time with him was over.

'Farewell, my lord.' A better curtsey this time, more controlled.

'My lord of Gloucester, are you there?' bawled a voice.

'Dickon, where are you?'

Richard looked in the direction of the sounds. 'It is Lovell,' he murmured. 'Stay, lady, I pray you.'

Frantic, I caught his sleeve. 'Sir, there will be trouble if my lady of Bedford finds I have left my post!' I whispered. 'Sir, I beg you, do not speak of it, or I shall be disgraced.'

He turned swiftly. 'I shall tell no one, least of all the Dowager Duchess,' he said, with a biting edge. Then he took my hand again, and I burned in the flame of him. 'For were you discovered I doubt you could return tomorrow evening and that would grieve me. For it seems a lonesome nook for one, a happy place for two.'

I listened without belief. I clung to his hand to steady my trembling.

'You'll come?' he said.

The sounds were coming closer, shouts and laughter. A commotion as someone fell downstairs.

'God keep my lord,' I said, and tore myself from the hand that would detain me, feeling as a trapped fox which, to achieve freedom, bites through and leaves a part behind.

I dreamed no longer of my faceless knight. I dreamed that I stood on the gallery with Richard Plantagenet, that we danced together, and he told me of the White Boar and his lips brushed my hair. And on awakening I was sad that such a fair dream must fade, until

* In mediaeval times, boar was spelled 'bore' and it is thought that Richard's device was an anagram for EBOR (York).

the frosty sun brought remembrance, and I roused Elysande with a hearty kiss which set her grumbling mightily, for she swore I had tossed and groaned night-long and had now broken the best of her slumber. She pushed me out of our bed and I sat on the floor and sang about the Nut-Brown Maid, while all the other women in our chamber looked affrighted, thinking I had had my brains addled by an incubus in sleep. They reckoned me a wanton little thing in any event, coming unheralded from the country under the mantle of my smile, and plying my wheedling craft upon my lady of Bedford until (they vowed) it sickened them.

Yea, and I willingly served her, disagreeable though she was that day, for 'twas through her I had attained my bliss. I massaged and perfumed her aged body, poured praises over her with the rose-water and, as if she were young and beautiful, spent hours tiring her meagre locks. I fetched her her potions and physics, held the mirror up and flattered its reflection with honey breath. She preened herself. And all the while that morning, after the dreaming night, I served her thus with great distaste in my heart, thinking about Sir Thomas Cook and the arras, and of the way the Woodvilles used Richard, with their cold glittering looks, their sharp elbows thrusting him from the King.

Of him I did not need to think. He was part of me already; wrapped close within my heart, warm and safe, with his dark eyes, fire and ice, his quiet voice, his hands that were hard and gentle. When I heard the sixty voices of the choristers in the Royal Chapel sweetly raised in the *Gloria*, I smiled for joy, for his kneeling image came so sharp and clear I knew myself in spirit at his side.

But all this made the Duchess no less capricious and tiresome. She complained of her liver, saying that the banquet last evening had not been to her taste, though Elysande whispered that she had eaten overmuch of green figs, and this was doubtless the truth. She moaned and muttered; I flew about frantically, soothing her with possets and sacred amulets upon her stomach. The Queen sent Master Dominic to tend her; he who had made such a jest out of himself at the birth of the Princess Elizabeth by so firmly prophesying a male heir; but my lady would have none of him. He in turn would have sought the skill of Doctor Serigo, the chief royal physician, but she ranted against this with such passion that he finally spread his hands despairingly and slid away to juggle with his almanac, in the chamber hung with cabalistic signs and thick with the reek of herbs. It was all most wearying, and catching a glimpse of my face I saw that I was pale, with bruises under my eyes. This cast me down, for I wished to look fresh and fair for my tryst that evening.

That he would not come I did not for a moment think. There was that in him better than honour; a lack of light-mindedness, and the cognizance of one who keeps a promise no matter to whom it is made. This trait shone from him, wordless, yet lacking no expression. My hands shook. I must be doubly careful not to spill anything, to fall prey to clumsiness and enrage the Duchess. I felt like the tumbling-women at the May-Games, balanced on sword-points, each nerve stretched in a dangerous skill. For I knew it would take but a little annoyance to drive the Duchess back to Grafton, and then I would need to work my wiles upon the Queen, a very different matter, for Elizabeth was of iron, and had plenty greater than I to flatter her. Also I had bound the Duchess to me with my sweet considerations, and I doubted she would let me leave her. So the other women shook their heads in wonder at my ceaseless toil and, murmuring that I did the work of four, shrugged their shoulders and snatched a little more leisure themselves, thanking me for a fool.

In the afternoon, Anthony Woodville came to visit the Duchess in her apartments, bringing some translations of the verses of Christine de Pisan that he had made. The gentlewomen fluttered like birds, for he was handsome. Attired like the most royal of princes, he strode through the gold-hung chamber in a journade of white velvet edged with ermine. Stylishly, he carried a tall hat on the end of his cane with an affected air. The pikes of his shoes, a quarter ell in length, were caught up at the toe and buckled about the knee with gold chains. He walked with caution. He had two new rings: a sapphire the size of a small walnut, and a pearl-and-enamel thumb-ring shaped like the royal rose. Very recently had the King bestowed on him the Order of the Garter. He knelt to kiss his mother's hand. All the women withdrew to a modest distance. Elysande pulled me down beside her on to cushions. She gave me a little shadowy smile, with a teasing cock of her head in Sir Anthony's direction.

'You see his shoes? Jesu, I wonder he does not braid his legs and tumble on his face!'

I smothered a laugh.

'The Pope has sent a Bull into England,' whispered one of the other women. 'He's sorely vexed at the worldliness of this new style, and says he'll excommunicate any cordwainer who fashions such long pikes.'

'My cordwainer says his Holiness's curse won't kill a fly,' said someone.

'Are you well, Madame?' enquired Anthony Woodville tenderly of the Duchess.

She gave a loud groan. 'Nay, sir, I fear I am sick in my stomach. I'll remain in my chamber this day.'

'Shall we not see you at the feasting tonight, my lady?' he asked. 'I vow you'll enjoy the sport. The Lord of Misrule holds sway this evening.'

I held my breath. Holy Mother of God, let her decide to go! I prayed. This was a turn of events I had not foreseen, The Duchess paused for a long space, while I bit my lips as if by pain I could will the right words from her.

'I cannot say yea or nay at this time,' she answered finally, and I lusted to leap across the room and shake her till her teeth chattered.

She peered at her son.

'How goes the sport?'

'I have been in the tiltyard at Eltham, and have unhorsed eight knights without a break,' he said with satisfaction.

'So you are champion again,' she said delightedly, and he smirked with pleasure.

'Yea, Madame, as on every day,' he answered, and went on to tell her of the ingenious new harness he had designed himself, cunningly fashioned to overthrow any opponent, or so he said.

He kissed her hand again before departing, and turned at the door to bid her finally farewell.

'I trust we shall have your company this evening, madam my mother,' he said, but still she would not decide, and I began to shiver and grow chill at the thought of not being able to slip away. As he made to leave, his cold grey eyes flicked idly round the mute circle of gentlewomen and came last to me. No recognition crossed his face and I was glad of it, for as I looked at him I remembered the dark chamber of Grafton Regis, and my fear. 'Flogged, at the cart's tail.'

I went swiftly to the Duchess. 'Are you too warm, my lady?' I murmured. 'Though for sure, the fire has brought a pretty colour to your face, dare I say it.'

She looked at me, and I thought she was about to grumble, but she said:

'You are a good child—thoughtful and kindly—would that all were the same,' and she shot an evil glance at Elysande who, truth to tell, often shirked a duty, if she thought she could do so undiscovered,

'Bring me some gowns,' she commanded. 'I will choose one to wear this evening.' And my heart sprang up with gladness, for tonight I could go to the gallery; and see again the face of my love.

The Duchess sifted through damask and velvet, and sighed heavily that none pleased her.

'This one becomes you well, Madame,' and I drew out an orange satin lined with marten's fur. She threw it to the floor.

'I'll not wear that gown,' she said angrily. 'The last time I appeared in it, there were those that mocked me.'

The gentlewomen gasped in chorus. 'Never, my lady,' said Lady Scrope. 'What churl would dare?'

'I saw my lord of Warwick smile,' she said grimly, and the whole chamber seemed to darken with the venom of her look. She cast the dress away with the point of her shoe. 'Take it,' she told me. 'It needs but a little threadwork to fit you.'

Stroking the slippery richness, I murmured my thanks. Elysande was beside me, caressing the fur, eyes lowered in admiration. 'You'll look like Venus,' she whispered. My heart turned one of Patch's somersaults; now I could appear before him fittingly clad, worthy and fine. Meanwhile the Duchess tried on dress after dress. And still she would not decide.

At four o'clock, pages brought up a light meal for the Duchess, who picked at it with little heart, and if her stomach was sick, mine was sicker, with my dread that she would abstain from the feasting. At seven she vowed she would take a short rest on her couch, and at nine she still slumbered, her mouth open, the jewels at her breast catching the light as they rose and fell. Elysande and I stood watching her.

'Could you not pour a sleeping draught between her jaws to quiet her for all night?' I whispered desperately. Elysande choked on merriment.

'Would you have us both end our days in the Fleet?' she sighed, weeping with laughter. She looked at me sideways. More than ever her eyes minded me of cursed Gyb, though they were green, not yellow.

'You are passing anxious to rid us of my lady by some means,' she murmured. 'I saw how you ran around like a frenzied stoat in your desire to robe her, and now you would have her drugged—by the Rood, that gallery must be an enchanted place! I myself have always found it too cold to stay long—but you spend half the night there and come to bed an icicle.'

'It's a diversion,' I said. 'No more.' And I turned from her, suddenly weary, all my bright dreams cold as tomorrow's fire, knowing that I had made much of naught. A few words, a dance, a kiss on the crown of the head—or had I imagined even that? A maid with long vixen-coloured hair—a moment's politeness—and all forgotten in the chase, in the tiltyard, or checking supplies in the armoury?

At ten, one of the Queen's henchmen tapped on the door of the outer chamber, and I spoke to him. He asked whether my lady would be descending to the Hall, as all were concerned for her health. I found great difficulty in answering, and held wide the door so that he could see through into the Duchess's apartment, where the gentlewomen drowsed, Elysande kept vigil and my lady snored.

'What a thing it is to be cursed with years,' he observed. 'My Lord of Misrule holds court below, and I warrant there will be much lusty sport, with men and women doing what they will! Do you not wish you were one of his subjects, mistress?' and he winked lewdly.

Wild imaginings burned my mind—Richard—the cool Duke of Gloucester, inflamed mayhap by some wanton, noble lady… I put my hand flat on the liveried chest, right over the royal badge, and gave it a shove.

'Not all have their minds crammed with bedsport, false mischiefs…' I gasped. 'Go! My lady sleeps and so shall we, soon.'

He twisted his body about in horrible gestures.

'Alone, mistress?' he mocked. ''Tis passing sad.'

From the Great Hall a roar ascended. Female shrieks and loud laughter followed. I glanced hopefully to where the Duchess lay, praying that the clamour might have awakened her, but I was disappointed.

'King Misrule will have them all kissing by now,' went on the page. 'So why should we two not kiss—fair mistress, give me your lips, I pray you.'

He lunged at me. He had been drinking ale, in some quiet corner. I thought sadly of *my* quiet corner, as I slammed the door in his face. The cold stones would be colder tonight, without me to warm them with my frail burning, and the torch flame would mutter to itself, unless others spoke and danced and touched lightly in its leaping glare. For he would not have come. I was now convinced of it.

And if by chance he had come and found me missing, a shrug of the shoulders would end that which had scarcely begun.

I could picture him, walking away, slender and agile, his jewels and his eyes of ice and fire the only points of light in the darkness of him. With his swift controlled step he would be descending the stairs, entering the Great Hall to link arms with his friend, the unseen Lovell of last evening, the fortunate one who called him Dickon.

Then they would exchange the old glances of young men.

'Did she come? Was she there? What happened?'

A shake of the head, a dagger of disdain sheathed in laughter—a draught of wine and eyes bright, seeking fresh faces to charm.

I had never seen an execution but had heard plenty of tales; how the bowels are dragged from the belly and burnt while the victim lives. I thought my pain akin to that pain. I turned and walked to where Elysande sat at her tapestry frame.

'Sweet holy Mother of God!' she cried softly. 'I vow I've never seen such a sad countenance in all my days! Grafton Regis must be the dullest place in the realm!'

'It's quiet enough. Why?' I said. The pain was growing more brutal, more real every minute.

'Well,' she said, laughing, 'it seems that having tasted the joys of spying on the great ones, you can't live without such nightly diversion! But I remember, when I came to court, I felt the same. It soon palls. Why, by St Catherine, maiden, you're weeping!'

And she sat without moving to comfort me, but looking at me with a quizzical gaze, mocking and pitying at the same time, while her face rippled and moved before my tear-filled eyes like stones on a river bed.

'Do not snivel like a slubberdegullion,' she said, sharply kind, and this was the best physic for me, for I collected myself, and managed to smile at her, weakly.

'There's more to this,' she spoke firmly. 'Will you tell me—we are friends, are we not?'

She was ever anxious to be my friend, and I was glad of it. But I could not trust myself to answer.

'You have a lover!' she said suddenly, in a pleased voice,

'No lover,' I answered. And minded the times I had said this to others who had asked me, and my reply had mattered no more to me than the death of a falling leaf. But now the case was changed anew; I had no lover, and I was in love. I thought of my love as a perfect pearl, gleaming and warm to the touch, richly sweet as honey, fragrant as the Rose, fierce as the Boar. It had been held out to me for a little space. Unfulfilled, it must be hidden in my heart. I wondered if a heart could contain all that rich and painful sweetness, without splitting clear in two.

'No lover, Elysande,' I said again.

'But you had an assignation,' she went on, guessing, eager, kind. I shook my head, and then the Duchess stirred. She was awakening, too late. The glance I gave her was sorrowful but it held no anger. She was only the tool used by unkindly Providence, to break me up.

'I have slept well,' she announced, and Elysande and I looked at each other, lost for words.

'Do you desire aught, Madame?' I asked her, though I knew there was little method in seizing the chance to go below on an errand. My gallery would be empty, empty. It was habit that made me solicitous for her needs.

'I'll have my hair brushed,' said the Duchess 'I feel quite renewed after my slumber. We will have a game of cards shortly,' and she clapped her hands with a fiend's delight, throwing all the nodding women into a frenzy of awakening.

So, for an hour, I brushed the Duchess's hair, and through a thin veil of unnoticed tears, I played a game that these were other locks I stroked; dark hair shining with life about a pale, noble, dangerous young face. It was difficult though; every time I made the feeling come alive, and closed my eyes the better to imagine, my lady railed at me for sleeping.

On my way to the launderer's in the morning, I passed the gallery, and stood a moment to bid it farewell. It was no longer an enchanted place. In daylight it seemed smaller and not the chamber of delight where once, long ago, he and I had been handfasted. The torch was black where it had burned through. An evil omen. There were a few people about; divers ladies of the court, white and wan with kiss-marks on their necks, and satiety hung on the air like over-heavy perfume in a hot room. I swept low as George of Clarence passed, gilt-haired, aloof, his fair brows drawn together in a headache knot.

I shifted the weight of clothes from one arm to the other and sighed. A heavier sigh from the lungs of a clever mimic, whistled past my ear. Only Patch, I thought, could have come so inopportunely; if he jests with me now, I will strike him in the face. But I had misjudged him. He seemed to sense my misery.

'Be not so doleful,' he counselled. 'I'll carry the gowns for you—Jesu! they are heavy!' He staggered under the weight of damask and fine linen.

'Give them back to me, Patch,' I said, mistrusting him. 'My lady's still wroth that one of her shifts went astray last week. God knows, you might steal one of these to wear for sport, and get me into trouble.'

Hurt, he whined: 'Cruel maid. You should know I wish you naught but good.'

So I pleaded pardon, and squeezed his arm. 'I'm in a foul humour this day, Patch,' I said.

'Then, like cat and dog, this spikes my own affection,' he answered. 'For I am joyful in truth... maiden, last night I had a great triumph. I was Lord of Misrule to the court, and set them all by the ears! God's bones, you never did see such sport!' and he laughed aloud with glee.

'That I can well believe,' I said, hiding my sorrow.

'I looked for you on the gallery,' he continued. 'I wished to share the laughter with you, sweeting. We could have watched them below, all in turmoil, and got great joy from it. But you never came, or at least I did not see you.'

'My lady was sick, and needed me,' I said, and turned to go, unable to bear more.

'Some folk keep strange custom,' he mused, picking up one of the Duchess's stockings which had escaped the bundle. 'For sure, I came up here to seek you, long past midnight. Yet I did but meet with Dickon of Gloucester, and I know not who was the more startled, he or I.'

Elysande had seen me talking to Patch, and noting my swift change from despair to gladness, reckoned it was he who was my paramour; and now that I had seen his wrinkled face and curving mouth again, all was well with me. So, to please her, I laughed, and thought on Piers, or Patch, for a brief space. He was clever, and scholarly, and his star was rising higher in the service of King Edward, so skilled and jocund was he. He was not ungently born and he was, I suspected, wealthy; neither was he freakish nor dwarfed, like some entertainers—he was fairly enough of proportions and far from unpleasing to look at. There would be few raised brows should I choose to be betrothed to him. Truly it seemed that marriage for me had faded into non-existence, these days. My mistress had gained her heart's desire—Lady Grey was Queen of England; and she had her relatives to look to in matters of suitable betrothal. She had many wards—I was useful no doubt in a minor way but of no consequence. As for my thoughts on marriage?

There was but one to whom I would belong. And had he been poor as the humblest cottar's son, ragged, lame, blind, ignorant, and yet capable of offering me the wedding ring, I would have taken him on the moment, with not one look behind, so long as he had Richard's face, and Richard's voice, and Richard's spirit, to burn me with a steady fire, to warm me with its young heat and make each day May Day for me.

'But you do not marry them,' I said in a whisper. By rank far distant, and by riches further apart than the topmost star. Elysande swam back into my vision.

'Fools, I mean.'

'Well, sweet, he is a man,' she said, laughing, and I saw suddenly the use of this silly delusion, and caught at it gladly.

'Yes, he is. He is, indeed,' I said, feigning coyness, and she looked hard at me, as if unsure of her own mind.

She was hard to fathom, Elysande. French in descent, she gave away little in confidence, never lost her temper through weariness as did the others, and she seemed to know many at court, some of noble birth. I had seen her only lately having fair speech with a woman, the strangest little person I had ever seen. She was even lower in stature than I, not a deal higher than the comic dwarfs King Edward kept for his pleasure, to juggle and ride the great hounds around the Hall. Far from well-favoured was this tiny lady, with a face all bones and sharply defined as an axe, small flashing eyes and hollow cheeks. Yet she had had two husbands, Elysande told me, for this was Lady Margaret Beaufort. Daughter of the Lancastrian Duke of Somerset, she had first wedded Edmund Tudor, Earl of Richmond, when she was thirteen, bearing a son, Henry, two months after the death of her knight.

Patch plagued me with tales of these Tudors; he seemed to know all their history. They were some kind of distant cousin to the King. He had witnessed a rare scene, had Patch, in Hereford, the town where he was born.

'I can see it now,' he said, more than once. 'Old Owen Tudor, kneeling in the market square—one blow, and he lacked a head... then came this madwoman...'

'And combed his hair and stroked his face and wept and lighted candles all around him,' I said wearily.

'I was but a little knave,' he said, uncaring. 'Jesu, that woman must have loved him sore. Then, if a Queen loved him, why not a witless wench?'

Surprised, I murmured: 'Did a Queen love him?'

'Yea, Queen Katherine, widow of Harry the Fifth—Harry of Agincourt. That is why they smote off his head, I vow. Slain for love,' he said romantically and sighed, rolling his eyes at me and conveniently contriving to forget all about old Owen's Lancastrian loyalties.

'Edmund Tudor was their bastard issue,' he maundered. 'Jasper and Owen and Edmund, Margaret Beaufort's first husband. Maiden, think you she has heard my tale of high romance and sorrow? Mayhap one day I will seek to interest her with it,' he said happily.

'I doubt not she is well familiar with it, Patch, as are we all.' I sighed and turned up my eyes to make him cease. And then I realized it was nearing dusk, and Tudors and Lady Beaufort fled from my mind. For they were all but as the pastry figures fashioned by cooks for the subtleties at the King's table, and my thoughts all drew together and ran to meet Richard, as I prayed for night to come swiftly.

I vowed I would wait for him until dawn. I donned the Duchess's gift as soon as she was safely below. Elysande brushed out my hair, as if I were a noble lady. The other women played at dice, casting resigned looks in our direction as we murmured and shook with mirth, though there were some who smiled to themselves, having faint remembrance of their own youth; they were all past thirty.

'They think you *lack-wit to love a fool*,' Elysande whispered, and we clutched each other and wept with our laughter. And I laughed more merrily than she at the secret jest which I enjoyed, until a sudden thought shattered my joy. In truth, I had likened Patch to a troublesome fly before, but this night, if my lord came and spoke with me, and bewitched me with his steady gaze and the clasp of his hand, the fool might prove more dangerous; a fly? nay, a hornet, with sharp jealous sting. I fell to gnawing my nails, and when Elysande asked me, sighing *what ailed me now*, I could not answer her.

She snuffed a few candles, and the chamber grew large and dark with this new riddle peering at me from the shadows. Two of the women already slept, and their quiet breathing mingled with the rattling dice and the faint music coming from below. I sat motionless.

'Your sweetheart will be looking for you,' Elysande whispered. 'Take your cloak, it is colder tonight.'

I drew the hood up over my hair.

'Why do you dally?' she hissed, holding the door open. A chill breath from the passage crept in. 'If you don't go soon, you'll not be back when my lady returns.'

'Ah, Jesu, Elysande,' I whispered. 'Will she return soon, think you?'

She smiled. 'Nay, child, she's in fine fettle tonight. From the way she spoke, she rued slumbering through the gaiety last evening.'

The door closed softly behind me. Shaken by a trembling that had naught to do with the cold, I moved vixen-silent through the familiar darkness. Around the corner, the flickering torch burned high, beckoning me with its elf-light. I heard the music and the raised voices, which by now I could almost tell apart. The King's laugh was a mighty sound, rich and golden as he, and I recognized Clarence's bibulous chuckle. Tenderly, I bent my body against the pillar, greeting the carved faces with my fingers, and looked down. I was safe from Patch for a time in any event, for a figure, all blazing yellow and red, jingling bells, leaped witlessly about before the royal dais. He had possessed himself of the gold carcanet from the neck of some knight, and was skipping with it in the manner of a young child. He will need to be careful, I thought. His glory of last night makes him wax stout and proud. For his sake, I hoped that the lord he had robbed was cup-shotten and careless.

The Woodvilles dominated the Hall. They were all gathered, and tonight also there was Lionel Woodville, lately made Bishop of Salisbury. In fine robes, he nodded and smiled at the wholesome folly before him. There was Lord Hastings, looking sour. Lord Stanley and his brother William. Katherine of Desmond, Dick and Thomas Grey, George of Clarence, and my lord of Warwick. My eyes found Warwick, found his companion, and searched no further.

He was the very reason for my birth. He was my lord, and he stood next to the Earl of Warwick, slender and elegant, dangerous and sad, and I felt my heart give one clapping rush out to him like the wings of a dying bird; and my eyes set upon him in longing love, and I heard myself, like someone far away, come forth with a little rush of loving words, and his name, said over and over in the darkness. It was a moment or two before I realized that all was not well with him. He was talking to Warwick, very fast. He was pale as death. He held one hand hard down upon the hilt of his dagger as if he feared it would suddenly take on life, and kill. He was angry.

Warwick, much taller than Richard, bent his handsome head languidly to listen. A little smile fidgeted his mouth. I mistrusted that smile. And George of Clarence came strolling into the tableau, also smiling, with full pouting lips, with condescension and unmistakable mockery. And Richard talked on and on, as I watched him, his hands; the clenched fist, the spread fingers, the clasped hands like a prayer; and his brows drawing together, and his eyes bright with this unknown anger and sadness. He glanced towards the King, then back to Warwick, talking, talking. And all the time Warwick smiled that arrogant, cruel smile, and Clarence chuckled in his wine-cup.

Then Warwick laid his hand upon his own heart and spoke. One short phrase, and Clarence laughed out loud, and the colour touched

Richard's face, as if each cheek had been held before the fire. Then in the next instant he was pale again, pale as one long dead.

Warwick placed an arm about George of Clarence's shoulders, and together they walked away.

Richard was looking at the King. Edward, with a moody good-humour, filled a goblet with wine and pushed it across the table, beckoning his brother to come and drink. Richard walked over to the dais. He made to lift the jewelled cup, when the Queen forestalled him. With a masterly coquetry and a cat's swiftness, she took the cup herself, pledging the King over it with large eyes. She touched it to her lips. Then she handed it over her shoulder to Anthony Woodville, who raised it high.

'The King, my lords!' he cried. 'The Sun in Splendour! Perdition to his enemies!'

With a roar, the court rose, goblets aflame. I saw them all, as if frozen in a pose, the gay court acclaiming its King, the royal pair smiling their pleasure, and the King's brother, young, solitary, fierce, his foot upon the step of the dais, glaring about as at those who sought his death. The only one to lack a cup for the loyal toast.

'Holy Jesu! Cruel, cruel!' I said out loud, and clung to the pillar, shaking.

I had been against the Countess of Desmond because she danced with him, but I loved her the next second, for it was she who brought salvation. Snatching up a half-empty hanap from one of the side tables, she tendered it discreetly towards Richard. And Patch, the troublesome fly, the witless fool, I loved him too. For he nipped it swiftly from her hand and gave it to my lord, with a courtly bow and a wink that held no mockery. So the wheels began to turn again, and the throats of men moved in their swallow, and the thud of goblets being set down merged with the minstrels' gay tune, and the moment passed.

My heart pounded, and my palms were wet. I fixed a killing glance upon the Queen but it did not touch her, for she fluttered her lashes and her hands, and the King ogled her with looks that spoke of bed. It was only when I surveyed the company again that I saw my lord of Warwick had not drained his cup, but held it brimming still. The smile on his countenance was bland and fierce. And now the gay colours, the glory, meant little. I smelled the storm, the hidden hate. It rose up and beat about me.

Warwick bent the knee before his King. He was departing, the carved smile still on his lips, and as I marked his progress through the door, I realized that another, the other, the only one, had left before him. And I had not even watched him go; it was like a betrayal, for I had sworn I would not let him from my sight, would protect him with my gaze as his own patron saint.

I sighed. He would not come now—that was certain, for he was too distressed by whatever had befallen him down there in that hell of hot laughter. And I would not even have the chance to offer him solace. It was as I thought thus, I wondered how best I might comfort him, and lacked conclusion, for how shall one, who has no quality, who is shadow and not substance, know aught of succouring a prince of the blood?

Cold and alone, I stood for a long time. My heart ached. I was full of longing and sorrow and shame, shame at myself. Last night, while the Duchess slumbered, I had tormented myself with thoughts of my love, deeming him a lightsome courtier, wayward in look and desire. Now I knew he was not even a part of the seething court; I saw him old beyond his years, constantly tortured; pricked by intrigue and spite, baited by circumstance as a bear by feast-day mastiffs. And the worst of it was I did not know all. I could not reckon what it was that branded his face with that look of angry sorrow. And, thinking how gladly I would have shared his trouble, no matter what, I drew my cloak about me and began to make my way, sadly, back towards the Duchess's apartments.

I felt a tugging at my skirts, and turned, frightened. A pale face stared up at me, level with my waist. A child's face, a faery face, disembodied above a suit of dark livery, and green-white with fatigue. A tiny page, come by night on an errand of which he was too young and too weary to know overmuch. Very hesitantly he asked my name and looked satisfied when I nodded. Then he fumbled for my cloaked hand and gripped its coldness. He began to tug me back towards the gallery. 'Mistress, come with me,' he muttered.

'Where?' I stood firm, while he heaved at my hand and breathed gustily as if to draw me after him by sheer strength.

'It is a command,' he insisted, and my blood turned to dreadful ice. Only the King commands. My first thought was that I had been espied on the gallery by night and that the Comptroller of the Household had been ordered to reprimand me. Or some doing of the Queen! My guilt summond wild images of Elizabeth's displeasure. I remembered too that I wore my lady of Bedford's gown. It came to my mind that she might not recall giving it to me. I sought to hide its rich folds from the torchlight and the child's weary eyes.

'Who so commands?' I whispered. The page shook his head, mute with sleep-lust.

'Madame, 'tis this way,' he breathed, his foot pawing the ground like a pony anchored by too great a weight. And so in pity and resignation I steeled myself and went with him, along the dark ways, past the drowsy guard, who winked at me as at any fair female face, answering my uneasy smile. We ascended narrow spiralling steps to another broad passage, descended a staircase, crossed a deserted hallway and entered a part of the Palace where I had not ventured. My captor halted before an oaken door, and bruised his knuckles hammering upon it. We waited. The page looked at me, and I at him, and he twitched his pale lips in a comic grimace.

'I suppose we had better enter,' he muttered, and threw his weight against the handle. I followed him into the empty chamber, and, in the light of many candles and a great fire, saw that upon his livery was blazoned the Boar, the White Boar, and my blood turned from ice to flame.

My hand was still imprisoned. He had a duty to fulfil, and none would chide him for shirking it. I managed to smile at him.

'I shall not flee, child,' I said gently. 'How cold your hand is! Come to the warmth.'

He came, willingly, and sat in the hearth, his knees under their proud livery drawn up to his chin, while I looked around the chamber, drinking in the things that were Richard, and which gave me joy.

'Where is my lord of Gloucester?' I asked, walking about on the rich carpet.

'He was here when I left, but he must have gone about some affairs,' said the child anxiously.

'Don't fret,' I said. Now I could hardly speak. 'He will come soon.'

His chessboard lay open upon a small table, the pieces frozen in an intricate move. My fingers hovered over a bishop; then dropped to my side, for I knew little of the game. I wondered with whom he had been playing, and guessed again at Lovell, his friend of the dark staircase. A fluttering sigh came from the corner. On a rod crouched a perigrine falcon, his round eye fixing me like an angry jewel. A lute lay on a chair near by and I touched it softly. The little discord rippled and hung sobbing on the air.

I walked to his writing table. Sheets of parchment lay strewn, and some had fallen to the floor. Pens and ink—a broken quill, and a pattern of fierce words leaping to my eye. I bent to read and saw with love, his signature... R. Gloucester; and three words, repeated over and over, the writing a fine Italic script growing wilder and ending with an ink-smear and paper torn by a savage pen. Very recent, that writing, the last line still wet. Three words only, time and again…

Loyaulte me lie.

The fire spurted and hissed as it licked damp wood.

I went through into the adjoining chamber, for the door was open, and gazed at Richard's narrow bed. It looked hard, though the sheets were damask, the covers edged with ermine. The White Boar, worked in silver thread, savaged the coverlet with its tusks. Above the couch shone a tiny light, steadfast and comfortable, illuminating the statue of St George. In silence I stared at the saint, and asked his blessing on Richard Plantagenet.

'I wish he would come,' said a small voice from the antechamber. I went back to the fire and was about to try to cheer the page, when the door opened, and he did come: all my joy, all my safety and all my bliss.

He entered smiling and he too had felt the cold, for he had thrown a long cloak of dark velvet about him. He gave me no time for any curtsey; he strode across the chamber and took my hands.

'Mistress, I am happy to see you again,' he said. His voice was as I remembered it. The joy became a pain, striking my depths.

'Sir, you commanded my presence; I am happy to obey,' I said softly. He must have felt the heartbeat in my wrist; beating, beating, like a song, like a tabor. But his glance swept to the page, and his smile faded a little.

'What's this?' he demanded. 'Harry, you are becoming hard of hearing now you are old and have fully eight years! I mentioned no word of command—I did but say you were to ask the lady.'

The page's mouth opened convulsively as if to set up a bawling. Richard bent hastily and took him in his arms, setting him on the table, so that his legs dangled.

'My lord, forgive my folly,' whimpered the child. 'I have a passing bad memory—I pray you, don't beat me.' And he shot a sly glance from under his lashes, cringing and fawning like a cur who begs morsels beneath the table.

'Folly indeed,' muttered Richard. 'When have I beaten you, you knave?'

'Never, my lord,' said the page primly.

Then Richard laughed. 'Well, sir, thanks for your faithful service this night. You look over-ripe for your bed. Be gone!' and he tossed a coin up in the air which the page caught deftly, tucked into a pouch that a faery might own, and, grinning, twinkled his legs across the chamber and heaved the door shut behind him.

And we were alone; and the fire blazed and chattered on the hearth, and we stood looking at each other across a chasm of unspoken words and my thoughts that leaped and swooned and grew bright.

He was the first to move. He crossed to me and my heart raced swifter for I thought... I know not what I thought, but he took my cloak from about me and his glance fell on my hair and he paled slightly.

'I pray you, be seated, mistress; be comfortable.' He drew a chair for me with as much courtesy as I had been the Queen. He laid our cloaks together across the table. 'I looked for you last evening,' he said, but his voice did not reproach me. His tone was rather that of one who expects to be disappointed.

'My lord, I would gladly have talked with you on the gallery again,' I said. 'But my lady of Bedford had need of my services.'

The look of kind politeness vanished from his face as if cloven off by a sword, and he gave a bitter laugh.

'Ah, holy God!' he said, and his quiet voice was even quieter. 'It is wondrous mirthful, for even in this, as in all my affairs, that company conspires to thwart me.'

He turned, with his restless, trained walk moving over to where stood a flagon of wine and cups.

'Will you drink, damoiselle?' he said, holding up the crested flagon, and I sprang from my chair, for it was unseemly for him to serve me.

'I will attend you, my lord,' I said hastily, seeking to take the wine from him. He covered my hand with his own, and his dark eyes held mine as he smiled a half-smile.

'You are my guest, mistress,' he said. 'Be seated, I pray; let us have no more folly. No posturing, no sham.'

Through my wild joy, he handed me the cup. He sat opposite me, the fire burning bright between us, and stretched his legs in the hearth, the time-honoured male gesture.

'This is better than that chill nook where first we met,' he said, and smiled at me over the top of his hanap. He drank, slowly, without taking his eyes from me. Then he whispered:

'Jesu! You are fair!'

I sat and tried to be calm, feeling myself becoming fairer under his look.

'Can you play chess?' he said suddenly.

Surprised, I shook my head. 'But I will learn, my lord, if that is your desire,' I murmured.

He waved his hand dismissively. 'It matters not,' he said. 'It is a good game, however, and one that all should know. It teaches a man strategy and tactics, and, by God, I vow that in this place one should be born cognizant of such matters!'

I longed to ask him more, help him unburden himself, but I knew I must wait until he chose to speak of that which troubled and angered him so much.

'How do you find the court?' he asked me, and I was sorely vexed for an answer.

'The jewels and the dresses are wonderous fine,' I ventured, and he hid a smile in his wine-cup, shaking his head, no doubt, at the light-mindedness of women.

'But I see little of the court itself, my lord, for I am neither one thing nor the other...' I babbled on. 'I am greater than some and lesser than some, and to speak the truth, I have not yet found my rightful place. I am pulled this way and that by standards of society, for though I came from the Queen's house at Grafton Regis, I am not of noble birth.'

He gazed at me, and there was that in his eye which reminded me of the falcon's stare, looking right through and out the other side.

'Noble birth,' he said slowly. 'Jesu, mistress, I have seen the humblest vassal conduct himself with more grace than some of noble birth! And I have seen those who, hiding their policies behind a lovesome smile, feign nobility as they were born to it. While their hands clutch power as greedily as any cutpurse in the street!'

I knew of whom he spoke, and I kept silence, though my mind shrieked agreement.

'But we are talking of you, mistress,' he said gently. 'It intrigues me much to hear you describe yourself thus—neither one thing nor the other, for I too have known this feeling, and it is strong in me tonight.'

I spread my hands, assaying to make a jest of it.

''Tis the best I can do,' I smiled. 'Like Patch, in his motley; half red, half yellow! That is I.'

He set down his wine, and sighed. 'And I,' he said.

Let us merge the red and the yellow then, I thought in my heart. Looking at him, dark and gleaming like a raven in the firelight, I wondered if I could contrive to touch his hand; and instantly, he must have read my thought, for his fingers reached out and closed about mine. We sat motionless, while a loving ache from his touch crept up my arm and settled in my breast.

He was quiet for so long a space, I felt bound to amuse him with conversation.

'We saw a passing marvellous sight, when we came by London Bridge,' I said. 'All the people were shouting and clamouring and everything halted for my lord of Warwick, as he rode...'

I bit my words off on a gasp of pain, as his hand tightened on mine like the steel of a trap. I sat enduring the agony, questioning the pallor of his face.

'Certes, the people love Warwick,' he said, through his teeth. 'It was always so, for he won their hearts with his kindliness and courtesy—none was too lowly for his notice... all love him, as I did.'

It was the firelight, there could be no tears in his eyes; that was impossible, I thought, for he was hard and shining like steel; a royal Duke, a King's brother, and such do not weep easily. Before I could decide, he had leaped from the chair, to lean against the polished sweep of the brass chimney-piece. He rested his forehead on his arm for a brief second. When he looked at me again, his face was so composed I thought I had imagined it. It was the firelight.

'I loved Warwick,' he said, and it was as if he spoke to an empty room. 'He was like my father, and he trained me in the arts of war as bravely as I were truly his son. I cannot bear to think of those happy times at Middleham, but when I breathe the corruption down there' he gestured fiercely in the direction of the Great Hall—'then I mind how sweet were the cold moors of Wensleydale with their sharp cleansing gales and haunted mists. There a man could come close to God and know himself at last. Here... there is naught but greed and spite and lechery...'

He smote the chimney-piece with his fist, and it gave off a dull booming sound. I sat quiet, and trembled.

'I wonder often, of a night when I lie sleepless,' he whispered, 'why I was blessed, or cursed, with a heart that knows one way only, and cleaves to that way as a priest to his breviary. It is easy for George—he was ever feckless and light- minded, and lets himself be swayed by the breeze of fortune whither it will. But I have cast my loves into the dust to honour my allegiance to his Grace... to my brother Edward. The Sun in Splendour, hidden now behind a foul cloud of locusts!'

His emotion rent me to the bone. His pain was mine.

'Do not distress yourself so, my lord,' I whispered. He did not hear me.

'When I was fourteen, I attended a great banquet,' he continued. 'My lord of Warwick made much of me, and I wore the Garter. Warwick seated me with his ladies, the Countess, Isabel, and little Anne... I was so honoured and happy, until I realized what he was about. He would have me turn traitor to the King. I would not take his bait, so he washed his hands of me. Did you see what befell tonight?' he demanded, turning his fiery gaze upon me.

'Yes, my lord, I knew much sadness,' I murmured.

'Jesu!' he muttered. 'He called me... a Woodville-lover! I, of all people, who would rather have died than see my beloved... his Grace, netted by that loathsome brood. And then the Queen caused me to lose face, deliberately, before all!'

His colour came and went, frighteningly, with his fierce breath. I rose and stood beside him.

'My lady of Desmond aided you,' I reminded him gently, and his frenzy ebbed a little.

'Yea, the dear Countess. She's a good friend to me… and one who has suffered much at… at the hands of Edward's Queen.'

As if he thought he had said too much, he glanced at me sharply. 'I may not speak of it,' he murmured. Then, in almost the same breath he said softly: 'She is widowed.' He looked at the fire. The leaping flames were red in the dark eyes. 'And worse,' he whispered. 'The shedding of infants' blood… Slaying women is bad enough, and no Plantagenet has ever done so, but the monstrous crime of takinng children's lives deserves eternal torment.'

We were silent again, a long silence, broken only by the chirping of burning logs; and the falcon's wings softly stirring in sleep. I knew that he spoke of some secret foulness of the Queen, and wondered if he remembered that I slept by Jacquetta of Bedford. In that instant he turned to me with a faint smile.

'I will say no more,' he said. 'It is not that I do not trust your gentle face, for there is that in it which moves me to confidence. And the King knows I am loyal and would not let the Woodvilles harm me. But you are in the service of Elizabeth's mother, and open to attack. So it is better now that I should teach you chess, if that would pleasure you.'

But we remained looking at each other, and he took my hands in that same tender clasp.

'I would not betray you, my lord,' I said steadily.

'Suffice it to say this is why the Countess of Desmond and I talk together and sometimes dance in the Great Hall,' he answered. 'We find some little comfort in each other's company. And I have need of such.'

I could scarcely catch his last sentence. With my heart I watched him, for I longed to keep his image with me for ever: his dark slenderness, his pale face. I marked every aspect of him; seeing that he looked worn now from his outburst of the past few moments; that his black brows were straight as if drawn by a steady pen; that his right shoulder was slightly uneven as against the left; that he was very unhappy. For all his polished manners and his knightly grace, he was young, and woefully unhappy, and I loved him, with a love sharp as death.

He still held my hands, and my gaze, with his own.

'Have you known loneliness?' he said without emotion. And I thought of Grafton Regis, after the old nurse died, and Agnes went away, and I nodded. All the time my limbs quivered, like branches under lightning—I was the tree, and he the storm.

'I would tell you something now, that I have not said in this past hour of high passion which I fear has wearied you,' he said. 'I am glad indeed that I wandered up to the gallery the other night... it gave me much pleasure when I saw you there, so fair, so kind, and welcoming me with a sweet smile and outstretched hand. Indeed, I would thank you for that, damoiselle, and for the dance we had together, and for this night, when you have listened, and soothed me with your gentle words. I feel you are a good maid. I would you were my friend.'

'I have done little, my lord,' I murmured.

'I was wroth with Harry this night,' he said, above my head. 'I did not command you to visit my apartments—that word tastes of the old *droit de seigneur*... I doubt not you thought I wished you here... to possess you, as if you were a peasant wench to tumble for an hour, when it was naught like that.'

And for all these bold and soldierly words, which could have come from the lips of Warwick himself, his voice shook slightly.

Slowly I looked at him, and, as I heard his breath quicken, knew that he would not dismiss me thus, without a kiss, and with only cool words of friendship. I shook my hair, so that it came free of my gown's collar and streamed about me, a gleaming fall, the colour of the fire.

'Call me by my name,' he whispered.

But I held it so dear my tongue could not shape the word, even to its owner.

And he reached for me with open arms, and we came together trembling, and I know not which of us shook the more, he or I, as if we lay in coldest snow, although we held each other standing in the hearth, and after a while I felt the flames warm upon the side of my gown.

'We shall be in the fire, my lord,' I said, trying to laugh, and the laugh got caught up in my throat.

'We are in the fire already,' he muttered, his face in my hair. 'We are in the fire, and burning.' And he tightened his arms about me so that I could scarcely breathe, and I felt his hard young body against mine, all steel and strength and honour, and behind my closed eyes I had a vision of him riding in Wensleydale, through the smoke of the mists, his hair tossed by the wind, and part of the wildness.

He kissed my eyes, and my throat, and my cheeks, and wound his hands in my hair, and I became as the soft wax of the candles and leaned back in his arms, wondering if this was how it felt to die, and attain Paradise.

The fire burned low as we stood thus in the press of love, and when he spoke his words slipped into my dream and became part of it.

'Lady, I have known no woman,' he murmured. I clasped my arms around his slender back.

'Then we are both 'prentices in love, my lord,' I said, softly smiling. 'For how can I teach you a craft of which I know naught?'

And we laughed together, all sorrow fled, and he lifted me in his arms, and I was as light as a twig. He took me to his bed and lay down with me, and we were very still for a long space, except for his hands stroking the hair which lay strewn across my cheek. He lifted his head and looked in my eyes.

'Call me by my name,' he whispered. 'Sweet heart, say it to me.'

'Richard,' I said, trembling. 'Richard, my love.'

His took me in his arms. He laid his lips on mine. And a flame sprang up and caught us, and we sighed in it, and were consumed by it, and there was naught in the world save its fierce glory. And he was no longer Duke of Gloucester, Earl of Cambridge, a prince of the blood, or the King's brother.

He was but Richard, and for a little space he was mine, and I was his true maid, his Nut-Brown Maid, who loved but him alone.

★

O Lord, what is this worldis bliss
That changeth as the moon!
My summer's day in lusty May
Is darked before the noon.
I hear you say, farewell: Nay, nay,
We depart not so soon.
Why say ye so? whither will ye go?

Alas! what have ye done?
All my welfare to sorrow and care
Should change, if ye were gone:
For in my mind, of all mankind
I love but you alone.

(The Nut-Brown Maid)

Now, I was part of the spring. Benevolent Saints, how I loved him! and how happy were those months! Even now, when I am old, and my body is sickly and weak so that I need the aid of others sprightlier than I that I may kneel for Lauds, I still mind that time. When the young green leaves sprouted tender as kisses, and the birds sang a merrier tune than any minstrel could pipe. When the pleasaunce at Greenwich and Shene boasted a crush of blossom nudging the velvet lawns, with brave iris and gillyflower, lilac and narcissus jousting with one another for acclaim. When the evening was haunted by lilies which, shaking in the breeze like censers, gave off a headier scent than the holy things they sought to ape, and the Rose, the White Rose, shed its splendour over all.

Yea, I have full remembrance of that time; but as my heart lies under tangling weeds and a rough stone slab, it is all as that read long ago in an old romance, and there is no movement in me, not even of sadness. Because—and for this I thank the Father in all His mercy—without a heart, there can be no sorrow, nor can there be joy. Thus, a heartless state is best during the days of waiting, which I pray will soon be over.

Yet from the time of Epiphany, when the revels ended, and order was restored to the jocund court, it became sorely difficult for Richard and me to meet. I dared not go too often to the gallery for two reasons: first because my lady of Bedford was ever demanding, lusting for this or that whim to be fulfilled, and secondly because there was no pleasure in watching him below at a distance, when I could not be in his arms. Though I did see him at the board, seated a thousand miles away at the other end of the Hall, seated below the Woodvilles, sometimes between Dick and Thomas Grey, toying with his knife, eating little, saying less, drawing his brows together as he gazed at the King, who was ever engrossed by Elizabeth's lively kinsfolk. He was all dignity and grace, sombre in the dark clothes he liked to wear, as ever courteous to all since that one burst of passion when Warwick had wounded him with words, the same night he and I first held each other—in pain, in bliss, in scorching, tender consummation.

We had been together less than a dozen times, yet I was happy beyond words. I remembered each meeting so perfectly, for I had to feed on it until the next; and once I saw him for ten minutes only, behind the tall yew hedge in the pleasaunce, while from very near the sound of the mallets in the forbidden game of 'closh' mingled with guilty laughter. There, we had stood and kissed each other softly for a few moments. I felt the sun warm on my closed eyes, my lifted face. He had said: 'Sweet heart, I had sore need of you last evening, for my heart was heavy.' And I had answered: 'My lord, my love, my heart was sad *because* I needed you.' There, in a nutshell, was the difference between us.

And that ten minutes served me for the next two weeks, for Richard was never idle, was ever conferring with older men who listened to his words with a smile, none the less impressed by his wisdom. He was meticulous over matters of policy, his commissions of oyer and terminer, and as I knew how much it pleased him when the King gave him tasks to do, I did assay to be happy on his behalf, but as he was not with me, I found it nigh impossible. Happy I was, yea, but I felt always as if the spring were gliding by too swiftly and that I was alone in the sunshine, with my own shadow darkening the gleam.

Then one evening all was well again, for Harry sought me on the spiralling stair, under the arras of gold, and I took his little hand as if we were children together and we went along light of heart in the gloom, to where the gentlemen ushers and grooms of the bedchamber turned their heads away and bent to their dice in the passages and whispered, though not of me, for they were wise men and sympathetic to the wants of lords, although they knew not what great love and joy passed between us. And Richard's chambers were deserted save for him; and if they called King Edward the Rose of Rouen, the Sun in Splendour, his youngest brother surpassed him in my eyes. Three hours I spent with him that evening, and we talked quietly of one another, of our hopes and our troubles, and our kisses grew stronger, and we were unable to withstand the whirlwind, the torrent, that burst within us. And we clung together, and forgot all but the longing to be enwrapped and enfolded within each other. And he was mine again, for three hours; and he tried to teach me to play chess, but as I sat upon his knee for the lesson and my hair swept the pieces off the board each time I turned to kiss him, it was not a success.

I wished in my heart that he had been born a cottar's son, and I betrothed to him at the village porch with a wreath of roses on my head, and the family standing ale-flushed and merry about us, and that we had been bedded together with rude mirth and left to live out our simple lives; rearing babes, toiling with smiles and frowns and days of gloom and hunger even, with our small pleasures, our bereavements, our feast days and our May Days... though each day would be May Day if Richard had been born thus.

Noblemen took lemen for lust, and the women went gladly through ambition, using their bodies as snares for gold and power. But he was not one of these, neither was I; for he turned to me out of the mazes of his loneliness, and I to him from the web of my love.

We were no longer 'prentices in love.

Warwick was seen no more at court. Patch, who seemed to have an ear at every door, was worse than any woman for whispering tales to me. He told me that the Earl, after a brief and unexpected Christmas appearance, had gone to his manor at Cambridge. Further, it was rumoured that George of Clarence communicated with him, and that there was more talk of Isabel, the frail fair lady with her vast estates.

'A right comely wench,' he said. 'But sickly, like her sister Anne. Though I doubt not that were she as hideous as I, the prospect of ridding London of the Woodvilles would aid Duke George to love her.'

He was waiting for me to say he was not hideous. All I said was: 'How would marrying Isabel harm the Woodvilles?'

'I fancy Lord Warwick has promised George that he will engineer this,' grinned Patch. 'But I fear 'tis delusion. You mind that Warwick was one of the Calais Earls?'

I did not, but let him continue.

'King Louis of France is a craftsman at flattery,' said the fool. 'Not long after he took the throne he made a ploy for Warwick—sought his advice on hunting dogs, wrote him fair letters at Calais, and Warwick bloomed like a peach.'

'Yet Warwick fought for Edward, and set him on the throne,' I said, confused.

'True,' he answered. 'And Warwick had the notion that once peace was made with Louis, there would be no more attacks from Margaret of Anjou. But this would mean crushing Burgundy. Edward would never agree to that. And in any event, as Elizabeth snatched the King from Bona of Savoy, Louis's sister by marriage, all Warwick's plans were halted in mid-gallop. Thus my lord loathes the Woodvilles.'

My mind flew back to an old conversation. I saw John Skelton's handsome face, heard the tale of Richard's flight to the Low Countries, and the saving of his life.

'Nay,' I said very softly. 'They would never break with Burgundy, for the Burgundians are passing kind.'

Patch laughed. 'Hardly could they, with the King's sister married to Charles, Burgundy's own Duke!'

He knew much more of politics than I. I said: 'Warwick still plots with George, then, think you?'

'Yes, and he would have done with Dickon, too,' said the fool, and my witless heart started its old dance, floundering and prancing at the name.

'I wonder if he will ever weaken,' Patch mused. 'I doubt not Warwick would give him Anne as a reward... 'Twould be easier if my lord had both brothers ranged against the King.'

Elysande had spoken of Richard; she had thought I was not listening. To Anne Haute she had said: 'The pull of Warwick is very strong.' Then, I did not understand. Now, I could say seriously to Patch: 'He will never yield his cause,' and the fool cocked his head to look into my face, which I kept passionless.

'As you say, mistress,' he said, and kissed my hand lightly, and bit it, and of a sudden his last speech echoed in my mind, disquieting.

'Little Anne Neville—how old is she?'.

'Oh, she is not so little,' said he carelessly. 'About thirteen years now—slight, golden-haired. Had Earl Warwick brought his ladies here for Yule you would have seen her.'

I thought of myself at thirteen, at twelve, on my joy-day, my May Day, which I would cherish for ever together with the song, which had brought my love to me. Then, as Patch was in a confiding mood,

I asked him about Katherine of Desmond, and of the matter at which Richard had only hinted. He wrenched his face about in grimaces meant to distract me, but finally told me that which all knew, but never mentioned.

'The Earl of Desmond was beheaded on a flimsy charge,' he said, in a voice even quieter than Richard's had been. 'He jested about the Queen soon after Edward married her. Last year, when the King was away, the Great Seal was purloined, and Desmond's execution ordered. They say his Grace was wroth when he returned and discovered this. Also, the Earl's two little knaves were murdered soon after their father's death, though none can swear who wrought this... nay, none can swear,' he said grimly, 'but all can guess.'

Then he sought to cheer me by capering about.

'How white you are,' he said cheerily. 'Come, sit a while. I have a new story, cunningly rhymed. Let me assay to cheer your dreary life a whit!'

I was about to tell him that my life was not so dreary, was indeed a perfect poem of bliss, on which his words had cast a fleeting shadow, when suddenly I saw, leaning on the terrace wall not far from us, the reason for my gladness.

He turned to look at me. The brightness of his look mocked the sun.

*

So later, when I sat with my distaff in the Duchess's apartments, assaulted by the monotonous twang of harp and lute, my thoughts could weave their own skein while my fingers idled. For though the day outside was still fair, and I must remain at my lady's side, I had seen him again. We had walked together in the quiet ways, through the Italian gardens, where none came, and for a brief time he had held my hand. His hand was not soft like that of most courtiers, but the palm was a little calloused from leather and steel, the fingers were fine-boned and delicate, the heavy rings a sweet small pain in his unconsciously hard grip. He did not link my last finger in his, custom of lovers, but walked slowly with his whole hand closed about mine. He was serious, aloof, until my frail jests brought about the swift, sweet smile peculiar to him alone.

Yet he did not smile when I mentioned the name now on everyone's lips, the name which hummed through the Palace, subject for conjecture. I had thought it romantic and said so, and he told me it was not for jesting: this Robin of Redesdale was a plaguey agitator who was stirring the whole of the north parts into a boil.

'You mark how he started the first rising in Yorkshire,' I heard his tone grow mellow on the beloved word. 'Then up springs another Robin...'

'Robin of Holderness,' I murmured. 'I like not that name so well.'

'As Northumberland cut him down,' he said with a little irony, 'you need not trouble about his name. But Robin of Redesdale has raised a strong following in Lancashire now. It should be quelled, and soon.'

He was frowning.

'I pray he is not becoming unwary, complacent,' he said under his breath. He often spoke of his Grace the King as if I were not with him; I did not know whether to be sad that his thoughts went from me so often, or flattered that he trusted me. In any event it was Richard's way, and therefore a joy.

'Will there be real trouble?' I asked him, remembering the omens with which Patch had tried to frighten me. 'People spoke some time past of bloody rain and a child that cried out in the womb...'

He dropped my hand to cross himself.

'Who is Robin of Redesdale, Richard?' I asked suddenly. 'Some say he is a man of the people, others that he is the agent of some alien power sent to stir mischief. Who is he?'

He looked at me; a swift, shrewd look. I lifted my face; the sun, or his glance, danced on my eyelashes. His expression melted; became charmed, and over serious words he smiled as if he could not help it.

'My love, would that I knew,' he said. 'But I can vow this is all more than just an agitation set up by the northern citizens. Though they yelled for the return of Percy as Earl of Northumberland, saying they misliked Warwick's jurisdiction, this trouble stems from deeper things. I am convinced of it.'

Then we had reached a favourite arbour, which to my joy was unoccupied by amorous couples gowned in indolence. And we stepped softly within the shell of roses and green leaves, and like lightning I doffed my headdress for he had no need to tell me how my hair pleased him. And again he held me in his arms, and kissed my mouth, with a trembling fierceness, while I clung, breathing my love into him on a sigh. Others came soon, heralding their approach with brittle mirth.

That was the pattern of my days; to meet, to kiss and part, for privacy was more precious than the finest gems, rare as true love in this place, this time. A fleeting figure, I wondered what they thought, who came to see my lord of Gloucester sitting alone in a lover's bower?

King Edward nearly discovered us that day. I had need to run swiftly, though I do not doubt he would have been glad to know his brother had a mistress. He came along the pleasaunce path, singing about lemen and Maying, and he had on many occasions been heard to remark that all men were frail. So he might have been pleased. Ah, I wonder.

Daily we sat with our distaffs or broidery frames in the Duchess's apartments, and the weeks slid by. Each night I lay wakeful, burned with a fever for which there was but one cure, and that denied me.

A yelp from one of the women roused me from my thoughts. A wasp had flown in through the open window. The Duchess of Bedford, who had been nodding, woke and flapped her hands angrily, and watching her, I thought how she had aged these last months. Her hair was snow white and the lines on her face deeply scored.

Elysande whispered: 'Sleep is good for the aged: but you are like a woman dead. Wake up! Answer me!'

'Forgive me,' I said. Vaguely I knew she had been asking me something, an urgent question on a breath.

'Who is Robin of Redesdale?' she murmured. 'Really, I mean. Any fool knows that name cloaks some angry lord. Who is he, say?'

The woman who had been stung rubbed her neck, listening. 'Yes, who is he?' she echoed.

''Tis the French Queen's captain,' said another. 'The whore of Anjou's liegeman, Beaufort of Somerset.'

'For God's sake, soft,' said Lady Scrope. Margaret Beaufort had but lately come and gone, visiting the Duchess. Bemused on all sides, I sought diplomacy, said naught, wishing I were out, roaming the grassy fields of Bloomsbury with my lord, my love.

'Beaufort!' said another.

'Why do you not ask the fool, Patch?' Elysande said slyly. 'He seems to know all of policy; you two are hand in glove.'

'Beaufort is not in England, surely,' said Anne Haute.

The others had lost interest. They were playing with the lap-dogs, yawning, picking at comfit-dishes. Elysande pulled her chair close to mine.

'By the Rood!' she whispered. 'Fools make fair paramours!'

My eyes on my work, I said: 'Why think you thus?'

She laughed softly. I was minded of Gyb's lilting purr.

'Why, maiden, you come to bed some nights with your flesh afire, blazing like the sun—I cannot bear to touch you, that I vow.' She shuddered, she watched me for some little space, her hands busy at her spindle, smiling her kind, cat's smile.

'Well, for sure,' declared Anne Haute, though none listened, 'England is safe from the Lancastrians, for my lord of Warwick's fleet lies in the Channel warding off invaders.'

The Duchess roused herself, spoke roughly. The harshness in her voice shocked me from my fading dream.

'By Christ's Blood, I would know mine enemy,' she said. 'I would know who labours against me and mine.'

Elysande whispered: 'Is Patch a fine lover? Lusty and lickerish, and hot to bed a maid?'

Removed by a thin veil from her friendly, bawdy talk, my spirit soared. I thought of Richard, and his tender, ardent lovemaking, and thought that young as he was, the fiery blood of his brother the King surely ran in his veins, for Edward had bastards which were openly acknowledged and all the maids he had bedded had long queues of knights clamouring for their hand, for that which had pleased so fair a prince was a prize in truth.

I thought thus and my heart grew heavy. For I would not now even be able to meet him of an evening, to find some chamber or terrace where we could clasp each other, kiss lingeringly, talk quietly. For tonight I must sleep at the foot of my lady's couch, and another six weeks would pass before I found my stealthy freedom, as we all served a tour of two moons tending her during the night, and this gave rise to a great sigh. And Elysande read my thought. She breathed in my ear:

'Far be it for me to stand between a lover and his maid,' she whispered. 'Would it please you, sweeting, if I cosseted my lady tonight and left you to seek your heart's lust?'

'But she clings to me,' I whispered back. 'Only I can comfort her at night.'

The Duchess had awful dreams, waking screaming and roaring.

'Men do say she is a witch,' breathed Elysande even lower, and looked at me.

There was the night at Grafton Regis, mewed up in my mind, now loosened by my friend's words. I thrust it away, took refuge in Elysande's own light laughing speech.

'You will have us thrown in the Fleet!' I said, as she had done, once.

'I jest,' said Elysande. 'But I thought you might have heard tales,' and her lips curved, and she looked down.

'I know naught,' I said. 'I have heard naught.'

'But—to our little strategy—it would please you?'

'It would delight me,' I answered.

'So be it, then,' said Elysande, and went straightway to Jacquetta of Bedford, wringing out cold cloths for her wrists against the heat, whispering sweetness in her wrinkled ear.

Seeking delight and sweetness both, I sought Richard that night, straying with trembling near to his apartments. I noticed much activity all about, even apart from the comings and goings of the esquires and yeomen of the bedchamber and the great unruly hounds. There was one face that I knew: Harry, the little page, who lingered to comfort me with saddening news, because while I would gladly have entered Richard's chamber with arms that craved him, he was not even there. For Harry told me that the King had finally listened to his advisers, and there was a council of war that night, and Richard sat on it, together with Lord Hastings and the Woodvilles; and that the King was arraying an army against Robin of Redesdale at last.

Now it was I thought I should never set eyes on him again, for although Elysande out of her charity kept the Duchess well satisfied and swore she never noticed the difference between us of a night, Richard was ever closeted with the King and his councillors. And if I knew him at all he must have been so joyful at being included in the discussions that he bore equably the presence of the Woodvilles. For, as was to be expected, King Edward's chief advisers were the Queen's father, Earl Rivers, Sir John Woodville, and Lord Anthony, laying his verses and his jousts aside to turn his talent to war.

I hung about the passages, shameless, all my conceit blown from me by the blast of my longing to be near Richard, if only for an instant, to hold his hand, to look into his unfathomable eyes. I even sought out Harry for news of him.

'How does my lord?' I asked him one evening, when thunder muffled the air and my head ached to match my heart.

He shrugged. The White Boar rose and fell on his doublet. 'There is that which gnaws at him,' he said, and my hopes leaped high for a moment, because I fancied he spoke of our separation.

'Harry...' I said, and ceased while he cocked an attentive brow. 'You know how dearly I love his Grace...'

'Mistress, I see naught, and hear less,' he said, folding his pink lips together like a night-flower, and I was moved to think how soon children grew old in this place; babes were youths, and youths, men.

'Tell him, Harry, if you see him... that I long to know he is in good health and spirits, I pray you,' I said miserably.

'This I'd do gladly,' he answered. 'But I scarcely have time to snatch a word with him myself—it's as if he sees me not—or any of us, for that matter. He is ever flying to the King's chambers, begging for audience, and he is in there half the night when the King has space to see him.'

'Of what do they talk?'

'Mistress,' said the little page patiently, 'how should I know what is discussed between great princes?'

'Of course,' I said, bending to kiss the small face swiftly, for the sole fact that he served Richard and had led me to his arms by night. He flinched from my sad lips and ran away.

Then one day I saw him, but he was completely surrounded by henchmen and esquires, young men who laughed with strong teeth and looked about them as if they looked at life itself and loved it. He did not laugh; his countenance was full of thoughts and he withdrew into them. He did not look around but strode on relentlessly, with full purpose and I would fain have known his mission. I stepped aside as they passed, and there were one or two who looked at me with the expression I longed to see in my lord's eyes. I willed him to see me with all my power.

But he strode on, so full of strength and grace and seriousness that my heart rose up to bursting at the sight and knowledge of him, and my lips grew cold for the touch of his. I would have thought he heard my mind crying of my long desire; for having tasted the apple no other food could sate me now, so deep in love was I.

I burned him with my gaze, and he walked on by. He was on his way to the King's chamber, on business of which I knew naught. He walked on by and did not look at me.

He had forgotten my existence.

News came to us that Robin of Redesdale rioted merrily in Lancashire. There were lootings, slayings, burning of property, but I was still curious to see this man. I was sure that he wore green and carried the long-bow, and that mayhap Maid Marian, with her false breasts, trailed wearily behind him.

The court was bored with his name by now, and new dances and sports would have taken the place of speculation, but the King wished for none of it. There was a change in him. The gallant courtier had disappeared and in his place was a stern and martial campaigner, the veteran of fearful Towton Field and Mortimer's Cross, with its holy sign of the Three Suns. Yet, paradoxically, he lingered at London, though he had ordered his tents and artillery and hundreds of jackets of murrey to be carried to Fotheringhay, whence he planned to direct his attack upon the rebels. With him he planned to take two favourite captains, Sir John Howard and Louis de Bretaylle; and Edward Brampton, a great, beetle-browed Portuguese warrior, added excitement by his arrival at court. Now the armourers polished the harness to blue-black fire, and the blacksmiths honed the swords and axes to a deadly tooth, and the banner of England with the leopards and lilies and the supporting standards of suns and roses sprouted like great dangerous blossoms wherever the eye turned. And in my heart I was glad, that though Richard could listen to those older than he laying their plans in the council chamber, all knew that the King thought him too young to join the affray. George of Clarence showed no interest in this time of preparation, for he was on one of his manors, attended by two hundred servants, basking in the sun and doubtless thinking of Isabel Neville. So men said.

The Duchess of Bedford said, waking and sleeping: 'I would know mine enemy.' I heard her without comprehension, through my shell of sick-heartedness. For Richard was daily cloistered with the King, and no man knew what passed between them, until I met with him again, on the last day of May.

The Duchess had been bathed and bedded, and there were few abroad save for the anonymous, hurrying servants in the passages, and I spoke with Elysande before she seated herself with her tapestry at the foot of my lady's couch.

'Think you she'll sleep?' I whispered. Come to think of it, most of our conversation took place in whispers. 'I must go out.'

Elysande's pointed teeth winked in her smile.

'Certes, what a lusty lover he must be!' she teased. 'And constant too! All these weeks you have languished for his arms!'

That I have, I thought, then gathered my wits as again she alluded to his motley dress and I was hard put to find a jocund answer. With little hope I strayed aimlessly up towards the gallery and, as it happened, I did see Patch, wandering, lack-wit as a sprite.

'I never see you now,' he said ill-humouredly.

'Well, we are on the edge of an array,' I answered. 'Shall you too put on harness?'

'I was trained for mirth not slaughter,' said he.

'Have you seen my lord of Gloucester of late?' I asked, throwing caution away.

'Certes, yesterday,' he said instantly. 'And he too was doleful as a drunkard in a dry tavern. I know not what ails folk these days... And as for you, mistress, become much more slender and I shall be able to nip your waist with one hand, so...'

I would have turned on him out of sheer misery as he stretched out what was only the hand of comfort, when my eyes fell on a small figure, patient, motionless under the torchlight a few feet away.

'Patch, good night!' I said, and left him, trying not to run, feeling his stare probing my back.

Harry took my hand.

'My lord commands...' he said. He had not learned his lesson. Light as air we flew, running together round and round the ascending stair, across the hall, the breeze of our passing disturbing the skirts of some tiny noble lady. 'By Saint Denis!' she cried. 'God's curse on these churlish manners!' Lady Margaret Beaufort, I thought; and she was already left far behind, to damn the sound of Harry's laughter as we ran, we flew, air-light, dove-light, down the Hall, and I remembered just in time to pull my hood across my face before we knocked on the oaken door, the fairest oaken door in Christendom. A squire of the bedchamber opened to us, passed with downcast eyes, and departed as we entered.

Had it not been for Harry's lingering I would have rushed wantonly into the arms of my lord, but I waited standing before him till I heard the door close behind the page and I lifted my face and felt Richard's lips, hard and soft, cool and burning, on my brow, my eyelids, and my mouth, and I wound my arms tight about his neck, and he tasted my tears.

The chamber was the same, though it might have been a year since I was last within its loving walls. There was one addition, though. His sword, and a pair of steel gauntlets lay across the table. For all my joy, a little cold spot began to form in my mind at the sight of these accoutrements.

'Don't weep,' he said softly.

At this I had to smile, a poor watery smile, for men never know a loving woman's heart. Poor fools we are, ruled by the moon, and variable, prone to her waxing and waning, all our tides sorrow and gladness. Men never know a woman's love.

He led me to the couch where we sat hand in hand and I gazed at him. Gently I smoothed the hair from his brow. He seemed excited, and I knew that in a moment he would be up again and pacing the chamber, for I fancied I knew him as I knew myself. Still he smiled.

'My lord, my love,' I whispered. 'I am joyful we are met together again.'

And he laid his hands about my face and looked at me with that look that turned a blade in my heart, and he smiled.

'You are happy,' I murmured.

'Sweet heart,' he said, in a cramped, glad voice, 'wait till you hear my news.' I could only say: 'Whatever pleases my lord, lightens my heart.' And he held me at arm's length, and already he seemed far from me. I had a precognition of what he was going to say.

'His Highness,' he whispered. 'His most noble Grace King Edward...' and he swallowed his excitement and continued, calmer. '... After many days I have at last persuaded the King that I shall ride with him against Robin of Redesdale. We leave the day after tomorrow... God grant we are in time, for we should have been north long ago to crush this rising... Is it not fair news? Now, by St Paul, I shall have chance to prove myself, utterly fearless, utterly loyal... But I am ranting on like a woman,' he finished, with an anxious laugh, and took me to him roughly and laughed again.

With difficulty I said: 'Your first campaign, Richard.' My voice sounded distant. 'I wish you joy, my dearest lord.'

He jumped up and walked about. And it was in that moment, all the sweetness mixed with the sour, that I knew I loved one born under the planet Mars. I fought my dismay, saying: 'I will make a novena for you, beloved.' And, because I had visions of mighty battles, thousands slain, I continued:

'I will pray that you shall smite this Robin a dolorous blow, and return in glory.'

He laughed gently. 'It will be but a little skirmish. But it is enough for my purpose. My esquires stand ready, my good friends Robert Percy, John Parr, and I shall wage more men to ride with me. His Grace will not find me lacking in resourcefulness...'

Then he looked at me. His eyes were tender as I ever remember them.

'Sweet heart,' he said, and he spoke my name, and sought my lips, and war battled with love in the mind and was unhorsed for a little while. I shelved my dolour while he held me in his arms, and tried to forget that the day after tomorrow he would ride north, and I knew not when I should see him again. For I ranked myself as the loving woman of a soldier, and I vowed I would train myself to be as others of that ilk, and not weep.

So when, too soon, I parted from him, and we kissed and blessed one another, I smiled a tinsel smile and carried a mask as gay as any of the nice disguisy things the mummers wore at Yule-tide. And he could have known no difference in me, for again, when Elysande opened the door to me and brushed her hand against my breast in the darkness, she shrank as if scalded and whispered, laughing, of the ardour of fools. Though that jest was rubbing a little thin.

It was very lonely when they had gone. Few remained at court, for most of the lords had left with the King's army, leading their own small levies, intending to wage men en route to the camp at Fotheringhay. The King's mother lived there, and, thinking of her for the first time, I remembered that she was Richard's mother too, and wondered about her. She had not visited the court since I was there, for it was said that she too had little love for the Woodvilles; and besides, was pious and devout more so than many widows; she still wore mourning for the Duke of York. Men called her the Rose of Raby—she had been wondrous fair.

I did not see my lord ride away. I had been in pursuit of a duty, and when at length I had managed to reach a window the last of the baggage trains was grinding and clattering through the gate, and the stiff new banner of Gloucester, with its grim boar's head, no longer splashed its pride against the sky.

I had not even Patch to talk to, as the King had given him leave to visit his mother, who kept a cookshop in Chepe; and for this reason I was able to resume my duties at Jacquetta's side. For if my lover had gone, why should there be need for Elysande to play proxy for me? I found the Duchess something altered; harder to please mayhap, I could not tell, but Elysande had little ways to which she had grown accustomed, and she grumbled more fiercely when I could not anticipate her whim.

So I withdrew into my own mind, and dreamed of my beloved; of his lips and his eyes, and of the words he had murmured to me in his quiet voice; how he had talked again, sadly, of his loves. For Clarence and Warwick had rejected him for what they mistook as the cowardice of youth, and Clarence was his tall and golden brother, lightsome and frivolous, as Richard could never be. He had told me, with a frowning smile, how the Lord Mayor of London had fallen asleep during a hearing of oyer and terminer: 'Speak softly, sirs, for the Mayor is asleep'—Clarence had provoked mirth by his wit on this occasion. It struck me that Richard, while counterfeiting disapproval, envied in secret his splendid, feckless brother. 'I know I am too serious,' he had said, and so I had assayed to make him laugh, with my foolish, loving ways, and often succeeded.

And Warwick! there the hurt lay deeper still, for Warwick had been his lord during the years when the will was formed, the pattern followed closely until it becomes the fabric of the soul. Warwick! who now, for the first time, disdained to ride with the King, no doubt eschewing the little skirmish as small meat for his blade to bite upon.

Richard had turned his back on Warwick, for of all his loves, there was but one. Would that it had been me.

I had alluded to the writing I had seen on that first night in his apartments, the French words of power.

'That is the code I live by,' he had said, his eyes like steel. 'Loyalty binds me. So will it always, to the Crown of England, to his Grace King Edward, and to all his kin.'

He had spoken these last five words as if they were dragged from him, for he had seen King Edward, as had all men, grow sleek and careless under the touch of a bewitching woman; one who stole the Great Seal to avenge her vanity.

'A hard road to ride,' I murmured.

'Yea, hard, foul and devious,' he said violently, and I knew that when he was violent he was sad, so I kissed his hand and held it to my cheek, for all his sorrow was my sorrow.

And now I guessed he would be glad as I was doleful, for he rode under the banner of England, and his golden brother's smile.

The flowers waved in the fair green gardens, but only in mockery. The sun had ceased to shine; the sky was blue no longer. The Duchess had a little slavering dog which jumped on my lap, shrieking shrilly. Sharp pains fleeted through my head. My lady was full of rancour and small malices. The Queen's bread was new-baked; mine was four days old, like the trenchers. I had no taste. Though the Palace still scampered with life, all who ran and walked and diced were creatures unearthly. Their voices reached me through a mist. Their faces were unreal.

I tried to conjure up his countenance, crushing my eyes closed, but I could not see him. At times a vague figure, armed and mounted, rushed through my mind, flanked by a fog of faces that mouthed silently, drowning his voice. I had no notion of how long it would take them to ride to where the rebellion flamed, but already my ears rang with the slithering crash of steel, loud formless noises, spewed out by my ignorance. My knees I wore red in prayer.

Queen Elizabeth remained calm, playing at merels and chess with her ladies; cool, with a carved coolness, retiring early to a great bed to which no tall young form strode to visit her, and she betrayed no longings, no lusting for his arms.

It was I who quivered and shed secret tears. It was she who smiled, prayed gently, drew on again the veil of the widow of Grafton Regis, patient and resigned. Then I remembered she was more than twice my age, and thought that with the years, passions burn fainter, lips lose their clinging strength, pulses grow weaker; and I thought of Richard, and knew in my mind I lied.

Had I thought to appease my hunger by that last encounter with him, I misled myself cruelly. It soothed me for a day, two days, and then began again the pain. Once I slipped like a spy into his chambers and lay for a moment on his couch, breathing the lost scent of him, to be chased from the room by an outraged butler.

I thought of him, upon his first campaign, and grew sick with fear. I minded John Skelton's words: 'He was seventeen. And they took his head and... speared on pikes at the Mickle Gate.' Edmund, young Edmund Plantagenet, and sharp points in my mind for Richard his brother.

On the ninth day of this torment, I paid no heed to Elysande flinging clothes into a chest, or her anguished cries for help, until she came to shake me.

'Am I to toil alone, then?' she cried. 'I vow you are as useless as yonder popinjay!' and she gave the bird's cage a vicious clout, making it scream.

Listlessly I turned to her.

'Will they have crushed Robin of Redesdale yet, Elysande?' She dropped the lid of the chest in a burst of exasperated laughter.

'Holy Mother of God, you are the most witless... the most...' She stopped suddenly as the Duchess entered, glowering, muttering *I would know my enemy*, the old incantation.

'Do you never listen?' Elysande said softly. 'Her Grace has declared the Palace needs sweetening, and for sure, the stink is enough to make you swoon. And it was arranged before they left that...'

I looked out of the window again. I did not care if the Palace stank like a midden. I could not even smell the vast bed of white roses below me.

'Help me,' she pleaded.

'How long will it take them to journey north?'

'Oh, the King will not hurry,' she said easily. 'They ride first to Norwich, then to pray at Our Lady of Walsingham, then Lynn, I think, and thereafter up the Nene to meet with us at Fotheringhay.'

'What say you?' I whispered.

'Fotheringhay, half-wit!' she said patiently. 'And if you don't help me with the packing, we shall not be there until Christmas next coming.'

Right in front of her I fell to my knees, crossing my breast, my mindless thanks soaring like smoke. Hastily she lifted me, glancing round.

'They will be bringing a priest to exorcize you,' she muttered. 'Now fold these gowns, while I assay to cram my lady's vanities into this box, which is far too small.'

So we went to Fotheringhay, and I had to control myself, for I feared they would think me truly mad and have me hidden away somewhere with the gibbering and the dying, when I wanted to laugh and live. So I curbed the smile on my face and travelled cool, sparing of words, with the Duchess's new pet upon my lap; a monkey that bit me often, and whose teeth I did not feel. Fotheringhay sprawled on the north bank of the river, bounded on one side by a double moat, gazing lonely and proud over the marshes from whence came the hoarse roar of bittern and the beat of herons' wings, mingled with the seagull's lament as it winged back and forth from the distant sea. A massive place, with mighty battlements, it was built in the fetterlock shape of the old Yorkist badge. As we trundled over the drawbridge I remembered that this was Richard's birthplace, where he had grown, sickly and brave and single-hearted. And once more thought of John Skelton, and the first time I heard the name of my beloved.

We were installed in a rather bleak apartment, but one which I loved, for I could hear the wind mocking over the fens, and smell the salt sea faintly in the darkness, and I could lie listening for the sound of the King's army, for none knew quite when they would arrive. And I could not contain my longing to meet with Richard again, to feel the soft hardness of his lips and hear his whispered voice, and I planned the things I would do to make him glad, the things I would say to make him merry, when he came to me at last. At a distance, I saw the Rose of Raby. I marked her coolness when she greeted the Queen, the same courteous ice I had seen in her youngest son. She wore the widow's barbe and wimple, and on her breast hung a great reliquary like a fetter, and there was something of Richard in her face. I thought her handsome, though Elysande murmured that she was also known as 'Proud Cis' and in these parts was much envied and feared.

Vast wagon-loads of armaments rolled in, and then came soldiery, all ages, some coarse, all dusty from the dry roads with their gaping pitfalls; a few laughing, some looking up in wonder at the great castle as they assembled tents for their officers and supplies within and without the bailey. And July was almost out when a barge came up the Nene, and in it were King Edward, Earl Rivers and his sons, the Lord Chamberlain Lord Hastings, and the King's youngest brother, together with a fistful of retainers.

They came in over the drawbridge and I watched them, unseen, while the Queen stood on the castle steps with the Duchess of York. Queen Elizabeth lowered her blue eyes and smiled as the King halted below her on the stair, but the King's mother remained gazing at him, with the same steady unfathomable look I had seen in Richard's eyes. I saw these things for only the briefest moment, for I looked for Richard and found him, lithe and swift in his dark travelling cloak, ascending the steps to kiss the hands of the Queen and his mother. The Duchess of York set her lips on his cheek. The blood in my body boiled to do the same.

On the next day I saw him again. I saw him at the other end of the dining hall. I saw that he was glad, and smiled twice, and laughed once, and ate his meat, and when the royal party walked through the bowing throng to leave, he passed quite close to me. I could almost have touched him, but for two women who sat between me and the door. He wore his gold carcanet with the ruby-eyed boar, which had grazed my flesh and burnt me like a brand. His hair was sleek as the plumes of a raven; I had smoothed it from his brow. The bones of his face were as delicate as ever; I had soothed them with my fingers. His eyes were like no other eyes in this world. Strive as I might to catch them, I had no success.

For the next seven days I earned a week from my allotted span of Purgatory. Though he was in Fotheringhay, he might have been in France, for all I saw of him. I endeavoured to keep track of him, and knew that he spent most of the day below on the camp, attending to various duties, or laced into a tent together with the other officers, though I could only guess vaguely at that which they spoke of and what they planned. And each night I must tend the Duchess of Bedford, whom I had learned to hate.

The King had soft speech with his Queen daily, and lay with her nightly, and I grew wondrous pale and my girdle slid about my waist, and I knew a terrible ache in my heart, and not only my heart.

So when Elysande said: 'They ride tomorrow, then,' as a matter of casual conversation, I could contain myself no more. All my sorrow broke its bounds, refreshing as a waterspout, draining as the bodily blood, reminder of Eve's fall, that purges us monthly.

'Come aloft,' she said suddenly, and taking my arm, led me up to the breezy battlements of the keep, where I saw, through the silk of my tears, the serpent Nene cleaving its coil through the marshes. And there was Richard, far below, seen as in a dream. From his horse he was talking with his mother, and he had a hawk balanced on his wrist. Slowly he stroked its feathers, as the King rode up beside them, his steed backing and tossing with its urgency, like my spirit. As they rode through the gate to their sport, I turned to Elysande. She patted the stone beside her, and we sat dangerously on top of the battlements, the wind tossing our veils.

'What's amiss?' Her voice was quiet.

My laugh was stillborn.

'You must think me blind,' she said. 'I will help you, if I can. I am your friend, am I not?'

She was, as I have said, ever anxious to be my friend. I watched the tiny figures against the blue-green marsh. The hawks were flying at heron, the snow of Edward's white gerfalcon catching the sun on its wings as it sped faster and faster through blue haze.

'You are deep in love,' she murmured. 'And yet he loves you not, for he remains in London, while you pine and wax slender, here with the Queen's household.'

So completely had I forgotten Patch's existence that I turned with a frown, and that frown told her all.

'Hey, hey!' she said. 'After all this, 'tis not the fool.'

'Of course it is not the fool.'

'Do not tell me you have been smitten by one of these,' she said, pointing with her slim hand down to the infantry's tents. 'Half of them are wedded, and will tell any tale to win a fresh maidenhead.'

I thought of my heart's lust. 'Prentice in love. I had to smile. Then I felt Elysande's hands loosening my headdress, unpinning my hair.

'Tell me his name,' she said. 'Tell me his name, and I will lie by my lady tonight, and you can seek him in the dark, and none shall know of it, save you and I.'

She began to stroke my hair gently. It waved about my face, blinding me, and her hands were like Richard's. The King's falcon was at the height of its stoop, powerful and clear against the azure mist. Silent, I watched as it dropped, beak and talons opening in a savage joy.

'Tell me his name,' she whispered. I shook my head.

Her hands clung to me. 'What does he call you?'

'Sweet heart, at times,' I whispered. I bent my head, closing my eyes under her strong, soft hands. She caressed the back of my neck, and truly it could have been Richard.

'Sweet heart,' she said very softly. 'Sweet heart, tell me his name! It will give you joy to speak it. I am your friend. I share your every woe.'

Edward's hawk had taken the heron. Like lovers, they dropped through the air, in the tender embrace of death.

'I am he,' Elysande whispered. 'Call me by my name.'

Without another thought, I told her. The gentle, stroking hands ceased for an instant.

'Certes, they fly high,' she murmured, with a little laugh.

'Who do?' I asked, in a dream.

'Why, the hawks, dear heart!' Her fingers caressed. The moments passed, grains slipping silent into eternity. I could not call them back.

'I never really thought of him in that wise,' she said. 'He looks so quiet, so serious. And yet, you have been paramours for some little time?'

'Ah, Richard,' I said, only half hearing her.

She lifted my hair from the nape of my neck, rubbing its mass between her fingers, tangling it into a skein.

'Is he a...'

I grew rigid. 'Ask me no more. I will not speak of it.' I closed my eyes. It was Richard who played with my hair, absently, his mind on something else.

'Tell me this, at any rate,' she said, over a tender laugh. 'I cannot ask the gentlemen of the bedchamber; they would think me wanton indeed, but you and I are dear friends and love each other. I'm curious. Sweeting, is it true, one shoulder is hideously malformed and he pads out his doublet to feign equality?'

I sprang to face her. 'Jesu, Elysande!' I cried. 'How do such tales begin?'

She shrugged; her hands stroked mine; she was my falconer, and I a trembling goshawk. 'You know how whispers wax fat from tongue to tongue,' she murmured. 'Let us therefore know the truth.'

Whatever the truth was, I would not speak of it to Elysande, and she abandoned the chase, and picked up my headdress from the stones, smoothing its windblown veil.

'I will serve the Duchess tonight, sweeting,' she said, and as I looked at her I marked how the sunlight turned her green eyes yellow, but thought her wondrous kind. We stood on the battlements and kissed each other tenderly; and a breeze sprang up and caught us. We swayed in it, and there was naught in the world save its fierce glory…

'I would know mine enemy,' muttered the Duchess of Bedford. The monkey chattered and wound its thin little arms about her neck.

All that long day Elysande cosseted me, staying close, smiling her gentle smile, whispering cheer as the hours wore on. She asked me no more questions about him, but made herself exceedingly useful to me, for she filtered about the castle as I would never dare, in soft enquiry as to his plans. I watched her with love and admiration, for she was clever in the way she spoke with the unfamiliar servants, the strange guards of Fotheringhay: gleaning knowledge by a half-sentence, a casual eyebrow, a disinterested nod. Certes, she was clever, Elysande.

At evening she returned triumphant.

'Proud Cis is giving a banquet in her stateroom,' she murmured. 'Let us get my lady dressed swiftly; for the sooner they have finished the feasting the earlier they will retire... that is, some will retire.' And she gave me a clip round the waist and I kissed her cheek, though an anxiousness fell upon me as I said:

'Dearest, I know not even where he lies, and there is none here who will guide me to him.'

She laughed. 'I was speaking of the King's Grace,' she said softly. 'Is it not natural that he should take his pleasure with the Queen this night, for they may not meet again in weeks. As for the other, if he keeps his usual custom, he will be down in camp, counting his men!' She covered a smile, as if she was loath to wound my feelings by jesting about him. 'They say he is so joyful at the following he has collected to ride under his blazon, he must visit them nightly, for all they were a handful of gems!'

And we laughed merrily, and cast ourselves about, until the Duchess came out from her bedchamber, and we both sped to attend her.

Much, much later, when the bed-curtains were fast on steady breathing, Elysande came to the door to bid me God-speed.

'One thing, dear heart,' she whispered.

'Anything, Elysande.'

'Ask him who is Robin of Redesdale,' she said, and I fancied her voice was a little higher than normal. But I was mad to go to him and I gave her my word. For although she did not know it, I had already asked Richard, and he had been as baffled as were we all, so I could tell her this after, and it would be truth.

It was a close evening, and the marsh mists swirled dank and warm about the castle, and I was a part of them. I clove like a ghost near to the walls until I had crossed the ward and could mingle easily with the hastening servants, grooms, carriers and soldiers who, in lantern-light, prepared for morning departure. Few lights were burning in the great fortress behind me as I threw it one last glance before halting near the drawbridge. A cart containing the chalices and trappings for the Mass was rolling towards it, and the sentinel, laughing with a fellow, casually waved it on. Covered from head to foot in my dark cloak, I ran unnoticed in the wagon's shadow across the moat, and felt the silken suck of the meadow under my soles. There were men everywhere. Never had I seen so many men. And there were horses, the great destriers of war, with hooves big as serving dishes, shifting restively at their tethers, or, forked by strong shadows, surging across my path like moving boulders of power. There was the smell of steel and sweat; and distantly, the marsh-fires burned green, brighter that night, for the demons that tended them were curious, aroused by all the activity. I crossed myself for I was more afraid than I had dreamed, and I thought of the Nut-Brown Maid, who would follow her lord into the wilds and the desolate places.

The waged men, the mercenaries, formed a vast circle. I saw their laughing faces in the light of camp fires. They were playing cards and dicing, using their leathern shields for a board, and, as I approached the dimlit shapes of the officers' tents, I saw for the first time there were women too, among the common soldiery. In one way I was glad, for I could mix with the bawds and the wenches from the nearby hamlet and none would question my presence; then, I was sorry, for as I scuttled past a little knot of men, two dark shapes rose on my either side, and I felt the touch of rough hands.

One of them kissed me, the other pulled off my hood. I felt a beard sharp on my skin. They both laughed, and they would have wrought further, for I felt fingers at my cloak's fastenings, and I screamed. A third figure appeared carrying a light, outlined against the glimmering marsh.

'Christ's Mercy!' said a voice wearily. 'Do we ravish children? See how small she is, you great ox!'

The one who had kissed me dropped his arms and muttered something unintelligible.

'Fat Mab awaits you. On the edge of camp,' pursued the man with the lantern. I crept closer to him.

'Sir,' I whispered, 'sir, I'm no camp-follower. Bid them let me pass, I pray you.'

'Are you from the castle?' he said.

Wildly, I stretched my mind, babbling, 'I have a message...'

'I'll take it then; and you can go back before this pack molest you any more,' he said slowly. I guessed then he must be one of the newly-waged men, or he would have asked why they had not sent one of the castle guard or a manservant, and not a young maid.

'It is a private message and urgent,' I whispered. 'I don't know you, sir.'

'Calthorp, mistress,' he said shortly. 'Bound in arms under my lord Duke of Gloucester.'

In all these hundreds of soldiers I had fallen on one of Richard's men. I had a message, but not one I could transmit by Master Calthorp.

'For his ears only,' I muttered, and in the lantern light, saw his mouth curve, and knew him as quite young, despite his serious way; the kind of man my lord would pick, I thought, and answered his smile.

'So be it' he answered, and we took our way through the lines of men. Some of them were polishing their weapons, talking quietly; one was writing a letter by firelight, chewing his nails to ease the labour of it. But, dangerously near the tents, a soldier possessed one of the village trulls, unhurriedly, half-burying her in the coarse grass, and in the gloom I felt my face scarlet and closed my ears to their sighing moans. Master Calthorp whisked me past, catching my elbow as I tripped over tussocks and the edge of my cloak.

'This is my first campaign,' he said, to cover my shame. Then, inconsequentially: 'I like the Duke of Gloucester well.' Jesu, take me to him then, I thought. For I too like the Duke of Gloucester.

Suddenly, I saw him. He was standing by an open tent-flap, talking with three young men. I faltered and shrank, and Master Calthorp looked round to see why I hung back.

'There he is, mistress,' he said cheerfully.

I stood and watched Richard. With the exact gesture of his brother the King, he threw his arm about the shoulder of one young man; friendly, assured, disquietingly royal. They laughed together. He seemed very joyful, and I felt lonely and lost. Calthorp strode up to him while I trailed behind, huddled in my cloak. An esquire, whom I recognized as Lord Percy's son, stepped forward protectively, hiding Richard for a moment.

'Here is one with a message for his Grace,' said Calthorp, and I drew my hood far across my face and felt the stuff quiver under my lips.

Richard turned his head as he caught the words, and waited. The three young men waited. Robert Percy waited, and so long did they all wait that Richard came forward and Calthorp held the lantern up so that it shone in my eyes. I saw Richard's hand stray to his dagger and I knew that I must present a strange, shapeless figure, half human, neither young nor old, and I feared they might think me Robin of Redesdale himself, mayhap, come south to murder them. So I turned my back on the others, and for Richard's eyes alone, dropped the veil from my face, and saw his expression change. I had never seen him angry, but he was passing wroth, then, and his fingers left his knife and he started turning his finger-rings round and round, as a cat lashes its tail. 'My thanks, Master Calthorp,' he said. His voice was like the cold stones in my gallery.

Calthorp bowed swiftly and faded away. The three young men shuffled their feet.

'Good night to you, Bernard, Barney, Broom,' said Richard, and he ran their names together so that it sounded like one of Patch's conundrums, and I wanted to laugh, and cry.

'Is all well?' Robert Percy said.

'This person is my acquaintance, and doubtless brings word from the castle,' said Richard. 'I will speak alone with her.'

'As your good lordship desires,' said Percy. 'I will remain and escort you to your apartments.'

'Nay, Robert,' Richard said. 'Get you to bed. We must be up betimes.' He held the tent-flap open for me as Percy vanished in the murk, and he followed me in, and there we were, among all the turmoil of preparation. Pieces of harness stood everywhere. Richard's sword, his banner with the Boar emblem, leather jackets on a couch, a silver basin and ewer in the corner. Brigandines, and fierce, eyeless casquetals. He came and stood before me.

'Why did you come down here?' he asked quietly.

I could not answer.

'You should not have come,' he repeated, and turned away, and stood looking out of the tent-flap into the misty darkness.

'I crave your Grace's pardon,' I said, and I think there was a little hauteur in my tone, for he had welcomed my presence when he was lonely and sad, and now he was glad and occupied in the King's service, it seemed he had no further need of me.

'I will leave you, my lord, straightway, and beg your indulgence for this misconduct,' I said formally, and I heard my voice quaver. Still he did not answer, standing straight and slender of waist, with his uneven shoulders and his smooth hair falling to his neck, a dark shadow against the tent wall. So I made to walk past him and would have dived out into the unfriendly night, but his hand caught my wrist and gripped it, with a hard tenderness.

'You are angry with me,' I whispered.

He looked down, and my eyes drooped, for his glance was the same as it ever was, deeply cool and burning and loving.

'Not with you, damoiselle, but with your folly,' he said. Then, anxiously: 'Have any harmed you, sweet heart?'

Gladness nudged at my bones. I shook my head.

'Sweet mistress, this is a world of men.' It was as though my dead father spoke to me. 'No place for you, among the rude soldiery and the harlots. Women, children, things of weakness in this time of strife.'

And I marvelled at the way he spoke, calm and controlled, full of wisdom and concern as if he were old beyond his years. And while he began softly to stroke my hair, I remarked on it, aloud.

'Yes, I may seem thus,' he said, then stopped, and I said gently: 'Yea, my lord, my love?'

'My childhood ended when I was seven years old,' he said, and a heavy silence hung between us. He lowered his hand from my hair, and we both thought of the heads on Micklegate Bar.

'You know what the King did?' he murmured. I shook my head.

'A ceremony of remembrance,' he said slowly. 'Five years ago, here in this very place. We rode behind a great death carriage, to the memory of my father and my brother. Under the banner of Christ in Majesty, Christ on a rainbow, flanked by the suns and roses. Gilded angels were fashioned, to cherish their souls. They lived again, that day. Then, through God's grace, and his own kingly might, Edward avenged their death. He brought peace to the realm.'

His voice shook. He turned to face me again.

'Thus, through my gratitude, have I striven to grow wise and strong, that I may be his right hand always. Great Jesu! I love him.'

A pain in my heart. Kings come and go. If only he could have said: 'Great Jesu! I love thee.' But in face of this strong and bitter love, I was no more than one of the village trulls, moaning in the long grass. I think it was then I decided my love must do for the two of us.

He went on: 'So, I will be true to him, and to his heirs, so long as I shall live.'

In the distance a woman's chuckling shriek, lewd and profane, sullied the grave quietness. For no reason at all, I thought of little Lady Beaufort.

Richard glanced round, anxiously. He put his hands over my ears, my hair, so that I should not hear the coarse sounds. 'Sweet heart, you should not be here,' he said, his voice coming faintly through a dim, rushing noise.

Then he said: 'Why did you come?'

I put my hands on his, and he held me, on either side of my head. I had never told him how I loved him, for it would not be seemly, but this night, I felt, with a strange sadness, might be the only time I should have the chance. So I told him, all of it, and when I had ceased, his hands were trembling under mine, and the rushing in my ears became a roar.

His voice sounded quite loud when he took his hands away. 'I wonder,' he said thoughtfully, 'if I am worthy of such love.'

I could not speak, for I was weeping, and I was angry with myself, for this was not what I had planned; I had wanted to make him glad, not bring him dolour.

I therefore took his hand and kissed it, and his rings were cold to my mouth. And he put his arm tenderly about my neck, and my hair came loose and streamed over his wrist down to the ground, as I leaned back and felt his lips on my throat, my heart.

And before I left him, because it was such a warm, damp night and he looked weary, I took a cloth with water from the ewer and washed his face as he lay on the couch. He closed his eyes for an instant and he could have been dead, with his high-boned countenance and his pallor. So hastily, to chase a demon, I signed his brow with the Cross and kissed him, and he clasped his arms tight about me, saying I was a true maid and had brought him much joy and comfort. He summoned a sleepy young man to escort me back to the castle, one who had but lately come on duty, so that none should know, for the greenish dawn was rising over the fens and the camp would soon be stirring. He raised his hand to me as he stood between the tent-flaps, and there was a light about him that was not earthly; or it may have been the marsh fiends dimming their night-lamps behind him; I did not know.

Neither did I know that I should not see Richard Plantagenet again for many years, and then he would be greatly changed.

I never had such a friend as Elysande; and Elysande had a new dress. It was green as a willow and suited her golden skin and tilted eyes. She was kind and lovesome and I loved her. It seemed I had more need of her than ever, particularly the day they left to meet with Robin, riding to Newark in their martial blue, for to save my soul I could not watch them go. I wanted to remember him as he stood in the lambent dawn, dark figure of my fate, holding all my happiness in one lifted hand.

Elysande sat beside me, stroking my cold fingers, for no flame burned in me. Only a block of ice, and I knew not why, for he had said: 'God keep you, sweet lady, be comfortable. When we have put down this pesky rising I shall come back and all will be well with us again.'

Yet all was not well with me, for, overlaying my great sadness, another shadow had fallen upon me, out of the past, and I was full of fear.

When I was returning from Richard, walking as in a deep sleep and still with him in spirit, I had not seen the tall figure advancing noiselessly along the twilit passage until we collided fiercely. Candlelight flared above me and a drop of hot wax fell on my neck. Like a blare of trumpets, I heard the warning that tore through my mind. I raised my face and saw Anthony Woodville gazing down at me from his slender height. He had just come from saying a Night Office, and his rosary beads were twisted round his fingers. Instead of frowning and passing by, he stopped and his eyes roved over me: my tumbling hair, my exposed throat and breast; my guilt.

'Well, madam?' he said. 'You are late abroad, or should I say early?'

And I was a child again, another oath broken, for I had sworn he would never again bring me fear.

'I know you, mistress, do I not?' His voice was kind, as a sword is kind until you feel the edge. I pulled my careless cloak together, confused. He had seen me more than once, sitting quietly in his mother's apartments.

'I had not recognized you before now,' he said, just as if he had read my thoughts. 'I vow—'tis those incredible headpieces you ladies wear, but now 'tis all plain ... were you not with us at Grafton Regis?'

It was undoubtedly true. With my hair fashionably hidden, the forehead shaved for height, I owned a different countenance. Without my wealth of hair, I was but another little pale face.

His eyes, cold depths of a winter lake, held mine. My gaze showed unease, I know, but strangely so did his, as if I were some little wild animal of uncertain temper. For a moment we looked at one another, and my heart, lately lulled to bliss by Richard's touch, began to leap and bound as do the birds cruel boys fasten to stakes and stone to death.

'Yes...' he said, very slowly, and that one word held more meaning than the longest speech. Then suddenly he turned on his heel and strode in the direction of the Duchess's apartments, while I stayed, paralysed with dismay, for there Elysande waited to let me in. I saw him halt outside my lady's door, musing deeply, and he must have thought the hour too late or too early, for he moved away without knocking, and vanished down the staircase, his tall shadow following him.

Now fear such as I had never known held me fast. He had remembered me, and with that remembrance, had come a reprise of that night at Grafton Regis, when he had bullied me into forgetting what I had seen. And what had I seen? Something not clearly understood, something evil and dangerous. He was plainly haunted. And I feared the outcome of his malaise.

'Holy Jesu!' I whispered outside the Duchess's door. 'He will send me back to Grafton!'

He would send me back to Grafton, and I would never see Richard again. Elysande slid back the bolt and I fell into her arms, weeping as loudly as I dared.

Now she was pressing my hand gently. She had been looking out of the window.

'He rides with Edward Brampton, the Portuguese,' she murmured. 'They make a goodly show—all of them...' stealing a sideways glance. 'He loved you right well last night?' she whispered, and I nodded, because she was a dear friend to me and full of understanding that love was not always carnal sin, as the priests said.

'You were courageous,' she whispered. 'To venture among all the military. I warrant you saw sights to bring the colour to your face.'

Even as she spoke, I knew for certainty that she herself must have made like journeys in her time, and wondered if she had loved a soldier ever, and knew the feeling. All the while she smiled; it was as if she applied the smile with her face-paint.

'Did you ask him?' she said.

I had to tell my little lie, truth as it was, that Richard did not know the real face of Robin of Redesdale. Her smile grew broader as if it were stretched and the paint on her lips cracked a little with the sweetness of her smile.

And then, that day, Lord Anthony entered, giving us all a fair good-day, and passed through to the Duchess's chamber. And strong terror gripped me, more than I could bear, and I turned trembling to Elysande, who put her arm about me as if she had only been waiting for me to tell her the old secret that had plagued me for years.

So while my lord was closeted with his mother, I sought comfort and reassurance from sweet Elysande, and I told her all about it; the moonlight, and the manikins and the black cat, and the herb garden, and Elizabeth Woodville's uncertainty as to the wisdom of their actions, and her mother's fierce words. I told her all, and waxed fat in the telling, for she was a kind and tender audience, and hung on every word and her eyes grew wide and she asked me many questions and showed horror and sympathy.

Then she told me to set it all from my mind, as if it were one of my bad dreams, to forget it all and be glad and think only of my dear love. How could Sir Anthony send me back to Grafton for that which was not my fault? Sure enough she was right, for naught dreadful happened, as when my lord and his mother came out of the chamber they did not even look at me.

So I ceased to be disquieted, and was only full of love-longing instead, and I know which was the heavier burden.

He had told me he had written a letter to a friend while he was at Rising, for he had had no money with which to pay his men, and he had even jested about it, as we lay in each other's arms.

I wished he would write *me* a letter, but I knew he would be far too busy for that.

There came August, and a day so full of sorrow that only one other summer day can best it for its anguish and that I cannot speak of yet.

Elysande's dress was red this day, like a fair red rose, like blood, but we were not sitting quietly together on this occasion. We were at Westminster, running here and there, throwing things into chests, packing urgently, while the Household flew about as feverishly as did the panicking crowds in the street below.

For the King was taken. The King was a prisoner, and his captor was the man who had been his friend, the one who had set him on the throne, the knight Richard had loved.

Robin of Redesdale was not Robin Hood after all: he was Sir John Conyers, cousin of the Earl of Warwick; and Warwick had taken the King. Edward had left matters too late, with his hawking and his bedsport and his dalliance at Fotheringhay. While he pleasured himself thus, and his wise young brother chafed to be off, the man who made and unmade kings had been wondrous busy.

Horsemen on steaming beasts cried frenzy through London. Elysande cursed under her breath and I sought to calm my churning stomach, while we piled clothing and jewellery into coffers, bed-linen and arras into cases, helped by pallid manservants with the smell of fear about them. Hoarse shouting came in gusts over the screams of the mob. I rushed to a window; whenever I made out the word 'slain' or 'beheaded', a ghastly grinning spectre rose up to wave at me through the panes. Of a sudden I dropped the end of a Turkish rug and rushed out into the teeming passages, frantic for the news I dreaded. In a niche in the stones sat a small figure, weeping. I had never seen Harry cry before. In the midst of my demented progress I stopped and knelt to him. He pressed his face against me, his tears fell on my bosom. He would not be comforted.

'The King's Grace is taken,' he sobbed. 'I am so afraid.'

'Don't weep, Harry,' I said, as bravely as I could. 'All will be well.'

'My sweet lord,' he whispered through snuffling tears. All my heart's blood massed in a red, icy knot.

'What say you?' I cried.

'He was wondrous kind to me,' he choked. 'Men say he has been slain.'

I rose and staggered on my feet, bruising my back against the carved pillar. Then I started, witlessly, to run, seeking the street, to seize the stirrup of the nearest courier and demand he give this terrible news the lie. I stumbled, and arms caught me; arms that I fought, screaming into a lined face no longer merry.

'God's Passion,' said Patch. 'Must all fly about like slaughtered fowls?' He held me fast. 'Sweeting, calm yourself.'

'Patch,' I cried. 'Patch!'

He grinned. His face looked strained and meagre; a skull-like face.

'Mary have mercy!' he said. 'I thought you had more courage than to cry havoc with the rest. So the King is taken! Was he not warned, time and again? Why all this wonder, that the great Warwick seeks vengeance on the Woodvilles?'

'Pembroke and Devon are headless now.
More necks will bleed ere long, I trow.'

He made a little jingle out of it. Then for a brief moment his face crumpled with grief, he crossed himself, said: 'Christ preserve the King,' and pulled me down beside him on a window-ledge.

'Ah, I love you, maiden,' he said, and I could have struck him for jesting at such a time, but felt too weak to raise my hand.

'Give me the news,' I said, trembling. 'Who is beheaded, who slain?'

'The King's favourites,' said Patch calmly. 'Sir Richard Woodville, John Woodville... Warwick will have the whole family's blood. Clarence stands at his right hand, now that Isabel is his bride.'

'George of Clarence—has wedded Warwick's daughter?' I cried. Patch nodded, and winked and said: 'In Calais, lately.'

'They will destroy the Woodvilles?' I gasped.

'In all ways possible,' said the fool. 'Tend well your mistress, maiden, for she'll need your prayers.'

I knew not what he meant, but when he started babbling again about love, and he still could not tell me where was Richard in all this, I sprang up and flew to Elysande, but she was nowhere to be seen. The Duchess's chamber was bolted from the inside, while two men stood without and spoke her name, sternly. They had a small retinue of henchmen, who wore the Bear and Ragged Staff, Warwick's livery. They stayed a few moments, then quit the chamber purposefully, while the gentlewomen huddled like terrified pigeons. Snatches of their speech crept to my ears.

'Redesdale's Proclamation likened his Grace to Richard the Second, Harry the Sixth,' said a shaking voice. 'All deposed monarchs...'

'Yea, and Edward the Second,' said Anne Haute, in horrified tones. She was deathly white and I remembered that she too was a Woodville. Then I thought of the King, and Richard, and of poor, unnatural Edward the Second, with his bowels burned out at Berkeley, and my stomach came up into my throat. When the blackness faded into light, Elysande was with me. She was not smiling when I opened my eyes, but as soon as I was sensible she kissed me, a loving sister. Her red gown hurt my gaze. The voices whispered on.

'The Archbishop of York... is in the Palace...'

'A Neville!' hissed another.

'Yea, and Clarence sits on the Council...'

'Warwick has summoned a Parliament...'

'The Duchess!' someone murmured anxiously.

'Who were those men... What have they done to her?'

Their whispers flew like arrows, rebounding on to bafflement.

Suddenly the Duchess came out from her chamber. She was yellowish, and her grim jaws were clamped together. Angrily she waved her hand at the gibbering group of women. She leaned firmly on her ivory cane, white-knuckled.

'Leave me—all of you!' she snapped.

Yet Elysande and I flew to her side, for we feared she might collapse, as the others rustled out hastily, with many a glance behind.

Ignoring me, the Duchess glared at Elysande.

'You failed me in your duty,' she said icily, and Elysande was out of countenance for a moment, and her eyes gave off sparks.

'Sweet madam, I wrought all I could, but the source ran dry,' she said, and I was bemused by her strange words.

'Where is Hastings?' asked the Duchess, and she uttered the Lord Chamberlain's name as if it were a poison on her tongue.

Elysande shrugged, as the French do.

'And young Gloucester?' My heart leaped in my throat. Before Elysande could reply, a stout knocking came on the outer door. The same two men returned who had waited to speak with the Duchess. They had waited vainly and now they would not be gainsaid. One said his name was Thomas Wake.

A panic fire had started somewhere down the street. I could hear the cracking of timber and the surging shouts from the crowd. Smoke drifted under the window.

The two men were courteous. They bowed to the Duchess, then one of them placed a parchment between her fingers.

'Madame, we will attend your presence in answer to this charge,' Thomas Wake said formally. Swiftly they left, walking clean and upright. One of them was dark and pale, like Richard.

The Duchess's fingers were stiff and curled, and the parchment dropped from her hand, so I bent to pick it up. There were many long words, and one of them was 'necromancy'.

'Holy God,' whispered Elysande.

'Ask her Grace to come,' said the Duchess firmly. I marvelled at her composure.

Elysande left and returned shortly with the Queen. For the first time ever, she came without her retinue of gentlewomen, servants, chaplains. On my knees, I glanced up at her. She was ivory-faced, but it became her, against her black dress with the jewelled girdle and the priceless reliquary Edward had given her. I wondered if she wept and feared for him as I did for my love.

'Madame, they have taken Master Daunger,' said the Duchess. And at the name I saw again, clear as crystal, the whey-faced clerk sitting at table on May Eve with the unquiet Elizabeth Woodville; galloping on May Day to Grafton Regis.

'So I am informed,' said the Queen. She also was serene, though less so. She frowned at the old woman and swept into the inner chamber, beckoning her mother to follow. Elysande and I waited. Low murmurings came from behind the closed door. I looked at my friend, and her eyes were yellow, like a wolf's eyes.

'They have Daunger,' she said, and looked at me. I said naught. I was trying to collect my thoughts, straining my ears for the cries of men bringing news of the rebellion; news of Richard.

'How fortunate that he is their only witness,' she said musingly. And then I felt afraid. The voices within were louder, raised in anger... that was the Queen...

'Even if they have his feet in the fire?'

'He will not say aught, my daughter...' And it was Grafton Regis all over again when she said: 'It is written, it is written... he is a stubborn man, and clever.'

'So there is naught to fear,' said Elizabeth, the door now ajar.

As they came out, I sought to exchange comforting glances with Elysande. She gave me a right lovesome smile. Then she stepped forward with a deep curtsey before the Queen.

'Your most noble Grace,' she said softly, and despite this formal address there was a certain familiarity in her tone as if she had known the Queen years ago, in France, mayhap, when Elizabeth served Margaret of Anjou. The Queen looked at her expressionlessly.

'Madame, there is one here,' said Elysande slowly, 'who speaks of necromancy, and sorcery... I know naught of it myself, for I am loyal and love your Grace. But one has told me tales of moonlight on the last day of April... things seen and heard. I am your servant and would safeguard you.'

She took the Queen's hand and kissed it gracefully, and Elizabeth laid her own white hand on the shoulder of my dear friend, Elysande.

They all turned and looked closely at me, while I stood shaking, and it was as if their three faces were one, with the same cold hard glance, ruthless, appraising, as if I were a pear to be plucked, a stone to be priced, a sheep to be butchered. The Duchess spoke first.

'And what folly does this one say, mistress?'

Elysande smiled. 'All, Madame. Something about evil rites and words, and ravings about fickle men and "*the other*".' She finished with the casual air of one who imparts the insignificant. The Queen's ivory face turned to chalk.

'Jesu, mercy,' she said quietly. Then, in the next breath and as if I were not there: 'She was but a child...'

'She would never withstand an inquisition,' said one of them, but by now I was falling into a black tomb and did not know who spoke.

'She is of little importance... she will not speak.'

I opened my mouth, to swear eternal silence.

'She may already have spoken,' said a voice, and knew it by its sweetness to be that of Elysande. She came and stood beside me. I caught a glint of her red gown through a fog of fear. And Elysande said, in a voice like running water:

'Know you not, your Grace, that this one'—she indicated me with a slender sleeve-swish—'this one lies o'night with my lord of Gloucester, and doubtless bears many a pretty tale?'

It was what Richard would have called a flank attack. While I was engaged with the dangerous enemy before me, she had come down out of a mist of smiles and lovesomeness to destroy me. It was now that I knew she was truly a Woodville-lover and always had been, despite her provoking words in my presence, her soft mocking of the sleeping Duchess. She had betrayed me.

I fell at the Queen's feet.

'You should thank me,' Elysande said. She was at the window, watching the reflections of the mob fire. Dark was falling. The glow lit up the great chamber like blood. They had been waiting for the night, for they were going to dispose of me. My mind ran rings of terror; the Tower yawned; nay, I thought, Warwick would examine all prisoners now that he was in power, and I would be of use to him.

The Queen was in Sanctuary; Elysande was on the point of joining her and the Duchess.

Ah, holy Jesu! I thought. They will kill me. They will murder me, as they did Desmond's boys. A small cry broke from me.

'I have saved your life,' said Elysande, and mayhap she did not want my blood on her slender hands, for she continued: 'The King loves Gloucester, and you are his harlot.'

I felt tears spring to my eyes at the word, for such were they who lay in long grass with soldiers, and did not give their whole heart and love to one alone.

'Young Gloucester has no power; yet if you died, and he complained to the King, Edward would be angry... the risk is too great. Thus you will live, cursed and forgotten.'

'He may seek me,' I said through frozen lips.

Elysande laughed, throwing back her head. 'He will not wish to seek you,' she said gaily. 'You will have vanished from the sight of men; and you have betrayed his confidence.'

'I have never betrayed him,' I whispered, shaking.

'You have spoken of him to me,' Elysande said. 'Doubtless he will believe you have carried tales of his policies to Jacquetta of Bedford. All know there is no love lost between Richard and the Queen's kin. Has he not spoken to you of things other than love?'

I thought how I asked him about Robin of Redesdale—in his eyes I would be a Woodville spy. I thought of his swift disdainful anger and the way he had toyed with his knife at my cloaked anonymity. My tears began to fall. Elysande went on, softly:

'He will think you to be a witch; that you had part in the rites and this is why you are no longer at court... a dangerous witness... a necromancer. One who helped secure the King for Elizabeth Woodville.'

I asked her: 'And who shall speak such foul lies?'

'Whispers wax fat,' she said, her favourite expression.

'He will seek me,' I said, and I knew I lied for comfort's sake, for there was none to succour me.

'Others will soon replace you,' she said, and watched me carefully, enjoying my anguish. 'And anyway that witless loyalty of his will destroy him... all the Woodvilles are scattered but Warwick's men are everywhere. I doubt not they have cut him down already on the road, together with his followers.'

'Warwick would never slay him!' I cried. 'They were as father and son!'

'Jesu! what a fool you are!' she said contemptuously. 'In war, men slay their own kin.'

And I thought with sorrow of Richard who, if he still lived, would need to ride against George of Clarence and the great Neville, and my tears turned inward, and shrouded him.

Then I heard the tramp of boots, the voices of men.

'Now all the dresses and the praises will be mine,' said Elysande, softly smiling. Outside the steps halted, and a key turned.

'You have sold me for a gown?' I cried, and she shook her head, the smile gone. 'I bore you no real malice, for I thought you want-wit, harmless, until one day,' she murmured. 'Yet you have flown exceedingly high, and striven to ape your betters, and may God have mercy...' and I knew she spoke of Elizabeth Woodville and the King, and Richard and me.

So they came and took me. They were silent men and we passed quickly out through the teeming streets, with the citizens with brows clubbed bloody, and here and there the glow of a fire gilding the leaning house gables. We left behind the heaps of filth and ordure which steamed and stank on the cobbles, while far above them a hundred spires pointed to Paradise. And the great Tower faded, all faded, behind the veil of my tears, light as a spider's dwelling on a May dawn; and I heard them speak of the north parties of the realm, which phrase I clung to, Yorkshire being part of my lord, and therefore of me.

I wished that I had learned to play chess as he had tried to teach me, for as he said, one should be born cognizant of strategy and cunning in this world. Therefore I kept my own counsel ever afterwards, and the only words I spoke during that long rough journey northward through danger were but to ask them not to ride so fast. For I had something to protect. Under my cloak I kept my arms crossed tight, safeguarding one last small and secret joy.

The royal child, the Plantagenet. The child of my beloved.

HERE THE MAIDEN'S TALE IS BROKEN

Part Two

The Fool

NOW-A-DAYS	*Also I have a wife; her name is Rachell.*
	Betwixt her and me was a great battle;
	And fain of you would I here tell
	Who was the most master.
NOUGHT	*Thy wife, Rachell, I dare 20 lies.*
NOW-A-DAYS	*Who spake to thee, fool? Thou art not wise!*

Mankind (*ca.* 1470)

I fear something's amiss with my eyes. A pale shadow dims them at moments. Should it continue, I shall go back to the wise woman, over the river at Southwark, among the stews and taverns which flourish as briskly as in the old days. She will sell me the toadstone and whisper her charms, placing her hand on my brow, and I shall almost believe it is my sweet lady. Although her hands are sisters to the lilies, and I lose no chance of kissing them; this I do needlessly, often. We are good friends, if such a thing is possible between a Queen and a mocker, a diverter of courtiers, one who hides his wit behind idiocy and keeps a well-tuned ear. I am content; I serve the one I love; men treat me with respect, and he likes me, for he pays me, and that is great bounty from such as his Divine Majesty. I see him now, wandering in the pleasaunce, a tatterdemalion, wine-stains down his sparse robe, scratching in his little account-book. His long face is drawn in despair over some outrageous extravagance, such as a tun of malmsey for the Spanish Ambassador last month, or one dozen candles for my lord Stanley's apartments. Poor fellow! Henry, 'tis a passing heavy business, this being a King.

This evening I will play cards, with my lady. I will sit on the floor for there are few chairs since the last inventory, and the ladies will have their cushions strewn around us. There are a few pleasures left in this life, if one knows how to look at them, as one might watch a disguising, absorbing its message until one is drawn in thread by thread, to become part of the picture.

We do not speak of King Richard now. Years past, she would lean the barest inch closer to me, give that small anxious cough and say:

'Tell me, Sir Fool, do you remember that revel when...'

And I would say, very low: 'A dreadful night, madam; when the mummers' wildman costumes caught fire and poor Geffrey was burned...'

Of necessity, I am a diverter. Laughing, she'd fall a little woeful at the remembrance of a real tragedy, but be amused by my evasiveness and continue the game, and I would know she thought of the last Christmas before the turning of the tide... I have these trouble-some eyes, and she laughs less than once she did; she looks weary, anxious about Arthur, for all his beauty frail enough to be blown off by a sneeze. Once, her mind was full of torment and courage and resignation, and wore mourning—truly. The darkness of it shone in her glance.

I do not know how old I am exactly, but I must be past my half century. My Queen has great understanding, and should I repeat the rhyme I pleased her with yesterday she merely smiles like the sun. Should she desire more riotous sport, dancing, tumbling, she will call one of the younger men, Scot, or Jakes, more agile than I. It is not that my mind is wanting; more that I seem to live in two dimensions, past and present, and sometimes the two merge and the former cuts sharply through the soft outlines of reality. There I am back again, in the merry days of my lady's father, whom God assoil. The Maiden dances, dances, alone on the gallery. Was it only six moons she stayed at court? It seemed a lifetime; would to all the Saints it had been so!

King Henry has a stable full of fools. If my sight worsens, I may be blessed with a small pension and end my days in a monkery. Yet I cannot brook the thought of parting from my sweet lady. I have loved two women in my life, and they could not have been less alike, save for one trait. Pure goodness, of which many prate but few observe, for all the Masses that they hear. The court is still full of the small triumphs and betrayals which echo the bigger ones that cost the lives of men, and kings. Under the glitter, the ritual splendours, lie serpents, dormant now, but once they writhed and clung and their fangs bit deep.

Two women. One whom I have loved since she was old enough to run and tug my flaunting sleeve, beg a conundrum or a game. Elizabeth, growing into a tall flower, a beauty, destined to be Queen-Consort of England soon after the battle-blood was sunk into the ground and the dark star of Richard Plantagenet fallen for ever. The Maiden was not a deal older when I gave her my heart, and she laughed at me. She was a one for laughing. Her portrait is a second skin over my mind: her huge eyes of dark velvet, and her tiny swift body, flashing through the forbidden ways, diving with a lilt under the arms of startled guards; dodging the Dowager Duchess of Bedford in all places at once, so that even I with my trained young agility could not match her.

We have had little ado here since the business of Master Perkin Warbeck. I stood in the courtyard the day they brought him in chains to confront the King. He had masqueraded as the Duke of York, my royal lady's brother, vanished long since in the bloody mist that wreathes the Tower, along with the Prince of Wales, and their uncle's reputation. Golden-haired Warbeck was a Plantagenet; one glance was enough to show, and the thought that came to me was King Edward's fondness for a pretty face, and that not always of Elizabeth Woodville. Our sovereign faced the tall rebel. Changing emotions frolicked on his sallow countenance like squirrels on a lawn. He reddened and bit his lips, and under all the just anger and coldness I saw something else, gone in an eyelid's bat—a glance like a hairshirt, a demon-haunted look.

I lingered near my lady, for I reckoned she might feel sad at the sight of such an obvious relative and a bastard. For a short space she too had known the shame of bastardy, until King Henry, in his goodness, legitimized her for their holy union. I always thought him born under a lucky planet, for had his lovely consort's brothers still been alive, he would have had to choose between her and the throne of England. Some men truly attain bliss.

I had a little monkey on my shoulder that day, and it clung close, binding its hard scaly tail about my throat. How long since they hanged Perkin? I forget. Kings are no longer addressed 'Your Grace'—their new title befits better the truly divine, the sons of Cadwallader; His Majesty is negotiating with Spain for the hand of the Infanta Caterina for Prince Arthur. That boy looks more fitted for rest and cosseting than the marriage mart.

I have been married; she died, of the new plague, the sweating sickness brought over by our King's French mercenaries when they came in 1485. I scarcely remember her; I have loved but two women.

1471

There are particular days which seem good, when the sun shines brighter and the cobbles are not so hard under the soles of new shoes with the upturned points; on such a day I strolled down Jewry and up Chepe to visit my mother, like a dutiful son. I had no notion why I felt so gay, unless it was that I had just seen a wench who reminded me of the Maiden; something in her gait and the shape of her eyes stirred me, but when I smiled at her she only swished her gown haughtily past my legs and was gone, into the press of people. Nor did I dwell on her, or on the one she resembled, but went, high-spirited, abroad the bright street. Though we had been out of Sanctuary for nearly a month, the sonorous plainsong of the monks still trod my mind, reminding me of my frailties. I had chosen to bide with the Queen this last time, not only for safety, but so that I could be near the Princess Elizabeth. For her I would play the dragon or the griffon, cavorting fearsomely, while she, leaning on her nurse's lap, bubbled like my mother's smallest stew-pot coming to the boil. There was naught could frighten her; in her there was more of her father, less of her mother, that gilded icicle.

Her Grace had first flown into Westminster Sanctuary after the collapse of that ill-starred campaign against Robin of Redesdale, when London hovered on the lip of mob rule and blow after blow rained on the Woodvilles. Warwick had shown no quarter. Hard to say who had been smitten the most: mayhap the Dowager Duchess of Bedford. No sooner had the sorcery indictment been dropped than she had to mourn a husband and a son. Sir John Woodville and Earl Rivers were beheaded outside Coventry. This last had sent her half witless for a while. Men had murmured she wrought witchcraft for many years, but there had been no witnesses to prove a thing. Now she crept about, a murmuring dark mound, widowed, thought-entombed.

Anthony Woodville had embraced the religious life. I do not mean he had taken to cloister, or to going barefoot in monkish garb, for he rode to battle with the rest. Yet the gossiping esquires whispered he wore a hairshirt under his peer's velvet. Though he still penned verses, he was given to God, he declared. Thus can the breeze of fear blow men heavenward.

After King Edward's capture by Warwick, he had been taken by George Neville, Archbishop of York, to Coventry to meet his princely adversaries. Warwick and George of Clarence were both well-flown with triumph. His Grace displayed great cunning: he spoke his captors fair, bowed to their every wish, and went with them to Warwick Castle, then north to desolate Middleham, by night. While, in London, chaos blazed. I remained with my mother, barricading the cookshop door, while the cressets of threatening and threatened flickered past the window, and the cookboys tucked themselves under the counter, crying.

Bereft of its King, England went wild. Old enemies seized the chance to settle ancient scores—disturbances flared all over the realm. Ironically, it was such a one that proved Warwick's first undoing: while slackening his hold on the royal captive to quell a Lancastrian rising initiated by one of his own cousins, he found himself pulled up sharp. Not a soul would answer to his call until they knew the King was safe. Thus, after less than a month, King Edward revealed himself to the people of York. Lord Hastings and Richard of Gloucester rode hot to where the King lay. Neither Warwick nor his brother the Archbishop could do aught but allow these lords to escort the King whither he wished. So Edward came triumphant again to London, with his Lord Chamberlain and his youngest brother, with Suffolk, Henry, Duke of Buckingham, Essex and Arundel, Dacre and Mountjoy, and the one Neville who had remained loyal to him, John, Earl of Northumberland.

With a thousand horse they were received into London's bosom. All rejoiced, poor fools. I marvel now there was not another torrent of bloody rain to spoil the washing of good housewives, for all the mischief that lay ahead.

Misliking the Woodvilles as I did, it gave me some amusement to see young Gloucester appointed Constable of England for life in place of Lord Rivers. Although this nullified the patent for this office that was implicit in Earl Rivers's death, the King made no bones about his pride in his brother. Doubtless his Grace compared Richard's loyalty to the treachery of George of Clarence. As for Gloucester—he actually smiled, on more than one occasion. In his new capacity as chief steward of Wales and the Marches, he quelled risings swiftly, was made Chief Justice and Chamberlain of South Wales, and Viceroy of those entire parts. Irony again, for these powers had lately belonged to the Earl of Warwick, with whom the King then sought to be reconciled. He had gone so far as to betroth my sweet Elizabeth to John Neville's young son, and had sought in other ways to woo Warwick, to settle the disputes without strife. To little avail though, for there came another upheaval in Lincolnshire, started by Lords Welles and Dymmock, and it was like Robin of Redesdale all over again: another ghostly, rumour-ridden attempt to shake the throne, and again, Warwick and Clarence behind it.

Welles and Dymmock went to the block after a scuffle at Empingham, and at the end of March, in the year of Our Lord 1470, the King proclaimed his brother George and the Earl of Warwick traitors. Some there were who joined forces with the two noble rebels, among them Lord Stanley; I used to see him often at court, and he was another who smiled scantily; he had a long, shrewd face, with gloomy, nervous lips, and a manner all hiver-hover. I had watched him at the board, and he was exceeding hard to please, forever waving away one dish and calling for another, as if unable to make up his mind.

Did I say the King rewarded loyalty well? Unfathomable monarch—in the midst of all the ado, he robbed the faithful John Neville of his earldom of Northumberland, restoring it to Henry Percy, that most arrogant knight. The Marquisate of Montagu seemed a poor substitute, given thus to one who had deserted his own brothers to uphold his King.

One skirmish followed another; Warwick and Clarence rode westward to join Lord Stanley; Richard of Gloucester rode after them and scattered Stanley's men. Stanley was indignant, and complained to the King! And almost as soon as Edward had proclaimed that peace was to be kept between Stanley and Gloucester, we heard, in London, how the bigger quarry had evaded him.

Warwick, Clarence, and their ladies had fled to France, to be welcomed in princely style by King Louis—'King Spider'—and to bow over the chill hand of Margaret of Anjou. And the bond to seal the bargain with Lancaster? The fair, frail Anne Neville, for the French Queen's son, Edward, Prince of Wales.

Then fortunes turned, in the bat of an eye. It was folly that King Edward wrought, robbing the Marquis of Montagu of his earldom, for that one swore he had been 'given a paltry title, and a pie's nest to maintain it with'. In September he showed his displeasure, turning on the King when he lay at Doncaster, and the next we knew was that Edward, Hastings, Rivers and Gloucester were fugitives, exiled in the Low Countries. Back to town came Warwick wrenching half-witted Harry the Sixth from his prayers in the Tower to lead the poor wight through London, as a kind of sad harbinger of his French wife's due invasion. By this time the Queen, great with child, her ladies and her three daughters were crammed into Sanctuary, with Mother Cobb the midwife, and there was a chill corner for the King's jesters and mountebanks, all among the holy men. I could thank God for my safety—I could play with the Princess Elizabeth, and duly marvel at the new royal heir—and think of the Maiden through the sober quietness. It was not a bad time, yet we ached for news. When we heard that the King and Richard of Gloucester had landed at Ravenspur and gained York through some cunning policy, we were heartened. When we knew that the King offered Warwick and Clarence pardon or the haze of battle, we were hopeful; and when we learned that Clarence at least was reconciled with his brothers, we rejoiced.

Yet again, the Nevilles paraded Harry Six through London in a ploy to rally Lancaster. Pitiful dolt! with his emblem of two foxtails on a staff drooping in the mizzling rain—men said it shamed the stomach. Then, suddenly, his Grace strode into Sanctuary, taking the Queen in his arms, kissing all the ladies, offering prayers in thanks for the fair babe. He even gripped me by the shoulder for an instant, and shed one tear of gladness. That was the sign for general weeping from all the women. I thought I should be driven mad by their noise. So I stole over to the Princess Elizabeth and saw that she was laughing, as she ever did, and that her uncle of Gloucester laughed with her.

Then the fierce struggles at Barnet, at Tewkesbury, and the thousands slain, among which were the French Queen's son, and the man who made and unmade kings, Richard Neville, Earl of Warwick.

Noble, hot-humoured Warwick, the flamboyant baron for whom the people once shouted so gladly, was dead. For Warwick had schooled his cousin well in the diversities of war and policy, and the princely pupil had overmatched him. I could not deny a vague regret—though I was right heartily the King's lover, it was as if Warwick had donned the crown and sword of Gabriel, to drive corruption from Paradise. Although there were now fewer Woodvilles, they still fed on the realm, and its bounty.

And the Sanctuary of Westminster was free of us once more; of the women and children, the servants and the nervous dogs, of the sweet Princesses, and the new heir to England, whose entry into the sinful world had brought the omens of complete victory to Edward, his father. So I walked up Chepe with the ground sunny under my soles and the taste of freedom in my belly, with only one little bit of sour.

For beside all the great personages, there was one truly insignificant but exceeding dear, of whom I had no news, for she had vanished as if she had never been.

I carried a staff along Eastchepe, to guard me from the 'prentices, who would as soon pick a quarrel as sell you an oyster-pie. Loud and impertinent, they sought to emulate the quality, dressing beyond their means, wearing tall hats, piked shoes. Their finery was the spoils of gambling; today they would lose on the dice and pawn their doublet, tomorrow be peacocking in a friend's attire, won at cards. Thus, thought I, the way of the world, the fortunes of York and Lancaster, and I smiled.

The door of the cookshop felt greasy to my palm. I went inside the brisk heat and bustle. Trade was good. Shortly before my father's death, my mother had started this enterprise, moving from Hereford to London, while I played noble houses, itinerant with a group of minstrels, and learning my craft daily. My father was a fool, his father before him, and, in the days of Coeur de Lion, my ancestor was a jongleur, and rich rewarded.

A knot of cookboys toiled at the fire, and my mother came welcoming. Short-statured like myself, she was plump as a pigeon, with grey eyes and small firm mouth. I bussed her on the cheek; it was months since we last met. We talked of small family matters, and then of the King and Queen—she was glad of a diversion from labour and heat, though all the while there seemed to be some trouble peering round her shoulder.

'So England has an heir at last.'

'Yea, the prettiest prince,' I answered. She leaped from thought to thought.

'Did you see them bring the French Queen through the City?' She laughed. 'A right draggletail, and her eyes were mindless. Some hurled filth at her but'—she lowered her voice—'I felt pity—ask me not why.'

'She's lost everything,' I said. 'Her pride and her solace, her Silver Swan.' (So they called him, this dead prince, this Anjou witch's son.)

'What of his widow?' she asked. 'Anne of Warwick?'

I told her the little I knew, from the time when Warwick had gathered up his ladies and sped them overseas. Anne and the Countess, George of Clarence's wife Isabel, great with child. The hand of the youngest daughter for the French Queen's son, and King Louis rubbing his palms over the prospect of Burgundy under his belt, and a fruitful harvest for Lancaster.

'Is it the truth?' asked my mother. 'That proud Margaret kept the Earl on his knees a full hour before she'd consent to the match?'

'Some say a half-hour, some ten minutes,' I chuckled. 'Their children were wedded at Angers, at any rate; thus is Anne Neville widowed at sixteen and lies at her sister's house. They must be right doleful together. Isabel mourns her dead child—the one born aboard ship, off the French coast.'

I gave her shreds of gossip; how Isabel's babe had been buried at sea; how it was Richard of Gloucester who persuaded Clarence to leave the ranks of his father-in-law and rejoin his brothers, before

Barnet; how the swirling mists of that battle were said by some to be the product of sorcery, by others the benison of God. She drank it all, yawning at my description of the battle blows, but keen to hear everything concerning those of the blood royal and their rebellious kin.

'I did hear,' said she, 'that the Duke of Gloucester hankered to marry Anne of Warwick, time past.'

'He still does.'

She turned to clout a cookboy, who had let a pan of eels in gravy singe. When she came back her face was full of wonder.

'Why, she's under attainder, disgraced,' she murmured.

'Love makes fools of all,' I chaffed. 'And were they not children together at Middleham?'

'So has she vast estates, through her mother the Countess,' she reminded me, sharp at my sentimental drift. A woman of affairs, my mother.

'He might feel kinship, sympathy. You pitied Margaret of Anjou,' I mocked, and she coloured and dealt me a buffet in the chest, laughing.

'We shall see what manner of man he is,' she said. 'I saw him last month, heading the procession, with the banners waving and his Grace smiling behind him. How they differ, Richard and the King! Such a pale, set countenance. So sombre.'

'He's a brave fighter,' I said ungrudgingly. I admired his prowess, but otherwise I preferred Edward. There was a man, full of laughter and love, colour and light. I stole a hot sausage from the cookshop counter and blew on it. 'And a bold leader,' I added.

'And now, you say, he seeks to prove the lover,' said my mother, smiling.

I ate my sausage, good and spicy as it was, thought on Gloucester briefly, tipped him from my thoughts.

'And what of your own affairs of the heart?' I said suddenly, remembering something. 'What of Master Fray?'

'Do not speak of Daniel Fray,' she said, and angry little scars of temper bloomed on her forehead.

'Has he offended you?'

'Certes, he offends me constantly,' she said. 'I'll not speak of it before the knaves.'

She took me to the upper chamber and yielded an intelligence that made my blood simmer like the cookpots. Scarcely had she ceased when one of the kitchen maids intruded a head, saying that there was one without who would speak with her mistress. She admitted someone more like a ferret than any I have seen popping into a badger's hide. A face the colour of curds and eyes like watery rubies, he was no more than nineteen. Hesitant too. He had not even the manners to doff his greasy cap—I lifted it gently from his head with my cane. He cast a glance at me as if unsure of my humour; my mother, too, looked strangely as if she wished I were gone. I asked his business.

'My uncle and master, of the Eagle, sends words for this dame's ears,' he said, scarcely civil, and I laughed, saying: 'Prate of devils and they appear,' for I knew him now as nephew to Fray the tavern-keeper. An unsavoury house was that, in a mean court off Butchers Lane. They watered the wine there, and harboured thieves. It had offended me at first to hear that Dan Fray dared woo my mother, then I had been amused, to hear how he came creaking lean-shanked into her shop with his declarations, vowing he sought to protect the comely widow. I was confident she could look to herself.

'Well?' I demanded.

He swivelled his red eye at my mother. 'My master your kinsman desires a final answer,' he said, wriggling his feet about in their worn-out boots.

'You speak of kinship!' I cried, before she would reply. 'What nonsense is this? Daniel Fray is naught to me or mine, and well you know it.'

My mother looked weary.

'He vows he has proof of such, distant as it is on your father's side,' she said. 'He has shown me letters—deeds of title; Master Priest has read them to me. He cannot make much of them, but there is something of validity.'

Forgeries, I thought. I said sharply: 'Deeds of title?'

'To half this property,' said Fray's nephew, and cast a glance around the parlour where a nice arras hung, gift from some long-deceased lord whom my father had contrived to amuse. Costly it was, woven all over with hawking knights and ladies, and bordered with hounds and grapes. His eyes took inventory; there was a fine glass window on to the street, a small coffer of Spanish chestnut, several carved oaken chairs. My mother was silent. I looked from one face to the other, starting a sweat of incredulous anger.

'My master's a fair man, sir and mistress,' said the youth. 'He bids me acquaint you again of his devotion and seeks your agreement to his proposal.'

To my relief she shook her head.

'I will have none of him.' Her voice was faint but steady. 'As to this claim to half my livelode, it is all fog and mist.'

'He will secure it without you, then,' said the ferret-face, while I gaped at him. 'Choose, dame, and I will bear your message back to my uncle. He would get these affairs settled once and for all.'

I have a temper. Looking at this young oaf, knock-kneed, his doublet foul with ale, then at my mother in her clean trim apron and neat kerchief, I came to the boil and overflowed.

'Get you gone,' I said, my words hot in my throat.

'I will go when I wish,' answered the ferret in a squeaking voice. 'Master Dan has not yet his answer.'

I stepped up close. 'Nor will he get one,' said I in a fury. 'For he sends a puling whelp to do a man's work. All you see here is rightly my mother's, by her own labour, and no poxy falsified deed can say otherwise. This shop was hers while your uncle was busy stealing the rings off slain soldiers in France, and you were still at pap.'

He put up his fist to me, and I laughed out loud. I took my staff to his head, and the blood flowed on to my mother's clean boards, while he howled like a dog, folding his arms over his skull.

'Take this message to your master,' I said, and he flew downstairs, through the seething shop and out into the street. I spun his oily cap after him through the window.

I turned back to my mother, triumphant.

'It was well that I came by this day,' I said.

Her hands were trembling. 'I am not so sure,' she, said anxiously. 'You should not have struck him—his uncle will be wroth indeed. Oh! and to think that villain spoke me so fair these past months!'

'There'll be no more business from that soapy pack,' I said; but I realized her feelings were wounded—that she had taken some pleasure in thinking she was still a woman to evoke tenderness.

'He will send others,' she said, distressed. 'Men stronger than that boy—he will set this place by the ears; others whispered that he wrought them ill but I didn't believe it.'

'Others?' I said.

'Mistress Petson.' Her lips were tight. 'Some tale of how he claimed she owed him money. She stood fast, and had her windows smashed by night—ruffians that ran too swiftly for the Watch to take them.'

'Extortion! In Chepe!' I cried. 'Certes, I would have thought folk were too well dined here for such ill-humoured tricks.'

'He has not been to dine with me lately—oh, let's have no more ado with it,' she said suddenly, descending again into the sweaty shop. 'I have a marriage party to look to in an hour.'

She squeezed my arm. 'Come back again to see me,' she whispered, and I promised to return soon, advising her to bar her doors by night—though I was secretly well pleased that I had sent Fray's lout off with such a straight answer, and thought we would hear no more of it.

There had been one last assault from the Lancastrians, when the Bastard of Fauconberg, with his force of Kentish men, made an attack on the south gate of London. Lords Essex and Rivers drove him back and held his army in abeyance until the King's advance guard arrived, whereupon Fauconberg took fright and fled to where his ships lay in Sandwich harbour.

Then King Edward sent his brother Gloucester to quell the Bastard. It seemed no time at all before he returned, with the penitent Fauconberg suing for peace. This was the final campaign. I remember feeling a mixture of gratitude to God and a vague treasonable pity for those who had suffered most; the pawns on a great battle-board, a fierce game that, with real knights toppling, queens and would-be queens befouled with mud and curses.

Old, mad Harry the Sixth lay on a catafalque in St Paul's. I went with the rest to look at the waxen white face of saint or idiot, none would ever know. Still and exposed he was, between the straight figures of a guard of honour. A strangely eerie sight. The church seemed full of ghosts that shrieked silently in fury or torment. I was glad to leave the vaulted quietness and rejoin the sun-drenched crowds outside, now gaping at a new spectacle.

It was the Duke of Gloucester returning from Kent, with Fauconberg riding meekly behind him under the White Boar standard. Gloucester marked the crush of people outside Paul's, turned to his esquire with a question. 'Old Harry's dead,' they were saying. 'He pined and dwined of sheer melancholy.' For an instant I saw Gloucester's face. It whitened, he bit his lip. Some said he loved the saintly, traitorous old fool.

So peace came to England, and though his Grace laboured long of days to restore his shaken government, the merry nights returned; oh yes, we capered. And thus it befell that though I was far from forgetting my mother's anxiety and the threats of Master Dan, I had no chance to visit her for many weeks, because of my duty to the King. To amuse the Princesses was a joy, not a labour; but their mother! Marry, there was scant humour in her. More regal than any born of a long line of monarchs, she seldom thawed to a smile. Great diamonds she wore, and pigeon-blood rubies, Italian collars of silver weeping pearls large as a finger's nail, and more rings even than the French bitch was wont to wear. Mostly her gown was black—she spent hours in the Royal Chapel, and her pale confessors were seen to wander wearily after her wherever she would go.

That summer we rode down to Eltham while Baynard's Castle was being cleansed and I was glad, for I had feared we might move to Greenwich, and I had memories both sweet and sour... there it was I used to steal up on to the gallery to talk with the Maiden. Little did she know or care that I could have lost my post through it—each time I skipped away my heart was in my mouth that the King would look for diversion among his fools and find one missing. The Maiden beggared protocol. Once, I brought her up a red apple, I who would have given her rubies, and she tossed the core over the balustrade at Thomas Grey, who turned in anger on his brother Dick, while the Maiden laughed among the shadows like a witless woman. The tears rolled down her face; I marvelled how she wept for a space long after the end of laughter. She would not tell me why.

I tried to guard that little damsel when I had the chance. I know that folk try to make out there's no such thing as love, only barter and bargain, and that women lead us all to Hell, but I loved her. I think she was fond of me, and others must have thought the same. Often I came up against that French-born witch of a friend of hers, that Elysande, who looked sly and mocking at me and spoke of paramours. I would like to have turned her skirts over her head. She was a mischief-weaver, and more than that, for the last I heard of her was in France, where she had flown to the kin of her dead husband, changing her allegiance like a running hare.

We had the jousting and the games at Eltham. Despite his hair shirt, Anthony Rivers excelled once more at all things; and when they had packed up the tents and banners and loaded the carts with all the groaning knights who had been maimed in the fierce sport, we returned to Westminster. I rode by the serjeant of the minstrels, Master Alexander Carlile. King Edward was very agreeable to him; it was the serjeant who had roused him in the middle of the night when John Neville's men were breaking down the gates at Doncaster. Doubtless this swift action saved the lives of his Grace and Lords Hastings, Rivers and Gloucester. He told me of that wild crossing to the Low Countries, and the five months' maddening exile in Bruges and Flushing.

Also we spoke of the jousting lately ended, and of old tourneys, reliving with a little mirth the most famous occasion of all: that contest between Rivers and Antoine of Burgundy, a day nearly ending in disaster.

'His Grace the Bastard of Burgundy vowed my lord used illegal harness, and weapons of trickery,' said Master Carlile.

'When he did but fight with a nag's head,' I gibed. For a time we conjured again the whole spectacle: the loges at Smithfield blazing with tapestries and the satin and silk of the nobility; King Edward in purple with the Garter; foreign diplomats dotting the stands like a pox—the ambassador of Charolais, come to finalize plans for the marriage of Edward's sister Margaret with Duke Charles; Olivier de la Marche, the Burgundian chronicler, anxious to trap every moment; Butcher Tiptoft of Worcester, Arbiter of Chivalry for the day, smiling in complacent gladness. Then the preliminary skirmishing with swords, dismay and scandal. For when the two knights tilted fiercely at each other, the Burgundian's horse rammed its head into Lord Rivers's saddle and fell dead. The noble rider lay still, pinned beneath the destrier's weight, while the crowd rose with a thundering roar of disbelief.

'Do you recall how exceedingly displeased he seemed?'

'Yea, for when his Grace asked if he wished another mount, he replied it was "no season" and retired.'

'Twas well he was unharmed,' I said. I had at that moment remembered that even then Warwick was conniving in France with King Louis.

Riding through fields of harvest, the hay-apple smell sweet and bitter, we spoke of Warwick, and as night follows day, we spoke of his widow, immured in Beaulieu Sanctuary, and of his youngest daughter Anne, whom Richard of Gloucester hankered to marry.

'I think his Grace will have Anne Neville,' said Master Carlile, with an unshakable air.

'I heard the King forbade the match,' I said cautiously.

'Yes, while her father lived and the Duke would not go against him; but now he seeks his reward, and he's earned it, certes. Though George of Clarence is wrath—he is her self-appointed guardian. Vast estates she has. But the King loves Gloucester.'

Something in this tickled my spleen. I remembered the little Neville well; thin and fair and flaxen, with a gentle smile and small, anxious hands. 'Now he seeks his reward,' Master Carlile had said. Her mother's lands were forfeit to the Crown. With a sudden distaste I thought of Dan Fray, who had talked of love to my mother, and to what purpose, and then envisaged Gloucester, distant and frowning these past weeks. I had seen him wandering about the Palace at evening, preoccupied with what thoughts one could only guess at. George had married Isabel Neville—Richard's almost perverse loyalty had curbed his own ambition. As we rode I wondered whether there was a spark of tenderness in him for poor, beleaguered Anne, and saw the red eyes of greed in the face of Fray's nephew, sweeping up the contents of my mother's parlour with a glance.

'He has not seen her of late,' I said. The serjeant looked oddly at me.

'So? He saw her, and so did I, after Tewkesbury. I had blown my last attack and the enemy were cut to pieces or drowning in the stream; my lord Stanley came to take the French Queen. She had just learned that her son was slain. By my loyalty! her screams rang in my head for days.'

'And Warwick's daughter?'

'Still, she sat, and the colour of a tallow dip. Eyes open, seeing naught. Then up rode Gloucester—harness shining with blood—even his horse's coat black with it—and he doffed his helm and looked at her. Hair wild, eyes rimmed with blood and mire on his face. And the maid, corpse-mute, staring as if he were the foul fiend.'

'Did he speak?' I asked.

'Nay, not a word. Yet he looked at her, for a long space, with a strange look. Then he turned and rode off to join the King, while Anne was taken under the protection of Duke George, to her sister's house. The Neville affairs are entirely in his hands, so he says. Thus her inheritance lies safe within his walls, until the maiden shall be married.'

I had noted the dark glances between Clarence and Gloucester. The picture was emerging.

'And yet,' he continued, 'I think my lord of Gloucester will have his way. For the King's Grace is inclined to dismiss Clarence's right of wardship as nebulous.'

I saw life as a spread chessboard neatly partitioned, though some of the black ran into the white at times. It shifted and wavered in my vision. The smallest pawn was Anne of Warwick, a little ivory figure. The Maiden and I were not on the board—we were of no importance, and I was glad of it.

Then suddenly we had reached the top of Shooters Hill, and there was London, again lying like a wanton along the breast of the swift river, while in the distance all the green turned blue as it merged with the hills of Hampstead and Highgate. Down the slope we came with a throng of people all hurrying to be within the walls by sunset. Their frantic haste put me in mind of a rhyme. I took out my tablets to snare it, and the fortunes of the nobility faded and were gone.

The Master of the Revels had his eye on me. I knew it, and he knew that I knew it. He was minded that my jests were too bold, and would have had me booted from the court had not the King unwittingly shielded me with his ready smile. None could gainsay his Grace in matters of pleasure, and I was a very small matter for dissent. Though there were a few, deeply devout, who would fain have called the Church down about our ears, with their rumblings that we trouvères—to wit, 'jesters, jugglers, histrios, dancing women and harlots'—were lewd leaders to damnation and the Devil. Strong words these, for the belly of one who worked hard for his money. I would have found solace in giving the Revels Master my task for a day. He would have taken his bed a wearier man, and stiff of limb.

One late summer evening he was watching me, and he was robed and regal and ready to frown. We, the joculatores, skilled in singing, in recounting of fable spiced with mime and posture, had been summoned to the King's chamber. It was an island of informality betwixt the outer hall of reception and the inner mysteries of Edward's bedroom. Within this middle haunt the King would snatch his pleasure after hours of wrangling in the chair of Council. He sat fair-humouredly, his astute brain free to wander, like his well-shaped hands to the dish of grapes and walnuts near his couch. A few of his intimates stood about him. There was a lady there, Elizabeth Lucey, whose husband had met his death fighting for the Royal House... the King made much of her. Did I not say he rewarded loyalty well? In her butterfly headgear and gown of sapphire silk, she looked queenly. There is treason. Lord Hastings had his gaze on her, as she sat on her little velvet cushion, and his smooth jaw quivered with the fullness of his thoughts.

And the Master of the Revels had his eye on me.

I fancied I excelled myself at reciting one of the *Gesta Romanorum*, one of those tales fashioned by the monk Pierre Bercheur at the convent of Saint Eloi. Latin lends well to a double meaning. The King beckoned me nearer. I shot a sly complacent glance at my mentor as I drew a new pack of cards from my sleeve. I threw them high in a rainbow skein from one hand to the other. Some charlatans use a silk thread through the pack: I first mastered the trick when I was eight years old and was beaten if I dared to let them drop thereafter.

'If you, most dread Sire, would...'

'Take a card,' laughed Edward. He reached out his fingers. He liked cards. Dame Elizabeth Lucey stretched her fair neck like a flower. I palmed the Death Card quickly ere he should take it. Kings must only see and hear what is good. The royal astrologer stood near, fingering his pearl reliquary. Edward's hand hovered over the blind, spread fan of cards. A distant sound, growing louder, came to our ears. Heads turned at the noise of two sharp voices outside. A henchman tapped, entered, knelt. He announced that the Dukes of Clarence and Gloucester sought audience. Edward raised his eyebrows.

'Bid them come.'

I stayed, one foot lightly on the dais, my eyes on my cards. Under my lids I could study George and Dickon as they entered. Clarence came first, laughing a little ill-temperedly. He flew the pink flag of temper on his cheek, but he was full of grace as he kissed the King's hand.

'Talk! talk! by my faith, it's thirsty work,' he remarked. Crossing to a side table, he lifted and drained a cup of hypocras. Edward's keen eyes smiled.

'Come, my lord, here's something to intrigue—a new piece of magic from our friend. He seeks to blind us with swift skill.'

Clarence leaned over me. The smell of wine was a heavy song on his breath. His bright hair fell about his rosy cheeks. A young pagan god was he, tall and gilded, but alas! the hand that touched the cards was over-plump, and trembled.

'Good fellow, what is it?'

Edward said softly: 'A game of chance, fair prince,' and for a brief instant the plump hand was rigid, and I knew that even my little diversion had its use, the reminder of old sins.

George laughed too loud. He straightened his back. 'I'm done with such,' he said with a candour that made me squirm. 'Besides, I am lucky in love—' He turned to include the silent Gloucester in his charming smile. 'Therefore I should not meddle with these nice tricky pastimes, neither will I.'

Gloucester moved forward into my sight. White as a ghost, more slender than ever, he looked as if he could be broken in two. His hair shone dark, and his eyes smouldered. Quietly he said: 'Your Grace, I would speak with you on a matter of gravest importance.'

'Concerning?' said Edward gently.

Richard glanced at my intruding figure almost with hatred. He fiddled with his finger-rings. In the privacy of our stable, we fools often mimicked him; but then we aped everyone, from the Dowager Duchess downwards; it was sport. Discreetly I huddled from the step, and watched him. I would have thought he might have looked happier, for lately he had again earned the King's praise. There had been trouble on the Scottish border. The North was a seat of unrest, and the King was cautious in his attitude to Lord Percy, Earl of Northumberland. Thus he had accorded his youngest brother the Wardenship of the North, all dead Warwick's commands. Richard had resigned his offices of Chief Justice and Chamberlain of Wales to the new Earl of Pembroke and now, with his northern holdings went Warwick's estates: Sheriff Hutton, Penrith and, above all, his beloved Middleham. He should have looked happier, but by his demeanour, these things were not enough. Something vexed him, and judging by Clarence's uncomfortably high spirits, I knew what it was. Earl Warwick's lands were Richard's, but not the Countess's, and the marriage ring was not yet on her daughter's finger. I heard Anne Neville's name, and knew that Gloucester still hankered. Little Anne, buffeted and tossed from the arms of the fierce, arrogant Silver Swan to those of the strange, unsmiling Silver Boar. Anne, who had looked with terror on the bloody Richard at Tewkesbury and who trailed the fetters of vast wealth. I glared at Gloucester, and catching his long dark eye, hastily turned my baleful look into a fool's grimace.

I was thinking that I must go back and see my mother, and that all men were acquisitive save for myself, who would have wedded the Maiden in the shift she stood up in, when a sudden explosion from the dais came.

'O Jesu! Cannot you, my lords, be at peace one with another?' The King's jovial mood was gone. He sat bolt upright on the couch, glowering at his brothers. Elizabeth Lucey scuttled off her cushion and fled. Lord Hastings studied his nails, while Thomas Grey smirked openly from behind the dais.

'Sire,' said Richard, 'how shall I live happily with one who will not give me answer?'

The King turned his fierce look upon Clarence.

'How say you, my lord?' he demanded. 'It seems the lady Anne is no longer in your household. Where shall my brother find her?'

Clarence turned up his eyes. 'Fair Sire,' he said eventually, 'it grieves me, by my loyalty, that I cannot ease our noble brother. Though I know he desires the lady my sister-in-law, how can I help? For, since Your Grace would have it that I own no wardship over her—her whereabouts are surely no concern of mine.'

George's tongue was gold. This statement was a mingling of airy simplicity and innocent amazement. Richard kept silence under the King's troubled gaze.

'Well, sir?' said Edward.

'I'm of the opinion,' said Richard with difficulty, 'that she is concealed somewhere.'

Clarence laughed gently. 'Likely, good brother,' he murmured. 'But 'tis naught to me. London is a great place, likewise York, or Canterbury or any other fair town. She is but a little maid,' he mused.

He came over to me, where I still held the cards fanned out.

'Let us play one game of hazard, Dickon,' he said kindly, and under cover of his sleeve flicked up the cards for a lightning look. Richard stood mute, his hands behind his back. I could almost hear his thoughts, as the Countess of Warwick's lands, so nearly gained, were slipping from his grasp.

'Come!' George said. 'Won't you tempt Dame Fortune? Draw a card, and see if the omens are good!'

Gloucester was silent.

'Then I must play alone,' sighed George, and with thumb and finger tweaked out a card. I knew what it was for I had placed them; so did he, for he had cheated. Richard's face, when confronted by the Queen of Diamonds, betrayed little, and the jest went sour. He made an obeisance to the frowning King, and quit the room. The minstrels quietly gathered up their instruments.

'Certes, I found a lady,' murmured Clarence. 'A grey-eyed lady for my noble brother, but he misliked her.' I followed the tall prince in the wake of a soft French air that drifted from his lips and on the terrace waylaid him. There I showed him a little game—played with three walnut shells and a pea, and he achieved much skill with it, laughed for full five minutes, and gave me a mark.

Richard had gone, tight-lipped, down to the armoury, or I would have sought to please him with it too. Would I though? There was no humour in him, and I knew I would only be wasting my time.

⋆

Robert Hawkins played the shawm, John Green the lute, and exceptionally tuneful were they, in sounds both sacred and secular. Also they had another love, that being gambling. So, through my lord of Gloucester's whim, I had a wager of two marks with John, and the price of a good pair of hose with Robert, and I would have had the stakes doubled had it not been for their cautiousness, so sure of victory was I.

'My lord went down into Southwark two days ago,' Robert said uneasily. 'He took with him a train of henchmen, two knights and some fellows in jacks and sallets—while yesterday he was combing the ward of Bishopsgate and had an hour's talk with the Prioress of St Mary Spital.'

I laughed merrily and measured my leg against his, for the new hose.

'I will have them in green,' I said. 'And sure enough 'tis a fool that will place them on my feet. For does his Grace seek to find the lady all among the Bishop of Winchester's geese?'

This was a time-honoured jest among us. Once, the bagnios that housed the whores over the river paid rent to the Bishop's bailiffs, and brought him in a tidy sum.

'Today he went alone, and on foot,' said John. 'With but two squires to guard him.' He sighed. 'Jesu! he loves her.'

'There's no such thing as love,' I said. And I tried to believe it, for my own heart's peace.

John took up his lute. His voice was pure, falsetto, silver, to set the hair on your head tingling.

'Belle, qui tiens ma vie
Captive de tes yeux
Qui ma l'âme ravie
Ton souris gracieux.
Vientôt me secourir
Ou me faudra mourir.'

'Pretty,' said I. 'But he will never find her. He may have slain her husband at Tewkesbury, but she'll stay widowed if my lord of Clarence has half the wit...'

John rested his lute on his knee. 'I never knew it was Gloucester that killed the French Queen's son,' he said, interested.

'My cousin was in the battle's thick,' I boasted. 'Were not the young princes rivals for Anne of Warwick?'

I embroidered, as Alexander Carlile had done, and my colours were even brighter than his. So is history made. Detail and truth both done to death for drama's sake, with hard bright fact concealed under the pretty swirl of histrionics. I am no worse, no better. Others have done it. But so is truth butchered, for the sake of a song.

They hung on my words, and they composed a sad little tune.

'His horse's bardings—black with the gore of. the fallen.'

This I liked well, and should it be the lady's husband's blood, splashed up from Gloucester's blade, an even more thrilling ballad could be fashioned. Unluckily for me, a few words of this lay (which smacked of unchivalry) crept to my cousin's ears. He sent a boy to fetch me to where he was practising at the butts. I watched him admiringly as he drew his bow. Muscle the size of an orange blossomed under the fine hide of each sleeve. The thrum and swish of his dart caused the heads of the watching esquires to turn; against the cloudless sky it cleaved an arc, striking the target just south of the bull. My cousin swore softly, but I clapped hands and cried bravo. Anthony Rivers took up his turn, standing a good yard back from my cousin's mark, and loosed a clean quill. Under the cries of acclaim, my cousin said softly: 'So you deem yourself a chronicler, kinsman,' and flashed his steel-grey eyes at me. I was a little put out and busied myself applauding Lord Stanley's shot.

'I've heard your account of Tewkesbury,' he continued drily. 'I knew naught of my little cousin's war-lust. Mayhap I can arrange a battle for you to see all first-hand.'

The thought of fighting made me quake. 'Sir, what have I said?'

'Lies, tales of murder in the field,' he growled.

So I stood on one leg and sang:

'I saw a codfish corn sow,
And a worm a whistle blow,
And a pie treading a crow,
I will have the whetstone, and I may.'

'Fool,' he muttered.

'Yea, 'tis my calling,' said I.

'You may yet have the whetstone,' he said. 'Hung about your neck for perjuring my account of a bloody battle nobly fought.'

'I'll do penance,' I whined. Only last week I'd seen a convicted liar in the market-place, with folk sharpening their knives on the great stone around his throat.

'Sit, then,' he commanded. 'I'll tell you of Tewkesbury.'

So I sat, and the sun was hot, and I closed my eyes the better to hear his tale; and woke with a jump to a cool breeze and his voice, quieter now, saying: 'Thus ended the House of Lancaster. Not, good friend, with silly tales of stabbings over a maid's hand, but in dust, and heat, and honour.'

'It's a fine story,' I said, blinking. He looked so sternly at me I wondered if he knew I'd been asleep. All he said was:

'More credible than yours,' and I answered meekly:

'I will have the whetstone, kinsman,' and left him. I had thought to mention Dan Fray and my mother, but I thought he might wax wroth at my clouting the nephew and risking a brawl, so I thought better of it and went to visit her myself.

The cookshop was hotter than ever. The smell of dead dinners clung to the buckram hangings of the kitchen-chamber and the rushes were greasy with fat-splashes. I leaned on one side of the fireplace until the cook, with a heavy politeness, told me I was in his way. So I retreated to watch all the diversities of cunning employed by the cook-knaves. One was preparing a venison frumenty; he had leched the meat into strips and had his wheaten soup made ready, to which he was adding egg yolks, salt and sugar. Another, more ambitious, struggled uneasily with a *fylettes en galantyne*, stirring chopped roast pork and onions into beef broth boiled with pepper, cinnamon, cloves and mace. Old Mary was grinding fresh brawn in a mortar. I watched her temper it with almond meats and strain the mess into an earthenware dish, boiling the mixture with sugar and cloves, thickening it with cinnamon and ginger. The near-solid mass took shape—a hare, was it? a hog? I was about to ask her, when my mother appeared, beckoning me from half-way up the stairs. In the upper room, I knew there had been trouble. Her face said it.

'He's been back,' I murmured.

'Yea, and none of your persuasions have swayed the uncle, for he came himself, and snared me in my own parlour, chasing me round the table. I was distressed enough to go say an Ave and a Pater at your father's tomb, I who had his Month's Mind kept all these past years.'

Rageful and sorely anxious, I said: 'You should have married Butcher Gould. You know as well as I how widows are fair game. Even now 'tis not too late to get you to the Minories.'

'Never!' she cried. 'I am not shaped for the cloister, and I'll marry none. This'—she gestured around—'is my all. 'Twill take more than Master Fray to drive me out.'

I gave her a moment to cool and she ran downstairs; she said she smelled burning and was anxious for a special order—a dozen eel-and-grape pies, coming to their peak. When she returned I asked: 'Has his nephew's pate healed yet? Tell me, that I may break it again.'

'I feared for that, too. He talked of summonsing you for assault on the lad. He held this over me if I did not submit.'

'I'm in his Grace's service,' I said wildly. Even so, I thought of John Davy, late favourite of the King, who had had his hand cut off for striking a man in front of King's Bench at Westminster Hall. I saw myself fleeing again into Sanctuary, wading into the sea after my forty days' grace crying: 'Passage, for the love of God and King Edward!' like any common felon. And the King would take unkindly to my fleeing the judgement of his Mayor—hiding beneath the clergy's mantle. Then, with relief, I remembered that Fray, with a tavern full of whores in their striped rays and Lancastrian spies thick as roaches, would be ill-advised to seek a lawsuit. All ale-sellers were reckoned guilty; whatever the matter.

'He would find no sympathy at the sessions, I'd dare my next feastday wage,' I said. 'We'll have him for trespass—we'll appeal to the Gild. He has been uttering threats against your person.'

An unwilling smile curved her mouth.

'The Gild is not much concerned with personal matters,' she murmured. 'Anyway, he said that all he offered was an honourable proposal of marriage—no threat has passed his lips—he did but offer me protection.'

'By God!' I said sourly. 'He is as cunning as Clarence! Naught to lay hold of, and in his ways as stubborn as a mule.'

She was instantly distracted.

'Ah, poor young Gloucester!' she said. 'All the City watch for him daily. My boys were in Smithfield yesterday and saw him questioning the horse-copers. Billingsgate likewise, among the fish merchants. He has paid his respects to every Abbess in town. The lady Anne has vanished from human sight, and Gloucester's like one of Arthur's knights in search of the Grail.'

'Cast in solid gold and weighty with gems,' I remarked.

'So!' she said keenly. 'Is there love?'

'Barter,' said I.

'What of Clarence?'

I told her about the playing cards and she grimaced. 'A bad jest,' and then: 'But I would not speak against Clarence outside these walls.' She gestured, east.

'Three doors down,' she said. 'Although they are under Duke George's patronage, I mislike that woman. She whispered that I gave short weight in my mutton pasties and since Corpus Christi last our dealings have been few.'

She laughed at my indignation.

'Put up your staff, before you break more heads. It will be a long while before they hang my pies about my neck on Cornhill. Words can't hurt me when I know my merchandise is good.'

'We have strayed,' I said. 'What had Fray to say finally?'

'He gave me till Michaelmas for the banns to be cried. I told him the same answer, so he waved his plaguey deeds of title before my face. I said he would have to bring this before the justices of this ward and the courts are jammed with suits. We shall have a few months' breathing space.'

'But you can't go on like this!' I cried. 'Tell him to go to the Devil!'

She squared her shoulders. 'That was my last injunction. I'll take what he brings, and I'll best him.' I leaped from the table and embraced her.

'If there's trouble...'

'Can I call on you?' she said timidly.

'Yes, ask Butcher Gould to send a boy to the Palace—the King thinks much of him since he succoured Elizabeth in Sanctuary. They'll give a message.'

'Only if there's real mischief.'

'I shall come straightway.' To end a disquieting hour with jesting, I told her of my wager, and bade her commend me to her silkmaid at Michaelmas to make me a costly new hose; that is, if the Duke of Gloucester had not found his lady by then.

I walked down Eastchepe into the widening strip of Candlewick Street with its lines of mercers' and drapers' shops displaying rich cloth; then, because I had time to spare, strolled up Tower Street. I stopped for a swift mazer of ale in the Boar's Head. Sir John Howard was there, entertaining strangers; I made way with full courtesy, and the commonalty in turn fell back for me. The crenellated turrets of the Tower stood stark against the haze of the September afternoon. Within that building I had often entertained the King. My mind turned idly to the woman who doubtless now paced up and down behind one of those faraway slits in the great white fortress. Margaret of Anjou: I'd heard that her hair had turned grey from the loss of her son. I wondered if she wept, too, for old Harry. And Somerset—Beaufort had been her last link with a dead love; men said his father, the old Earl, had bedded with the French Queen. Like Owen Tudor and Queen Katherine.

Thinking of the slain Prince, I thought again of Anne Neville, Richard Gloucester, and the wager. I had given John and Robert until Michaelmas, and knew my money safe. He would never find her. Idly I wondered where she was, and decided she had got herself out of England—but to whom? In my mind I saw her little, childish face, blonde-framed. I had seen it often at court before the rift with Warwick; to deem her friendless made me rather sad.

That evening I brought a goat into the Hall and made a parody of John Lydgate's 'Little Short Ditty against Horns', I dressed the beast in a hennin filched from a Flemish dancing maid, and there was much mirth and not a few red faces under the extravagant headgear of the court ladies. I plied my craft with gusto and genuine feeling—I have thought it a shame to conceal a woman's hair, her fairest possession—and when I plucked out a few hairs from the goat's brow, aping a tiring wench, and caused it to bleat and butt me in the nether end—the company laughed like demons. Therefore one did not heed the few glum and abstracted persons who sat, toying with their trenchers and staring into air. Richard Gloucester was one of these. He had come in late, a little footsore I swear and glad to be seated, his face worn and weary and unsmiling. My own magical powers took hold of me and I half-killed myself trying to make him laugh, but to no avail. By the end of the entertainment I had the strangest feeling of kinship with him. For I, too, had wandered many weeks in search of my love, and I remembered how people had chaffed me. This feeling grew stronger until I reminded myself of

Gloucester's motives; I drew a callous skin over my soul and thought of how Anne Neville, if she remained hidden, would make of me a fashionable man.

Neither did the Queen smile. When the Maiden was at court, we would talk of Elizabeth—I got some sly kind of sport from the days of Grafton Regis, when food was sparse and the rod heavy on my poor sweeting's back. King Edward's wooing—ah, God! that sweet, innocent conversation:

'Lady Grey went for a walk in Whittlebury Forest and was nearly run down by the King's horse.'

Marry, what would Lady Grey expect? Everyone knew that Whittlebury was a royal chase. If that were an accident that she were there on that day, holding a fatherless boy by each hand under the Queen's Oak, then I had six toes on either foot. All sorrowful beauty would she be, suing piteously for the restoration of Bradgate, her children's inheritance. They had been dispossessed following the defeat of Lancaster at St Alban's. Sir John Grey had been knighted by Mad Harry at Colney in the spring of 1461, but had died of his wounds shortly afterwards. No wonder food was short at Grafton; Elizabeth Woodville had been near destitution. Fortune smiles on the fair. And the not so fair. As early as 1461 the King had affectionately considered the benefit of Jacquetta Duchess of Bedford, his cozen's mother. He paid her an annual stipend of 300 marks—and 100 livres in advance. Lust makes fools of all. Even Kings.

I bowed low before the royal pair, and the goat got loose and bolted round the hall, sweeping a tablecloth off with its horns. The Master of the Revels made a note in his book and looked at me, and I gave him obeisance.

In the space between the end of dinner, and supper at four, John, Robert and I, and others employed in the sweet pursuit of do-naught, would gather near the entry to Westminster Hall. There we would watch the world and his wife, and some exceeding pretty wives there were, in truth. We stood under the Clock House, and as the last deep note throbbed and burgeoned and died (and we waited for our hearing to return) Lady Elizabeth Lucey rode out from the Palace on a splendid bay. Green velvet she wore, and her headgear was almost as high as the Clochard spire with its three giant bells which, men said, soured all the drink in the town. John affected a swoon at sight of the lady. Robert said, soft and knowing:

'His Grace had me make music for that sweet face in his inner chamber.'

We trusted one another. I said: 'Love songs, I doubt not.'

He nodded. 'Well, the Queen had the costliest new device. Italianate silverwork collar and baubles for her ears—a fair bargain.'

'Riches or love, which would you?' asked Robert. I thought of Gloucester and shrugged, saying: ''Tis all the same, it seems.'

None could resist the King; I reckoned no surprise at it, so beautiful a person was he, and for the sheer pleasure of the words on my tongue, I quoted gently:

'Now is the Rose of Rouen grown to great honour
Therefore sing we every one blessed be that flower
I warn ye every one that he shall understand
There sprang a Rose in Rouen that spread to England
Had not the Rose of Rouen been, all England had been dour,
Y-blessed be the time God ever spread that flower.'

So we sang Edward's Coronation song, and continued to watch: the serjeants of the Crown in their silken hoods and the lawyers in long gowns of striped ray hurrying in and out the door of the great Hall of Westminster; jammed with suits, as my mother had said, like any other City Court. That splendid building was erected by King William the Red, and rebuilt in magnificence by Richard of Bordeaux; whose wife was Anne. The fellow Gloucester was on my mind again, and I shook him off like a flea. There were comings and goings from the Hall; above was the Court of Chancery, and the busy Exchequer and Star Chamber, womb of many stern laws. The Court of Common Pleas too lay within, and King's Bench, where Edward had sat for three days together at the start of his reign. All about milled the plaintiffs and defendants, the suitors and witnesses, the red robes of aldermen mingling with the commonalty's poor worsted. Flemings, in the sad-coloured smocks and hanging liripipes hawked pins and spectacles and fine felt hats, while nearby an amateur fiddler scraped a hideous noise for groats. Fierce-eyed cook-knaves, their manners more thrusting even than in Eastchepe, blustered of fine fare at the gate, clutching at hastening lawyers with their cries. Wretches hang that jurymen may dine.

Barefoot, travel-seamed, in a dusty-grey habit, a Franciscan touched my sleeve. He gave me a blessing. 'Sir, I seek the London lodging of my house.'

'You'll hear the Jesus bells of St Paul's, Father,' I told him. 'North of Paul on Newgate you'll find your church and cloister.'

'And the library?' His weary eyes lit up. 'That which the Sun of Marchandy, Sir Richard Whittington, so generously endowed?'

I nodded. 'You've travelled far?'

'From Norwich.' He fingered his wooden crucifix. 'God's mercy on all there.'

I heard the inrush of breath behind me.

'Plague,' I said softly... He smiled wanly as John and Robert shrank from him.

'Fear naught,' he murmured. 'Weeks I lay, my bones dissolving to water, but the Lord spared me. I am whole again.'

I felt for a coin—he was not importunate, and it was luck to fill his wooden bowl. 'God be good to your house,' I said.

A slender dark shadow fell across us. I looked into the face of the Duke of Gloucester and saw it to be weary and grim with a look of restless days and nights. The Franciscan's bowl was still extended and Richard dropped a gold piece and bowed his head briefly, passing on. The friar looked after him wistfully.

'*Benedicite*,' he whispered.

'His Grace of Gloucester,' I told him.

'I have seen him before, my son,' he said gently. 'Two years ago, before all the troubles in this realm, be came to Our Lady of Walsingham with the King. I spoke with him then, though he could not have remembered me.'

But he had remembered him, I thought. As the friar blessed us and moved away, I wondered deeply. What manner of man was Richard? There was no doubt in my mind: after two years, he had given recognition to an impoverished and anonymous friar. For some reason I began to feel much incensed. I heard the others whispering.

'He should not have come to London,' Robert said grimly. 'Death can be carried—by God, I didn't know they had plague in Norwich.'

'Nor I,' whispered John, all jelly-trembling.

'You should wear the bezoar stone,' I said, laughing again, and I fingered my talisman, smooth and round within my pouch. While I jested and saw their courage returning, I felt cold, thinking of the sudden crippling dizziness that assailed a man even in the ale-house; the orange-sized hard swelling in the armpit, the black vomit, the fires of Hell...

So I comforted them.

'*Carpe diem*,' Robert said: 'When his Grace sent us to play at Bungay six weeks gone, I heard no talk of plague at Norwich, for I and the King's bearward were only speaking of sickness.'

'They had no plague in Norwich,' said John, 'since August five years past, when hundreds died. Mistress Paston's household left town for fear of it.'

'One case,' Robert argued. 'The Lady Eleanor Butler. She died in the house of the Carmelites three years ago.'

'That was not the plague,' John insisted. 'At first they thought it lung fever—but she died bewitched—no prayers or simples could aid her. They said she courted death, and went willingly.'

'What talk for a fine day!' I cried. 'Pestilence, and tombs, and white faces, and my lord of Gloucester wandering the streets like a walking curse. All be merry, as I!' and I snatched a pair of spectacles from a Flemish pedlar, donned them and, blinded instantly, walked smack into a wall.

'Patch, I mislike this wager of ours,' said Robert.

'So you'd withdraw,' I said. 'You have not the wherewithal to pay me when I win.'

'Nay,' said Robert. He thought it too sorry a matter for gambling on. The Lady Anne was the Lord knew where, and her mother, Countess of Warwick, was in durance in the Sanctuary of Beaulieu, and it was, in effect, her money we were gaming on.

'She has petitioned the Commons that she has never done aught to offend the King; she has sought safe-conduct in vain, all her estates being forfeit. She has written most piteously to the Queen's Grace, the Duchess of York, the King's daughters, and the Dowager Duchess of Bedford, all in her own hand in the absence of clerks. She tells of great affection between herself and her daughter Anne, and craves her whereabouts. What we are about seems knavish,' he said lamely.

'God's Passion!' I cried. 'What harm can it do?' John looked down, and shuffled his feet.

'I too,' he said. 'Last night I sang a song, and incurred my lord of Gloucester's displeasure, for he looked at me with a most terrible look.'

He raised his pure boy's voice and sang a dolorous French song so beautiful it made me want to howl like a wolf. People passing smiled with joy.

'Sing it in English,' I said. 'I thought you attended the *scholae minstrallorum* in Paris—yet your accent mazes me utterly.'

He reddened. 'I had ado with many Southerners,' he said.

'Alas, of you I should indeed complain
If it please you not that I see you again
My love, who has my soul enchained.
For without I see you wherever I be
All I behold displeases me
Nor, until then, shall I sated be.'

He spoke the words.

'It loses pith in the translation.'

I thought of the Maiden, and the sun went behind a cloud.

Butcher Gould's 'prentice rode a sweating palfrey, and the beast was nearly done. He had ridden hard to Westminster Palace, nearly a league's distance, and was short of breath himself, while the horse, its sides pumping in and out, stood making water on the cobbles outside the Palace gate, a thing forbidden in the meanest streets. I had thrown my cloak on inside out in my frenzy, and was clad in my worst suiting, for I had that evening been in rehearsal—trying out the dramatization of Ovid's *Art of Love*, with many effects *ad libitum*, and I had no mind for ruining good clothes by rolling on the floor with Flemish Jeane, so ill-prepared for a night's foray was I. I had not yet dared ask the boy what kind of trouble was afoot—the one gasped word was enough.

I had been bedwards and on my way to the panterer's to get my bread and ale and candle-ends when the message came. The King was sitting late in Council; there had been no entertainment. The gateman grumbled as he let me out, but he had that very day taken two shillings from me at dice so I clattered unrebuked on my mare into the September night to where Gould's boy waited. Together we rode in the direction of the Strand. There was a last gleam in the sky as we reached Temple Bar, but the serjeant closed the gate behind us and I was fast in the City for the night. So be it, I thought. If she needs me, I will risk reprimand. Our horses' hooves crashed on the cobbles in a dangerous, slippery ride. Few people were abroad; only the cressets of the Watch flickering on the edge of Candlewick Street, and the occasional ragged bundle in the gutter, groaning under a hunger-dream. Few people; that is, until we came into Eastchepe and saw a fair crowd. Then I knew, with sinking belly, what kind of mischief this was. The most dread enemy, after plague. Outside my mother's shop I threw my reins to one of the gawping crowd and ran into the fierce light of flames that feasted on dry timber, chuckled over greasy rushes, and roared approval as they fed.

My mother was wondrous calm. She was marshalling affairs, standing at the head of the line, swinging each bucket of water as it came to her hand through the blazing cookshop window. It looked as if the fire had been started just within, under the sill, and the frame was already destroyed. Now and then loose slivers of glass crashed to the ground. The lintel of the doorpost had caught. I seized a bucket, just as the cart drawn by two unquiet horses ground to a halt on iron wheels. 'Good man!' I cried to the driver, and filled my bucket from the slopping barrels aboard the wain. Others, silent and grimed, bent alongside me. Mistress Petson, shameless in her bedwrap, her long grey hair flying, stood wringing her hands, and I yelled to her to come fill a pail, but she seemed to have lost her reason. The frightened horses backed and plunged, so that the water barrels overflowed. Great wet patches flowed on to the cobbles, blood-red from the fire's reflection. The neighbours worked tirelessly—a swing, a splash, a deafening hiss as water fought flame. Yet the fire grew. I looked up to see the latten sign above the doorway bending in the heat, the whole square of metal drooping like a defeated banner, the gay colours blackening. A great terrible rage took hold of me. I fought my way to my mother's side.

'This is devil's work!'

'Not the devil, but his henchman.' She swung her bucket—the fire spat mockingly. I looked hard into a leaping flame and wished I saw Fray's tortured face in its midst. 'He warned me,' she gasped. 'God's curse on him.'

The barrels were empty again. With painful sloth, the wagon turned in the narrow street and made for the conduit in lumbering haste. But all the while the fire raged madly. All around were anxious faces.

'The whole street will go,' I heard.

'Yea, by cock!'

'Mother of God, how slow it is!' And two or three ran up the street to meet the approaching cart, filling their pails before the terrified horses had halted, racing back to cast the pitifully small streams of water through the roaring doorway. Someone had foreseen to save divers belongings: I saw the arras hastily rolled and leaning against the wall. The knights still hawked upon it, the grapes still bloomed. My mother's little chestnut coffer sat impassively on the cobbles.

The cookboys were doing their best, and I joined them in beating at the flames with strips of buckram torn from the walls. One of them, Walter Cleeve, whom I had ever thought half-wit, was worse than useless. In fact, when the rats, disturbed by the heat, started to run out of the doorway in dark, firelit streaks, he set his terrier on them, crying: 'Sa, sa, cy, avaunt, sohow!' like a lord in King Edward's otter-chase. I turned and dealt him a great buffet, and shoved a pail in his hand, just as the night Watch arrived, sternly demanding that firehooks be used. My mother pleaded with them.

'Sirs, don't pull it down—the roof remains untouched! Sirs, we'll save it!' She choked on a hot gust of smoke. I looked up to see billowing black blotting out the narrow gap of sky between the houses. They could not pull down the shop. The smarting in my eyes had naught to do with smoke. Again the water-cart trundled up—willing hands dipped and threw and dipped and wiped their brows, and cursing mingled with the pluming black haze.

My mother grasped my arm. 'The well!' she screamed.

I shook my head, dull, uncomprehending. 'We have no well,' I muttered, but she pointed to where, three doors down, the woman who said my mother gave short weight, who enjoyed the Duke of Clarence's patronage, was calmly soaking her own door-frame with water.

'She has a well in her courtyard—hurry,' and I ran off, halting grimly and dishevelled before the lady, who looked at me aloofly.

'Dame, we need water.'

'You have buckets?' she said, strangely cool and pointed through to the dark recesses of her shop and I yelled to the others to follow me, while the lady went on damping her door-frame as if she were alone in the world, and in no danger. It was a good deep well and the winch well oiled. Butcher Gould and I pulled on the rope like madmen, taking the skin off our hands, running back to cast water on the laughing flames until my chest felt it would burst asunder. On my sixth journey I had to stop for an instant, and then it was I saw another leather pail, half-way up the stairs; a welcome sight for there were scarcely enough to go round. So I ran up to seize it, not caring what the unfriendly owner might say—there was a maiden coming down as I went up and we met abruptly. She carried a candle; she was frightened, for the flame quivered and shook for all that she came so steadily. I sought to pass her, and she stepped the same way. The candle almost seared my eyebrow. I dodged round the other side of her, and she had the same idea. It was a mad dance, this tripping from side to side on the stairs. We darted and feinted at one another like fighting cocks in a Southwark pit. I had to take her by the elbow, and her bones were as small as a lark's.

'Mistress, for God's love let me by!' I cried. I took the candle from her for she was all a-quiver and dangerous. Her eyes looked into mine, and in that frantic instant I marked them as pretty eyes, nay, eyes of great beauty, the colour of woodsmoke, and filled with tears.

She said: 'Are we in danger?' She wore a serving maid's white coif and I spoke her free, for I had had many happy hours of kissing and clipping, years gone, with such as she. That is, before I rose in the ranks and attained the court.

'No danger, sweet, but you would be better outside.'

She shrank from me, tears brimming.

'I cannot,' she whispered, and the next moment took the candle back from me with a thin, work-red hand; a hand so delicate that the light shone through it. And gallant as ever, in all my distress, I snatched her other hand and gave it a kiss, closing my nose to the stench of garlic and onions that perfumed it; for she was a lovesome creature, if undoubtedly somewhat loony. I could not tarry when she tore her fingers from mine and whirled away back into the upper part of the house. Seizing the pail from the stair, I hastened to fill it and ran back, just as the door-frame of my mother's shop collapsed, one beam leaning like the endpost of a gallows. I wished Fray on the gallows, and I started to pray.

I felt for my Christopher, who shielded me on summer forays when I rode forth to entertain the nobles—but it was scarcely a fit occasion for that sweet saint. I thought wildly of Barbara, to whom men call in thunder and in cannon-fire; and then remembered St Florian. Though he had been dead for twelve hundred years, I fancied him the very man for this work, and so I cried aloud to Florian of Lorch, to make the water flow faster and the helpers run swifter, and for a miracle to save my mother's shop.

Blessed St Florian, you have ever a special place in my heart. It had been overcast all day, yet, when the first drops of rain, large as pennies, spattered on my brow, coming swift and blessedly cool, straight from Heaven's own well, I could not believe it true and thought the moisture but my own mingling tears and sweat. Then, as I heard the downpour hissing on the smouldering broken gable and the red-hot beams, and saw the cobbles awash and the disappointed flames beaten from their supper, I gave thanks from a full heart and held my mother close, in an arm so stiff from bucket-carrying I thought I would never raise it again to quaff my ale.

We had a little reprimand from the Watch of course, but my mother drew the serjeant aside and spoke to him, and he glanced across at Mistress Petson's house and nodded. The man responsible for storing the ladders and firehooks packed up his gear and we were glad to see him go. Then we inspected the damage. The counter had been destroyed, and most of the shop frontage, but it could have been a thousand times worse. A neighbour offered to make a new sign for the door, and my mother thanked him prettily. I saw then why cursed Dan Fray wanted to wed her, quite apart from her flourishing business. They carried the arras and goods back upstairs for her; and men with axes knocked away parts of the house still reckoned dangerously warm. My mother bade stupid Walter Cleeve bring up beer for all who had helped so valorously. When all were seated on those oak chairs of which she was so proud, and the boys were sweeping out the water into the street, she beckoned me and together with

Agnes Petson—now conscious of her wanton appearance and full of shame—we went into that dame's house and stopped in front of her spice cupboard. A bag of pepper had burst inside it, and the sneezes of Fray's nephew mingled with his cries and thumps.

'I am sorry, mistress, to burden you with such a guest,' my mother told Agnes politely, though her lips twitched. If I have any humour in me, and men say I make them laugh, I swear I owe it to my mother. If I have any courage, that, too, is from her blood. On her own she had caught the devil's henchman, though not before he had tossed his pitch-soaked brand in through the shop window. His nose was red with pepper when the Watch came for him, and he seemed almost glad to be out of that cupboard.

'I could not lock him in my own place, in case he burned to death,' she said. I told her she was too merciful, and she quoted to me: 'Vengeance is mine, saith the Lord,' then fashioned a paradox by saying she hoped they would hang the uncle first and make an example of him.

Later we rehearsed the case against Fray, and the boys were brought in to prepare their evidence, and they told how they had been roused by the flash of flame as they slept under the counter, going to my mother's aid as she felled the nephew. And I was impressed by their wits, with the exception of Walter Cleeve, sitting stroking the dog, who had slain four rats. I compared them favourably with the servants of my mother's neighbours.

'What witless wenches she keeps,' I said, pointing towards the uncivil one's shop. My mother looked surprised.

'I always thought Jane Thomson and Dyonsia to be rather sharp young maids,' she said.

'I met one on the stairs who seemed half out of her mind,' I said, but I was yawning by now, and I looked out of the window and saw, in the square of reflected light from our chamber, my poor horse hanging her head. So I shoved her in the stall behind the shop with my mother's black pony and a sumpter horse left in pledge by some fellow who had dined and could not pay, and I bedded on the floor with the cook-boys, and it was right chill there, the shop front being open to the wind. What with the smell of charred timbers and the cold, I slept exceeding ill. My body was one ache from running and throwing, my hands throbbed from their skinning on the well-rope.

I lived through the whole night again, and when I rose before dawn, anxious to regain Westminster in time for Mass, I was still half-dreaming. I had been dodging the strange wild maiden on the stairs. Her mist-grey eyes looked into mine, her eyes of smoke with all their trouble and anguish; and in my dreaming I saw other things that my haste had marked without the realization. The little, drooping mouth, the small round chin. As I hastened with the Household to the Royal Chapel, her face floated ahead of me—I could not move it from my mind. Behind my eyes as I prayed her hands—the hands too fine of bone for a cook-wench-—clutched at me, and her face came closer. As the sweet boyish voices rose to the arch above me, I pictured that face smiling. Then all fell into place, though I would fain have dismissed it as foolishness. I would gladly have cast such thoughts aside, for she was but a cook maid, toiling long hours, lacking privileges, abject of a bullying mistress. Yet had she smiled...

Those heavy eyes could easily have smiled, and I would have marked that smile journeying to the small mouth and the chin round as a child's. And, at the holy season of Christmas, four years gone, that childish face had watched my antics, and had smiled most delightfully. But then she had been seated with the Earl of Warwick, her noble father.

Up in the nave, together with others of the blood royal, Gloucester knelt. I saw his hard, pale profile; the set lips, the rigid chin.

The truth beat at me and I shrank from it.

I had found Anne Neville.

'Lo, now comes in a Fiend,' intoned the herald.

The mermaid sat wrapped in long silvery hair, with a tinsel tail made of oyster-shells. Anxious eyes peeped from under the counterfeit locks. The rosebud mouth pouted. With one hand, the mermaid held up the nether wall of a painted cave as if he feared, with good reason, it might collapse. An unpleasant youth, that mermaid, and an amateur, brought in that evening under the auspices of George of Clarence, who had been impressed by his talent at the manor. We had had words already, the mermaid and I.

'Now comes in a Fiend!' bawled the herald. I felt a thrust behind, and turned to see Alexander Carlile. Cold with horror, I realized I had missed my entrance. Robert Hawkins watched—and he ran out of spit—it's not easy to play the shawm and laugh at the same time. Some kindly soul struck flint and tinder and lit my firecrackers, and, hideously late on cue, I leaped across the Hall in a burst of flame. It's a dangerous game, the Profession.

'Sir, mind the tent,' hissed the mermaid, then broke into his wailing song, his voice like a cold douche of water. I capered about, menacing him—I swear his fear was unfeigned. Closer I danced, answering his piteous song with gleeful growling—I do not pretend to have a voice; my magical powers are compensation enough. Out of mischief I brushed the cave wall on my progress, and it shook alarmingly. 'Charlatan,' whispered the mermaid, and I roared like a lion. I was enjoying myself. The Princess Elizabeth had been brought down for the entertainment. I heard her laughter, free and joyful as a lark's high blue song. Glancing up to see the pleasure of her, little and round as a peach beside the formidable Lady Scrope, I filled my eyes with the rest of the royal family, and my fleeting joy vanished. For the King was not even watching the play. His countenance was grim. Yet it had been he who had commissioned tonight's show—'to divert him from affairs'—so the Steward of the Household sent word to us. And I had a good notion what it was that troubled my royal and most beloved master. Gloucester: he and his fruitless quest. Gloucester's anxiety was mirrored in the King's fair face. The King loved Gloucester; and I wondered whether he himself, who had chosen the woman he craved in the face of Warwick's anger, found his sympathy enhanced by old desires. But then, the King had been in love, lustful love; and of love, Gloucester knew naught. So I thought... I like men that laugh, warm men of lusty heart.

All the time, near me, was a devil, a conscience devil, slowly taking shape. For why should God have chosen me as the key to this baleful mystery? It was my duty to tell Gloucester all I knew. I should have gone straightway from the cookshop to the Duke, roused him from bed, mayhap, as Alexander Carlile had roused the King at Doncaster. It was as much of a duty as that. In failing Gloucester, I had failed the King. For I could not betray Anne Neville, although my devil told me nightly that the maid was weary and soiled and very afraid. God help me, I sighed, and forgot my words.

St George stood behind the screen, his plumes wavering in a draught. He looked distraught, waiting for his cue. I was extemporizing wildly—he should have entered minutes ago, to slay me.

'And hurl us into Hell, ho, ho!' I cried, and saw St George consulting with the prompter. Under his lifted visor his face was a troubled mask. I gave up and struck my final attitude, leaning satanically upon an unsteady rock draped with buckram at the cave mouth. A brief struggle with the Saint followed, and I writhed in a death-agony. I heard him muttering 'Be still' as he prodded me with his lead-tipped sword. 'Fool I may be, but you ask much of folly,' I replied, under cover of some rather faint-hearted applause. I rolled aside as he stabbed his point into the rushes an inch from my nose. A friend of mine was butchered thus, once, and all in play. As I made myself invisible and ran from the Hall I saw that Gloucester's place was empty and remembered he had ridden north in search of Anne. I hoped he might remain there. I stood behind the screen and endured the reproofs of the Master of Revels for a poor performance, craved his pardon, and crept away to wrestle alone with my devil.

In the passage, I heard George Clarence congratulating his protégé. He was full of smiles and wine. I wondered if he knew what I knew, and what my knowledge was worth to him. In that unworthy moment I wished I had my own private confessor to run to like the King and Queen. I asked myself: how much of a sin was it? I had it in my power to ease the King, and did not do so. The King's brother was being denied the right to augment his estates, and this troubled the King. I had done nothing to alter the situation. Therefore my sin was that of non-action. My sin was silence.

I told myself for the tenth time that I had been mistaken. It was a maiden very like Warwick's daughter; a spookish trick of light, the hallucination of my frenzy. Or mayhap—and here my skin began to creep—it was a phantom. Anne Neville was dead, and because I had thought about her often lately, her spirit had wandered in my direction, appearing when I was weary and fraught and distressed for my loved ones. That night, when I slept, I shouted in slumber and woke the others. When I had made a light and sat among the straw all asweat, I saw fear on the faces of my friends.

'Jesu, he affrighted me,' said John.

'Such wild words,' whispered the man who played the rebec.

'What was I saying?' I muttered.

'Of Death, and a maiden, and the mandrake root,' he said softly, and to a man, they crossed their breasts and turned from me; in the dark, I heard them whispering, and knew they thought me possessed. As indeed I was. I closed my fingers on the crucifix my mother had given me when I was a child. Yet the devil still sat near my head, and nibbled at me with questions. Why had I appointed myself the warden of her peace? She was a gentlewoman of lineage so rich and ancient it was almost lost in time, a Plantagenet, cousin to the King. I cringed as I remembered how I'd called her 'sweet'. She was a noble lady, such as those for whom knights maim each other in the lists. She was a pawn in the game of acquisition. The devil nudged me, and then the answer came flooding clear. She was little, and lost. She was a maiden, slender and fragile, like my own Maiden, and such pluck at my heart. Thus stands the case.

Then I slept, and the Maiden came to me in a vision. I stretched out my arms to her, and she stood in a dress the colour of water and her ardent eyes big and brown and her hair streamed about her, full of flame.

'Be happy,' she whispered. 'Dear one, be merry and glad. Be no more sad…' the words from that very song she loved so much, that paltry song.

I cried and ran to her, and then I saw that her loving gaze looked past me into grouped dark shadows, and the shine in her eyes grew and grew until it consumed her and she wavered into fire; and someone said: 'They are burning a witch.'

I sobbed, 'Nay! 'tis but the glory of her soul ablaze!' and woke, glad to wake, to find the year was dying, and cold to my bones.

Two days I lay sick. Word went about and his Grace sent one of Master Dominic's assistants—there was never such a King as Edward. The young physician told me that the sovereign had heard of my illness and was sorry. I asked how the King did, and he looked sober, saying that his Grace was troubled still for his brother's sake, and that other things too disquieted him. I drank a foul potion to mend me and probed further.

'The astrologer,' he said furtively. 'He has finished the charts, and men say he has told his Grace...' He stopped abruptly.

'Well?'

'No more.' He plucked the swollen leeches from my flesh, laid a toad-cold hand on my brow, made the Holy Sign over me and rose to go. I frowned imploringly.

'Can you not tell me?'

'I should never have begun,' he said. Then, on reaching the door, he halted, itching to share his secret, full of wavering indiscretion.

He said: 'It concerned the royal succession,' and departed. I recovered swiftly after that, for it seemed that events were busying themselves and I was gossip-hungry. Upon rising from my bed I found that the astrologer's prophecy was not so much a secret as the doctor had made out. John had it, from one of the Chapel boys, who got it from a clerk belonging to Bishop Morton of Ely, who learned it from the under-falconer, and he was enamoured of one of the Queen's tire-women, who were part of the furnishings and knew everything.

'Her Grace became sorely agitated,' John told me. 'She sent for the Dowager Duchess of Bedford and they had high words together. Her mother said she was becoming too old to do aught and went to her prayers ill-pleased. Construe it how you will.'

'And the astrologer said?'

His warm breath tickled my ear. 'That the next King's name will begin with G.'

'Surely,' I said softly, 'George Clarence would never dare aspire again to the throne, as when Warwick was alive. Pardoned, enriched, he holds all the cards.'

'Clarence was ever reckless,' said John, and we were so near talking treason, with its old familiar fearful excitement, that I had to check him swiftly.

'The Duchess Isabel is ailing,' John said.

'As ever,' I replied. 'She and her sister were always frail in body...' and I ceased suddenly, for with the thought of Anne there was my devil, full and venomous and real, as real as the man standing next to me. He was peering round the ribbed stone arches of the Great Hall high above, ready to spring.

There was less than a week to Michaelmas, when I could claim my wager, but the thought gave me no joy. I went down into the City one day when the river was mantled with haze, and took a penny-boat from just below Westminster Hall. I tried to enjoy the voyage; at any other time I would have risked the ebb tide and the treacherous currents under the Bridge, for with a clever boatman this could be fierce sport, but not that day. The gilt and azure and crimson of barges floated magnificently among a throng of lesser vessels. We rocked on the swell of the Earl of Essex's carved boat, sailed near the gold-hung splendour of Lord Hasting's craft. The misty river echoed the strains of pipe and viol from the barges' depths. Under the flaming banners liveried oarsmen rowed lustily, with great dipping strokes. All the way from Blackfriars to the Tower great cranes bristled bowed-headed among the myriad quays and warehouses. We passed the massive pile of Baynard's Castle and the stone fortress of the Steelyard, home of the strange, martial Hanse traders. On the southern end of the Bridge sat three heads, staring with great melancholy over the city through which their legs had walked the week before. Two galleys stocked with tuns of good Bordeaux were anchored at the Vintners' Wharf. Next moment we were beneath the Bridge, and the roar of hooves and wheels above competed with the rushing water that lapped us for a few dark moments. I saw the wooden starlings over my head, slime-green and crusted. On the other side, Brown's Wharf was boiling with trade. A Spanish merchantman was tied up low in the water from a cargo of iron and madder and oil. At the next quay a vessel Calais-bound and laden with sarplers of wool was hoisting sail. Towards St Catherine's a Flemish carvel, carrying fine Holland cloth, came slowly, like a great indolent bird.

The eel-ships were tied up at Marlowe's, and the voices of housewives fighting to board them rose shrill and impatient. The water-bailiff's men held them back while their master searched for red or undersized eels, and the women railed at his sloth. The rush-boats were in. I saw Palace servants, bent like cripples, running with their great green loads. As we pulled towards Billingsgate, the salt-cod smell wafted to my nose from an Icelandic trawler.

There was a high-masted Venetian galley wharved below the Tower, weighted with damask, velvet, and rare spices for sure, judging by the perfume. The crew were like monkeys, little and dark with gesticulating hands. My pilot spat over the side of the boat at them, and their outlandish tongue. On either bank the peter-nets lay like floating spiderwebs, dripping water as the fishers hauled in, a load of salmon and barbel and flounder. The autumn sun turned the drops to jewels. A swan took flight astern of us, flying strongly east, the thin light gilding its wings. I pushed my devil to one side and tried to be happy.

I disembarked and fought the seething crush in Petty Wales, dodging the carriers and wains, assaulted by the dreadful language of the carters, vaguely comforted by the presence of that violent life. Down Thames Street I went, turned up from the river, came into Mincing Lane and walked westward into Eastchepe. There I met Beatrice the wimple-washer with her maids all loaded with laundry, and she had linen cloths for my mother in her bundle. I took these and went on down to the cookshop. The men were chipping away plaster to fit the new door-frame in and the master carpenter told me, with shaking head, that it would be a long work, and costly. Yet we laughed together at the news of Dan Fray and his nephew, lying hungry in the Fleet. To be in jail is an expensive business too.

'One meal a day, if he can pay,' said the carpenter smoothing the fractured gable.

'Or eat the rats!' said I merrily, and went into the shop to find the borrowed fire-bucket. I then made my way to the house three doors down.

I contrived to look into the back room. She was still there: Anne of Warwick, late Princess of Wales. There was no doubt in me as I watched her, slender and wearied, plunging her arms deep in greasy washing-up water. Her little chin sank on her chest. She did not look up. I marked her sorrow, felt her loneliness. The other wenches gave her sharp words, pushed past her, wearing the livery of resentment. She was an upstart, an unskilled stranger in their domain. Sick-hearted, I sought the owner, to return her bucket. I had no lust to stay. The mistress of the house raised sparse brows at me as if I were some rare beast. I stared her out. I spoke her soft. I thanked her for the loan of the fire-bucket.

''Twas naught,' she said. There was truly a nip in the air as I passed out on to the street, wishing I could leave my devil within to sour her salmon morteux.

Walter Cleeve was killing a sucking-pig when I returned. It shrieked as he smote it in the middle—I could hardly hear my mother's voice. She was full of smiles. She had appealed to the Gild; they would loan her money; not enough, mind, but better than naught. We went aloft.

'You've been sick,' she said. 'What ails you?'

I longed to tell her. I told her half of it.

'I know where Anne Neville is,' I said softly.

She said instantly: 'You have acquainted the Duke of Gloucester of this?' and when I confessed I had not, her face grew livid and her eyes like stones. Never had I seen her so angry.

''Tis your duty.' I strode maddened about the parlour, trying to explain that which made nonsense. Shortly she cooled and tried reasoning with me.

'Every maiden has a dowry—wedlock is a business... you have not the right.'

I knew all that, I said. I repeated Clarence's mocking words: 'She's but a little maid,' then my own thoughts: 'Alone, unloved.'

'Mary have mercy!' cried my mother. 'I have reared an idiot!' An hour we wrangled, and I grew stubborn and would tell her no more. I sought comfort and advice; she advised me and left me comfortless, only enhancing my guilt. 'The King loves Gloucester,' she said.

The King loves Gloucester, and is troubled by his trouble. God help me.

'Do not fail in your duty,' she repeated.

Thus I left her. I was shaking, and thought of going to the Boar's Head for a drink and idle talk. But instead I went past the tavern and found myself at the London Stone; and on a whim went into St Swithin's, where it was dark and the wings of God beat through the mutterings of the Mass. There I knelt for an hour. The devil came into church with me and tried to look devout, sitting with folded hands on the stall-carvings above my head.

When I came out into the thin air and falling leaves of the churchyard, my mind was clear. The things about me were no longer misted as on the river trip, but sharp and solid. An old beggar lying dead against the iron bars of London Stone. A grey cat, disembowelled on the cobbles. Two disreputable players of the *scurrae vagi*, prancing to the noise of fife and tabor. A merchant, wife and daughter, dismounting outside the church. He rode a fine bay. The women shared a big white mare. I looked at the daughter, and she at me. Pale, big-breasted, with black eyes, she stared at me as her father helped her from the horse. She toyed with her beads and her gaze was unflickering. Even in my anguish of spirit I marked the wanton sparkle of that look. I fancied I saw ardour in it; a promise of forgetfulness, came the chance. Then, that warmth dazzled me—for how could I know that this was but the kindling embers of a foul humour—and that she would use me very unkindly throughout our wedded life.

I spoke of my devil to none, but there were those who, I fancied, gave me strange looks, and I had need to be doubly foolish and gay to belie my dread. Actually, my devil was not an ill-favoured fellow by any means. He had horns, for sure, and a neat little beard, and I think his feet were cloven, but as he usually had them tucked under him I could not swear to it. His face was mild and gentle, with large eyes and a protruding mouth; it was only the expression on it that chilled me, and the reproving way he wagged his head. When I was busily occupied he let me alone, but when I stopped and thought of Lady Anne Neville, abandoned among the slubberdegullions, he came nimbly down from his little niche or dropped from a flying buttress and spoke me soft. He would say: 'Go to him,' and I would shake my head, for my mind—which at one time I had thought made up—had once more turned traitor.

Gloucester was back from Sheriff Hutton, more grim-visaged than ever. Still he searched. He sent letters, he questioned folk, he took barge upriver and back again; he walked leagues, attended by his household knights. He went from the great sprawling wards of Cripplegate and Farringdon Without, to the Priory of St Bart's and the Inns of Chancery, the shops of Fleet Street, the Temple. Along the Street he walked, the Poultry, the Vintry, Jewry, up Bread Street and Milk Street; north he rode to the Grand Priory of Holy Trinity. He wandered through Moorfields, and in all these forays he spoke with an hundred holy men and women, abbots, prioresses and clerks. He dispatched emissaries to the sanctuaries with sealed writings. He was unsparing and unwearying. He grew thin and hard and eager, and the King glowered at him with an impatient, loving look. Clarence departed to tend his sick wife, the Neville inheritance still secure within his hand. I thought of Anne, and the devil swung from the vaultings and tweaked my hair.

'Tell him,' he said.

'Avaunt, Lucifer!' said I, and he looked injured. 'Give one good reason why not,' he asked. 'She is afraid,' I said. 'She is wretched,' answered the devil. 'You bear a bond for Clarence? While the maid lies low *he* is rich. You are his man in this matter?'

Nay, I was not for George Clarence, fair and jocund though he was, for he was a silly fellow to betray the King with Warwick and lucky, yea lucky, to escape retribution. The devil listened, his head on one side.

'Certes, Barnet,' he said. ''Twas Richard who was the peacemaker there. Blessed are they...' and it seemed so strange to hear a devil quoting the Scriptures that I tried to look him in the eye but it was impossible. He would just fade and become part of the stonework or curl himself up into one of the bosses on the ceiling. He was at my other ear now. 'Of what is she afraid?'

'Of being wed to Gloucester,' I said.

'All must marry,' said the devil sensibly.

'She has been married,' I said. 'A wretched, treacherous marriage—to the Lancastrian. She has been bludgeoned with bad tidings. Alone, bereft of husband, father, mother, attainted, disgraced. A pawn,' I said, and nearly choked. 'A movable.'

'Why a pawn?' he asked with interest. 'Pawns are not flesh and blood—they are ivory. Inanimate. Devoid of feeling.'

And I said, 'But she has feeling; I saw her tears, looked in her eyes. She should be cosseted, not hunted down for her fortune. If she must marry, let it be to a loving husband who cares not a jot for her livelode!'

The devil squinted at me and his horns moved a trifle. 'You speak as if you have designs,' he murmured. 'Were she not the Lady Anne—but I forget, you love another...'

At this I was so incensed that I struck at him with the cane I carried, and he flew up to the roof in a fury, shrieking: 'Tell him! Tell him! Tell him!'

I saw one of the pages turn green and cross himself and walk right speedily past me down the corridor, and I realized I had better put my affairs in order before they brought in a priest.

The weather snapped into coldness. Every morning mist lingered on the Thames until dinner, and drew down sharply at dusk. We were nearly in October and the birds were taking their leave for the other edge of the world. And as the birds departed, men and women began to thread back into the city. We had watched them go in late spring, with staff and pouch, heavy with sin. Under the hot suns of Galicia they had offered a waxen leg to St James for their deliverance, and now they came from *La-Dame-sous-Terre* and from Rome, dusty yet cleansed, and lighter of purse. Trailing the severed links of their fetters they came, bearing back all that had been healed by the sight of those sacred relics: their sick hawks, their limbs, their souls. They came with a wool-thread from the chasuble of a saint; a spoonful of dust lifted from the grounds of a shrine. The shell of Compostella adorned their hat brims. They came from abroad, and from Canterbury, where a thousand candles reflected the glory of Henry Plantagenet's penitence. I had made that journey once, to see, in its canopy of beaten gold, the Regal of France, finest ruby in the realm. So they came: they had journeyed leagues and returned satisfied. Yet the Duke of Gloucester tramped London town, and came back empty.

I withdrew from the wager with John and Robert. They were surprised yet pleased with my new-found sense of propriety. Did I do it to safeguard my own interests? I was not even sure myself; I knew only that the whole matter had become too odious a jest. On the day prior to the Feast of St Michael, because I could not hear the conversation of my friends for my devil's whispering, I went down to the stables to seek a mule that I might train for the coming Christmas festival. We would soon be in rehearsal and I reckoned to get all my properties in good array. I wondered whom the King would choose for Revels Master over the twelve days. Gloom ruled my every thought, I who was so merry. Along the terrace I went in my day's pale grey. In the courtyard, the pigeons searched amid sodden red leaves; the pavement was silken with damp. I went under the arches into the smell of hay and horses. I looked at the mules. Two were too docile for my purpose but the third had mischief in its gait. I set up a tub for its forelegs to stand on, in practice for when it would reach the King's dais, with me aboard. Two household stewards were grooming Lyard Duras and Lyard Lewes. Sir John Howard had chosen well in his gift to the royal couple—the fair coursers were everything that a horse should be. They struck at each other in play, with swift squealing blows. Lyard Duras kicked out, jarring a hoof on the stones.

'They can smell the mares,' said a steward. 'Even the mule won't quiet them today.'

Lyard Lewes rose on end and cried of his own beauty with quivering nostrils. His coat was silver, his haunches whorled and dappled like soaring smoke.

'He's as brave as he is fair,' called the groom, grinning. 'Today he killed a hound—cleft his skull like a nut.'

My mule was snuffing at something small behind us, something that moved and chuckled. 'Holy Mary,' whispered the groom. He lunged for the Princess Elizabeth as she ran laughing away. I never saw a five-year-old maid move so swiftly. She wanted to fondle the fair horses. She sped on across the courtyard—once, my fingers grazed her gown, but she was a hare, a light pink and golden bird, a faery. She was enjoying herself. Horsemen were approaching from the outer gate, their hooves resounding under the archway. She changed course and flew to meet them. They came strongly, their surcotes shimmering in the mist—I saw only the strong legs of the horses pounding air. She would be trampled to pulp. I foresaw her end—my sweet Elizabeth—and every man present jigging at Tyburn.

One of the front line of horsemen leaped from his mount. With a stride he was upon the Princess, grasping her by her flying hair. He wore the livery of the White Boar, and there mounted behind him was the Duke himself. The horsemen milled in a circle, exclaiming harshly, looking to see if the child had been harmed. The young knight who had caught her had been rough in his handling, and Elizabeth was on the point of tears. At that moment her nurse, the accursed, witless old fool, came panting flatfootedly across the yard. Gloucester dismounted, and the Princess ran to him. She threw herself against his legs—he lifted her up. He was chiding her gently, calling her 'sweet Bess'. She wound her arms around him, burying her face in his fur collar.

Gloucester spoke to the nurse. He did not raise his voice, but its tone sent frissons down my spine.

'Well, dame?' he said, while the Princess peeped out at us with one eye.

The nurse fell to her knees, weeping and wailing.

'Is this how you guard the blood royal?' he asked. His voice was soft; soft and dangerous.

'Your Grace, I did but turn my back an instant...' she whimpered.

'An instant,' he repeated. 'I doubt not it would have been likewise with the Prince Edward! An instant's heinous idling—a hound at the cradle—a spark from the fire...' He bit his words back in fury. 'It seems that princes are cheaply begotten.' He turned to two of the pallid guard. 'Put this woman under arrest.'

'They'll flog her,' whispered the groom.

'They'll hang her, if he's a mind to it,' said the steward who was trying to gentle Lyard Duras. 'If he takes a leaf from the Butcher's book.'

So I thought on our last Constable of England, Tiptoft Earl of Worcester, who had devised new wondrous methods of impalement for felons... a brave man, who requested his own head shorn off in three strokes to honour the Trinity. As they led the weeping woman away Gloucester took the Princess up higher in his arms. She clasped and prattled. 'Bess, my love,' I heard him say.

My devil took shape beside me, romping in the day's dour colours, pleased at the aura of recent fear.

'He is capable of tenderness,' he murmured, and I instructed him to depart to his master, whoever that might be; while I heard Gloucester telling the Princess it was wrong to wander off, she all the time putting up great arguments—her nurse bored her and she would sooner be out of doors.

'We must all do things we mislike,' he said seriously, but she took it upon her to start kissing him, all over his face. She was more generous with kisses than protocol allowed; she had once kissed me before I could stop her. I have been kissed by a Queen.

'What great wrath lies in him too,' whispered the devil. He was beginning to talk more subtly to me these days. 'Your Grace,' I said, in a strangled voice, but by now the Duke was disappearing through the archway. Elizabeth's hair caught the wind of their passing and lifted, cloth of gold but richer.

I feared his anger which was rare as his smile, but I also marked his gentleness with the child and sought portents in all this. But then my portents came so thick and fast I did not know what to believe, and the next thing I knew I was on my way, drearily, to his apartments. One of the young pages opened and asked my business, so I told him it was none of his. When I said it was an urgent and secret matter he seemed impressed. A pinelog fire burned in the hearth and one of Gloucester's huge hounds lay before it. It was a room of paradoxes: there was a lute, a set of tables, and Caxton's new printed book on chess, loaned from Flanders, but the Duke had a suit of harness piled against the wall, and I wondered if he contemplated joining forces with the Easterling traders, it being their custom to keep armour in every room. Then I remembered the purpose of my visit, and my heart started knocking at my ribs.

'His Grace is taking a bath,' announced the henchman.

The hound eyed me and growled. Murmuring voices came from behind the closed door of the bedchamber. I turned tail. I would shirk this odious duty. I had just convinced the page that what was important to me was of no consequence to the Duke, and was talking my way across the room when the bedchamber door opened. I heard Richard's voice as one of the Yeomen of the Body came through.

'If you will bring the book, Jervais, I'll prove both you and Lord Anthony wrong,' he called out. There was laughter.

Jervais picked up Caxton's book lovingly.

'They're arguing a point,' he told the page. 'Last night Lord Anthony vowed…' He saw me and raised his brows.

'You wish to see the Duke?'

'Who is it?' said the Duke from his bath.

I knew then that matters were out of my hands. The henchmen whispered together and Jervais went through to the inner room. Miserably I heard him repeat my own words 'urgent and secret' and let them escort me to where Richard sat up to his armpits in warm water. He and I faced each other through curtains and steam. The aroma of coriander and rose-water tickled my nose. He looked at me apparently without recognition and the man Jervais bent over the bathing tent and murmured: 'One of the histrios, sir,' an unkind designation which at other times would have made me burst with rancour, but now I did not care. Richard nodded, then he said:

'What is this matter concerning me?'

I tried to speak and found myself dumb.

'This good man seems ailing,' Richard said mildly. 'Give him a drink.'

I gulped down a cup of Rhenish, which went straight to my head. I saw them all, grouped expectantly, save for the body servants who went on calmly pouring hot herbals over the Duke's neck and back. Francis Lovell glanced up from the *Game and Play of the Chess* and smiled. I always liked him—he had a lucky face. Richard gazed quizzically at me over the high tub. I whispered my secret.

'Come nearer,' he said with impatience, and as I did not wish him to take me for a fool, I marched up to the parted curtains of the bathing tent and told him what I knew, louder than I had intended. Something strange befell his face. He waxed white and then rosy red and the skin seemed to be stretched tight over his cheeks as his normal pallor returned.

'Help me out,' he said and extended a hand on either side. Jervais caught one, and I the other. I took the Duke's wet hand, all slippery with fine Bristol soap, and nearly had my fingers mangled by his inhuman grip. He was as thin as a whip, straight though not overtall, and well made, particularly about the shoulders. After my curiosity was sated I looked at his eyes, and ever afterwards he held my gaze with his, while they dressed him and I stood plaiting my fingers behind my back.

They dressed him with care. While one knight tied the points of his hose, the other put over his head an applebloom shirt of the finest Rennes cloth. They clothed him in the purple, the narrow-waisted doublet edged with gris, and with the new-fangled sleeves like bladders, arranging the tucks of the tunic to achieve the desired triangular effect. Two esquires knelt to introduce his legs into the soft leather thighboots with the grey silk lining. Jervais fastened the gold collar of York about his chest, and gave him his velvet bonnet with the pendant bauble of rubies and he said, without taking his eyes from mine:

'Now I am ready, Frank, to go a-wooing.' And under young Lovell's soft mirth, I felt murder in my soul at so sickly a jest.

He slung his cloak about him, and it too mocked my sad thoughts of Anne Neville, for it was velvet on velvet, precedent of the highest nobility. Yes, you are very grand, Dickon, I thought. I hope that the stench of onions and greasy water will not taint you. Soon you will be even wealthier. May she spit on you.

London is dirtier now, under Henry Tudor. Ugly little houses clog the streets, though this is not, of course, the fault of his Divine Majesty. He has put much hard-earned money into the building of his Chapel to the Virgin at Westminster, where they sing Masses night and day for the souls of the dead. Speaking of death, he has given directions for his own funeral, commanding royal and proper magnificence but no outrageous superfluities. Such a King he is.

As I say, now it's dirtier, but on the day I walked through town with Richard of Gloucester, going a-courting, I thought I had seldom seen it so foul and knew a peculiar shame for the filthy alleys and the stench which rose about me and my sumptuous companion. I was horrified that he had decided to walk anyway—I thought we would go by boat at least, and when he marched out of the Palace gate into the howling thoroughfare, I stopped in amazement.

'I'll get horses for your Grace,' I murmured. He said grimly: 'Friend, I have walked miles on this errand which ends today. I'll see it through in like fashion,' and added, as if to himself: 'They marched further to Tewkesbury.' I reckoned he was just rambling, being so full of triumph. We went together along the Strand, with the bishops' palaces lining the south side, past Temple Bar and through Ludgate where the press thickened. I had need to run to keep up with him—all the while I was fearful that he might be assaulted or robbed, and I leaped from side to side of the street endeavouring to guard him. My disquiet must have been apparent, for at one point he stopped while I panted at his elbow.

'My lord, why have we no esquires to ease your passage?' I gasped. A smile crept over his face and he murmured:

'Good fellow, there are times when one goes where no other should penetrate,' and with that smile there was something in the back of his eyes that perplexed me utterly; that, coupled with the really mischievous look, man to man, which he gave me. I had never seen him with a woman; his habits were not those of the King and Clarence, both of whom had bastards all over England; then I remembered talk of Richard and a woman of Bruges, whom he had got with child.

Eastchepe was crammed, redolent of food and filth. I whacked the cook-knaves aside as they clutched with foul hands at us both. The Gild had prohibited the practice of soliciting, but they still did it. 'Hot sheep's feet!' they yelled. 'Ribs o' beef!' I saw a grease-smear on the Duke's velvet cloak, and, surreptitiously sponging at it with my glove, wished I had never been born. A ragged band playing harp, pipe and psaltery impeded us—they sang of 'Jenkin and Julian'. The fishmongers shouted their melwell and mackerel earsplittingly. Even the oaths sounded worse in a prince's presence. The window overhead flew open and a wife, with careless cry of 'Gardy loo!' hurled the contents of her pot almost on top of us. A dead dog, maggot-white, stank in the gutter. This was my Eastchepe, and, for the first time, I felt shame for it. 'Good lord, excuse this foulness,' I said, and was angry with myself as soon as the words were out.

'Is it all of your making, then?' he said, with a cool dark look. 'Southwark is also somewhat unsavoury, but it has a fine inn.'

'The Tabard,' I said eagerly.

'Yea, Geoffrey Chaucer's tavern. All one hears is Chaucer. He has still an ardent following, and rightly so.'

'His works would fit Master Caxton's skill,' said I, fawning. Kiss-your-arse Patch, I was. Am.

'Of course you're more familiar with such gestes than I,' he said, and I caught the hint that he thought I could be more honourably employed than amusing the court with my fellow joculatores. But his wit was only slightly barbed and we talked culture. Of course he knew more than I, yet we enjoyed the same things, and as we walked, he recited 'The Love Unfeigned', and very well too; and when he came to the line *This world, that passeth soon as flowers fair*, I wanted to weep, as ever, and came near liking him. But then we neared the cook-shop and, remembering who lay within, I thought the title of 'Dan' Chaucer's poem, coming from him, in poor taste.

My mother's shop, as we approached, looked a rather pitiful sight, and I would fain have hurried him past, but he slowed and looked up at it. 'Whose place is this?' he said, and squirming, I told him. I knew he would now think I was serving him for a reward and I felt like Judas Iscariot already without the thirty pieces being added.

'She should have compensation,' he announced, and I said that the Gild had matters in hand. He said 'Hmmm,' and was loath to drop the affair, but the next minute we were at our destination.

I went first, and the haughty mistress stepped from behind her counter unsmiling, but when Richard of Gloucester darkened the doorway in his velvet and jewels and with his eyes like arrowheads, she swept to the ground, all her hauteur gone. As Gloucester only stood and looked about, I enquired of the mistress where the young lady might be found. Speechless, she pointed aloft, and I hung back as Richard strode through the shop. To my great dismay, for I had thought my task was done, he beckoned me from the foot of the stairs.

'Give me a watch while I talk with the Lady Anne,' he said, and turning, I saw the popping eyes of the cook-knaves. They were creeping imperceptibly towards the stairs, leaving their pies to catch at this latest entertainment. The owner was gone, I assume, to fashion an explanation for George of Clarence.

I followed Gloucester upstairs. 'Dismiss her servants,' he said, then sharply asked me why I laughed and I told him; the lady's status was not now what might be expected of Warwick's daughter, and he would find her much altered. He swore a most fearful oath, and struck the door a rap with the hilt of his knife. My heart went into my boots as Anne opened the door. Now I have witnessed many executions, and taken my due lesson from them, as is intended. I have seen the faces of those about to be hanged, disembowelled and cut up, burned in barrels, and beheaded. They have a mingling of abject terror and resignation, patched over with a fierce bravado. This vanishes into mist at the first touch of the knife. Anne Neville carried that look. I knew better than any how Judas felt.

Richard said, 'Wait here;' then: 'Let none come up,' and I saw Anne's little white face, with the blonde hair dull from grease and her white coif smudged with dirt, blotted out by the Duke's dark shadow, as he closed the door behind him. The servants were grouped at the stairfoot. They were straining to hear like a pack of hounds at a treed quarry, but in vain. I, on the other hand, had no wish to know what went on behind that door. But it had great cracks where the oak had shrunk, and I could hear every word.

At first I thought on Daniel Fray and his lust for my mother's livelode, and wondered if that old play would be performed within, before realizing that lords do not, as a rule, chase women round tables, although the Maiden once told me a fantastic tale about King Edward threatening Elizabeth with his dagger at Grafton Regis. Well, the King was one on his own.

There was such a long silence that I was full of anguish. If he harms her, I said to myself, trembling fiercely, I will knock and enter, asking if they wish for wine. I will risk his wrath. Lord Jesu, keep my tongue still.

His first words were shockingly clear.

'This is an unseemly place to find you, my lady.'

He got no answer to this, so he said: 'Are you well, Madame?'

Had he no eyes? He could surely see she was far from well. Again she did not reply.

'I have come to fetch you away.'

'I thought you would come,' she said.

'You heard that I was seeking you;' he continued. 'Why did you not send word of your whereabouts?'

She coughed. She said, very fast: 'I was warned of you, my lord.' Then, more softly: 'I was afraid.'

'Warned? By whom? By Clarence?'

No answer.

'Yea, by my brother,' he said. He laughed harshly. 'Lord, how flown are some with ambition, how unbelievably cunning and devious...' Then, less bitterly: 'And you? What of your feelings in this… this conspiracy?'

'I was not consulted, your Grace,' she said, her voice battling with tears.

'He brought you here by force,' said Richard.

'Nay, not by force. He said it would be better...' her words started to run away, tripping over each other '...that you were so full of spleen, so hot in your desire for my mother's estates... so full of fury because of my treasonous marriage you wished me ill. I was afraid,' she said again, and changed it. 'I am afraid.'

Do not weep, I thought. Support your soul before him, for the love of God.

'The day I called at his manor he would not let me see you,' Richard said. 'He told me you were sick—was this the truth?'

She was silent.

'Three days I waited, close by,' he said inexorably. 'Then I returned, to learn you were so ailing you could not be disturbed. And then you were vanished, utterly. I've journeyed miles to find you.'

'And now you have,' she said wearily. 'What do you wish of me, my lord?'

'Why, to have you with me, of course!' he cried. His voice dropped as he said: 'We have been apart too long.'

'There has been too much blood shed,' she said sadly.

The boards creaked as he started to walk about the room.

''Tis true, that in his Grace's service I rode against your father. Of your husband I will not speak, but you know well my one-time affection for Richard Neville. That foolish, gallant knight,' he said softly.

Her voice trembling, she said: 'Did you see him die?'

'Oxford had fled, Montagu was cut down. The Earl of Warwick made for Wrotham Wood and the Barnet Road. He was pursued and slain. Once, through the fog, I saw his standard, then I was unhorsed. My esquires were dead—I was still embroiled in the fray. Then I saw his standard flew no more, but I heard only of his death when I was in the surgeon's tent.'

''Tis hard for me to brook these thoughts,' she said, in great sorrow.

'And for me. I too remember Yorkshire, and happier days. But you, my lady, have been constantly in my mind.'

'The last time we met was after Tewkesbury,' she replied. 'You had a terrible aspect. You did not speak to me.'

'I was too overmatched, Madame. And, unlike my brothers, I am unlettered in fair speeches. I could but look at you and love you. Be sure of this, I shall not let you go again.'

'When we were children,' she said slowly, 'I thought you loved me... but that was long ago.'

'At Middleham,' he said. 'My feelings have not changed. Anne, come to me.'

'I will not wed you, my lord,' she said. 'And I'm too good to be your leman.'

Her voice was that of proud Warwick's daughter. I was seized by a fit of horrid mirth, for these last words were the very same used by Elizabeth Woodville, when the King's desire ran high, as told to me by the Maiden.

'As you wish,' he said coldly, and exhaled his breath in a long sigh. The floor squeaked under his pacing, then suddenly he gave a great cry. I broke into a sweat.

'Blessed Mother of God!'

'Oh, what is it?' she said terrified.

'Anne, your hands! Your little hands! O Lord, to think that things should have come to this!'

Her steps neared the door as she evaded him. The latch lifted, the door opened a crack and slammed shut beneath the weight of his arm.

'Let me kiss them,' he said, and there was a taut silence, broken by a curious little noise like the last choking sob a child makes after bawling—full up with tears, struggling to scream again.

'Don't weep,' he said fiercely. 'Don't weep, Anne. Ah, Anne, I love you.'

'Your Grace,' she cried. 'I pray you, do not kneel to me. Do not kneel. Richard, get up.'

'Your little hands, Anne, red and broken as a scullion's,' he repeated, like a madman. 'I will restore them—before God, I'll restore you. To Middleham...'

'That was once my home,' she said sadly.

'Our home, Anne! Where I'll give you every joy, I swear it.'

Another silence followed, then she said: 'I am aweary of it all. Take me, Richard, do what you will. My mother's possessions are forfeit. I feel but a chattel, a necessary part of the movables, past caring. The estates are yours, and so am I.'

'To the Devil with the estates!' he cried, and my skin tingled as I realized he could shout as loud as the King when he chose. 'Anne, Anne, I love you. Love me.'

And then the silence grew longer and longer and was heavy-hung with dreaming, and I curled my toes and rolled about against the wall, feeling exceeding guilty for being there. The touch of her must have aroused old memories, for he said quite roughly: 'I have had paramours, you should know this. I have also a son, whom I shall acknowledge. Will you be wounded if he lives with us in Yorkshire?'

She did not answer for a moment.

'He is called John,' Richard said. 'He's a fine babe.'

'I love children,' Anne Neville said softly.

'I will give you children, Anne. God will bless us with many children. Brave sons. Sweet Anne.'

'The Prince Edward of Lancaster...' she began, and he said, his voice rigid again: 'I would rather not know of that.'

She laughed gently through her tears.

'Queen Margaret would not allow him alone with me. She swore the union should not be consummated until Lancaster was strong in England. Ah, Richard, he was an arrogant, fearsome creature—he spoke only of war and beheadings.'

'I, too, know of war,' he said. 'Enough to long for peace and tranquillity with you for wife, and my friends about me...'

She was weeping now in earnest, and he said: 'Come, my lady, my love. Let's leave this dismal place. Lean on me.'

He opened the door so suddenly I was transfixed. However, he scarcely looked at me, only saying: 'Bring round a horse, I pray you,' and disappeared again into the chamber. My mother was out. I took her black palfrey without leave and brushed its coat. I hoped it would be a fitting mount for the Lady Anne. I tethered it outside the shop and ran up the stairs once more, into the upper room, with but a swift knocking and out again right hastily, red-eared. The Duke of Gloucester had Anne Neville close in his arms, and his mouth on hers, and in the moment of my intrusion I saw her lift her arms slowly and clasp him tightly to her, like a weary child who waits to be carried into sleep.

It was chill when we came out and moisture clung to our hair and slid down the carved beams and pentices of the houses either side of Eastchepe. Richard of Gloucester cupped his hands for Anne's foot and tossed her up lightly into the saddle and laughed, a laugh which I had seldom heard and did not recognize. She smiled down at him and her face was rose pink; and already the lady of Christmas revels, merry and safe beside a strong man, was returning. I thought he would take her back to Westminster, but he did not. On the other side of the street I walked. I walked with them and yet away from them. Their eyes never wavered from the road ahead. Once he halted, took off his fair velvet cloak and wrapped it about her, where it draped her from neck to ankles as she sat the pony. Once she touched his hand and he bore her fingers to his lips. Yet all the while they looked ahead, as if they had no wish to glance behind as long as they lived.

We went slowly along Budge Row and Watling Street as far as St Paul's churchyard and passed under the sombre shadow of the church through into Chepeside and towards Aldersgate until we saw the crenellations of the Wall. There, he halted the pony at the Sanctuary of St-Martin-le-Grand, and together they went in. He emerged alone after a little space; on his face joy and sadness gathered, overlaid with the look of one who anticipates a wearisome campaign.

My devil took flight and sped over the housetops, webbed black wings beating lustily: I never realized he had wings. Gone, no doubt, to plague some other wretch.

In a February-grey dawn I watched London, and Westminster, and all dear and familiar to me, vanish to the south-east. Coming up through Sheen, with the fingers of winter catching at my mouth, I watched it go. The Palace, and the river with its dipping cranes doing obeisance to trade, sank out of sight as we hit Watling Street, which was frost-foul. This was no May Day sally to entertain ducal households. Those were occasions spiced with good humour, singing through summer days with the minstrels and the bear loping behind on his chain, and, following, the children from every village dancing after for a league. Then I would be at the height of my power, jesting with a ceaseless cascade of fable and rhyme, and often, if time decreed, halting at a hamlet to entrap the peasants with my wit and skill. Thus had I once been myself enchanted, on the green at Stoney Stratford, by a child with hair the colour of ripe hazel nuts. I do not need to speak her name—to me, she was always but the Maiden, and save for a Queen, there was never her equal.

This was no blossomy pilgrimage of mirth, to divert Lord Hastings at Ashby, or Sir John Howard, or Sir John Fastolfe. Nor were we bound to tell sacred gestes and holy lays for mitred abbots like those at Glastonbury and St Alban's. Jolly times were those, riding forth between cowslip fields shouting with colour, and not only because the lords we pleasured were generous, but for another reason. We knew that, after our task was done, we the emissaries of the King's gaiety would be returning to London. And London was life itself to me. All those I loved were there, save she whom I had lost. All the things I knew best were there—the taverns, the reek, the jostle, the sparkling court. The sweet Princess Elizabeth. The King, who had betrayed me.

King Edward had dismissed me from his service, I that loved him so well. From the best and most innocent of intentions, he had bidden my departure on a day still edged with winter. When the Comptroller sent word to me I thought at first it was only a bad jest.

'You, sir, are to ride to Middleham, in the north parts,' said the messenger, cringing a little at my aspect, which must have shown many things.

'Alone?' I could only fashion the one word.

'You, sir, Masters Green and Hawkins—it is the royal wish,' he said, and, as there was naught to add, departed.

The King had made a gift of me to Dickon of Gloucester. A marriage gift, for Richard was wedded at last, and in a fine hurry after the final Council meeting at Sheen. Anne Neville had come forth out of Sanctuary to be his bride. After four months of Council-chatter they were man and wife, and gone from London in haste, vanishing into the wilds of the north, which I knew for a fact to be haunted by evil demons, and cheerless indeed. John had made music at the consecration of their union, and he now rode a little behind me through the foggy morning, with the Chilterns rising gloomily to the west and the rime cracking underfoot like an ill-smitten tabor. We were seven, riding north. Ahead I could see the broad backs of Sir James Tyrell and his two esquires. Directly in front of me a young tonsured clerk sat a dejected mule. I could hear John touching his lute as he rode at my rear, and Robert, lagging behind, seemed to be half asleep. We were for the cold castle of Middleham and a master still an unknown quantity. Behind me lay the royal court and all its fond memories. It seemed my days of joy and play were over, and ill fortune surely mine: I had felt this since December lately gone.

It had been a doleful Christmas. Yet we had feasted enough and been rewarded for our revel-labours, and I had ruled over Misrule once more and had got my twenty shillings from the King. Anthony Woodville fashioned a most holy play which took all our wit to justify, and I saw the Princess Elizabeth every day. Yet, as I looked to my royal master for his pleasure, and saw him fumbling and sad under a dangerous golden smile, my joy was much confined. Though I rode my mule around the hall, right up to the cloth of estate and with ringing cries summoned the lords to gamble dice, which they did right heartily. Fifty joculatores crammed the Hall, wearing their tunics of blue and gold, and the guises of wildmen and angels to mask the sweating faces beneath. The pageant wagons churned through the rushes, and King Neptune sat, high on the foremost ship, dressed in green cloth of gold. We played Samson, too, pulling down a temple that almost grazed the roof. One of the master-cooks invented a Nativity for the royal table so glorious that it became his swansong, for after fashioning the last gold star set in a spun-sugar sky above the Holy Child, he felt a fainting in his leg and sat down, and soon died.

The Queen's sisters danced lustily. They twirled and swooned in the bransle and saltarello, while their noble husbands, Essex, Bourchier, Kent, Lord Dunster, postured and bowed with wonderful elegance, their satin thighs stealing the torch glow from the ladies' jewels. There was a covey of holy men: Bishops Morton, Russell, Rotherham, Lionel Woodville of Salisbury. They pledged his Grace in spiced malmsey and hypocras, and if they thought the dancing wild, they did not say so.

The Queen, great with child again, was gay. The pastry-cook had moulded the Virgin's face in likeness to her Grace. This pleased her, likewise the collar of rubies and the sapphire girdle presented by the King's herald on gift-night. Anthony Woodville was lordly and high-hearted with prowess in the lists and at the rhyming. Young Thomas Dorset and Richard Grey were thrustingly merry, looking about with eyes that asked who dared drink deeper, dance more gracefully—and the candle of those eyes burned hot, seeking the thrown gauntlet.

And my sovereign lord? Well, truly he feasted twice, once after the vomit—in the high Roman manner, and passing bad for the belly, I have always reckoned; but I loved him no less for it. He cut a fair caper, and had he not been King I would fain have recruited him for my troupe of actors, so well did he disguise his thunderous heart. The reason for this hidden trouble was still Richard of Gloucester, whom, after the service I had done him, I had thought to see no more at court. He danced but once, and that with the Countess of Desmond, and he kissed her cheek in a filial way when all were flown with wine and goodwill. He drank but one cup to toast the King, and he stood out like a ramping tooth—Death at the feast. Ever he toyed with those accursed rings and his eyes were changing—from soft determination to hard melancholy.

George Clarence evaded the King's glance, and drank cup after cup with Lord Hastings who, like himself, shunned the Queen's kin as much as diplomacy would allow. Clarence feigned gaiety over wrath, and at times looked like a naughty infant who stamps its feet for a plaything and dares a beating. His wife Isabel was there, waxing faint after a short dance, with a wonderful red colour in her thin cheeks. Clarence cherished her well, for the bright blood in that face was Neville blood. All this I saw, and because I would have had my King merry in soul and body at Yule I became furious. I therefore found satisfaction in persecuting Clarence's poxy mermaid, who was with us again, angel-voiced and simpering. For Clarence it was who had caused my King's well-disguised disquietude. He had suffered a change of humour.

I had not been wandering when I marked Gloucester's expression as he came from St-Martin-le-Grand. I said he looked as one who sees the need to do battle, and I was in sympathy with him. As soon as I had overheard his oath: 'To the Devil with the estates!' I longed to see him settled, and King Edward too. Richard had spoken to me during the Twelve Days. Half-demented from my exertions, I had gone aloft to the gallery. Now this was not like the gallery at Greenwich, with its souvenirs of the Maiden; that was just a little stone recess where one could stand very close, and mayhap trip a measure for the sheer, silly childish joy of it. This was a broad passage with the moon coming through the openings between the corbels, and great chambers leading off on one side. Into one of these I skipped to quiet my pounding heart, and there, without candles, was Gloucester, his elbows on the window-ledge. I muttered apology, but he turned, friendly, from the night sky and I made a light for him. His face was all hollows and bones in the solitary flame. He knew me then. I would have assayed a jest and gone, but he said:

'I didn't acknowledge the service you did me in September,' whereupon I replied: 'To serve your Grace warrants pride on the servant's part, naught else,' thinking all the time how little he knew he was nearly *not* so served.

'You will not find me ungrateful,' he said, still short and brusque, I wondered what made him so: just the absence of Anne, or was it ever his way? So I dared ask him how the Lady Anne was, and he answered she was weary of Sanctuary. He sounded sad, then.

So he must have anticipated trouble, and he was not disappointed. The court hummed with George's latest sleight-of-hand.

'A chop-house!' he had cried, feigning great wonder. 'Certes, the doings at Tewkesbury must have addled the maiden! Fortunate indeed that you found her, good brother.'

In the King's pleasure-chamber, John had twanged a false note in his excitement.

'I made a loathsome din,' he told me afterwards. 'But so amazed was I by Clarence's duplicity I forget all Master Bucheron's teaching. One should keep the thumb fixed so, behind the neck of my lady Lute and—'

'A plague on that,' I said. 'What did the King say?'

'He looked very hard at Clarence, as if deciding this playacting unworthy of comment. Then he turned to my lord of Gloucester, saying, "Let us now arrange your marriage with Lady Anne, and name your first-born after me." "With my whole heart, your Grace," said Gloucester, and was bending to kiss the King's hand, when Clarence gave a mighty shout. "Nay!" he cried. "He shall not have her! She is still my ward, and the Neville affairs are in my hands. Her sister is still my wife. He'll not marry her, and there's an end to it."

'The King rose and swept all his chessmen to the floor, and the blood came into his face. "By God's Blessed Lady," he said, "George, would you deny our brother the solace of marriage?" "Let him marry someone else," said Clarence, right sullen. Wherefore my lord of Gloucester murmured that this was not his desire, and I went on playing as best I could with my ears not on the tune, and got some strange looks from Master Carlile.'

Yet now they were married, after months of wrangling, and because it had so affected me, what with my devil and my anxieties, and now with my own future in the balance, I lusted to know the details. So I halted my mount until John and I rode knee to knee and spoke him soft, smothering my foul humour.

'They say it's a cheerless place, Middleham,' I murmured.

'Who says?' he asked scornfully. 'My Lady Anne seemed well disposed to ride there with her lord.'

'Tell me about the wedding.'

'It was as any other,' said he. 'The bells rang, the incense burned, the Sacrament was taken, the vows plighted. They were married.' I vowed he was an exceeding dull chronicler.

'Yet it was a quiet ado,' he mused. 'With scant ceremony. Unlike the Princess Margaret's union with Duke Charles le Téméraire.'

I scowled at him. He had been there too, in Burgundy, at the right place and time as usual. He chattered on.

'Only the direct members of the blood royal—all the Queen's kin and my lady's sister, ridden with Clarence from Warwick Castle.'

'So Clarence is at Warwick!'

'How wan of countenance she was,' he said tenderly, lost in his own drift.

'Lady Isabel is sick,' I reminded him.

'Nay, the Lady Anne. Her Grace the Queen looked proud,' he remarked, and with these few words drew a clear picture of Elizabeth, great with another royal child, all firm lips and high brow, condescending to bless the marriage of her brother-in-law with little Anne. Neville and Beauchamp Anne, before her noble father launched himself against the Woodvilles and the realm. Neville and Beauchamp still, but I could well imagine the disdainful looks from those whom the Earl once tried to overthrow.

I asked: 'What took place at the Council meeting? Clarence was so adamant.'

John said: 'Well, the brothers parted with affection, after the ceremony. Of the settlement I know little—there are more words than music in King's Chamber of Council.' He pointed ahead. 'He can sate your curiosity, if he has a mind.'

The clerk rode bowed-headed. His plainsong blew back through the brightening morning. The cold air pricked pimples on his tonsured scalp. I urged forward beside him. He was midway through a soft *Magnificat*, so I waited until he got to '*et in saecula saeculorum*' and joined him in the long '*Amen*'. He was bound for Dunstable Priory, with letters from his master, the Abbot of Croyland.

'We ride to Yorkshire,' I said, and he murmured, 'Ah, a wild part, with great abbeys and rolling heathlands,' and my heart became heavier for all this sounded somewhat gloomy. But there could be no casting back, now, and I was keen to hear his knowledge of the blood royal. I probed his mind, gently, like tickling a trout.

'I have yet to visit Croyland.' No sooner had the words left me than he was off, all a-shimmer with the Abbey's history.

'Holy St Guthlac founded it in the six hundred and ninety-ninth year of our Lord, when Croyland was bound by water,' said he. 'The house has withstood fire, and earthquake. Our carved rood screen is the finest. The footbridge in the market place spans three holy streams—my master is making a new chronicle which will compass all England and its times—my hands ache with the writing of it.'

He spoke of blessed streams, and his words ran on like one of them. He talked of St Benedict of Nursia, his patron. It seemed I would never draw him on to the subject of the Warwick estates. When he paused for air, I said with cautious haste: 'Sir Clerk, I would gladly know what your master wrote of the King's Council meetings at Sheen lately,' and he replied:

'Never have I heard so many arguments put forth on either side in respect of the Lady Anne. Nor have I heard before such eloquence as that possessed by my lord of Clarence. Even the lawyers were amazed by his ingenuity. Again and again he swore that the right of wardship was his and that Gloucester should have none of her.'

'How spoke King Edward?'

'When at first my lord of Gloucester offered to relinquish all... the King showed anger, as if he thought him over-generous.'

'He said this?'

'During a lapse in the sessions I heard him with raised voice. "Nay, sir," he told the lord Richard. "You are my loyal and beloved brother and I will not see you cheated. But Clarence must be handled with velvet or he will wax more stubborn." Gloucester answered: "All I want, Sire, is my wife—and Middleham." "It is not enough, by God's Blessed Lady!" said King Edward. He strode back into Council, and weeks longer they argued, Clarence full of orations, my lord of Gloucester standing quiet, and full only of thoughts.'

In my mind I could see him, pensive, unsmiling, rigid.

'Finally he grew passionate,' said the clerk. 'He marched towards the Bench and faced them, turning this way and that so that his royal brothers should know his mind. "My lords and honest citizens," he said. "I pray his Grace's indulgence, but my wish is only for marriage with the Lady Anne, and for the Castle of Middleham. My brother of Clarence can have the remainder of the Warwick lands given me by the King after Barnet Field. So can he also have my Great Chamberlainship of England. And the earldoms of Warwick and Salisbury. All I desire is my wife—and Middleham."

Warwick Castle alone was a prize. I could scarcely believe it.

'"And Sheriff Hutton, and Penrith," said the King sternly. "So be it," said my lord of Clarence, and a long sigh rushed round the chamber. There was then only the sound of parchment being rolled, and coughing and yawning, and a great black cloud, lifting.'

'You are a poet, Sir Clerk,' I said admiringly.

'And a Parliamentary roll ordaining that no grant of lands made to Clarence ever be revoked,' he added, reproving my frivolity.

We parted near Dunstable and he gave me his blessing, and I was glad of it, for London and all I loved were slipping further and further behind down Watling Street. The first night we lodged six leagues south of Northampton and I slept well, also the following night, outside Lincoln walls. But on the morning of the fourth day, with the towns getting fewer and the great flocks of sheep rolling across our path, I waxed doleful indeed. I wondered what the Princess Elizabeth was doing, and whether the King were pleased with his new fool. I thought on my mother and the last time we met. She had been wondrous merry, pert with some hidden humour like a young maid, and when I gave her the news of my impending departure, and into whose service, she clapped her hands, saying I was a fortunate man. She then made me admire the new shop front, which gleamed black and gilded, and the brave new sign clanking in the breeze, and all I could get from her was what a noble prince was my lord of Gloucester. 'Serve him well,' she said, and when I raised my brows, she did but repeat herself and went on stroking the new timbers, like a daft woman, lovelorn. I hate secrets.

Also she asked me when I was to be married. For, over that miserable winter of '71, I had in my great folly, become betrothed to the maiden seen for the first time outside St Swithin's Church. Maiden I say, but Mistress Grace was in fact a widow of two-and-twenty, and all aflame to marry again. Mourning had not suited her heart—she was a fickle, jealous, wayward creature and for a space she fascinated me. From the moment I accepted her invitation to dine at her parents' house, things were out of my hands. Her father was a grocer and apothecary with a shop in Bucklersbury Lane, where he sold treacle of Genoa, and honey and sugar-loaves and copperas and cubebs and liquorice, as well as coarse goods in bulk. He had a house in St Laurence's Lane, next to Blossom's Inn with its sign of St Laurence the Deacon in a border of flowers. He was wealthy, but I was not without the wherewithal by any account, and both my mother and Grace's family seemed delighted by the match. So we were troth-plight—bound as if by marriage, in God's sight. I had had a strange feeling on hearing my baptismal name, used so rarely: Piers, the man, or Patch, the fool: which would you? One afternoon she well nigh tempted me to sin, in her parents' parlour. She had black eyes. We were betrothed, and I knew not if I loved her. She had not wept when I left for the north. She had only looked at me as if she couldn't wait for my return; or as if she couldn't wait.

'I will send for you,' I had told her, and she had wrapped her arms about my neck, shuddering delicately.

'Dear heart, I couldn't brook those solitary parts,' she had said. 'Mayhap I will go to the Minories for a space,' but I knew she would not. She had too much of a roving eye to cloister herself among the droning nuns. None the less, I am what I am, weak and cautious, and would not commit myself to instant matrimony, so I said: 'I will come soon again to London,' and gave her a tawny gown furred with squirrel, and a coral beads, which she wrapped round her wrist in the fashionable manner. I suppose it must have been in the back of my mind that she was my surety for a return to London, for if I asked my lord of Gloucester for leave to visit my *betrothed*, after all that had passed between him and me, and his lady, he could surely not refuse me. In any event, it was done; and as I rode north I still knew not if I loved her.

By four of the clock we were in right wild country, with our mounts flagging from the undulations of the Fosse Way. Treacherous ice patches covered the small bogs in our path. We forded streams, plunged through thickets where the only life was the frightened duck and grouse and wild boar which started and squealed. It was as the Croyland monk had said, wild and awesome; we passed the sprawling grey shape of many an abbey and priory. Then, suddenly, a great mysterious hand threw a cloak upon us. Utterly bewildered, our company came to a stop.

'We're lost,' said John.

Ahead, I heard Sir James Tyrell in conversation with his esquires. Their voices and the chink of their horses' gear sounded dull and far in the still, enveloping greyness.

'What was that last holy dwelling?'

'Kirklees, or Hampole, my lord. I'm not sure.'

'We are off course,' said Sir James.

He murmured something else. One of the esquires rode back to us, his face a pale splash in the swirling cloud.

'We will seek shelter at the next abbey,' he told us. 'My lord says it's madness to go on.' He turned his horse, and vanished within an armsbreath. John clutched my sleeve, fear in his face.

'It's only fog,' I said kindly. 'Bear up.'

'I thought I saw...' He was muttering about demons, then asked with fresh terror if we were to spend the night at Kirklees, where the wicked nun bled Robin Hood to death, and Jesu preserve us all!

We approached neither Kirklees nor Hampole. I never knew the name of that holy house, but it was a grim, solitary place and the nun at the lodge gate loath to receive us.

'We've enough to feed already,' she said, then saw Sir James looming behind us on his great black horse, and became all a-flutter. 'Enter, sirs.'

We dismounted, aching from damp and the ride, and tramped through cloisters into the parlour, where the Prioress, no more than five-and-twenty, received us in rich robes. She sat motionless, a small dog on her lap. Jewels sparkled on her white hands. The *Romaunt de la Rose* lay open on the table. At the farther end of the room a fine peregrine sat on its rod. I looked keenly at the lady and decided that this was a very worldly nun. John also stared, under his lashes. I wondered if he were thinking of Master Hood, and looking for blood-irons.

'Sirs, please to be fed,' she said in a high, douce tone. 'There are two chambers you may use—we have parlour boarders here or I would house you better.' She rang a bell and a maiden entered. She was about thirteen; no nun's habit for her, nor jewelled rings. She wore a plain grey gown and limped.

'Mistress Edyth will guide you to the guesthouse,' said Madame. 'But soft, sirs, it is long past Compline.'

We followed the shadowy Edyth along the cloister out into the fog and the cloister-garth and through to the long low building which served the corrodians and there we ate mutton in an uneasy silence. Edyth hovered; she was pale, with sad dull eyes. There was a heavy atmosphere about the place. I felt it, as I stood with John and Robert in the passage waiting while Edyth brought candles. It was so still, yet fraught with past dooms. Unconsciously I felt for my knife as a jay-bird screamed. A dog howled, a woman laughed. I lingered for a moment while the others went towards bed. I know not why. As I stood I heard a quick, light tread, and saw a flickering light bloom in the dark distance. A woman was approaching— not a nun—she wore a neat headdress with a short veil. She was as small as a faery woman, with a handspan waist. She was the Maiden, and just as in my dreams, only better.

She stopped and peeped up at me, and it was as of old with the flame leaping round our heads and the chill darkness. The last time I had seen her she was distraught and weeping, while the King was captive and heads rolling all over the realm. Now she was calm, and older. Like a still portrait she stood with one hand on the crucifix at her breast, the other raised so that the light she held flooded us both and flickered in the draught. She had filled my thoughts for a long, long time, and I had thought to see her no more. And all my wit and power were stilled under the force of my love, and I knew not what to say to her. So I spoke her name, saying it over and over, and then I took and kissed her hand, the one that lay on the Cross. When she greeted me it was as if she were the jester, and I the maiden.

'Well, sir!' she said smiling. 'Is the King's fool to become a monk? If so, he has strayed into the wrong cloister, for we have no habit to fit him here. Or is it plans for some new disguising?'

I heard my own voice boom back from the vaulted passage. 'Sweetest of mistresses! Oh, sweet! How and what do you here, in God's name?'

She set the candle on the ledge and spread her hands, just as she used to do.

'I live here,' she said simply. 'This place is my husband in truth, for my dower feeds me, and clothes me...'

'I never guessed you were to buy a corrody,' I said, and she answered right swiftly: 'It was bought *for* me, my friend, and thus I eat heartily and pray long—that is, when I can, for the jargoning birds in church and dorter drive one senseless with their noise.'

So she was unhappy. To gain time I said: 'We were lost. We came here for succour. At first they were loath to open but Sir James...'

She cut into my speech and her lips curled scornfully.

'Pay no heed to their tales,' she said. 'It costs less to feed wayfarers than to flaunt in twenty shillings of fur on her mantle, as does the Prioress!'

When she was young, and I her only friend at court, I would hold her hand; at Christmas I had kissed her. I again took her hand and held on to it, and she curled her fingers around mine. Truly I had forgotten how deep I loved her. A sighing wind blew down the corridor and the little veil fluttered on either side of her face. I thought of her nut-brown hair, hidden this night, and I, too, sighed like the wind. Now I could rue my hasty betrothal. In the sight of God, Grace and I were one, and here was I, enchanted. The Maiden and I stared at each other, and the scent of my sorrow must have released hers, for she cried:

'Oh, Patch! this is a terrible place—there's no discipline, no peace. One of the nuns threw herself into the well, a month past.'

'Why, in heaven's name?'

'She was guilty of apostasy.'

'In what way?'

The Maiden smiled, a wonderful tight smile. 'She was in love.'

To change the subject I said: 'We are for Middleham,' and in the guttering candlelight I could have sworn her colour faded and came back.

'We can't talk here,' she said, after a pause. 'Come to the scriptorium.'

As we walked together, one of the shadows detached itself from a pillar and became the little Edyth. She took the Maiden's gown by its edge and went along with her like a dog. It was then I knew her witless, and wondered even on that, for I am far from such, yet would fain have been my sweet mistress's cur, fawning on her daily. The Maiden spoke her soft, saying: 'Go along, dear child; wait in my room,' then turned to me and murmured: 'She is not as marvellously dull as she appears; she is my beadswoman in heart and thought—indispensable.'

Yet Edyth tarried, looking at my lady with all the love I would fain have shown, until the Maiden said: 'Go! tend the jewel, she was coughing a half-hour back. I shall not be long.' And Edyth became a shadow again, merging with the darkness.

'A sick nun?' I asked.

She smiled and laughed and looked sad, all at once.

'As you wish. Aye, a young, sick nun.'

'Who is Edyth?'

'One such as I,' said my lady. 'One who rides the tide anchorless. She is gently born. A bastard. Now, what of the court?'

I drew my wits together and told her of London. Being cloistered she knew little of past events. She knew of Warwick, though.

'I cannot believe that he is dead,' she said slowly. 'Never will I forget my first sight of him—he was like one descended from Olympus.' Then she asked: 'How does the Queen's Grace, and all her many cousins?'

'Thriving,' said I. 'Waxing fat.'

'The Dowager Duchess of Bedford?'

'Dead and chested.' Remembering that the Maiden had served that lady intimately, I added, 'God assoil her.' I waited for her 'Amen' but her thoughts must have wandered for a space, for I did not hear it. She asked after Katherine and Elinor and Mary and Anne Haute and Elysande, and I was able to give her news of all these fair ones. She hounded me with questions.

'And the Princesses, and the new, blessed heir to England?' I told her of my sweet Elizabeth, raking through last autumn's leaves for titbits to enchant her. I told of the day when Elizabeth escaped her nurse, and the Duke of Gloucester's wrath. She became very still suddenly, with the stillness of a rose before its petals drop.

'You say—Richard was angry with the dame,' she said, as if it mattered.

'Aye, white with fury and concern.'

'He was rare in his wrath, as I remember.'

'Ah, you would not know Gloucester now,' I said. 'When you were at court he was but a youth, shy, ill-fitting among the gaiety. Now he is a man, with battle scars and a will of his own. Constable and Admiral of England, and Lord of the North. He rules these parts—from Wensleydale.' I pointed northward. 'From that gloomy fortress of his, where I am bound tomorrow.'

I hoped she would commiserate with me for she knew how I loved London. But she said, right soft: 'Wensleydale, with its sharp cleansing gales and haunted mists. There a man can come close to God and know himself at last,' and it sounded like a poem she had by rote, a song of someone else's making. 'Tell me of all the royal princes,' she said.

I knew not where to begin, but told of George of Clarence, recounting my part in the love-tale of Anne Neville. I spared no detail, for it was better than any ballad lately fashioned, being so packed with surprise and romance, and as I had been a protagonist in the strange events I recounted with gusto. And she was very quiet—the quietest audience I had had for many a geste-night.

When I paused for want of fresh embroidery she said: 'Tell on—so George thwarted the match,' and I said, with satisfaction, 'Yea, and with such cunning one could almost admire him.' Suddenly she cried: 'Friend, will you bear a letter for me?' She called for pen and paper, which the pale Edyth brought, with fresh candles. Thus she wrote, standing fine and slender like the carved scribe-stand against which she leaned, while I waited, drinking up her beauty. She rolled the paper and then she took from her pouch her seal which she held up, dark and heavy-gleaming, saying: 'My seal—at least they left me that.' She took the tallow to the flame and sealed the letter and addressed it: 'In secret, to his Grace the Duke of Gloucester,' and then as an afterthought, all his titles. She was about to give it to me when I said: 'But I didn't finish my story—do you not like it?' and added the parts I had missed, about my devil and his flying away, and she crossed herself to think of such a horrid demon plaguing me. She murmured: 'So they were wedded, eventually?' Her eyes were big and lustrous and I longed to kiss her, but on seeing her seal realized how little I had known of her, and of her family. She had always vowed herself humble, at court, with her dead father a landless knight, but in truth she had as much right there as any of the upstarts brought in over the years by the Woodvilles. It was then I felt bound to tell her a little of my thoughts, and plunged in, clumsy-footed.

'I had a dream of you last autumn.' She smiled softly. 'A fair dream, I hope?' So I told her how strange it was, and affrighting, and as I spoke I thought I saw something cousin to fear growing in her eyes. Then when I came to the end, where I fancied I saw her burning and heard the whisperings of necromancy, she cried: 'Ah, God! Do not! Say no more!' and turning from me fell upon her knees. I caught her shoulders and drew her up, full of remorse.

And all she could say, with sobs pouring, was: 'I am innocent—I had no part of it. All were lies,' and she raised her face, just the shape of a little shield, perfect and pointed. And looking at that face which was incapable of sin, I said: 'Sweet lady—it was but a foolish dream, and you never wrought witchcraft in your life, that I know.'

Yet she talked on wildly. 'You have told me, this night, that the Duchess of Bedford is dead and chested—I could have been served likewise. Ah, God help her!'

'Yes, she's dead,' I said, wondering.

She whispered: 'Was it—the block—the stake?'

'The Duchess died in her bed,' I said slowly. 'Peaceful, and shriven, with all her daughters round her, and the window wide for her spirit's passage. What talk is this of judgements?'

'But she bewitched the King!' said the Maiden, shuddering.

This I had not heard, and was full of horror for my lady's indiscretion. 'There was a charge of sorcery, indeed,' I said, very quiet. 'But it was my Lord of Warwick whom she was said to have enthralled. They said she made images of him with an iron band round his waist, to sap his strength. Not of his Grace, certes. There was a clerk named Daunger, whom Thomas Wake said had practised witchcraft years ago and knew the Duchess. But naught was proven. The arraignment was dropped, and all was fog and mist for there was none to testify.'

'Did they not speak of me?'

'At no time,' I said truthfully. I had only wished they had spoken of her, far she had vanished, and it seemed that none knew, or cared.

'Or—of love-sorcery?'

'Dear lady,' I said, patient, 'it was all a pitiful attempt to shake the Queen's kin during the rebellion—gone like summer haze. Be calm, for your soul's sake!'

She laughed, with no humour in it, more like weeping. I was nigh frantic, perplexed by her. I was almost glad when Edyth stole back into the chamber. To my lady she whispered: 'She is fretting for you.'

'Coming!' said the Maiden in a stronger voice. 'Farewell, Sir Fool.'

'Give me the letter,' I said, holding out my hand.

But she only smiled, and held the roll in the flame, and it burnt up bright and lit all our faces with a glow like Hell Mouth at the Gild plays, and was destroyed.

'God send you good fortune,' she laid her lips most sweetly on my cheek. She was leaving, and I could not bear it.

'St Catherine have you in her keeping,' I said with difficulty.

'We shall not meet again,' she said, and was gone the next instant.

Fool that I am, I wept.

His Majesty keeps mastiffs. They lie outside his chamber of a night. Soon after his coronation we had a big baiting at Smithfield: in its way an innovation because instead of a bull, he commanded that a lion should be tried against three of his dogs. When the great tawny beast lay dead, and the curs, all gaping gory wounds, stood panting froth, King Henry ordered a strange conclusion to the sport.

'Hang them,' he said in his high Welsh voice. 'Traitorous dogs shall not rise against a king.' It took long moments for the big animals to choke on the end of a felon's halter. Some of the ladies shuddered at the unnatural sight; my sweet Elizabeth merely smiled a curious little smile. But then she knows his Majesty's mind, being wedded to him, and sees reason where most ignorant folk cannot...

There were many dogs at Middleham. When I rode up from the market-place, a half-dozen of Richard's hounds ran to greet me. I waved my staff with its merry moonface jester's banner, crying: 'Call off your dogs, my lord! Here enters the king of mirth and none other. My sword is wit—yet, marry, though there be no bone in the tongue it has often broken a man's head!' All this was wasted—there were only the open-mouthed stable knaves and the smith to hear me. They shook their heads, muttering that I must be a Turk or a Frenchie, so odd were my ways. Nor could I reckon much of their northern speech. I dismounted and fondled Richard's dogs: great deer-hounds with a brush of wolf in them, slender running-whelps and harriers. Strong dogs.

That first evening, during supper, when I bounded into the Great Hall full of quips and favoured heraldic allusions, I looked to my new master's dais and was quite put at a loss. Though he sat under his cloth of estate with his wife and his friends about him, I had ado to recognize him. This was not the sombre, watchful young knight of the royal court. Those once guarded eyes had a light in them—like the renewed flame in those of one recovered from a dolorous sickness, or the gleam of those returning from blessed Compostella. Now and again his face broke up into smiles, as if he had no control over a deep gladness and comfort deep within. I looked along the table for the reason for his joy. In great Warwick's powerful day, my lady Anne was ever a lovesome little creature. Now it was not the rich jewels or the blue velvet that made her fair, though lovely indeed she was. She, too, had that same inner light.

He held her hand, shamelessly. Their joined hands lay on the damask; this made eating difficult, but quite often they disdained to eat, and looked at each other. My jests that night were a little diffident, as I was anxious to try the humour of this strange place, but my lord and lady laughed at everything I said, or did. I closed one eye at John and Robert. After a time the minstrels struck up '*Filles à marier*' which warns maidens against marriage because of its domestic hazards, and Anne Neville smiled, casting down her eyes, shaking her head.

Item, I had seen a friend when we passed through York. Coming up Stonegate, where they had brought the masonry to finish the fair Cathedral Church, I chanced to raise my eyes to the new houses and the gildsmen's high halls, and there, perched on a stone buttress, was my devil. I stared him out, saying under my breath: 'All this is your fault, fiend,' but to my surprise he only looked straight ahead, as if we had never been familiar, or argued about the fate of Lady Anne. I was quite wounded by his unmannerly ways.

Gloucester's friends sat about him at the high table: Francis Lovell, Robert Percy, James Harrington, William Parr, Richard Nele and Miles Metcalfe, lawyers both; and two of the Warwick kinsmen, Lord Scrope of Bolton and Baron Greystoke, Richard's loyal friends. James Tyrell was there, too. When the pale purple evening deepened to violet through the high windows, they brought torches and Gloucester beckoned me to the dais. It was for a moment reminiscent of King Edward's easy custom. He was not bent on mirth, Richard, however, for he leaned across and asked softly: 'Now, my friend, what of London?'

It seemed as if this was another pressing me for news, as if I knew more than the lords about him. I was curious, for Richard was not cloistered in a nunnery, like my sweet lady. Accordingly I gazed with innocent and lackwit eyes, saying:

'Marry, sir, the forests of Eltham mourn now that the noblest of Boars is departed,' and although his lips flickered upwards he said: 'Don't flatter me, Sir Fool,' and I thought how George of Clarence would have preened at my choice folly. I told him that the King was well, and his Queen, for diplomacy throwing in 'more beautiful than ever,' at which my lord turned to the Lady Anne. He murmured: 'Sir Fool prates of beauty. How should he know, when all beauty is at Middleham?' and this threw me adrift for a moment, to hear such words from one who had just condemned flattery—until, looking at their faces, I realized that he was in earnest.

'How does my brother of Clarence?' he said, turning to me again.

So I was to be his eyes and ears. I had warned the King, times past, about Warwick's rebellion, yet he had dallied. Richard knew of this. Men speak much before a fool—the name misguides them. In a low tone, I gave my master what I knew. George was again dabbling in conspiracy with the slippery Archbishop of York, George Neville—I cast many an anxious glance at the Lady Anne; it was a passing difficult situation for me. Richard listened and I saw his face begin to lose its lightness.

'The Archbishop is in touch with my lord of Oxford, in France,' I said. 'King Louis has tried attacking Calais, once...'

He gestured impatiently. 'Yea, I know of that. It's my brother who troubles me ... surely even he would not be so...'

He was about to say 'so rash, so witless' but checked himself. To try and find an excuse for witless Clarence I murmured, 'Mayhap my lord Astrologer was led by a false star.'

For the prophecy, I reckoned, had given George remembrance that he was in fact, King of England, having been declared heir by the Lancastrian Parliament in '70. Now with Prince Edward of Lancaster and Harry VI entombed, who else? Then I grew cold from the look on Richard's face.

'What prophecy?' he whispered.

Holy Jesu! I thought. He had not heard of it. Impossible but true—he had been too busy looking for Anne. I told him as lightly as I could, and with growing courage, for astrology cannot be treason, that 'the next King's name would begin with "G".' I saw him whiten and cross himself, and it was like a window opening in my mind, flooding me with cold light. I thought of my lord as 'Richard'—often, to myself, I called him 'Dickon'. The name George began with G, indeed—but so did Gloucester. We stared into each other's eyes: I, the fool, he, the Lord of the North. The Great Hall with its gently laughing throng, the clatter of silver, the scurrying servants, quivered into the distance around us. Anne's laughter, rich and soft, answered some gallantry of Francis Lovell.

Gloucester took a late rose from the bowl in front of him. Young and fresh and fair, like in Chaucer's poem. He twirled the little yellow bloom between his fingers. Then he spoke and sometimes, in these clouded days, I hear his words again.

'God forbid,' he said softly. 'This'—and he embraced the whole company with one slight gesture—'this is my kingdom.'

His kingdom was a right wild one. Behind his court, the moors rolled upward to the sky. Middleham had stood on the slope of that dale for more than three centuries, and even before that the Conqueror's men had raised a pile of stone, the remnants of which burgeoned against the waving grasses, the shape of motte and bailey still existing. Earlier still, the ancient Celts had built a palace there—it was old as time, this place, and mysterious.

After that first evening I took care to guard my tongue—I am paid to make men merry, not distress them. We never spoke again of the prophecy, though he talked often of Clarence, and once about sending his brother an invitation to stay a while at Middleham. He was all anxiousness; I thought of how he had drawn the flickering Duke over to the King's standard again, before Barnet Field.

In his kingdom he was absorbed. He knew every inch. The flying winds, the bold sunlight that slipped across the moors with dark cloud-banners following were in his blood, as was the swift-rushing Ure, foaming on its journey down to the Mill Gill force at Aysgarth. Secretly I would watch him—for I am curious about my masters—when he rode out hawking, strong and frail, a creature of paradoxes, with his great white gerfalcon on the gauntlet. Its silver bells would catch in the breeze and jingle. Spaniels ran beside, black silk and scent-eager. Spring was coming, and Lent around the corner, the day I challenged him, for a jape, to single combat. Unsmiling, he took me to the tiltyard and with one lance-thrust... well, I consider myself nimble, but I fancied he had broken my wrist. Thereupon he hoisted me up with a merry laugh and bound my arm, as a brother might do, roughly gentle. 'Try hawking,' he counselled me and thereafter I accompanied him over the long slopes which opened like the scroll of a manuscript, with the great abbeys, Fountains, Jervaulx, Rievaulx, for initial letters and the dotted thickets the lesser text. Often it was just he and I and the Lady Anne.

The blessed time of Passion and Resurrection was behind us soon. I remember how heavenly sweet the choristers lifted their voices. At one moment it seemed that their praises would burst right through the roof of the nave and up into the clear moorland air among the larks who carolled of our deliverance. There was a great freedom about that place, a sanctity. I rode down the dale with my lord and lady. Anne's mare, Cryseyde, stopped to nibble a hazel sapling. The new buds were tempting as almond milk—no matter how she tugged the rein, the beast wouldn't budge, so I disengaged horse from branch, and Lady Anne smiled her thanks, singing to herself all the while. The ballad she sang hurled my heart down into my parti-coloured boots.

'For if ye, as ye said,
Be so unkind to leave behind
Your love, the Nut-Brown Maid...

Why do you weep, Sir Fool?'

I shut my eyes hard, and laughed so loud that Gloucester turned back to see what we were about.

'That poor song ill-befits so fair a voice,' I said, and in a great burst of rodomontade, 'Marry, I have a song that I fancy may outshine it; if it does not please you, madame, then I will eat it, together with salt and pepper and a wing of the next duck your lord puts up.'

She clapped her hands together, joyful as a child. I had meant to hoard this poem for some special occasion, but I would fain change the tune on her lips, for at this moment, all the day's sweet was mixed with sour. So I cleared my sandy throat and gave forth with my poor effort, all in praise of the little Duchess. Her pale face flamed with pleasure. Gloucester watched her with a serious love. 'Brave, Patch,' he said. 'For that, you shall put up the first bird.'

I rode off, balancing my sparrowhawk, sending in the dogs, gently showing my hawk the light, then throwing her up into the winds. And when I looked back from the fluttering, diving birds, I saw Richard lifting his lady from her horse on to his. So gently he set his lips on her brow, on each eyelid, on her small, pale mouth. The spaniels started many birds that day, and all for me, for my master had lost interest. There are a lot of songs written about the toils of wedlock, and most of them by fools. As for the poem, the manuscript was lost long ago, but some of the lines bide with me:

'Now let a muse but murmur of her Grace
Her Grace's matchless grace is well nigh matched
For by the blessed beauty of her face
Poor souls made radiant are, and woes dispatched.
Hearts that behold her gentleness wax light,
With humble joy the winds her form caress,
*Heaven's tears dry up at sight of her liesse,**
And Winter yieldeth to a Rose so White.'

There was more, but only the last two lines remain:

'She has, and is, in Virtue every part,
Queen of the North, and noble Gloucester's heart.'

Let no man draw from my chronicle that noble Gloucester was all for dalliance. He was too full of affairs for that, but the day on the hill stays with me, for it was spring and the world the same green world as today, where such matters are concerned. He was twenty, and she sixteen. This world that passes soon, as flowers fair.

John was in love with the Duchess. I think he saw himself as one of the old-style trouvères, who would single out a married lady in secret and, still in secret, give her his heart. He was jealous of my poem, and endeavoured to better it, but in vain. But then, neither could I sing, so the coat was as long as large. And as my lady saw the face of no man but Gloucester, however handsome or devoted, the whole business was not worth a quarrel. Neither, strangest of

* Old French—'joy'.

all, did I feel inclined to quarrelling. I had thought to be restive at Middleham, full of London-longing, but I was not. I had looked for boredom and lonesomeness in the solitary north. I was happy. The summer wore on, and the heather bloomed on the moors, and the flying song of the bees caught my troubles drowsing more than once. I dare not dwell on all this, because when joy is flown the remembrance of that joy's making brings only pain. Then, though, there were no more mists to affright me, no devils to rend my feeble, faltering soul.

The *minstralli ducis gloucestriae* gained some little esteem, as we travelled the north country at intervals. We were two bands—John belonged to the Lady Anne, so he was satisfied at any rate. I can see him still and hear his beautiful singing voice in that upper chapel at Middleham, his eyes steady on the carved roof that was as delicate as a spider-web. So can I hear the rushing river pounding the moorland slope with its message of haste—a beckoning haste that then I did not understand. I can smell the flowers in Lady Anne's garden. I can remember the names of Richard's dogs, most of whom died of old age. I say I do not dwell on that time: I lie. There are things that remain: the flight of a falcon over the dale; the sound of music in the waters of Hell Gill Beck.

I remember—and I have forgotten. Fear and spleen have made me forget all this, yet it comes again and again to taunt and reproach me. For his Divine Majesty likes music too, but the tunes are loud to my old ears, and more devious. He also likes hunting, and is exceeding skilled. He flushes out his quarry from the most secret hides, and his hawks kill with such marvellous speed that a poor fool knows not whether yesterday is today, or today tomorrow.

My Grace wrote an ill-formed hand, with characters small and straggling, and I had ado to make much of her writings. I was impatient with this, for they were full of London news, interspersed with her new gown of muster-develers, her sarcenet bonnets and additions to her father's stable. Out of this formless jumble I learned that King Edward had nipped in the bud those fresh stirrings of rebellion in George of Clarence and the Nevilles.

'My Lord Archbishop lies imprisoned in Hammes Castle, off great Calais,' she wrote. 'Yet there be many flying tales in London still and men buy harness daily. It may be that Oxford will attack the realm. The King, whom Jesu preserve, keeps watch, moving from town to town. This day I saw the Princess Elizabeth go by barge to the Tower. She will grow into the fairest lady.'

Those were the lines to give me little pangs. The King, bright head grazing the clouds, sword in hand against Lancastrian foes. His eldest daughter, growing womanly.

'My mother has a green popinjay now that talks like a Christian. It pleases me you are happy at Middleham.' A great blot smeared the paper. I wondered if she had been enraged at the time of writing. I had seen her temper; she had sharp nails, and could shout as adeptly as she could wheedle and coax. We would be a right merry pair together, I thought, reading on.

'You speak much of my lord of Gloucester and his fair dealings with the northern citizens. There is like talk here, for some men of York were at my cousin's to dine and full of your good lordship. One said he offers good and indifferent justice to all, gentle or simple—would then that the sheriff of this ward had his ear, for Master Fray came before sessions two weeks gone and—'

I threw the letter away and leaped up, smote the stone wall a violent blow with my fist, then strode about nursing the pain. Dan Fray had been acquitted. Lack of evidence, wrote Grace, but her careful, blotched characters hid the truth. Secretly I had feared this outcome, but had bargained on my mother's testimony together with that of the cook-boys to secure Fray's conviction. But Fray had done men service in his time; lords who dabbled in this and that, and whose night-walking heralds were taciturn and cloaked. Wretches hang that jurymen may dine, indeed, yet should the wretch know the right words, the jury... I wept with rage.

'Why so wrathful, Sir Fool?' asked Gloucester, quietly behind me. His swift eyes caught the discarded roll of writing. 'Has mischief befallen you, or yours?' His tone was the same soft emotionless one I had heard him use on the occasions when, from a quiet niche, I watched him preside at the Council of the North. Wherever the Council met, whether at Sheriff Hutton, Pontefract, or Middleham, the scene would be the same—with Master John Kendall standing, pen poised, behind, Richard would sit in the chair of estate, his red robes a bright flood against the oak. His hands would be gently folded on the table, his eye keen and intent. When he heard news that pleased him, such as the repairing of Holy Trinity Priory at York, a lightning smile would cross his mouth. When he learned at Pontefract of a poor wife dispossessed by the land-hungry overlord, he drew off his ring on his last finger and replaced it, over and over. His face betrayed little; his hands were the heralds of his distress. Once, I had thought it anger that moved them. Long hours I studied him at these council meetings, sessions that left me with a strange feeling of ignorance. In plain words, he educated me in morals and philosophy, and to judge by the startled faces of his fellows, I was not alone. Often I smiled at the dropping jaws of Lords Scrope and Greystoke and the northern justices of the Peace, when Richard, confronted by a wrangling knot of citizens, pronounced a judgement so wonderful in its simplicity that the problem, whatever it was, seemed never to have existed. While I thought on this, he still stood by me waiting for my answer. But mine was too small a matter, I thought.

'My lady writes of bright green popinjays, your Grace, and I am jealous,' I carolled, thrusting out one red leg.

'How does your mother, at the cook-shop?' he asked, without a smile, and I was afraid he was in league with the devil and could read my thoughts. I dropped all folly on the instant.

'The villain who fired her shop walks free as air, and that displeases me.'

'A corrupt jury,' he said instantly.

'Yea, bought and sold,' I answered.

'Ah, holy God!' he cried. 'It displeases you, friend, but, by Our Lady, it *angers* me. 'Tis like a cursed, creeping plague that weakens the whole structure of our justice. Would that this matter had come before *my* Council!'

Then he asked what else, and I read on, the part not digested, and had ado to conceal a sour grin.

'Fray's nephew died in gaol,' I said. Then the satisfaction vanished, for I had no quarrel with the three yeomen and a knight, likewise chested through the same prison-fever.

'The charge was but flimsy,' wrote my betrothed. 'But they had lain in Fleet for three parts of a year so God took them, they being frail from poor diet. They will come before a higher court.' She had a keen and sarcastic wit, my lady. Richard was looking at me, pensively. He said: 'Sir Fool, what think you of this notion? If money can be exploited to sway justice, why should it not also serve to lighten the lot of those awaiting trial?'

'Pay for their victuals in gaol, my lord?'

He shook his head impatiently. 'Nay—take them from prison—rather have them stand surety in a friend's bond. Thus relieve the dreadful press within the gaols.' He looked sharp. 'Have you seen inside Ludgate, or the Fleet?'

'Never imprisoned, save by a lady's smile,' said I.

'Once I went out of curiosity,' he said softly. 'The sights stayed with me for days. It is a bitter education.'

I gaped. His reasoning had lost me long ago. Prisons were for felons; if you lay within, that was your bad fortune. An esquire came in to say the horses were ready.

'You are for London, my lord?' I asked, in a panic. They seemed to be on the point of departure, and I had not composed my reply to Grace.

'We ride to Nottingham, and the King,' he said, and gave a peculiar smile. 'A little private business,' and left me wondering.

He also left me to amuse his lady and her companions. We sat on the warm green slope with the Castle behind us and a flourishing oak for shade. Idle days, in the sun, with the fantail doves strutting like tiny peacocks at our feet. 'My lady,' I would say, 'it is your turn to play.'

I would stare at my hand for the best part of a quarter-hour, until I knew each card by heart. I also knew what Lady Anne held; she had poor cards but I was determined she should win. She was dolorous, far away in a dream. She was ever like this—worse perhaps when he went to Scotland to investigate the regular outbreaks of fighting there. She gave a long sigh.

'Dick... my lord has been gone five days,' she announced, as if I were a wayfarer newly come to the estate.

'I doubt not he has many pressing affairs for King Edward's ear,' I said lamely. There was no point in jesting with her. When he was gone, she was like a flower out of water, dying by inches. It was as well he never remained absent long.

'He said it was something that would please me,' she said woefully. 'A surprise. A secret, one I would have shared.'

'Oh, my life's sovereign pleasaunce! your good lord had his reasons!' I said, remembering he had hinted about folks in durance and wondering what it was all about. Then she asked me did I know aught of love? I knew not if she spoke of love of God, home and family, country, or of man to woman, so I diced on the latter.

'Yea, "Dan" Chaucer's "dreadful joy",' I said softly. Now that the sharing of our livelode was settled and Grace's dower decided, it was time I set the marriage date. The Maiden had dismissed me. 'We shall not meet again.' My turn to sigh now. How could she be so sure?

'I do crave oranges!' said Lady Anne.

A gasping cry of delight rushed round the circle of gentlewomen. The Duchess's face was sweetly comical in its innocence. I conjured a bright fruit from my sleeve to please her. Next week it would be lemons, no doubt, or pomegranates. My mother had been the same while carrying my youngest brother—

'Little Blaise
Lived but eight days.'

I thought of Isabel Neville's stillborn babe, and resolved an extra fervent prayer for the Duchess's safe travail when her time came. Like a child herself, she sat dabbing at the orange-drops that had splashed on her gown. Lady Harrington knelt beside her.

'Now you have a secret for your lord, dear mouse.'

'Marry, she has her lord in a cleft stick,' said I boldly; I was glad they would leave Anne to tell the Duke herself. I anticipated his joy. There was already a child at Middleham; John, Richard's little bastard son. Lady Anne had asked for him, complete with wet-nurse. She cuddled him often—he was a lovesome boy, though not pretty; the Plantagenet features were overstrong in the small face and he seemed to have inherited his father's seriousness. Watching her with this product of a gay or careless hour, I had longed to see her with a child of her own. So my day was lightened by an orange-feast.

John was called John of Gloucester, later. Years ago, I watched him go to the block, still serious, still strong of face. He died at twenty, brave Plantagenet. Traitorous dogs shall not rise against a King.

The Lady Anne's secret was very evident before my lord of Gloucester revealed his private business to any of us. He chose to surprise his wife at a great banquet one evening. The Great Hall was bulging with guests. Wreaths of poppies and roses trailed along the damask tablecloths. Pipes of hypocras and malmsey were borne in from the buttery, with baked swan and pheasant, roast capon and sucking-pig, doucettes and subtleties, and a great White Rose fashioned of frosting and honey. A barrowload of fragrant gillyflowers had been mingled with the rushes underfoot. Outside, against a greenish sky, bats dived and swooped past the window arches, and a drowsy thrush chortled. Anne Neville concealed her proud secret behind the high table; it was strange to see her so round, elsewhere she was exceeding slender. I teased her gently, saying I knew it would be the fairest babe ever, and in all virtues like her Grace, save in the 'very, very thing' for I knew Richard longed for an heir. He had given us all an increase in wages.

We had an honoured guest that evening: one whose shadow cast itself over my lord's affairs constantly: Lord Percy, Earl of Northumberland. Grim and arrogant, he had sworn before King's Council to respect Richard's superiority in the northern marches. Richard had likewise taken oath to be his good and gracious lord and give him due considerations in all matters of policy. My lord often entertained this awkward nobleman, made him joint arbiter in the disputes arising among the barons, and spoke him fair. Yet the vice Envy gnawed, and my master never touched Northumberland's heart. I capered and mocked and declaimed great double witted praises on the noble earl and his ancestry which I fancied he might be too slow to grasp, while John and Robert twanged and bugled in the gallery. Lord Percy fed on roast heron and sugared violets, while Richard discoursed with him upon the Scots wars and Middle March jurors, listening cordially to his opinions, firm and cool. Lord Percy could be offensive in a careful, veiled way, but Richard never showed a flicker. There they sat, these two great men: the young, royal Lord of the North, and Henry Percy, whose family had ruled that same North for generations with a heavy hand, and in whose belly this new arrangement lay right sour. Richard, however, had got him laughing when I looked up once from the floor of the Hall. I felt jealous; this was my job. Then I heard Gloucester say: 'They are late.' One of his henchmen leaned down from behind the cloth of estate and whispered. Richard smiled and turned to Lady Anne, pointing to the door, through which strode Sir James Tyrell, dusty from riding, and beside him a frail, ageing lady.

Richard rose and came down the steps to embrace the Countess of Warwick. Sciatica made her hobble at every step, her face was drawn. He kissed her on each cheek and led her to the vacant seat beside her daughter. I had mused about that empty place all evening. Anne was weeping. All she could say was: 'Ah, sweet mother!'

''Tis all thanks to your good lordship,' said the Countess of Warwick wearily. Richard leaned to wipe up tears with a napkin, signalled to me to start a jape, while the servers came forward with food for the fragile old dame.

This then was his well-kept secret. I found out afterwards that King Edward had taken some persuading. None knew why he was so reluctant to release the Countess from Beaulieu Sanctuary, but Richard's pleas at Nottingham had finally succeeded. And he had his reward in the one burning, loving look from his little wife. I would like a woman to look at me like that, if only once. But then, I am not Richard Plantagenet. I am of no importance, and alive.

'It is four winters since we plighted our troth,' wrote my lady. 'I find you a false wretch, as false a knave as ever my eyes beheld, for you say you cannot come to London and I could not support the cold of the north, without that I had a gown furred with the red fox and a dozen pairs of warm shoes, and such an unfeeling creature as yourself would seem ill-disposed to furnish me therewith. I trow you are without a heart.'

Lord! how she did rail! But to good cause, I admit, for over the sweet, fleeting years at Middleham I had become a craftsman in procrastination. None could hiver-hover like I. Yet I looked forward to her letters, for she still spoke of the King and the weather of policy in and around the capital, furnishing me with precious news.

'Since my lord Oxford found himself adrift on St Michael's Mount, he showed good sense in throwing himself upon the King's mercy. My lord Clarence is full proud and lusts for this and that supplementation, and maybe more than just added livelode. The lady Isabel's boy, now Earl of Warwick, thrives and will be the same age as your Duchess Anne's child, bearing the same name, that of his Grace. Katherine my sister is with child again and bound for Calais to succour her lord who received grievous wounds. His wool-ship was plundered by the heathen Scots three days out of Dover. I have a new brachet, bought me by an old friend, you do not know him, he is a gentleman. My lord Clarence left the King's Parliament lately right joyous now that he has Clavering in Essex and the manor of Le Herber, that which Earl Warwick used to own. It seems that the King has one thought and that only for his brothers to be at peace together.'

At one juncture it had seemed that Gloucester might lose Middleham. Anxious days those, while Clarence agitated again for the redistribution of the Warwick estates. Lady Anne had wept in the arms of her gentlewomen.

'Why must he have these cravings?' she sobbed. 'Can he not live in harmony?'

'There, dear heart,' said Lady Lovell uneasily.

'My lord thinks as I do. Today he said, "Why can he not be content as I?"'

Thereon I had burst into the room with mad grimace and silly song, and dried their tears within five minutes. Yea, the Church may frown on craftsmen like myself, but I vow there is virtue in folly at times. Then, Dame Jane Collins brought in her precious charge, Edward of Middleham, with his playfellow, and their sport together put mine to shame. For when Edward bumped his head, little John it was that bawled.

I will speak now of Edward, for he is as clear in my mind as the red rose I wear in my cap today. He was, as I had forecast, the fairest babe I ever saw: light and delicate as a rainbow, with the gentle features of his mother, and Gloucester's dark blue eyes. He wore a white velvet doublet and a tiny dagger, blunt as an old man's wits, and he played the soldier, challenging little John and besting him, for all that he lacked a year of his age.

'Item,' wrote Grace. 'I hear that by the means of the Duke of Gloucester my Lord Archbishop Neville has come home. It passes my understanding that your lord should so concern himself with one who has laboured so treacherously and should have other deserts. I saw the Archbishop leaving ship at St Catherine's. His time in prison has made an old man of him—he could scarce mount the steps. As for you, right worshipful and well beloved, I am likewise waxed frail in your absence, and would wear your ring soon for naught lasts ever, neither beauty, nor money, nor kindness, and my humours change daily, as the moon wanes and waxes. Let no earthly creature see this bill.'

I was about to tear it into shreds accordingly, when her scratched postscript caught my eye. 'Item, your mother is sick.'

Just that. If Grace had wanted to get me to London, she had chosen the right halter to lead me. The letter was a sennight old and the packman who brought it north must have been riding a snail. Not so the courier who arrived at Middleham an hour after I had finished reading my lady's hard words.

His horse was dying. It staggered on its feet, keeled over and lay with blown belly. The rider, a young harnessed knight, strode clear of the kicking hooves and made for the castle steps. He came swiftly, clutching his dispatches hard against his side and doffing his helm with its dark blue mantling. He was not one of the Middleham knights, but was gently born with the right to bear arms of the bend sinister, like Gloucester's John. I did not recognize the other charges on his tabard. Besides I was taken with his eyes. Cold eyes, the colour of ice, and a black ring round the pale candle, like the eyes in a mad horse. There was excitement in him—folk could smell it—they came hastily: the horse-leech and the slaughterman, the grooms and two of the guard. Then more sedately, a chantry priest and my friends Robert and John, fresh from the delightful toils of music. 'What news?'

The young man's eyes, when he smiled, were not cold at all.

'History in the making!' he said. 'I have gained the north in four days from London. Five spent horses and one squire weeping by the road without York! As for the news, you will hear it from his Grace. Where's my lord of Gloucester?'

The guard pointed across the drawbridge. In the long distance, two horsemen were approaching, tiny figures.

'The Duke rode to Rievaulx this day. Is that he returning?'

The strange knight stepped forward a pace. He looked for a long moment into the far blue and green of the spring day. 'Nay, that's Lord Percy's man,' he said finally. 'He bears the silver crescent on his shield.' He stared longer. 'And the Earl's son, Sir Robert, rides with him. He's smiling.'

No man had sight like that, I thought. I made up my mind that he was a braggart and began to chaff him delicately with riddles, while all the time the riders grew closer and closer and came up over the drawbridge and dismounted, hastily, with the same elated air as this keen-sighted gentleman at arms. And they were Robert Percy and his esquire, of the silver crescent and the smiling face.

'We are for France, and war!' they cried.

So it came that I did not ride London-ward alone. At first we were an hundred, then double that number, and by the time of reaching York walls, our band had burgeoned to five hundred northern men; armed knights, archers and swordsmen, on foot and mounted. They wore brigandines, spiked pauldrons at the shoulder, heavy greaves on the leg; they sported jacks and sallets, carried bright swords and bills and leaden mauls; and if the mail sat on some better than others, or there were weapons that had lain idle overlong, it was nevertheless a heartening sight. From Northallerton and Boroughbridge and Knaresborough and Pontefract they came, and at York the column swelled to a thousand and then five hundred more. I could not fight, but I could sing, and so we did, with lewd jests against King Spider, to be wound in his own web, and praises sung for Charles of Burgundy, awaiting at St Omer the flower of England's invading host. Their fathers had taught them the Agincourt song, and now was the time for its airing. So they rode to war, these men of the north—hard and swift of ire and slow to laughter, and they raised their steel-framed eyes often to the standard that flew above the long, glittering file: the snarling Boar of Gloucester.

I contented myself with riding up and down the line with quip and sally, dodging many a blow from men who could not wait to strike at something. One of these looked at me with scorn and muttered of coxcombs; whereon I rode knee to knee with him and strangled him with a paradox as we came to York, heart-high. On Lendal Bridge, the Friars of St Augustine raised blessing hands—Gloucester bowed; they were his friends. We clattered down Micklegate and either side was hemmed with women whose lords and husbands moved out to mingle with our throng. Under ghost-hung Mickle Bar we rode, and an old man wavered from the walls: 'Jesu preserve his Grace! God for England!' for he had fought beside King Harry, and come back limbless. This then was the army of the North; men bred in the cold moors' solitude, who knew little of the court and its silken coils. Their loves were those of Gloucester, and they were Gloucester's men.

My lord of Northumberland smiled a wonderful sour smile and set his shining back, for it was plain how these northern men loved Gloucester, who took the time to listen to their grievances in all the blaze of his great affairs, and once these had been Percy's people. To quote one small incident: there was that matter of the fishgarths. These traps, said the men of York, littered the Ouse and Humber to such a degree that poor folk could scarcely make a catch; but the Bishop of Durham and those like him needed this meat for their holy houses—an outrageous monopoly, vowed the northern magistrates. Such sacred souls are fat and powerful—it took a King's brother to find the solution. The plaintiffs came to the Council of the North with their pleas, and went away satisfied. So thereafter was fish on the table of clergy and laity alike, and one day fish on the Duke of Gloucester's board—perch and tench and demain bread and pipes of wine—gifts from the grateful aldermen of York. Oh, how that fish stuck in Lord Percy's craw!

When we emerged from Galtres Forest a party of knights awaited us at Bootham Bar. At that time I rode near the man of keen sight. I could only distinguish a vague shape of colour drifting from the standard bearer's pole, but the young knight said calmly: 'The Company of Taylors and Drapers—a goodly sight.' And again I would not give him credence until he murmured: 'Or, a pavilion purpure lined ermine on a chief azure, a lion's head cabooshed affronté or over all, two Robes of Estate ermine lined purpure. Is your name Thomas, by chance, Sir Fool?'

Throughout London they were arming. In Eastchepe the merchants were leaving their houses on richly caparisoned mounts. I went first to my mother's place, and stood aside for the band of archers who strode down the street, singing grimly.

'Godspeed, lads!' I called.

One stopped, mischievous-faced. 'Don't you wish you were coming, Sir Fool?' he cried. 'Frenchwomen are fair, I'm told, and fairer when they struggle!'

'Bring me a souvenir!'

'A French purse?'

'A French pox, more like!' I cried, then stepped into the cook-shop, my heart sinking, for there was the sickness smell, and no customers. My mother lay abed, small in a mountain of pillows. I pushed between the curtains and embraced her. My sister had come from

Kent and stood at the fireplace with her back to me, stoking the flames as if for a lying-in.

'Open the window,' my mother said. 'I would hear the men riding by.' This I did, and the sound of tramping feet rose clear from the cobbles, a never-ending clatter. 'I shall soon be well,' she said, and would not talk about her ailments, but gossiped with me as before, of the Royal household, London life, and trade, which had not been so good lately

'Folk have not the wherewithal,' she said. 'And there has been too much costly strife in London—quarrels breed heavy fines and besides, the King, God cherish him, asks much of his people.'

'How?'

'The *benevolences*, he calls them. Even here I've heard grumblings. You cannot milk a dry cow.'

'Why, I thought the King could pluck his jaybirds with such skill that they never cry out.'

'No more. And this war is expensive. God send him victorious.'

'Amen to that,' said I.

She smiled weakly. 'As for this French affair—it is his intent to cool their humours with a real battle.'

I felt a wish to see the King. She said, 'You may find him changed,' but would say no more, so I asked about his royal offspring.

'The Prince of Wales is at Ludlow,' she said. 'With his noble governor,' and pulled a little face, saying that some servants of Anthony Woodville, Earl Rivers, had been in the shop lately and brawled with Lord Hastings's men. There had been bloody noses and a table broken. 'Let us hope he is teaching the Prince Edward better manners.'

'The Earl is schooling him in all ways of urbanity and nurture,' said my sister from the fireplace, and I winked at her.

'Let us hope they will not make a milksop of him,' I said boldly, thinking of the Woodvilles' creeping elegance.

'Speaking of heirs,' my mother said, 'you must wed Mistress Grace.' This was the moment I had wished to avoid. I acted right shiftily, causing my mother to plead and my sister to frown.

'Do not deny me grandchildren,' said my mother. I told her I had affairs to see to, and left her with a kiss, trying not to notice her sad face. My sister followed me down; she was weeping.

‘’Tis canker,’ she whispered. ‘She has a growth on her belly the size of an orange. The doctor would have cut her, but it goes too deep. I mislike your lady Grace, but it would please our mother to see you settled and the line continued.’

‘Then *you* have a son,’ I said, bitter with grief.

‘My son died,’ she said, going pale. ‘I have been to Canterbury, but I am still barren.’

So I went out into the street, and made my way, heavy hearted, to Grace’s house. I had forgotten how foul London was. The streets were littered with filth that once I had hardly noticed. Had anyone, times past, told me I would crave the moors of Wensleydale, I would have struck him for a traitor.

On the corner of Fish Street I jostled a real popinjay of a fellow who cursed me. My mother had said that folk were tightening their belts against the press of Edward’s benevolences, but this man was exceedingly well-endowed. He was no nobleman yet he wore violet satin and carried a gold-headed cane. His hat was a green velvet carrot, with silver tassels. He had a fair, rosy, maiden’s face, and his voice, even when raised in oaths, was like a warbling thrush. It was Clarence’s mermaid, his protégé who sang so sweet. A member of the Profession, so I spoke him soft.

‘Life treats you well, friend.’ He smiled a double-edged smile at this.

‘Certes, I have a good master,’ he answered, and flickered past me into Candlewick Street. I watched him disappear into The Parys, a tavern frequented by the wealthiest lords, and I pondered on him all the way to the house of my betrothed.

Well, the banns were cried, and Grace and I were married, and my mother came to church in a litter borne by two of her oldest servants, who had burned to ride on the second Agincourt but were too full of years. The candles gleamed, and we plighted our eternal troth in God’s holy house, and took the wedding breakfast at my mother’s. There were smiles all round, even on my face, because not for naught was I trained as an actor. Then I took my lady and got her with child; and in the dark, she had very long, soft hair.

Grace was rounding to the grandchild which my mother would never see, the day I sat in the Boar’s Head and watched the men returning from war, and saw the faces no longer smiling and heard the voices that no longer sang. Some of them passed through the tavern without words and quaffed ale as if to sate a thirst for blood. Their faces were such I thought it more prudent to sit silent until a figure I knew entered. It was my cousin, who halted at my bench, standing splay-legged, tall and fearsome with eyes like iron bolts.

'You should have come with us,' he said, sickly with scorn. 'For that was a fool's errand, yea, a fool's errand, by Jesu!'

'How went the battle?' I said, frightened. He lobbed his spit over the table edge and down by my feet.

'You should have been there,' he repeated. 'For there was much hearty jesting, and dancing, and sport, sweet talk, fair words. By Our Lord, I need drink! Tapster, wine here!'

'And the fighting? How many casualties—how many men did Charles of Burgundy send?'

'Not a blow was struck,' he said, on a great swallow. 'Not one blow. And as for Burgundy...'

There was a clamour at the inn door and a company of young archers came in shouting. They were spoiling for a fight. There had been no booty, no plunder for them in France. Outside, a minor riot was developing among lewd soldiery who had ravished no women, plundered no dwellings. One of the archers was a little flown with drink.

'You liar!' he cried to a fellow. 'My father paid taxes to make war, not sign treaties!'

Blows followed, and the landlord seized a truncheon from the wall and ran among them. It looked a good fight—I fingered my staff, then felt my cousin's fingers gripping my arm. He was gazing through the window where could be seen the livery of the King's Peace officers. 'Be still,' he muttered, and I obeyed, watching while they entered and arrested four, five, six of these young hotbloods, clapping them in manacles and dragging them away, still foamy-mouthed with ale and passion. Then my kinsman told me all.

King Edward had signed a peace treaty with France on the bridge at Picquigny. Charles of Burgundy had never arrived at all; he had gone wandering off to besiege Neuss at the crucial moment. It had been a bloodless truce.

'Disgrace,' I whispered, feeling torn to pieces. 'Oh God, dishonour!'

'I warn you never to speak thus,' my cousin said grimly. 'His Grace has said farewell to mercy.'

He told me that times were a-changing; that the King now intended to punish—with the swiftness of the Almighty—all miscreants in word or deed: thieves, murderers, and those of seditious tongue. 'He may have signed for gold with Louis, but he is still our King, by God's grace, fearful and omnipotent. You'll see.'

'And all the lords stand with him,' I said miserably.

'Yea, they were well pleased with the fine presents King Louis showered… save for one, that is.'

'My lord of Gloucester?' I murmured, and he said, somewhat shortly, why did I ask him of the doings in France, if I knew them already?

'He was as angry as any out there.' He pointed to the grumble-haunted street.

'Don't ask me to believe he quarrelled with the King,' I said.

'The Devil have my soul, when I see that day,' said my cousin with a laugh. 'Louis sought to woo him full lovingly, but the more he smiled the more fiercely did Gloucester scowl. He would not dine with the French King, as did my lord of Clarence and de Bretaylle. At the King's direction he accepted Louis's presents, but with as much wrath as if he thought he'd sold himself.'

'Though the Boar is rooted in the Rose,' I mused. 'It seems our King could set the realm in flames and his brother would cleave to him.'

'I know not which he loves more, England or his Grace.'

'They are one and the same,' I said. 'Whatever the end, France is conquered.'

'And Hogan keeps his head.'

'That charlatan!' I roared. On all his perambulations round England the wily old soothsayer stirred up the people. No matter which way the wind blew he could lay claim to foresight and this day no exception. He had forecast that France would be conquered—so had she been, for 50,000 crowns a year and a trade agreement.

'The Princess Elizabeth is promised in marriage to the Dauphin.'

This was the end for me. 'I would leave London,' said I. 'I would go home.'

He smiled. 'So the north is now home to you. You've caught a tincture of its speech—d'you know it?'

Gloucester had taken his anger back to Middleham, yet I was still in London when they burned John Goos for heresy. My mother was fading fast and Grace's time near, like the ebb and flow of the tide. The cook-shop would be mine by my mother's will. Grace expressed the urge to manage it, though I would liefer have put in some trusted body to see to these affairs, and have my wife and child by me in Yorkshire. We quarrelled over it. If I ever conjure her into my mind these days, which I do rarely, I see my lady with her weapons of war to hand: a kettle, a pewter platter, a ginger-jar. Once, she heaved a whole pig's head, hot from the fire, at me. That was one missile I did not catch, but on the whole she fumed in impotence at my dexterity. Though she had her way over the shop.

'I will have no Month's Mind kept,' my mother said, in a whisper.

'If that be your wish,' I answered with regret. I wanted to remember her publicly and in honour, came the anniversary of her departing. The physician approached and set leeches to her temples. Her pallor deepened and her eyes closed in pain. I could not brook remaining in that hot room heavy with sickness and my sister's sorrow. Grace's kinfolk were there too: her haughty brothers and her sister Kate, who was tender to my mother as if she were truly of her blood. I walked with long marching steps through London. Aimlessly I went Tower-ward, where Margaret of Anjou no longer lay; for the King had ransomed her as part of the peace bargain with Louis, and she had returned to France, no longer fair, an old woman.

On Tower Hill there was a vast crowd and some who recognized me. So I gave them a heel-and-toe and a bawdy rhyme, before the real revel began and they led Master Goos, self-confessed Lollard, to the stake. The sheriffs and priests stood about him with stern pleading. He had a sallow, gentle face; and even at that late hour he spoke of Wyclif with quiet conviction as if the whole matter had been decided for him years ago. They beseeched him to die a Christian man but he shook his head. So they looked at one another with thunderous cold looks, and made fast the chains about his body. The smell of the pitch rose high as they soaked the faggots and touched them with flame.

One priest persisted, stepping close in the whirling smoke. 'My son, my son, is not the Holy Sacrament Christ's Body?'

'It is but bread,' gasped the heretic.

When the blackened head drooped, there was a woman who writhed on the ground and wept, despite the tuggings and hushing glances of her friends. There is ever, I have found, one woman who mourns a death. Many may weep but there is always one who loves, and most times she is unknown. Like the dame who cried for Owen Tydder, with his poll on the highest point of Hereford Market Cross. Some unwise philosophy made me say aloud: 'He died for what he thought was right.'

'Yea, he did and is damned for it,' said a great bellied cordwainer who stood by me, and spat towards the sinking flames.

There were many such sights that year. King Edward was better than his word. He said farewell to mercy and he spared none, not even his own domestic. There were hangings by the score, quarterings and beheadings. Ears were nailed to cart wheels and their owners given a knife and told to leave town. There was even a boiling, but I did not see it. The gaols were straining at the seams. But there were no more mutterings of England's dishonour, for the people were, in a strange way, comforted. They still had their strong fierce monarch, their Rose of Rouen, even if the Rose's petals had curled a little. I saw him a couple of times in the distance. On the first occasion I might have thought him slightly changed for there seemed an unfamiliar fullness about his person. The second time was on the day I returned from the graveyard, walking behind the empty carriage with its big black horses (many accompanied me; my mother was respected). My heart turned a little even in its sadness as the King passed. He was half hidden by his gentlemen-at-arms but what I saw seemed foggy, with no clear outline. It may have been the last of my grief confusing me, but he did not seem so strong and sharp as in my remembrance. It was to be twelve months before I knew the truth of this.

'Right worshipful husband,' wrote Grace after my return north. 'I have had occasion to dismiss Master Bates and Mistress Mary Slone, for idleness was upon them and the woman Slone was in the habit of wasting scraps on back-door vagrants. She was insolent and spoke of going to the Gild for settlement but my brothers talked with her and she will cause no trouble now.'

Mary had been with my mother for fifteen years. It had been her custom to feed beggars; my mother had turned a blind eye.

'My brothers have found a dozen fresh knaves for the work; they are stout fellows and loyal to us. We do not find business to be thriving as you told me, I know not why. Master Fray came in the shop last week. He said he hoped all was pardoned and we shook hands on it, as I see no call to harbour dead grudges.'

I began to wish she would cease to write me. Then the next bit caught my fancy. 'Duchess Isabel has been passing sick, and was brought to bed of a boy lately. Men say she will not live, her lungs are bad. It is hard to be warm in London, so you freeze, no doubt, in the north parts.' With this joyful thought she commended me to the Almighty, bidding me burn the letter. I turned it sideways to read the postscript.

'Item, the Duchess Isabel is dead.'

That cast a shadow on Lady Anne's Christmas, the year of 1476, though she herself was well, and rosy from the sharp weather. Edward throve, and little John waxed strong. My lord of Gloucester rode against the Scots and returned victorious. I made them good cheer and we were peaceful together—until the King summoned Gloucester to the Great Council at Westminster. There had been grave tidings of a death, and that of one more important than the quiet Isabel. Charles of Burgundy was dead; not of anger over the Picquigny scandal, but from a surfeit of steel in his noble body. Rash as his nickname, the Duke had been besieging Nancy with a depleted force. Thus, in January snow, perish great princes. I stood behind Lady Anne on the castle stairway and watched my lord depart. His company moved out of the gate and down the dale, and the spring day was a little dimmed for my Duchess.

'Truly, he seems never at home.'

'Duty robs Beauty, 'tis the thief of joy,' said I.

'He hates London,' she murmured.

King Louis had made a proclamation. Now that Charles was dead he declared Burgundy to be his, all its domains reverting to the Crown of France.

'This day I saw the lords ride to Westminster,' wrote my lady. 'His Grace, whom God uphold, has it in mind to stand with Burgundy, but he would liefer not upset the Frenchie. My lord of Gloucester has advised taking arms, but my lord of Clarence has the notion, men say, to wed the Princess Mary and thus rule Burgundy himself. He is wonderfully strong in his wishes, but I fancy the King does not share this ardour. Messengers take ship daily to the Duchess Margaret but none yet know her mind, that of her late lord's heir, or indeed, the mind of our King.

'Item, my sister's husband is sore afraid lest we fail to keep Flanders. Is it not enough that his ships have trouble with the false Scots and the Hanse traders? For another cargo of wool was taken three days past, and he fears that should we lose our ally, he will lose his livelode.

'Item, Mistress Petson's man was fined £1 this day for scalding hogs in the street. Your son has been sick, but is well again.'

We were to know the King's mind, and that of Clarence, before the end of summer. A company came back from London, among them minstrel John, laden with new songs for my lady's delectation. I met him near the smithy, in sunlight.

'This is a fair rondeau,' he said, joyful. '*J'ai pris amours de ma devise*.'

'That's the music of Flanders,' I said. 'And how are they singing in that realm?'

'There's most wonderful mischief.' He drew close. 'Clarence's suit was rebuffed.'

'By the Princess Mary?' I smiled. 'George stuck in her gorge, then?'

'Nay, 'twas the King would not allow it,' he said urgently. 'And as for names, the lady might fare worse to consider St Anthony Woodville.'

'Earl Rivers?'

''Tis the Queen's wish, but they say she will not have him, either. As for Clarence...'

'Tell me naught,' I chuckled. 'He is enraged, and stalks about the town, vowing the Woodvilles have blighted his troth. Blighted his plight, he wanders meatless and Maryless, making his moan.'

'Far worse. There was a woman hanged by his jurors, and they all in fear of their lives and property to prove other than her guilt.'

'What woman, why?'

'Ankarette Twynhoe,' he whispered.

I remembered Ankarette from the court days. She was Duchess Isabel's chamberwoman, a nice old soul. John told a strange tale.

'My lord swore she had poisoned the Duchess. He sent eighty armed men to her dwelling to drag her from her bed. She was tried speedily and hanged quicker. *Yet the one who should have dangled wears a crown.*'

'You're witless from fast London living,' I said, stupefied by this.

'Clarence vows it. He burst into the King's council chamber while his Grace was at Windsor and said all manner of terrible things. How that the King, the Queen and her kin had plotted against him, had given money to the woman Twynhoe for this murder. And that a Woodville servant had slain his infant son.'

'What else?' Could there be aught else, I wondered. The cards were surely stacked against George now.

'He has cast a taint upon the King's lineage,' he murmured. 'He would have it that he is the rightful sovereign, his Grace of bastard stock. His men whisper that the King has dabbled in the Black Art,' he said, crossing himself.

'Say no more.' This was treason of the worst kind.

'He courts disaster,' said gentle John, strangely bold. 'I'll say what I wish—there are no spies at Middleham. Not like London, where the Queen's kin are everywhere, whisper, whisper in the alehouse, in church. How that Clarence seeks the downfall of those who lie at Windsor and at Ludlow, surely as the blood of Sir John Woodville and his father stains the Duke's hands.'

'Robin of Redesdale, do his archers shoot from the grave?' I said, wondering.

'But men also say there is some secret Clarence holds,' murmured John. All this was too much for me. I got me to London, full as a plum with curiosity.

I bent to my wife's lips, and she gave me her cheek. So be it, I thought, and kissed my son instead, who knocked off my hat in a loving fury, seized the feather and endeavoured to choke himself with it. My pleasure was only dimmed when I saw him treat my wife's brothers in the same familiar fashion. I did not stay long; I was for the court, all agog to see the King again. The closer I came to him the more I longed to see his smile, his handsome face, and I asked Grace how he did, while clothing myself for the ride to Windsor.

'Easier now that Clarence lies at the Tower,' she replied.

'In the royal apartments?' I asked, lack-wit.

'In a dungeon, dolt!' she said. 'The Queen's kin did their work well. Guard your tongue, no man is safe.' We had one thing in common, my wife and I: the name Woodville bred a hearty mistrust.

'He'll soon pardon him again,' I said. 'Blood is thicker than water.'

'The King has a new leman,' she said suddenly. 'Mistress Shore.'

I burst out laughing. 'Not Will Shore's wife!'

'She is beautiful—none can resist her. She laughs excessively, and is kind besides.'

'I remember her,' I said. 'So it's farewell to lovely Lucey, and all the other queans, for the mercer's finest ware?'

'Oh, he still has others,' she replied. 'The holiest, the fairest, and Jane, the merriest harlot in the realm.' I hastened through the autumn noon to see for myself.

I met Anne Neville outside the royal apartments with her ladies and she gave me a pale smile; the journey south had wearied her. We had left Edward behind at Middleham, and I knew his little fair face haunted her. Richard was nowhere to be found. I had not yet seen the Rose of Rouen, but I had crossed swords with the King's resident fool, and he had bowed to my greater experience. So we had made a pact that he should sing and I would dance, we would both tumble, and when one grew weary the other should relieve him. I was armed with a thousand new jests, suited in purple and green with silver bells on my boots and a longing in my heart to hear the sovereign laughter. The King's laughter—he of the old royal blood. That evening Windsor Great Hall was the same, and the company therein, save for those who were dead or absent for other reasons; the hot perfumed air was as my dreaming nose recalled it. Queen Elizabeth sat lily-cool, and some witchcraft had chained the years at her door, for her beauty was untouched. Beside her, my King.

O Jesu! he was fat! he was well-nigh gross, and his complexion marred by threads of scarlet running down into the pouched flesh at his jowl. Those gem-like eyes were fighting for room above full cheeks. The rings cut into his fingers. No one had told me he would look like this. I had need to turn my grief into mockery, vowing that it was joy at seeing him which made me weep.

A printed book was being passed from hand to hand. Over the high wailing music I heard the remarks, and between the velvet sleeves of the Queen's kinfolk saw the flash of gems on its binding.

'What a mind! What a man! Truly the sayings of the Philosophers could have no finer translator. I felicitate you, my lord.' This was Doctor Morton, Master of the Rolls. Barbed whiskers at his chin, he leaned at Anthony Woodville's side.

'Master Caxton has laboured well too,' said my lord of Gloucester, in that emotionless voice. He had come midway through the revel, straight from Horton Quay where his Admiralty had been hearing a case. Soberly dressed, his plumage was markedly dull beside that of his companion. Henry Stafford, Duke of Buckingham, who stood with his arm through Gloucester's, was dizened like a peacock, with his device of the flaming wheel powdered on purple satin. At one time this young man had not excited my curiosity, being only the one wed to Kate Woodville so that the Queen's sister should not die a poor spinster, and the Queen's tears be staunched. Now he glittered, and Richard liked him. There was a lot of Clarence in young Buck, the same languid voice and fluent charm.

Earl Rivers bore his treasure to the King's dais, smirking, and Edward pored over it. I turned and set off round the hall at a run, flattering the ladies outrageously, conjuring eggs and serpents from the sleeves of bemused lords, capering on the bounds of what was seemly. I leaped on a table and down again, head over arse. I brought two monkeys and staged a wedding. The company loved me. Jane Shore's was a lovely name to juggle with. Better even than the princely stables and the King's Grey Mare.

'For Shore is gold a prince's treasure
And shorely he should take his pleasure.'

Or:

'I trow no sailor asks for more—
Than to come safely into Shore.'

(This last I kept for my friends.) She was fair, as Grace said, and there was much warmth in her. Rosy and round, a little thing, with elegant manners; much kindness did she for men, and her wit was almost equal to mine Still there were those who reckoned her last name should begin with W, not S, for varying reasons. She danced with Lord Hastings, and once brushed lightly against Gloucester as he stood with Anne and bright Buckingham. He bowed stiffly to her—his eyes were cold. He was sad that night—an Israelite in Babylon.

Some of the old faces had new husbands. Lady Margaret Beaufort was wed for the third time, now to Lord Stanley. King Edward had approved this gladly, so said my wife. For Margaret was Lancastrian as well as learned, and Stanley was loyal enough to curb these leanings.

'She brought her son to court, a month past,' Grace told me. 'Dressed like a peasant, with scarce a word to say for himself.'

King Edward had received young Henry Tudor generously, while the court muttered a little at Lady Margaret's effrontery. Some sniggered at his gaucherie and Welsh accent.

There are times when I feel I have lived too long, and seen overmuch. It makes an old man dizzy, the way the wheel spins.

Then there was the night we went down drinking in Southwark, and came out of the inn late, a little cup-shotten but not so mad with wine that we neglected to look well for the Watch or the special constables prowling the darkness. Robert was anxious lest he be locked out. John—well, I had ado to stop him singing. He reeled about and almost pulled me down, and some of his verses would have made the King roar and my Lord Gloucester look very sharp indeed. We rolled up the street, a fine uncaring trinity, being barked at by dogs and cursed by people already abed. It was I who had suggested this foray. Once again I was dolorous: not only because of the King's looks, his loss of something beautiful and remembered that pained me still. Richard seemed full of gloom, his lady choked with anxiety about her faraway son, and Grace—I had had occasion that day to remind her that there were penances for scolds, rich and poor alike, and hang the disgrace of it. It was the hour between dog and wolf, and as the drink soured in my belly old sins kept me company. I should not have been amazed to see my devil, and I had just decided to become a monk when a dreadful, groaning yell convinced me I was too late in my good intentions.

'O Jesu, what was that?' whispered John. He dropped our light in a patch of snow. Cursing, we stood in darkness. I could not find my tinder; I was shivering so much. Robert snatched up the lantern.

'You are a brace of old women,' he said angrily, but the flint was damp. He swore and struggled, while my fearful ears strained for other manifestations of Hell. Feet were approaching, their swift thudding accompanied by the sound of gasping breath. There were two people—earthly at that, but in the blackness we could only discern vague shapes. We cringed against the wall. Robert got the lantern going all of a sudden. It flamed up as the shadows passed at a jog-trot; I got a flash of half-hidden white faces, black cloaks, and the dull spark of steel. Then they were gone. We breathed again, drunkenly comforted by the absence of ghosts.

'Go carefully,' said Robert. We sidled round the next corner in our little isle of light. The snow was dirty underfoot from the day's traffic. I felt pity for a poor beggar lying in the gutter. He was rolled in a houpeland of fine cloth for such as he; his breath snored whistling through the filth of his pillow. As cup-shotten fools will do, we stood and contemplated him.

'Friends,' said John, 'let us lay him against the wall or he will be trampled.'

'Let him alone,' Robert said. 'Sleep's his only comfort.' And so, as is ever my way, I did the opposite and rolled the limp form an inch over the cobbles. I saw then that he had been stuck with a dagger; his fine wool doublet was sopped with blood all round the protruding hilt. I called Robert to bring down the light so I could see the face of this well-clad vagrant. It was Clarence's mermaid, and he was not quite dead. The snoring stopped and he gave a bubbling cough. I had found him arrogant but he was after all one of my ilk, an entertainer, so I took his head on my arm and he opened his eyes.

'Sir Fool, tell my lord,' he said, in quite a strong voice. I remembered how beautifully he sang, and I felt great sorrow.

'Peace, friend, lie quiet.'

His breath came quicker, horrible to hear.

'I have done my duty,' he gasped. Then he was babbling in a whisper, babbling and bubbling like a slaughtered beast, and my hands became sticky with his blood. He had a tale for my lord of Clarence, but Clarence was in the Tower, waiting on the abatement of the King's rage. So I tried to quiet the wanderings of this grievous wound, which were a jumble of nonsense, words plaited in a wanton skein, among them being… 'the house of the Carmelites' and something that sounded like either 'bastard whelps' or 'Bath and Wells'. I stroked his face with a chilling hand, trying to hush him, while he coughed and then became stark dead. We did not linger, of course. 'Did you know those two?' I asked, as we ran. Robert shook his head but John clutched my arm.

'The one I know,' he whispered. 'He writes ballads. Sometimes he sings.'

'Well, he has sung one there to death,' I said, frozen to the bone.

'He's Earl Rivers's man, I think,' John gasped, running on.

Lady Anne Neville stretched out her hand. 'My lord! Dickon, let me see the letter.' With great reluctance he gave her the precious missive lately received from Middleham, and he smiled for the first time in weeks.

'God be praised, he's well,' she sighed, reading. ''Twas a little fever he had. My sweet son!' She kissed the letter as if it were Edward himself. Anne had a cough. She was not so well in London, and touched her amulet constantly; she wore it against her continuing barrenness. We had been gambling in my lord's apartment; a nonsense game, for the Regal of France, the London Stone, and the Forest of Eltham, and I was winning all. While they both read and re-read the letter, their heads together like children, a rap came at the door, and quite a small company entered.

'We are honoured, my lord,' said Richard, rising. Anthony Woodville, Earl Rivers, was cordial in scarlet satin. Thomas Grey, Marquess of Dorset, looked about him with a little contempt. With them came two boys, neither of whom I had seen for years. Prince Edward had grown fair as a maid, and pouted like one. Richard, Duke of York, was smaller, a swift bright bird. He tugged impatiently at his heavy state robes as if he would fain have put them off. His sleeves were too long—he pushed back the ermine from his wrists like one keen to deal out blows. I knelt before our future monarch, who leaned, languor-pale, on Earl Rivers's arm.

'His princely Grace expressed the wish to see you, Sir,' said Rivers, and laughed rather unquietly.

'My brother wanted to hear about the fighting in Scotland,' said Prince Edward quietly. He stepped forward, but Rivers held his hand. There was no holding back the Duke of York, however. He nipped up and took the stance of a grown man, feet crossed, against the table where Gloucester sat. They gazed seriously at one another.

'Sir! Have you slain many men?' enquired the little Duke.

'As many as was needful, my lord,' said Gloucester, with a faint smile.

'How many?' asked Richard of York, and I could foresee a long conversation.

'As many as would have slain my troops, had matters gone otherwise,' replied Gloucester calmly.

'Why do you not recite your verses to his Grace?' asked Rivers, all hasty.

'How many dead?' said Richard of York. 'How many, I say? Did you use guns? Bang! Bang! I have a new pony,' he added. He darted closer to Gloucester, until he leaned on his knee.

'My lord uncle, excuse my brother. He's but an infant,' said the seven-year-old Prince. He disengaged from Rivers's clasp and came to stand by Richard. 'He's to be married soon,' he said confidentially, as if this explained the Duke's wildness.

'Is the lady fair, my lord?' asked Richard of Gloucester.

'She is the Duchess of Norfolk,' said Prince Edward.

'She's taller than me,' said the prospective bridegroom.

'So Richard shall have Anne,' said Gloucester. 'To me, that augurs well for future joy.'

'Did you go in a ship to Scotland?' said the Duke of York. 'Have you many ships? I went in a ship once... to a big place and there was a lady...'

'That was a barge,' said Prince Edward wearily. 'On the Thames. But I too would dearly love to sail the sea. My lord, when did you first take ship?'

Gloucester looked at the small boy, suddenly serious. 'When I was your age,' he replied, and his voice was quiet. Thomas Grey cleared his throat.

'My Prince, tell his Grace what you have learned of Cicero.' Edward remained, staring at his uncle. 'Sir, shall I be a soldier and captain like you?' he asked. At this, Gloucester looked straight into Earl Rivers's eyes, saying: 'The finest, good Prince. But better than I.

Like the King your father, who raised the great Sun banner and was rewarded by God, in snow, in fog, and in foul country. Skilled in war and courage, as well as in verse and music.' The way he said these last three words made me cringe, and hide my lute behind a cushion.

'What's necromancy?' asked the Duke of York, loud and sudden. Earl Rivers and Grey both moved forward at once.

'Come, my lords, it grows late.'

Obediently the Prince Edward gave his hand again to Earl Rivers, smiling up at him. But little York lingered, staring at my lord, on whose face there was a trace of the old grimness.

'Where's my uncle of Clarence?' the boy demanded suddenly. '*He* makes me laugh. Where's he gone?'

'Come, my lord,' said Thomas Grey. 'Your brother waits,' adding to Gloucester, with a charming smile, 'They are inseparable.' Dickon of York stumbled over his robes in the doorway. This seemed to unleash a tide of passion in him, and we listened to his diminishing shrieks. 'I want to see my Uncle George!'

'Here's a new rhyme,' I began, wriggling in anguish.

Neither my lord nor his lady paid any heed.

'He's Edward's age,' whispered Lady Anne. 'He cannot comprehend all.'

Richard rose slowly, white as a skull. 'Give me your prayers, my lady,' he said, and strode to the door. She stretched out her hands to him, but he was gone, marching through to the King's apartments in a fury of decision. I fidgeted, watching her. She was very thin, and sad.

'Read the letter,' I said, and soon she was lost in it again, murmuring little thoughts like beads. 'Dirick has made him new shoes. Green, silver buckles. Medcalf and Pacock took him to Aysgarth lately—they guard him well, those men.' So I left her and stole away. For that day was the Eve of St Nicholas the first night of the revels, and I had plans for a spectacular entrance. I would leap from the minstrels' gallery on to the shoulders of the Vice Titivillius 'who snares neglected prayers, words dropped at Mass', and hoped they would pick a sturdy fellow for the part. I had some measurements to make; it would be a mighty leap. So along the passage I went and into the gloom of the small recess, bumping over lecterns and scattering sheets of music. I leaned over the rail to study the drop, and there below, within spitting distance, was proceeding a play, a tragedy by the look of it. In the deserted Hall, the King held court. He had just returned from the chase; there was snow on his boots. The dull gold of his head throbbed in the twilight as he lay wearily in his chair. Richard of Gloucester knelt before him, gripping the sovereign robe by its hem. The Queen looked on. Her hand lay on the back of the King's chair, close to his neck. Her pointed pale face was in shadow but I saw the gleam of her little teeth as she chewed her lip. Edward's voice grated on my ear.

'I have shown mercy,' he said. 'He has betrayed me. Not once but many times, and I have pardoned him. No more.'

'Your most noble Grace,' said Richard, very low, 'does not our Saviour say: forgive not once, but seventy times seven?'

'My lord,' Edward answered heavily, 'I have spoken my mind. The traitor must be punished. It is God's will.'

Elizabeth's soft voice from the shadows said: 'Yea, my lord, the King's grace speaks wisely. For my children are not safe while Clarence lives.'

The King raised his hand, touched white fingers lightly.

'Soft, Bess,' he said gently. 'I have promised. None shall harm our blessed heirs.' She slid away in a rustle of dark satin and diamonds. King Edward rose from his chair, and Richard from his knees.

'Edward my lord,' Gloucester said, 'will you not hear me? Have you forgotten all we have known together? Have you forgotten we are of one blood?'

The King was not wroth. He leaned and kissed Richard, but his tone was stern.

'He is a traitor,' he repeated. 'He has called me bastard and practiser of witchcraft. He has sown death, and shall reap it. Leave me now.'

'Your Grace, he is my brother!' Gloucester's cry chilled me.

'He's mine also, Dickon,' the King said wearily. 'Go from me.'

I watched Gloucester quit the Hall. The Lord of the North—tears poured down his face. Quiet in the gallery, I thought many things as the King sat below, his head cupped in his hand. It seemed plain that the name Woodville had brought a deal of dolour to the Court, this way and that. A jest leaped to mind. I could not shame the Queen and live, but there were others. Edward was calling for wine.

'And I am dispirited,' he told the page. 'Summon Mistress Shore.'

I crept out.

The King was drunk early that night. Lord Hastings saw to that; he plied him with wine as if he gained more pleasure from double drunkenness. They shared a void with Jane, vowing that her lips gave added sweetness to the drink. St Nicholas paraded with his crook and mitre, and the Vice Titivillius was there, a strong lad, with his long pouch full of *Glorias* and *Misericordias* and all the other bits the priests gabble over. But I had a better entrance than the one planned previously. I waited patiently until Anthony Woodville was present. Behind the screen there were gasps at my costume; it was lewd in the extreme. The coat reached only to my middle and the hose—well, they would not be delivered of me uncut, for they revealed all: in plain words, my privy parts, so close were they shaped. The points of my shoes were long enough to stretch half across the Hall. In my hand I bore a marsh pike, and so I entered, to screams.

The King was not so flown; he blinked at me as I neared the cloth of estate.

'Ha, Sir Fool!' he said. 'Why this guise?'

I took a full breath, for a loud voice.

'Upon my word, Sir King,' said I, 'I have been absent from court too long. For I trow, the Rivers are so high in your realm, I could not hope to ford them without the help of this staff.'

Thinking back, 'twas a feeble jest, but they were ripe for it. All the old nobility whose noses had been disjointed by the Queen's kin bayed like dogs. Elizabeth froze. King Edward looked a little hard at me for a moment, startled to tremble, then opened his mouth with the fair white teeth and his wonderful rich laughter came pouring forth. He threw back his head. The portly chins vanished, and he was, for a brief space, the Rose of Rouen once more. All the company was mine, from that instant, and I would not let it rest there. All night I pranced in my shameless garb, tripping past Earl Rivers with my nose in the air, crying: 'High, high! By my loyalty, they are high!' It was a fair victory. As for the Queen's brother, he bore himself well; he smiled adequately though he was very tight of countenance. Once I caught him gazing at Gloucester, who had also raised a smile at my folly. I believe there were some who congratulated him on having such a clever fellow in his household. Those such as I wax fat on praise, and I listened afterwards to the comments. Lord Hastings had helped the King to bed and folk were dispersing, dizzy with wine and food, as I kept my ears wide in nook and cranny and torch-lit corridor. Thus it was I heard the opinion of Earl Rivers; he seemed displeased. He stood round a bend in the passage, the wind blowing chill on his shadow and that of his companion.

'It was but a harmless jest, my lord,' said Doctor Morton soothingly.

Rivers laughed sourly. 'Harmless indeed,' he said. 'The King took pleasure in it.'

'Do not trouble about the humour of his Grace's brother, my lord,' said Morton. 'He has doubtless grown unfamiliar with our culture, living his rude, far existence.'

Instead of comforting the Earl, this seemed to enrage him further.

'Yea, by God!' he said violently. 'He may have a tame popinjay to pipe his insults, but I have a prince in my schoolroom.'

'Soft, my lord,' said Morton uncomfortably.

'One day it may be Gloucester who needs a marsh pike to ford the realm,' said Rivers, and their voices grew fainter, and went away.

If a man stood in Petty Wales, between Billingsgate and the Tower, he could watch royal retinues issuing from the fine apartments. He could laugh heartily to see them fuming in the moil of traffic that barred their way. The carters did not care: they carried on; foul-mouthed, whipping their horses through spaces too narrow, upsetting drays laden with flax and rope, thread, grain and fish. A man could also listen for news of those who lay within Tower gaol. Whenever there was an execution, I found that the quickest way to gain the truth of the matter was to enter a cook-shop in that quarter, for within the hour all would come to my ears. It was simpler to chaff the tidings out of the wife of a loose-tongued under-warder than wait to be told in formal proclamation at Paul's Cross. The Tower in those days was like a beehive, heavy with gossip. Not so now; they are not such a jolly crew, and less informative. Or less informed.

I left behind a London that was partly scandalized, partly amused by the marvellous novelty of Clarence's demise. My friends at Middleham were inclined to disbelieve me, until I elaborated.

'He was drowned in wine,' I said. 'The doorway of his cell was too small, so they took him to the butt instead, trussed like a fowl. The malmsey was of the finest, and his favourite.'

'I would rather have my head struck off,' said Dirick the shoemaker. 'For I know I would try to drink deep, and be defeated.'

'Well, it was at his own request,' I said, feeling rather sickly. For I remembered Clarence: fair, jocund, lovesome traitor. This last gesture had in it a jesting princeliness, a snapping of the fingers at death. I could not help but wonder what became of the malmsey, after they drew out the dead Duke. Then all my frivolous thoughts fled away. From the chantry came a file of monks and priests and poor men from the village, all clad in sombre mourning. The great cross at the head of the procession caught the winking sunshine, the requiem bell tolled in time with each step. Behind the smallest pair of singing-boys came the lady Anne, holding her son by the hand, and last of all, my lord of Gloucester, in black, his eyes swollen with weeping.

The King had agreed to Gloucester's wish that he should found two colleges, one at Middleham, the other at Barnard Castle; and ceaselessly the bells were sounded at both establishments. Each day the priests named in solemn obituary those of the House of York who had gone: my lord's father Richard, his brother Rutland, his uncle Salisbury, and, latest in this company, the fair, foolish George of Clarence.

Gloucester went no more to court, but kept himself within the northern territories. He was often away from home, for King Edward kept him busy. So for the amusement of the lady Anne I wrote poems about him and his fierce punishment of the heathen Scots, and these gave her as much pleasure as her lord's martial exploits did the King. For King Louis had persuaded the Scottish James to violate his truce with England, and for want of the loving words I could not pen, I gave Grace the news in my southbound bills.

'Right well beloved wife, it may be that you will receive my fool's cap with the head yet inside of it, for we are to be besieged by those false kilted creatures north of us and I know not what will befall. I leave all in the hands of my lord of Gloucester, and through Him that sits higher than all earthly princes, we shall prevail. I read what you say about the tax which the King's government has levied upon our livelode; may the Saints attend his Grace's wisdom and may the pinch be worth the penny.'

In truth I only wrote thus to affright her, and in hopes perchance of a kind word or two, for I had no doubt whatever of

Richard Gloucester's strength and strategy. His blistering assaults upon Dumfries and Berwick, and his capture of Edinburgh without the loss of a single man; well, these are still talked of today, albeit softly. King Edward was full with his brother's success. He himself did not come northward; he had not the humour, he said. He wrote to his Holiness the Pope thanking the Giver of all good gifts for his most loving brother, whose proven success was enough to chastise the whole of Scotland.

'Right worshipful husband, I have taken as a parlour boarder the kinsman of Master Fray. He is a man skilled in penmanship and will help me with the accountancy. You will know that Calais was attacked lately; it is as well that your Duke of Gloucester has subdued the Scots though never did I think to see the day when England could call on those for aid, which state you say his lordship has brought about. Hogan sings loud as ever, he did say the Bull would swim and the Boar would triumph. Item, Louis of France has broken his son's troth with our Princess Elizabeth. This day I saw her, and she was more fair even than yesterday. She was merry. Yet marriage is a blissful state is it not? The price of hogs has risen.'

Elizabeth was not sad when she was young; not even when the Dauphin was withdrawn from her by his devious father.

Yet my Queen looks sad today. She has that look of anxious love familiar to me from the days with Lady Anne Neville. When Edward ailed and my lord was away she had a moonbeam look troubled by trailing clouds. I think it is Arthur who grieves my lady, and he has the look of Anne Neville, too white, too rosy. Life is full of paradoxes. Each mirrors the other.

I saw his Divine Majesty eye me last evening. I thought he was going to say I was too old to earn my money, but he did not. None the less, I tried to put on a younger aspect—then I thought he might say I was too wise. One must either be young and silly, or wise and feeble. I am what I am. I live in past and present, then suddenly both come together with a fierce clash like an axe on armour and I am shaken into confusion—ah, this white mist over my eyes...

There are particular days in life which seem good, when the sun shines and the air sings sweet down to the well of the lungs, and on such a day I walked through York for Corpus Christi. Long before dawn the Gild Masters readied the wagons for their slow journey around the City. Five hundred actors waited on Toft Green. I followed each pageant with eagerness, from Holy Trinity Priory on Micklegate, across to All Saints, Davygate, where they lighted the beacon for wayfarers in Lantern Tower. The wagons halted before the houses of great lords, who stood at their windows to watch the rise and fall of mankind, and threw gold for their lesson.

Eve was very fair, and shamed by her nakedness when the Prince of Darkness tempted her in serpent-guise. On Lendal Bridge Noah built his ark, and who better to advise him than the gildsmen of the Shipwrights, the Fishmongers and Mariners? The actors of the Vintners' Gild dealt with the Miracle at Cana, where Our Lord changed water into wine. The tyrant Herod was wonderfully fierce. He leaped from his chariot to buffet his head upon the stones, foaming at the mouth. He used lye soap and gunpowder for this; the Gild Master had fined him the year before for not having given enough pith to his part. As we moved towards the great new Cathedral Church, there came the soldiers of Herod who took and slew with daggers the Holy Innocents, wrenching them from their mothers' arms. The women's screams were like icicles. Lady Anne filled her large grey eyes with tears at the dreadful scene. My lord of Gloucester, as he watched, laid his hand upon his small son's head.

And as was right and proper, darkness had covered the City when they nailed Christ to the Tree, so that the faces of the singing boys wavered like the candle flames they carried, and there was soft sobbing in the dusk. Very low and sweet they sang the old carol, those little boys with their innocent faces.

Lully, lulley, lully, lulley,
The faucon has borne my make away.
He bare him up, he bare him down,
He bare him into an orchard brown,
In that orchard there was an hall
That was hanged with purple and pall.
And in that hall there was a bed
It was hanged with gold so red.
And in that bed there lieth a knight
His wounds bleeding both day and night.
By that bedside kneeleth a may

And she weepeth both night and day.
And by that bedside there standeth a stone,
Corpus Christi written thereon.

I could have been a devil at Doomsday had I paid pageant-pence and volunteered, but there seemed enough cunning players to drag humanity into Hell already. The discipline was strict: I saw one of the fraternity chastising a devil who came in late on his entrance after quaffing a mazer of ale behind Hell Mouth. They fined him four pence on the spot. In his black hose embroidered with pitchforks he leaped on the platform, declaring that he had been unjustly used. God, in six skins of white leather, frowned from his pinnacled throne. And they hurled them into Hell: the men and women, the lustful and those who had shown no charity, the adulterers and the murderers, those of unkind tongue and all who had taken no pity on those who lie in prison or are otherwise persecuted. For no reason that I can name I turned and emptied my purse into the hand of a blind man who stood behind me. He dropped some of the coins, they ran tinkling away. I looked up at the other side of the stage where the silver steps led to Heaven, and saw a great progress of angels and men ascending to the bright robes of Christ, and found myself weeping.

The following day they made my lord and his lady members of the Corpus Christi Gild. With bishops and priests they walked, glimpsed by the people through a forest of mitres and chasubles, shaded by the cloth of silver banners and crosses of gold. In its jewelled shrine the Host went before them and thus, from Holy Trinity they went all the way to the Cathedral Church. The air was full of singing. And, with my eternally curious ears, I listened to the men of York chanting a faux bourdon to these solemn hymns as my lord walked through town, straight and rigid with a soldier's step. Snips of thought were blown to my hearing like birds in a storm. 'Gloucester settled the matter, and all was well.' 'Through my lord's aid, we are friendly once more.' 'Because my man's father was sick, he...' 'I rode beside Richard—he fought like ten!' 'Our gracious Lord...' 'He set their kilts afire!' Laughter. 'Our son lay in gaol and he...' One booming voice, full of self-importance: 'You prate of small matters—when all was feared lost, he saved this City's charter!'

At the ale in Eden Berrys on Goodramgate it was 'Dickon, God preserve him!' from one roisterer who should have known better.

All the way it was Richard, Richard, Richard. From the Merchant Adventurers to the smallest craftsman. They loaded his table with the choicest food in Gildhall, they set before him the finest wines. They arrayed the aldermen in scarlet by the score and horsed them grandly for his welcome at Bootham Bar. The banners danced above him. The trumpets blared for his entrance. He wore York like a jewel in his bonnet.

Lord Percy rode a little behind him, and was deafened by the noise.

And there are days in life which start out so fair, and end up black, like the hand of God descending to chasten men for their sins, for none knows when the Day will be. Hogan and others had prophesied the world's end in the year 1500, but I still live to speak of a day I hold in my mind clearer than many.

The sun was shining. I was a little anxious about my sparrowhawk; she was baiting, and I took off her hood to look into her misted eye. She would not eat, not even the choicest morsels, and I did not want to spoil her for future sport with temptation, so I left her with the falconer and walked across the ward. The drawbridge was down, for a horseman had lately ridden in, flecked with spur-blood and spume. In the green meadow across the moat, I could see Edward on his pony, trotting in a circle, round and round like a leaf in the breeze. He was laughing. Little John sat on a sturdy bay in the corner of the meadow, watching Edward as a priest guards a shrine.

I walked back to the Castle. Folk were gathered at the foot of the steps and more were issuing from the great door. I raised my eyes to the battlements; they were lowering the standard that flew there in the moorland wind. At the same moment as a bell began to boom slowly, the horseman I had seen emerged and ran down the steps, unwashed, foam-spattered cloak wafting about him. He called for fresh horses. A page ran beside him, and passed close, so I caught at his sleeve. He wore Lord Hastings's livery.

'What news?' I said. He looked excited and fearfully pale.

'The King is dead,' he said, shrugging me off in his haste.

It was like a blow, a douche of icy water. The whole ward shimmered before me into something alien and fierce. I caught at the boy as he hurried past.

'You lie,' I said softly.

Then I looked again towards the Castle and saw Lady Anne, Lady Lovell and a few other women. Anne Neville was descending the steps; I fell on my knees and offered her my arm, for she almost stumbled in her haste to reach the level of the yard. She leaned on me briefly—like a willow tree she was, for she wore palest green and she trembled and shivered and swayed like a willow in the wind.

'What tidings, my lady?' I cried. 'Pray, go carefully,' for her feet caught in the hem of her gown. 'Ill tidings,' she whispered, as people came running to strain for her words. Her voice rose from a mere breath to a sorrowful cry.

'Our Sovereign Lord is dead!' Then, softer: 'O Jesu, Edward is dead! And Dick is in Scotland! He has been cold a week; our Sovereign Lord is dead!'

Over and over she cried it. We all knew it was impossible. Yet it was true.

Thus ended my time at Middleham.

The sun was brighter then.

HERE ENDS THE FOOL'S TALE

We Speak No Treason continues

Book 2

The White Rose Turned to Blood

Rosemary Hawley Jarman

The sweeping epic of England's last Plantagenet king continues with the testimony of Richard III's sworn man, Mark Archer, a sharp-sighted soldier, who follows his lord into an adventure-filled exile and beyond. Through the bloodiest battlefields and the devious atmosphere of a royal court where every other nobleman is a traitor, to the solitude of the cloister, this stormy, tragic tale concludes with the story of the Nut-Brown Maid who loved and lost Richard, her gruelling ordeals at the hands of unscrupulous nuns, her courage in the face of danger, and a fateful reunion as the wheel comes full circle...

July 2006

£6.99

0 7524 3942 1

TORC, an imprint of TEMPUS

We Speak No Treason
The Flowering of the Rose
ROSEMARY HAWLEY JARMAN
'Superb' ***The Sunday Mirror***
'Brilliant' ***The Sunday Express***
'Outstanding' ***The Guardian***
THE NUMBER ONE BESTSELLER
£6.99 0 7524 3941 3

We Speak No Treason
The White Rose Turned to Blood
ROSEMARY HAWLEY JARMAN
'A superb novel' ***The Sunday Express***
'I could not put it down' ***The Sunday Mirror***
'Ablaze with colour, smell and sound, for lovers of the historical novel, this is a feast' ***Vogue***
THE NUMBER ONE BESTSELLER
£6.99 0 7524 3942 1

Wife to the Bastard
HILDA LEWIS
'A spankingly good story about Matilda'
The Spectator
'Well documented historical fiction'
The Observer
'A work of quiet distinction' ***The Sunday Times***
£6.99 0 7524 3945 6

Wife to Charles II
HILDA LEWIS
'A lively story, full of plots and trials and executions... Fragrant is the word the tale brings to mind' ***The Observer***
'Filled with splendour, intrigue, violence and tragedy' ***The Yorkshire Post***
£6.99 0 7524 3948 0

Eleanor the Queen
NORAH LOFTS
'One of the most distinguished of English women novelists'
The Daily Telegraph
£6.99 0 7524 3944 8

The King's Pleasure
NORAH LOFTS
'This is everything that a good historic novel should be'
The Guardian
£6.99 0 7524 3946 4

Harlot Queen
HILDA LEWIS
'Hilda Lewis is not only mistress of her subject, but has the power to vitalise it'
The Daily Telegraph
£6.99 0 7524 3947 2

The Concubine
NORAH LOFTS
'Fascinating'
The Sunday Times
THE INTERNATIONAL BESTSELLER
£6.99 0 7524 3943 X

If you are interested in purchasing other books published by Tempus, or in case you have difficulty finding any Tempus books in your local bookshop, you can also place orders directly through our website

www.tempus-publishing.com